For more information, please visit www.rachelvincent.com

Blind Tiger

Wildcats Book 2

RACHEL VINCENT

ISBN-10: 0692848312
ISBN-13: 978-0692848319

To Jennifer Lynn Barnes.
Because this whole thing was your idea.

.

ACKNOWLEDGMENTS

Thanks, first and foremost, to my husband, who has put countless hours into my career in the form of artwork, web design, brainstorming, and moral support. You are my anchor and I love you.

Thanks also to Rinda Elliott, my long-time critique partner, who critiqued *Lion's Share* and *Blind Tiger* as well as the entire Shifters series.

Thanks to Jennifer Lynn Barnes who said, "You should write a billionaire werecat! He could be the shifter Batman!"

Thanks to Elizabeth Taylor, for an invaluable beta read.

And thanks most of all to all the Shifters fans who asked for more.

ONE

Robyn

Years ago, I saw a documentary about US detention centers. Most of them, it turns out, are made of some combination of steel bars, concrete, and shatter-proof acrylic walls. But there's another category of prison that neither the US Justice Department nor the producers of that documentary know about.

That category includes a certain large house on the outskirts of Atlanta, decorated by a woman with an excessive fondness for a soft shade of purple and an extravagant collection of ceramic angels.

I'd been a captive in that house for two months and eight days when I walked into the kitchen and saw Dr. Danny Carver cradling a steaming mug of coffee, his medical supply bag hanging from one shoulder. I swallowed a groan and crossed my arms over my chest. "Are you here for the conference, or did you come to break me out?"

His smile was small, but genuine. "No one considers you a prisoner, Robyn."

"Yet I'm not allowed to leave."

He set his mug on the counter and opened his bag of medical supplies. "You signed up for this."

"My options were pretty limited at the time, if you recall." A few months before, as a newly infected stray suffering from bloodlust and post-traumatic stress, I'd killed four human men. They totally deserved it, but murder is a capital crime in shifter society as it is in human society. However, because female werecats are rare and I am the first female stray confirmed to exist in the US, the territorial council offered me a deal. If I agreed to stay in the Southeast Territory and let them train me to control my inner-shifter, they wouldn't rip out my incisors. Or chop off the tips of my fingers, along with my claws.

Or execute me.

But the whole house arrest thing was supposed to be temporary. Only until I learned to control my new feline instincts and impulses. Which I never asked for, by the way. I was infected against my will, and that fact chafed my temper as surely as literal bindings would have abraded my wrists.

I considered myself fully rehabilitated, but every time I even hinted at the fact that I felt ready to leave the Southeast Territory, Umberto Di Carlo, my acting Alpha, doubled the guard. So I'd learned to keep my mouth shut.

Or at least to grumble quietly.

"Have a seat and roll your sleeves up please." Dr. Carver took a sterile syringe and several empty blood collection tubes from his bag and set them on the counter. Despite the disagreeable nature of his visit, he was a difficult man to stay mad at, considering that he legitimately believed that the violation of my veins was for the greater good.

The shifter world was desperate to understand why I'd survived infection when so many other women had died. That was the *real* reason I was still being held. One of them, anyway.

"You've come to poke me three times in one month?" I leaned against the kitchen doorframe, letting my obvious reluctance stand as my official protest. "People are starting to talk."

The doctor's chuckle produced a cluster of fine lines at the corners of his mouth and eyes, the only indicators that he was at least twenty years my senior. A handsome doctor with a gentle touch and a good sense of humor. In the human world, he would have been snapped up long before his mid-forties, but like the vast majority of the male shifters I'd met over the past couple of months, Carver was single, and as far as I could tell, completely without romantic prospects.

Not that I had any interest in changing that, even if he'd been closer to my age. I'd sworn off shifter men within minutes of meeting my first tomcat.

Still, it was a damn shame about Carver.

"What's it going to take to get you to cooperate?" The doctor pulled out a chair at the table for me, but I hardly glanced at it.

"That depends. What contraband were you able to smuggle in?"

His brows rose. "What do you want?"

"You are aware, are you not, that the Di Carlos don't get movie channels and don't have Wi-Fi? I've seen more History Channel documentaries in the past two months than any girl—even a history major—should ever have to suffer through. Take me to a movie, doc."

His smile faded a bit. "What would you say to a pint of ice cream and piping hot Starbucks? Venti."

"Do I get to pick them both up myself?" I asked, and his frown spoke volumes. "Not authorized to take me off the property, are you? Fine." I lowered my voice. "Give me ten minutes alone with your cell phone, and I'll bleed into every vial you brought." My phone was confiscated as part of my official sentence.

"Robyn…" He looked conflicted, but I knew from experience that his sympathy didn't mean he'd smuggle me off the grounds.

"Forget it." As frustrated as I was with my predicament, if it weren't for Dr. Carver's testimony on my behalf to the territorial council, I'd probably be much worse off. The good doctor was as close to an ally as I had. In the Southeast Territory, anyway.

Instead of sitting at the table, I hopped onto the kitchen counter with a fluid sort of feline grace. When I was a kid, my duplicate set of left feet were my biggest obstacle in life, and I bore the scars to attest to two broken arms, four broken toes, and a particularly traumatic tumble into a recently extinguished campfire.

Yet I hadn't lost my balance once in the four months since I'd been infected. But the upside was nowhere near enough to balance out my new lack of autonomy, impulse control, and the right to live as anonymously as I pleased. No tabby—the term for a female cat shifter—can live in peace in a society suffering an admittedly devastating gender imbalance.

On average, only one female werecat was born for every seven or eight males. Which meant that while most male shifters dated, few would ever get the chance to marry and have a family, because shifters were forbidden from disclosing their existence to humans.

That left the entire burden of bearing the next generation up to those one-in-seven-or-eight female shifters.

The imbalance was even more severe with strays, obviously.

I sympathized with the difficult situation. But the shifter world's lack of eligible bachelorettes was neither my fault nor my responsibility. Even if it had become my problem.

"So you're not going to the meeting?" I said, as Carver tore open the packaging around the sterile syringe.

"It's a council meeting. I'm not on the territorial council."

"Because you're not an Alpha?" I pushed the sleeve of my T-shirt up over my elbow.

Carver wrapped the rubber tourniquet a little tighter than it needed to be around my upper arm. "Go ahead. Rub it in." But he was still smiling.

In human society, many male doctors would be considered Alpha males, based on ego alone. The stereotypical "God complex" had its basis in truth, at least according to my personal dating history. Yet despite the fact that Dan Carver was the only medical doctor among the US shifter territories—though he was actually a medical examiner by trade—he lacked the toxic mix of aggression and ego necessary to claim a leadership position. Or a wife.

Which was fine by me. My opinion of Alphas differed very little from my opinion of tomcats in general.

"Don't they usually hold these meetings on the council chair's home turf?" I asked as Carver opened one of the vials.

The council chairman, Rick Wade, was the father of my best friend and former college roommate. I hadn't been allowed to talk to Abby Wade since my incarceration began, even though she'd saved my life when I was infected and kept me alive during the subsequent confusing, chaotic weeks.

I couldn't tell whether they were punishing Abby or me. Or both of us. Either way, since she'd renounced her loyalty to the council and defected to the free zone with her boyfriend—a disgraced former Alpha named Jace—everyone seemed worried that if I spoke to her, I might catch whatever rebellious inner demon had made her reject proper shifter society.

As if I needed Abby's influence for that.

"Yes, usually Rick Wade hosts council meetings." Carver took my right arm and examined the crook of my elbow for a good vein. "They're holding this one here because of you."

"The meeting's about me?" My pulse spiked at the thought. The last time all ten Alphas had gotten together, their purpose, in part, had been to decide my fate. If they were reconvening for the same reason, this time I would damn well be involved in the process. "Wait, I thought this was about Titus Alexander. I heard him talking through the door." Where I *might* have lingered, because the voice of the notorious "stray Alpha" was the only unfamiliar—and

6

deeply sexy—one coming from Bert Di Carlo's office.

"Yes, the Alphas are officially convening to hear Alexander's petition. But they're convening *here* for the excuse to observe your progress." Carver slid the needle into my vein with practiced ease. I hardly felt it. "Speaking of which, how's the training going?"

"Well, I was always good at fighting." And I found the exertion to be therapeutic. "That was part of the problem, remember?"

The doctor's small grin eased a little of my tension. My sense of humor functions as a defense mechanism, but no one other than the doctor seemed willing to make light of my crimes, even though every man I'd killed would have been executed by the council if they'd gotten the chance. I'd killed murderers. Very bad men. My actions were only considered crimes in shifter society because I committed them without permission from the council.

A technicality, as far as I was concerned.

"And the exercises? How's your control?"

"Flawless. I'm a fast learner." Both of which were only true under ideal circumstances. My impulse was still to shift into feline form when I felt angry or threatened, and resisting that very real physical pull was still the most difficult part of my daily routine. But I really *was* making progress…

"And the nightmares?"

"A thing of the past." Mostly because I rarely slept long enough to dream. "So feel free to tell them how very cured I am of the murderous rage. Seriously, I'm an asset to the community. Totally safe around both pets and small children."

"I'll be sure to pass that along." Dr. Carver

screwed one of the vials into the plastic sleeve at the end of the syringe, and I watched as my blood began to fill it. The contents of the vial looked so normal. One could never tell just from looking that somewhere in that DNA soup lay the answer to the huge question of my survival—and potentially of the entire shifter community.

Dr. Carver and his brother, a geneticist, were hoping to unlock the secrets of my successful infection. Making strays, including tabbies, is illegal, even though they—we—are in severely short supply. But if they could figure out how I'd survived, they could hopefully save any other women who were infected, whether through accident or intentional criminal act.

I totally supported the cause, which was the only reason I was participating so sweetly in the millionth withdrawal from the Robyn Sheffield Blood Bank.

"So what does the stray Alpha want?" I asked, as my blood continued to bubble into the vial. Titus Alexander was Jace and Abby's friend, and their host in the free zone, last I'd heard.

"He's come to request official recognition of his wildcat Pride by the council," Dr. Carver said as he unscrewed the full vial from the syringe.

"Why are there no stray Prides?"

"Because making strays is illegal, and the council is afraid that giving them official status will encourage the infection of more strays."

The thought made me feel sick to my stomach.

"So, how close are you to figuring me out?" I asked, as my blood filled the second vial. "I mean, you may as well stick a tap straight into my vein so you can draw more on demand. Like at a bar."

Carver chuckled again. "We're not drinking your blood. We're studying it."

"Maybe you should be studying how to prevent infection, rather than how to succeed at it, if making more like me is illegal." But I felt bad for saying that before the words had even faded into silence between us. I knew damn well that Carver wasn't trying to make more strays.

He disconnected the second vial and set it aside. "The only way to prevent infection is to prevent violent contact between humans and shifters. But that's a job for psychologists and enforcers, not doctors."

I thought about that while he removed the needle from my arm, covered the hole in my flesh with a bandage, and untied the tourniquet. Dr. Carver, I decided, was one of the good guys.

While he packed up his supplies and refilled his coffee mug, I wandered out of the kitchen and through the dining room, studying the framed photographs covering one long wall of the Di Carlos' most formal—and ceramic-angel-free—space. They rarely used the dining room, even though at least four of the territory's six live-in enforcers were present at every dinner.

I'd decided early on in my confinement that the room's lack of use was due to the faces staring at the diners from the wall. One face in particular.

"Who is she?"

I spun, startled by the unexpected yet familiar voice, to find a stranger standing behind me, leaning against the doorway. My gaze caught on him and stuck there, and for a moment, I could only stare at him with my mouth hanging open, like most of the toms around here look at me. His strong features and piercing eyes were unfamiliar—an unsettling rarity over the past two months—but one whiff of his scent provided his identity.

Stray.

Titus Alexander.

Why had no one told me the stray Alpha was *gorgeous*?

I glanced around the dining room, expecting to find one of the Southeast enforcers acting as escort for the guest. Bert Di Carlo *never* left me alone with strange toms, and this was the strangest—and prettiest—one I'd ever met.

Titus didn't wear dark clothes like an enforcer—intended to hide the inevitable bloodstains. He wore a suit, like the older generation of Alphas.

Yet he wore his suit *nothing* like the older generation of Alphas.

His steel-colored jacket exactly matched the shade of his eyes, and the material lay perfectly against every artfully sculpted plane and angle of his body. That suit hadn't come off a rack. Every stitch and fold was designed specifically for the man wearing it.

"Um…" I blinked, then tore my gaze away from him. I could feel my cheeks warming.

My hesitance seemed to amuse him, which only made my face burn hotter.

"Sara Di Carlo," I mumbled, forcing my focus back to the photo at the center of the arrangement on the wall. Like most tabbies, she'd been the youngest of her siblings, after a long line of sons.

The stray extended one hand toward me; he thought I was introducing myself.

"Not me. That was Sara." I gestured at the framed

photo. "I'm Robyn." When I clasped my hands behind me, declining his handshake, he withdrew his hand, yet somehow made the motion look...cool.

"Robyn Sheffield, the only American female stray." He inhaled subtly, confirming my identity with a whiff of my scent. "I'm Titus Alexander. The only stray Alpha. It seems we're both somewhat anomalous around here." His smile kindled an intimate fire deep inside me, and I scrambled to put out the flames. I did *not* like Alphas.

"Marc Ramos is a stray Alpha," I informed him. Though the truth was that Marc was his wife's co-Alpha. The council would never let him run a Pride on his own.

His smile faltered. "Yes. Of course." He cleared his throat and refocused on the photograph. "What happened to Sara?"

"She died. She and Abby—" And Faythe Sanders, the only female Alpha. "—um...ran into some trouble several years ago. Sara never made it home." I turned to point at another picture of a young man with beautiful blue eyes, just like his sister's. "Anthony died trying to get justice for her."

"The kidnapping." Titus nodded solemnly. "I heard about that."

"Abby told you?" I frowned. Abby *never* talked about whatever happened to her at the hands of those rogues.

"No." The realization that he'd said too much seemed to hit him all at once, and he shifted his weight onto one foot.

"Jace," I guessed.

"He only told me what I needed to know."

"As an Alpha?"

"And as their host," Titus clarified. "Sometimes Abby has nightmares."

Oh.

Whatever trauma Abby had suffered still haunted her. But not like it haunted Bert and Donna Di Carlo. Sara had been their only daughter, thus their Pride's only hope of producing a next generation. Losing her was both a personal and societal tragedy. I sympathized, though I also understood that when Donna looked at me, more often than not, she was seeing Sara. Figuratively, if not literally.

The Di Carlos seemed determined to protect me where they'd failed Sara. Even if that meant not letting me out of their sight until I was successfully rehabilitated—a moving target, at best.

"So, Jace and Abby are still staying with you?" I asked, looking up into the stray's dark gray eyes.

Titus shrugged, then slid his hands into his pockets, pulling his shirt tight against his chest beneath his open suit jacket. "The house is too big for one person."

But that wasn't the whole story. Several times since my incarceration, I'd overheard Donna Di Carlo worrying about Abby. Jace was exiled without his assets, and the Di Carlos seemed to think that Abby wouldn't be safe enough in the free zone to get a job. Because she was the only tabby in a territory full of male strays.

Titus had given Jace and Abby not just a place to stay, but a sanctuary, of sorts. Even if he wouldn't take credit for that.

"Mr. Alexander?" We both turned to see Teddy Di Carlo, the youngest of the Di Carlo boys and a senior Southeast Pride enforcer. "Did you get lost on the way to the bathroom?"

Titus smiled with a glance at me. "No, just...distracted."

"This way." Teddy gestured toward the guest bath. I watched them go long enough to determine that the back of Titus's suit fit as nicely as the front. Then I wandered toward Umberto Di Carlo's office.

Bert's enforcers had been picking Alphas up from the airport all day, but they were still waiting on a straggler before they could officially begin their meeting, and Teddy had left the office door cracked open.

I started to peek inside, then the mention of my name caught my attention, and I pressed myself against the wall instead. Eavesdropping without shame.

"So, which way is Robyn leaning?" The voice sounded gruff and middle-aged, and though I recognized it, I couldn't identify the owner. I'd only met most of the Alphas once, the day of the plea bargain that stuck me in this purple-walled, ceramic-angel hell, and I wasn't even sure I remembered all of their names.

"She isn't leaning at all," Bert answered. "That girl stands up straight every second of the day, afraid that if she bends even a little, we'll break her in half. She doesn't trust us."

"Do you blame her?" As the only woman on the council, Faythe's voice was easy to identify. "She wasn't born into this. Hell, I *was* born into this and still spent half my life rolling my eyes at you old coots. You're not exactly tuned in to the needs and wants of a young woman."

A smile snuck up on me. No wonder Abby liked

her.

Bert snorted. "Better not let Paul Blackwell hear you talk like that."

"If Paul Blackwell could hear anything, I might be worried," Faythe shot back, and several of the others laughed.

"My question stands," the first, unidentifiable voice said. "There are bigger issues at hand than the 'needs and wants' of one girl."

Spoken like a man in a position of power. I had to bite my tongue to keep a growl from rumbling up my throat.

"What are your thoughts on the matter, Bert?" a distinctive, deep voice asked, and that one I recognized. Abby's father, Rick Wade. The chairman of the territorial council. Maybe he would pass along a message to Abby, if I asked nicely…

Or maybe not. I wasn't even sure he was still in touch with his daughter since she'd defected to follow Jace into the free zone.

"Donna and I are hoping she takes to Teddy," Bert said. "They'd make a good match. He's interested, and since she arrived, he's developed a lot of potential."

"He's too young," the gruff voice insisted. "Teddy has too little experience."

"The circumstance makes the Alpha," a new voice countered, and a chorus of male voices seconded the platitude.

Alpha. *Teddy isn't an Alpha.*

All at once, I understood. If Teodoro Di Carlo displayed Alpha potential and I married him, he would *become* an Alpha. He would take over his father's Pride. I would become the daughter Bert and Donna had lost.

How neat and logical. My life was being planned out for me by a bunch of men, most of whom I'd hardly even met.

"Does she like him?" Faythe asked, her voice soft but strong, and my shocked inhalation tasted bitter. Abby described Faythe as an arrow piercing the shield of testosterone. Faythe had made her own rules and her own decisions from the day she was born, even when they conflicted with the wishes of the council. *Especially* when they conflicted with the wishes of the council. So why would she help them run my life?

Shouldn't she at least be bound by a sense of loyalty to a fellow member of the "girls' names containing extraneous Ys" club? We were as few as we were awesome.

"I can't tell that she likes anyone or anything." Bert cleared his throat while a lump formed in mine. "Time and trust will help some of that. Eventually, she has to understand that we have her best interests in mind."

"Do we, though?" Faythe asked. "At least Ed was honest; there are bigger issues at stake."

"Which is why we're prepared with an alternative," the first voice said, and now that I'd heard the name, I recognized its owner. Ed Taylor. "Abigail's defection had nothing to do with my son's ability to lead. Brian is still a perfectly viable option, and he'd like the chance to develop a connection. If Faythe thinks she can spare him for a while."

Brian Taylor. Abby's ex.

Brian was one of Faythe's enforcers in the South-Central territory. Did they really think they could just plug me into the gap Abby had left in everyone's lives? In their misplaced hopes?

My temper spiked along with my pulse, and my jaw began to ache.

The familiar sensation—the beginning of a shift—triggered an instant fear in me. If I couldn't control the impulse, they would never let me out of the Di Carlos' house. They would never stop running my life, "for my own good."

"Yes," Faythe said. "Brian came to me with the idea, but I'm not sure—"

"He's a good candidate," Ed Taylor snapped cutting her off in mid-sentence. "And if procreation proves possible with a female stray, he'd make an excellent sire."

Sire. As if Brian were a bull kept for breeding. As if I were a cow, good for nothing else.

The ache in my jaw became a sharp pain, and I shoved myself away from the wall. I shook my head over and over, but couldn't dislodge what I'd heard. What they were planning.

No wonder Abby ran. Not just into the free zone, but to college before that. No wonder she'd never talked about her family or her fiancé, even after I'd been infected. I hadn't truly understood what she was trying to shield me from until that very moment, listening outside my Alpha's office door.

Furious, I took off down the hall, moving silently, grinding my teeth to keep them from shifting. Rubbing my arms, as if that would keep fur from sprouting through my flesh. Dimly, I realized that the council's discussion had devolved into an argument—over whose son would get to father my kittens???—but little of it sank in. All I could think about was the future slipping through my fingers. The life I'd lost.

The door standing right in front of me.

Teddy was supposed to be guarding the front door, but he'd escorted Titus Alexander to the bathroom, to keep an eye on him. To make sure he didn't get "distracted" again.

No one expected me to sneak out of the house while the grounds were crawling with Alphas and their enforcer envoys. But the enforcers were all out by the pool house, drinking and cavorting with friends they hadn't seen since the last meeting. They were under orders to give me space, because no one thought I was cured yet.

They had no idea how right they were.

The door stood three feet away. Beyond it lay a driveway full of vehicles. Maybe someone had left keys in an ignition. Maybe…

I pushed the door open, then froze in my tracks.

The visiting Alphas and their entourages had all been picked up at the airport by Southeast Pride enforcers—Teddy Di Carlo and his coworkers. None of them drove anything more expensive than a Toyota Highlander. Which meant that the sleek, shiny black Mercedes SUV with Mississippi plates could only belong to…

Titus Alexander.

TWO

Titus

"Mr. Alexander, we've spent the past half hour listening to your statistics and your plans for this 'Pride,' should we grant your request." Milo Mitchell's use of air quotes told me exactly how seriously the majority of the council wasn't taking my presentation. I probably shouldn't have bothered with the spreadsheet. "So maybe now you could stop wasting our time and get to the point. Why, exactly, should we allow you to start your own Pride?"

"Respectfully, sir, I'm not asking for your permission." I closed my laptop and leaned against the folding table provided to me for my pitch—a decidedly less opulent setup than typically rolled out for my corporate boardroom meetings. But then, I wasn't there as a CEO, and my audience of Alphas couldn't have cared less about my day job. "I've already started my own Pride. In the former free zone now known as the Mississippi Valley Territory. I'm *already* an Alpha, and I already employ twelve full-time enforcers. That's a larger force than any of your Prides can sustain, even though my physical territory is smaller than any of yours. I'm just asking for official recognition from the council. For some legitimacy to support my position."

Faythe Sanders gave me a short warning shake of her head, but before I could rephrase, Jerold Pierce leaned forward in his chair, his eyes narrowed, his jaw tight. "A larger force? Is that a threat?"

Paul Blackwell scoffed, his bony grip tight on his knobby cane. "Hush, Jerold, the boy's not threatening us. The free zone is overrun with strays and rogues. He doesn't have enough time or resources—even with his dozen men—to make trouble for us."

The old man was right, but I knew better than to admit that. "I'm not threatening you. My point is that my Pride has been designed after the model you established. I've conformed to all of your requirements. And to answer your question, Mr. Mitchell, you should recognize my Pride because it will benefit you *all* to have the free zone under control. Those of you in the south can rest easier knowing that our border is friendly. Knowing that the men in my territory follow all the same rules your own members follow. Knowing that we're no threat. That we are, in fact, your allies."

For a second, Gardner, Pierce, and the young one—Abby's brother, Isaac Wade, who'd inherited Jace's Pride—seemed to be considering my points. Then...

"Why should we trust a stray?" Mitchell demanded.

Faythe held up one hand before I could unclench my jaw, and she carefully pushed herself to her feet, one hand on her round belly. "We agreed to hear Mr. Alexander out," she reminded the room in general.

"And bickering is beneath the stature of this council."

"Nonsense. Bickering is a time-honored council tradition," Blackwell insisted. A couple of the older men chuckled, and Isaac dared a hesitant smile.

"Do your strays want to be governed?" one of the Alphas asked, as the laughter faded, and I had to mentally grasp for his name.

Nick Davidson. Widowed Alpha of the New England Pride.

"Excuse me?" That was the last question I'd expected to be asked by a panel of mostly-men who'd been virtual dictators for their entire adult lives. Since when do they care whether their Pride members want to be governed? Shifter Prides are not a democracy.

"Your 'Pride' is made up of strays and rogues, right?" Davidson demanded softly. "The strays grew up human, and—like Robyn—they have no real concept of the Alpha-centric hierarchy. And the rogues presumably defected to the free zone specifically to escape that hierarchy. So my question is this: do they want you there at all? How are we supposed to believe you can control an element of our society that is, by definition, rebellious and out of control?"

I met his gaze. "You're supposed to believe I can do it because I've been doing it for more than a year now, without recognition or assistance from this council. And in that year, the number of infections and shifter-related homicides in the free zone has had a distinct downward trajectory, as my statistics clearly show." I laid one hand on my laptop, and one of the Alphas actually rolled his eyes. *So much for fair consideration.* "Can that be said about your own territories?"

Faythe groaned over my departure from the script. She, Marc, and Jace—the co-authors of my proposal—had given me detailed instructions about how best to address the council without pissing anyone off. But the Alphas weren't taking my respectful, sycophantic approach seriously. Time for a dose of the truth.

I stood straight and looked around the room, making eye contact with each Alpha. Making them look up at me. "Many of you seem to be misunderstanding my intent. I'm not asking for a favor. I'm offering to do *you* a favor. It's in *your* best interest to acknowledge my Pride and establish an open line of communication."

Mitchell snorted. "How is that?"

"For decades, you've been banishing strays and rogues from your territories, waiting for them to break one of your laws so that you can justify executing them. And eventually they *all* break the laws—rules they don't understand and aren't even always aware of—because you've thrown them out without any guidance or advice. You don't help them through scratch fever. You don't teach them to control their new instincts and impulses. You toss them out like garbage. I'm out there standing in the Dumpster, cleaning up the mess *you* made."

"Titus…" Faythe began, and I could practically see the warning building behind her eyes. "Never mind." She waved one hand for me to continue, then sank carefully into her spot on the left-hand couch. "They need to hear the truth. Give it to 'em."

So I turned back to the room full of scowls aimed at me. "Your council recognizes three free zones, and each of them is a dark spot on your collective radar.

I'm offering to turn the lights on in what was once the Mississippi free zone. To share information, so you know which of the strays and rogues in my territory are a threat to you and which could be assets."

"We don't need your assets," Ed Taylor, Alpha of the Midwest Pride insisted.

Faythe rolled her eyes. "Yes, we do, Ed."

"You're living in the past," I told them. "Information moves at the speed of Wi-Fi now, and if you keep shunning strays and rogues, they're going to break your secret to the world, and no threat of execution will be enough to keep them quiet. You've created a second class of citizens you can't monitor or control, and it's time to open the door and let them in. Let them work with you, rather than against you. I'm offering to help you do that."

"He's right." A bulge rippled across Faythe's belly as the baby kicked, and she rubbed it in small circles.

"The hell he is," Blackwell snapped, his fist tightening around his cane. "We didn't create this problem. We're not the ones out there making more strays. These days, its strays infecting other strays. Back in my day, we had a simple solution for that."

The old man's threat went unspoken, but we all knew what he wasn't saying. Back in Blackwell's day, strays had been executed on sight, to prevent the spread of infection.

If he were in charge, I'd be dead.

"Back in your day, forensics was an infant science and the internet wasn't even imagined." Faythe stood again and began pacing, stretching with every awkward step, as if she couldn't get comfortable. "We live in a different world now. It's time to open our eyes, gentlemen."

"Do you expect us to believe he's doing us a favor?" Mitchell demanded. "As if he and his strays wouldn't benefit?"

"Of course we would benefit," I admitted. No sense in denying that. "Right now, my men can't leave the free zones. They can't work or visit family in any of your territories or go to school there. They can't even drive through your territories on the way to other free zones. They're virtual prisoners of your making, and every aspect of their personal and professional lives is suffering because of that."

"Don't you mean *your* professional life?" Ed Taylor demanded, while Isaac Wade's focus shifted back and forth between us as if he were watching a tennis match. "Isn't this really about how the travel ban affects *your* business?"

I nodded. "Part of this is about opening the borders. Letting people live their lives. And you'll benefit from that as much as I will."

"That is not even remotely—" Blackwell sputtered, until Richard Wade, council chairman, stood and cut him off.

"Okay, I think that's enough for now. You've given us a lot to consider, Mr. Alexander, and you have my word that we'll do that."

"Thank you." I couldn't get a good read of Abby's dad. He was polite, certainly, but didn't seem to be taking a side on the issue, one way or another. "And thank you all for agreeing to hear me out."

Wade nodded. "And with that, I declare this meeting concluded. Gentlemen—and Faythe—I believe Donna Di Carlo has made something special for us this evening. I've smelled it cooking for the past hour. Is that beef Burgundy?"

The Alphas filed out of the office, following Umberto Di Carlo toward his kitchen, until only Rick Wade and Faythe remained.

"Well, that went better than expected," the council chair said as he closed the door behind his son Isaac.

I slid my laptop into its case. "So I should be pleased that Blackwell didn't try to have me executed on sight?"

"Yes, but don't take that personally," Faythe said with a grin. "He'd get rid of me too, if he could."

"It'd be best if you head out before they actually ask you to leave." Rick stuffed both hands into his pockets, beneath his suit jacket. "But you have my word that we'll discuss nothing else over dinner."

"Agreed." I shrugged. "I'm not a fan of beef Burgundy anyway."

Faythe laughed, one hand low on her stomach. "Neither is this little one. Donna's promised me a Margherita grilled cheese."

"Margarita, as in tequila and lime?"

"As in tomatoes and basil." She smiled. "The cravings this time around have been…interesting."

"How much longer?" I asked as I headed for the hall.

"Two months. Though I wouldn't object to an early arrival, as long as he's healthy."

"My little brother came early, and he was fine," I assured her. "I'll see you next time, Faythe. And Rick, thank you again for setting this up."

"It's the least we could do," Faythe said as she opened the door. "Literally the least," she added with a glance at the kitchen, where the other Alphas were gathered.

"I'll walk you out." Wade led me out the front door while Faythe went in search of her sandwich, and as I unlocked my SUV, he cleared his throat. "Titus, how's Abby doing? Is she safe?"

"Yes. You have my word." I met his gaze, letting him judge my sincerity for himself. "And she'll only be safer if and when the council recognizes our territory. An alliance would benefit us both. Your daughter could be officially in your life, Rick."

"I can't make any promises." His voice was carefully neutral, but I could see hope gathering behind his eyes. "This isn't a democracy, but it's not a dictatorship either. It's not solely my call. And it's a complicated issue."

I nodded, though to me, opening the borders and acknowledging everyone's right to exist seemed rather simple.

"Will you just... Will you tell her to call her mother?" Rick asked as I leaned into the car to drop my laptop case on the passenger seat.

I couldn't resist a laugh. "Abby doesn't take orders. But I'll *ask* her to call her mother."

"Thank you, Titus. You'll hear from us soon." Rick Wade watched me get into my car and start the engine. As I pulled out of the driveway, a small SUV followed me onto the road, and in the rearview mirror, I recognized the driver as Teddy Di Carlo, Bert Di Carlo's youngest remaining son. Teddy was my official escort out of the Southeast Territory.

I'd been driving for less than twenty minutes when my phone rang. Faythe's name appeared on the screen. I answered through the car's speakerphone. "Hey, Faythe. Do *not* tell me they've ruled against me already."

"No, they haven't started discussing it yet. This is about…" Her sentence faded, as if she were searching for a way to continue. "Titus, *please* tell me you don't have Robyn Sheffield."

I frowned at my phone, plugged into its travel charger. "I don't have Robyn Sheffield. Why would you even ask that?"

"She's missing. Everyone's out looking for her, but no one's seen her since before you left. So I thought…"

"You thought I, what? Just took her? Don't you think my helpful Southeast escort would notice if there were a passenger in my car?"

"Not if she were…hidden."

"Seriously? I would hope you know me better than that by now." Faythe, Marc, Jace, and I had been working together for nearly a year to put my proposal in front of the council.

"I do. I'm sorry." She sighed, and stress echoed in the sound. "I have to cover all the bases. I'm calling Abby next, to see if she's heard anything."

"Do you need her number?" Abby and Jace both had to get new cell phones when Jace's was passed to the new Alpha of his old Pride—Isaac Wade—and Abby's father took her off his family plan.

"No, I have it. Thanks, though. Will you let me know if you hear anything? She might tell you things she won't tell me these days."

"Of course." Though I wasn't entirely sure I meant that. Until and unless my Pride was officially recognized, my loyalty remained with my men. If Abby knew something and Robyn wasn't in any danger, I was inclined to let her keep her secret.

"Thanks." Faythe hung up, and I turned my

thoughts to the meeting as I drove, mentally going over every potential mistake I'd made during my presentation.

After several hours on the road, long after the sun had sunk beneath the western horizon in my windshield, I waved goodbye to Teddy Di Carlo at the territorial border, just east of the Mississippi state line. He nodded at me, acknowledging that I had officially vacated the Southeast Territory, but didn't crack even a hint of a smile.

Pride cats, in my experience, were entirely too serious.

A few miles later, I pulled into the state welcome center to use the restroom and buy a drink from the vending machine. As I was backing out of my parking spot, sipping from a bottle of sweet tea, a familiar scent suddenly washed over me.

I slammed on the breaks, my pulse racing in my ears, and movement in the rearview mirror caught my attention. A set of eyes blinked at me in the dark. From the cargo space in the back of my car.

"*Damn* it!" I slammed the gearshift into park and twisted in my seat so fast that tea sloshed over my hand. "Robyn? What the hell are you doing here?"

"Hi. I'm sorry." She flinched, and even in the dark, I could see guilt etched into the tiny worry lines forming around her frown. "I was going to hitch a ride into the free zone, and you would never have known I was here, but I drank two bottles of water and a huge mug of coffee before I settled in here, and now I *really* have to pee."

"You…? What…?" I dropped my bottle into the drink holder, and more splashed over.

"I have to pee. Like, right now. Sorry, but it's an

emergency." She climbed over the back seat and plopped down in the third row.

"Robyn, *why* are you in my car? And why do you smell like—?" *Me*. My scent clung to her, as if she'd been rolling around in my bed for hours.

With that thought, the image appeared in my head, helped along by the fact that her hair was disheveled from hours spent huddling beneath something in my car.

Robyn held something up, and I squinted into the near darkness at my spare shirt. "I found a change of clothes in a bag, and I covered myself with them. So you wouldn't smell me."

That took me a moment to process.

The only female stray confirmed to exist in the US—the Territorial Council's most guarded asset— had snuck out of her gilded birdcage and rolled around in my scent.

I shifted in my seat, struggling to stay focused on the problem because I'd never smelled a more arousing combination of scents in my life. Instincts I'd learned to control years before suddenly roared to life deep inside me. From the wild heart of my shifter half, which I'd managed to bottle up, but could never truly tame.

No. You cannot *have her*, my human half insisted. *She's going to get you killed.*

"Robyn, you can't be here." I spoke slowly. Careful to keep my thoughts out of my voice.

"I know that tone," she said as she climbed over another seat back and landed in the second row. "You can yell at me all you want in a few minutes. Right now, I have to pee."

"You're not getting out of this car. I'm driving you

straight back to—"

She opened the door and stepped into the parking lot.

"Damn it!" I spit as I pulled the SUV into the parking space and slammed the gear into park again. "Robyn!" I whispered fiercely as I got out and race-walked after her, across the dark expanse of crunchy February grass, trying not to notice how well her angry stride showed off her ass. "Get back here!"

A man looked up from helping his young daughter open a can of soda at the well-lit bank of vending machines.

"Robyn!" I caught up with her near the women's restroom and grabbed her arm. "You can't just leave. And you sure as *hell* can't involve me in whatever rebellion you're launching." I had a battle of my own to fight, which left me with neither the time nor the energy for hers. No matter how badly I wanted to kiss her and find out how she tasted.

She pulled her arm from my grip, staring up at me, and I wondered how any man in the world had ever refused those gorgeous blue eyes anything. "We'll discuss this after I empty my bladder."

"Get in the car." I reached for her again, and she stepped away, eyes flashing fiercely.

"I'll shout for help," she threatened through clenched teeth, nodding at the man and his daughter. "You can spend the evening in jail for assault, or you can let me go to the bathroom, after which I'll willingly get in your car."

Before I could answer, a family of five came out of the bright visitor's center into the dark night, clutching pamphlets advertising things to do on vacation in Mississippi.

Robyn wasn't bluffing. I could see that in the way she watched the family.

"Fine. Go pee. But if you try to run, I *will* chase you." Which would give me a legitimate excuse to watch her backside until I caught her. "You're going back to Atlanta even if I have to drag you there."

"By my hair?" she demanded softly, brows arched to make her point. Then she opened the door to the women's room and slipped inside.

I waited outside the door with my arms crossed over my chest, ignoring the blatant stares of the other motorists. I was well aware of how the situation looked from the outside. The big bad man in the suit won't even let his wife or girlfriend go to the bathroom in peace. But they had no idea what was really going on.

Every second that passed raised my blood pressure. If the sun were still up, I might already have been recognized, and every moment I stood there increased the chance of that happening.

I could *not* afford to be on the news again. Not like this.

A toilet flushed inside the bathroom and water ran softly. An electric hand dryer roared for a second before soft footsteps headed my way. I pulled open the door as she got to it and was rewarded with Robyn's surprised face staring out at me.

"That's creepy," she said, flicking several mineral-scented drops of water off her still-wet hands. Into my face.

"I believe the term you're looking for is 'courteous.'" I wiped the moisture off my face with my left hand. "That's what most people call it when one person opens a door for another."

"Unless that first person is planning to drag the second person back into captivity."

I started to argue with her characterization of the situation—until I realized how accurate it was. But that wasn't my fault. "Let's go."

"I'll get in your car because I promised I would," Robyn whispered as we walked toward my SUV. "But you're not taking me back to Atlanta."

I laughed, but the sound held no humor. "Where is it we're going, according to your delusion?"

"You're taking me home—that's the new plan. To *your* home. So I can talk to Abby."

Yes. Back to my home, where she really *could* roll around in my bed for hours.

I wish...

"This isn't a game, Robyn." I stopped and shoved my hands into my pocket, to make sure no one still watching would think I was threatening her. "Helping you escape into the free zone would ruin any chance I have of getting my Pride recognized," I hissed. "Any chance my men have of gaining rights and privileges you clearly take for granted."

Irritation flashed over her features. "Prison is not a privilege. And anyway, I'm already in the free zone."

"They don't have to know that." *Shit.* My forehead furrowed as the realization fell into place. "Except Teddy saw me cross the territorial line. You have no idea what you've done, do you?" I demanded. "A stray removing one of the council's tabbies from her territory will be considered an act of *war*. They will invade my territory and attack my men to get you back."

"You can't be serious," she insisted, blue eyes wide.

"Of course I'm serious. That's why Abby formally defected, instead of just running away. She did it in front of the entire council so that Jace couldn't be blamed. But you can't even do that, because you made a deal with them, didn't you?" A plea deal, according to Abby. "You have to go back." I reached for her arm again, and again she pulled away.

"No. I don't belong there." Her gaze landed on my mouth and seemed snagged there. "I want to stay with you."

A possessive rumble began deep inside me at her declaration, and it took every bit of self-control I had not to pull her closer and kiss her. The ache to touch her, as she stood there bathed in my scent, was almost more than I could resist.

What the hell is happening to me? It couldn't be the normal reaction to meeting a tabby. My body had never reacted like that to Faythe or Abby.

"I want to stay with Abby, I mean." She gave her head a little shake, as if to wake herself up. "At your house. She's the only friend I have."

"I'm sorry. I truly am." More than she would ever know. "But this isn't up to me."

Robyn's eyes widened, and the lights from the parking lot highlighted her impending panic. "I'm *not* going back. You're trying to make things better for strays, right? Well, I'm a stray, and I need help. They're trying to make me get married. They're *negotiating* with one another about whose son gets to knock me up."

That growl began again at the very *thought* of someone else touching her, and I swallowed hard, shoving it down. *She is not yours, Titus.*

"If you mean everything you said about making

32

things better, you *have* to help me." She took a deep breath and held my gaze with an impressive strength. "I demand sanctuary. As a stray."

My eyes fell closed, and I groaned as the predicament she'd put me in suddenly zoomed into crystal-clear focus.

I am so *screwed.*

THREE

Robyn

"Get in the car," Titus growled, pulling his phone from his pocket. "We're not going to have this argument in public."

I glanced across the welcome center, past a dark, empty playground and a bank of vending machines, at his SUV. "How do I know you won't drive me back to Atlanta?"

His scowl deepened. "You're the stowaway threatening to start a war in my territory. *I'm* the one who has a reason to distrust."

"I'm not threatening to start a war," I insisted as I headed toward his car. Slowly, in spite of the cold and the fact that I snuck out of the territory without my jacket.

His frown lingered on me as some battle I couldn't quite make sense of raged behind his steely gray eyes. "Yet that's exactly what will happen if they find out I have you and I refuse to return you."

"Look, I'm not trying to make life hard for you. I just want—"

"You can keep saying you don't want to start trouble." Titus clicked a button on his key fob as we drew closer to the parking lot, and his SUV's locks disengaged with a solid-sounding thump. "But as long as what you're actually doing is starting trouble, it's a little hard for me to believe you."

Okay, that's fair. "I admit I didn't think this through. I saw an opportunity and I took it. I couldn't stay in that house for *one more second.*"

Titus pulled the passenger's side door open for me, frowning. "They lock you in the house?"

"Well, no," I admitted as I slid onto the gray leather seat, setting his briefcase in my lap. He rolled his eyes and tried to close the door, but I held it open. "But they never let me leave the property, and they confiscated my phone, cutting off my access to the outside world. I'm under guard at all times. I'm a prisoner there."

"Yet somehow, you managed to sneak into my car without being seen."

"That was only possible because they trust you even less than they trust me," I insisted. "While they were watching you, I slipped through the cracks."

"And into my car." Titus slammed the door.

He rounded the front of the vehicle, then stopped suddenly, and I could practically see some new realization smack him on the forehead. Then he stomped to the driver's side and pulled his door open. "I already told them you weren't with me!"

"I heard. And I'm sorry. But your empty SUV was the only shot at freedom I've had in more than two months." If four hours spent hiding under a stranger's change of clothes didn't prove how desperate I'd been to get out of there, I wasn't sure what would. "Titus, if I'd stayed in that house, they would have turned me into some kind of feline Stepford wife and mother."

He slid into his seat and closed the door, leaving us in the dark when the interior light went out. Yet even in human form, I could still make out every silvery striation in his gray eyes, thanks to a cat's ability to see in low light. "I'm sure you misunder—"

"This is still the US, isn't it? I still have rights?" I demanded, my fist clenched around the door grip.

"Yes, but you made a deal with the council, and—"

"I was coerced. I was *threatened*. If I hadn't taken that deal, they would have ripped out my teeth or cut off the ends of my fingers to 'declaw' me. Have you seen what that looks like? Have you met Manx?" I saw her once, and a single glimpse of her mutilated hands had given me nightmares.

"No, but—"

"And there were veiled threats of execution. I had no choice but to accept their deal, not just for me, but for Abby. I did what I had to do to keep myself alive and to help her during her trial, but that doesn't mean the deal was fair. That doesn't give them the right to hand over my future to the Alpha with the most eligible son!"

"No, it doesn't." Anger flashed behind his eyes at the thought, and his reaction made something low and sensitive clench inside me. "But yours isn't the only life at stake here…" He started scrolling through the contacts list on his phone, and I realized I was losing him, in spite of the fact that he clearly agreed with me.

"Titus!" I waved my hand in front of his screen.

"If you send me to the Di Carlos, you have to admit that you're a sexist hypocrite!"

He arched both brows at me. "How the hell do you figure that?"

"You're offering protection and aid to all the strays in your territory, as long as they have a Y chromosome. That's textbook sexism."

He rolled his eyes. "You're the only stray in the country without a Y chromosome."

"Does that mean I don't deserve the same consideration as the men?"

"Of course not. But that's not the issue. When the council finds out I have you, they'll think I *lied*. They'll invade my territory to get you, and people will die. My Pride will never be recognized, and without the council's cooperation and resources, Life will never get better for strays in the free zone. I have to think about the greater good, Robyn."

I rolled my eyes. "And once again, the greater good of shifter society comes at the expense of one woman's liberty. You toms are all alike. Posturing, blustering, hypocritical bigots."

"*Stop talking*," Titus growled, and I recoiled from the anger in his voice instinctively.

Then hated myself for that.

I'd never shied away from a fight in my life, yet every feline instinct I'd been infected with was suddenly telling me to lower my eyes and slowly back away from the angry Alpha.

Screw that. If I'd learned anything from mandatory training, it was that I didn't have to give in to my shifter instincts. I was still as much human as feline. As was Titus.

He was also the only person in the world currently

in the position to give me what I needed.

Freedom. A little space. A chance to talk to Abby.

"You only have a problem if the council finds out. So don't tell the council." I shrugged, hoping he couldn't see—or somehow scent—my internal human-versus-feline battle of wills. "No one ever has to know how I broke out."

"They'll figure it out. You didn't leave any scent on the ground, and the only vehicle that left the Di Carlo property other than Teddy's was mine." He tapped a name on his phone, and Faythe Sanders's picture and phone number appeared. "If you really don't want to cause me trouble, call Faythe and tell her what you did." He tried to hand me his cell phone, but I pushed it away.

"Wait. Let's talk about this."

"We're not negotiating," he growled. "Call her, Robyn. That's an order."

I leaned against the passenger-side door, my arms crossed over my chest. Trying not to think about the wild, exciting nature of his scent—the warm, living version of the one I'd bathed in for four hours. "I don't take orders from you."

"If you want to belong to my Pride, you do."

Belong to his Pride? I'd asked for sanctuary, not membership. Were the two inextricable?

I had no interest in trading one Alpha's rules and machinations for another's—no matter how good he smelled. But if pretending I wanted to belong would keep him from sending me back to the Di Carlos...

Wait a minute.

"The way I see this, I win either way." I ticked the possibilities off on my fingers as I thought aloud, half convinced that I had overlooked some devastating detail. "If I join your Pride, I have to follow your orders, but you can't send me to Atlanta, because I won't belong there anymore. If I *don't* join your Pride, I *don't* have to follow your orders, which means you can tell me to go to Atlanta, but you'd be wasting your breath, because you're not the boss of me. Or am I thinking about this all wrong?"

He frowned at me in the dark, and even his scowl was somehow sexy. "Are you asking me to *help* you manipulate me?"

"I'm assuming that if you have a counterargument, you'll throw it at me. Soon, preferably."

"A counterargument." Titus slid his key into the ignition, and my pulse jumped when he started the car. "How's this: I'm going to drive you to the border and tell Teddy Di Carlo to come get you. He's less than an hour away."

"That would be the biggest mistake of your life."

Titus laughed, and the sound echoed through me, touching off little sparks everywhere it landed. "I'm pretty sure the biggest mistake of my life was following a shadow and a snort into a clump of brush during a corporate camping retreat three years ago." He untucked the tail of his button-down shirt and pulled it up to reveal four prominent white claw mark scars stretched across the defined ripples of his abs.

I reached out to touch them before I realized what I was doing. Then I jerked my hand away.

Stop it, Robyn. I shook my head, trying to dislodge the enticing mental image of his bare stomach. Yes, Titus was hot in an obvious sort of way that made my pulse race and my skin flush, but those reactions weren't real, and neither was any *totally* hypothetical attraction I felt toward him. Tabbies practically ovulating in the presence of an Alpha was hormonal witchcraft, and nothing more. Exactly the kind of shifter instinct I'd spent the past nine weeks learning that I didn't have to give in to.

Like bloodlust, and the overwhelming urge to shift when I got angry…

"But we play the cards we're dealt, right?" Titus continued, dragging my thoughts into focus.

Or you trade them in for a better hand. Which is what he wanted to do with me.

And what I wanted to do with my entire miserable existence. I'd been a semester from graduating with a degree in History from the University of Kentucky when I was sentenced to indefinite house arrest in Atlanta. I'd already been accepted into the graduate program, and my secret nerdy ambition had been to help eliminate educational bias by producing high school textbooks without culturally motivated omissions.

But that would never happen if I wound up married to some tom I hardly knew, popping out a baby every eighteen months for the next decade, not because I wanted kids, but because shifter society needed them.

"If you try to take me to the border, I'll jump from the moving vehicle. Or I'll call 911 and tell them I've been kidnapped. I'll do whatever it takes to stay in the free zone, and you can explain to the council how you not only removed a tabby from the Southeast Territory, but you *lost* her and wound up on the news."

His gray eyes narrowed. "You would throw my entire Pride and me under the bus just to get out of a deal *you* made?"

"Just to…?" I sat straighter and fought not to let him hear how desperate I was. "Have you ever been under house arrest? Ever been forced to live with strangers? Denied use of the telephone? Have you ever been told you can't go back to school, and you can't talk to your parents, and you can't even go for a walk by yourself? Have you ever had your every move studied and observed? Ever been the subject of endless medical testing? Ever had a guard stand outside the bathroom door while you shower, to make sure you're not prying the window open? Ever been told that you're worth nothing more than the secrets floating around in your bloodstream and the eggs waiting to be released into your uterus?"

"I don't actually have a uterus, so I'd have to say no." But his joke couldn't cover his discomfort. He understood why I had run. Yet he still wanted no part of my battle with the council.

"I'm sorry I dragged you into this, but…is there anything you wouldn't do to reclaim your own autonomy?"

He watched me for a moment, and I could see that he was giving the question actual thought. "Well, I'd like to think I wouldn't screw other people over in the pursuit of freedom."

"Again, I didn't realize I was doing that. And I'm sorry." If I could do it again, I'd certainly do it differently. "But what's done is done, and I can't go back. You don't have to take me to Abby. All you have to do is let me go." I reached for the door handle. "I'll be fine on my own."

His hand landed softly on my arm, and I fought the overwhelming and humiliating urge to press myself into his touch. "No, you won't."

"I heard part of your pitch today, before Dr. Carver came to run his tests. You told the council you've brought safety and stability to the free zone. If that's true, I'll be fine."

"I told them I'm *bringing* safety and stability to my territory," he corrected. "Present progressive tense. As in, the process is ongoing. The Mississippi free zone is like the wild west, Robyn. I'm the law, but the law is new, and there are still plenty of outlaws out here trying to raise hell."

I cocked my head to one side. "Did you seriously just use a cowboy analogy?"

He shrugged, and I missed the warmth when his hand left my arm. "It was more of a sheriff/desperado metaphor. But my point stands. I can't leave you here to fend for yourself."

"Fine. Let me see Abby, and I'll call the council and tell them you had no idea I was in the car until you pulled into your driveway."

His brows rose in the dark. "You'd lie to the council?"

"Would I lie to the governing body unfairly seeking to plot out my entire existence, without so much as asking my opinion? Hell. Yes."

Titus studied me while he weighed his options. "That won't stop them from coming to get you."

I shrugged. "You're an Alpha, right? I'm sure you can think of some way to keep the enemy out of your territory. If you can't, can you really call it 'your territory'?" If there was one thing I'd learned about Alphas, it was that they couldn't resist a challenge.

Titus growled again, but the words buried in that aggressive sound sent a thrill of excitement running through me. "Buckle up."

***

"This is your house?" I stared out the windshield at the front gate until we passed it, then I twisted in my seat to see it close behind us. "How did the gate know to open?"

"There's a sensor." Titus patted a small sticker on the lower right corner of his windshield, where my university parking pass had gone, back when I'd had a car. Back before a horrific camping trip had ended my academic career and sentenced me to an existence ruled by instincts I still didn't always understand.

By instincts, and by a council of ten Alphas governing my life by committee.

"When my car's within ten feet of the gate, it opens. When the car passes out of that range, it closes."

"That's awesome."

"Thank you." His deep voice echoed with pride. "My company developed the technology."

"Seriously?" I'd known he ran some business, and according to the Southeast enforcers, he was the most high-profile stray ever infected. But I'd had no idea his was a tech company. Or that he had such a *huge* house... "How many bedrooms do you have?"

Titus laughed. "Um...seven in the main house, I think. I haven't counted in a while."

Holy shit. "How many bathrooms?" I stared as we approached the three-story Greek Revival with sprawling lawns and manicured flower beds that looked colorful even in the winter. Even in the dark.

"Eight, I believe."

"Eight bathrooms." He could pee in a different

toilet from Sunday to Sunday, then start all over on Monday. That's not rich. That's *wealthy*.

Suddenly I felt like an idiot. What if he thought I'd hidden in his car because of...all this? That I was a tabby gold digger?

"It's just now midnight. It looks like someone's still awake." Titus looked toward the house, where lights were on in several rooms. "Probably Abby and Jace."

"How do you know?" I couldn't stop staring at the house. "Don't you have, like, a zillion enforcers?"

"A dozen. But most of them stay in the guest house, behind the pool. And at any given time, at least half of them are out on patrol. Right now, I have seven spread out around the territory, and five defending our home base." He gestured beyond the windshield at the property spread out around us.

"So, this is like any normal Pride? Only bigger."

"Kind of." Titus pulled the car to a stop on the half-circle drive between a massive set of curved brick steps and a three-tiered water fountain at the center of a semicircle formed by the arch of the driveway. "Geographically, my territory is the smallest in the country. But we have about twice the shifter population Jace said they have in the Appalachian Pride. Ninety percent strays."

"The other ten percent rogues?" Natural-born toms who left shifter society for one reason or another.

"Yes." He turned off the car.

"Donna Di Carlo says they're all criminals." My gaze roamed over the front of the house. "That your territory is nothing more than a penal colony."

Both Titus's smile and his eyes seemed to shine at

me in the dark. "We're much more than *just* a penal colony."

"So they *are* criminals?"

"According to the council's rulings? Yes. Most of them. Including Abby and Jace." His smile faded into a thoughtful look. "As are you."

I blinked, surprised. He was right. "I—"

The front door flew open, and Abby raced down the arched brick steps, leaving Jace's backlit silhouette in the doorway. "Titus! How did it go?" But then she stopped short, her jaw falling, when she saw me through the car window. "*Robyn?*"

"Hey." I pushed the door open and stepped into her hug, and the tension I'd been battling for the past hour of my car ride with Titus just melted away.

Abby was the only person in the world I *knew* I could trust. She'd risked her life to shield and protect me.

"Faythe said you were missing." She seemed to be trying to squeeze all the breath from my body. "Titus found you? Does the council know where you are?"

"No." Steps clomped down the stairs behind her, and I looked up to find Jace looking not at me, but over my shoulder. At Titus. "Faythe would have called us if they knew."

"Hey," a new voice said, as two more toms—one on two legs, one on four—stepped out of the house onto the porch. "What's going on?"

Titus cleared his throat as Abby finally let me go. "Robyn, this is Drew Borden, my lieutenant."

"In the 'right-hand man' sense of the word, not the G.I. Joe sense." Drew stuck his hand out, and I shook it. "I'm the lead enforcer in this Pride. This is Knox." He patted the glossy, black-furred head of the shifter standing next to him.

"Knox what? I assume he has a last name?"

"Actually, it's Alistair Knox," Drew said, and the cat standing next to him gave a throaty growl. "But he hates his first name, so we only use it when we want to piss him off. To what do we owe the pleasure...Robyn, right?"

"Yes. Robyn Sheffield." I turned to Titus, to see how he wanted to explain my presence.

He only crossed his arms over his very well-formed chest and shrugged. "That's your confession to make."

"Confession?" Drew's brows rose.

I couldn't imagine that Titus's men would be any happier than he was to hear about the position I'd put their Pride in. "Can I have something to drink first? Maybe a sandwich? I'm starving."

"Of course." Abby wound her arm through mine and tugged me toward the steps.

Titus stepped into our path. "No," he declared, his voice deep and...final. "Tell them."

"Titus?" Drew's posture tensed in response to his Alpha's tone. "Everything okay?"

"Robyn?" Abby looked worried now too.

I took a deep breath, then let go of her arm. "I kind of...defected. Unofficially. But I didn't know I'd be starting such a shitstorm."

"*Damn* it," Jace mumbled, and Knox gave another low growl, not of aggression, but of...displeasure.

I was starting to feel distinctly unwelcome.

Abby frowned. "What does that mean—unofficially?"

Titus exhaled, as if he were fighting for patience. "She snuck into my car and hitched an unauthorized ride out of the Southeast Territory. To see you."

Jace scrubbed one hand over his newly short brown waves. He met Titus's gaze. "We have to send her back."

"I'm staying." I sucked in a deep breath and met each set of eyes in turn. "They're trying to marry me off. I heard them. Your dad said that wouldn't happen, but I *heard* them!" I told Abby.

"I tried to tell her they won't do that," Titus said. "Faythe would never let that happen. Your dad would never let that happen."

"They didn't 'let' Jace get exiled, either, yet that happened," Drew pointed out.

"Technically, they can't make Robyn get married," Abby said, and though normally I hate being discussed as if I weren't present, that probably wasn't a good moment to start complaining. "But there are enough old-school Alphas left to make her life very difficult until she does what they want."

"Even with your brother on the council?" Titus asked. "Won't he take your dad's side?"

"Isaac might swing the other way just to show he's not biased. Either way, he's a pawn," Jace growled. "The council only accepted his Alpha status after they exiled me because they knew they could manipulate him."

"He's a good man in a tough position, Jace," Abby insisted. "You're holding a grudge because he got your sister pregnant."

Drew chuckled, and Knox gave an amused feline snort.

Jace rolled his eyes. "Good men can be pawns, Abby. Especially *young* good men, with no leadership ability, who have an intense desire to please their elders and safeguard their own status."

Abby shook her head with a glance at me. "He wouldn't—"

"If he thought making waves would endanger his position or make things rough for Melody, he would."

She frowned at Jace, but clearly had no argument for his point.

When an uncomfortable silence fell over us, I glanced from one face to the next. "So, I can stay?"

"No." Jace shook his head. "They'll come after you with everything they have."

"We can't just put her out on the street," Drew said, and Knox bobbed his muzzle. I gave them each a grateful smile.

"This is temporary." Titus clicked a button on his key fob, and his car locks thumped. "Drew, go tell the others that we have a guest, and I'll introduce everyone in the morning."

Drew nodded, and he and Knox took off into the huge house.

"Titus…" Jace's tone sounded like a warning, and Titus's bearing stiffened almost imperceptibly in response.

Two Alphas in one house. *I bet* that's *a laugh a minute…*

"She's going to call Faythe and tell the council that she ran on her own," Titus said.

"That won't absolve us," Jace insisted. "If we don't send her back, they'll have a concrete reason to turn down our request for formal recognition. Then they'll come in and take her."

Titus's eyes narrowed. "It won't come to that." But he was obviously as angry at the thought of his territory being invaded as he was at the thought of them hauling me into captivity.

"Okay, clearly we need a plan. Let's eat while we talk." Abby tugged me up the steps without waiting for a response from either of the toms. "It's okay," she whispered as we crossed the threshold into a three-story foyer crowned with a giant chandelier. "We'll work this out."

When the guys followed us inside, Abby pushed a mass of red curls from her face and forced a smile. "I'm starving. Let's make sandwiches." Then she took off down a central hallway, assuming we'd all follow.

We did.

Abby pulled out a bar stool for me at a massive granite island, then started taking sandwich supplies from a forty-eight-inch refrigerator.

Titus went straight for an upper cabinet, from which he pulled down a bottle of bourbon and four glasses. "You're old enough, right?"

"For anything you can imagine," I said. With no thought about how that might sound.

Titus's brows rose again.

Jace and Abby both glanced at me in surprise.

"I'm twenty-two," I clarified. "Old enough to drink, and to make my own decisions. At least in human society."

"Ham or turkey?" Abby asked at last, breaking the fragile silence.

"Yes," I said, and she laughed as she set a paper plate on the island in front of me.

"Fancy." I held up the disposable dish, to contrast it with the high-end appliances.

"No one likes doing dishes," Abby explained as she piled shaved ham onto a slice of bread on her plate.

"Time to make that phone call." Titus set his cell phone and a short, thick glass in front of me. Clearly, alcohol trumped the "no real dishes" policy.

"No." Jace slid the phone out of my reach. "Not until we work out what she's going to say."

"She's going to tell the council that I had nothing to do with breaking her out." Titus set his phone in front of me again. "And she's going to do it now, before they figure out on their own that we have her."

"Then what?" Jace demanded. "We can't tell them she's here until we're ready to send her back, and I don't think she's going to go willingly."

"If we don't tell them she's here, we're actively hiding her," Titus insisted. "And every second we spend hiding her gives them a stronger reason to consider us enemies and reject our petition!"

"Are they always like this?" I whispered to Abby, as I watched Jace and Titus argue.

"Not always. They're good friends. But two Alphas living under one roof is always a prickly situation."

I layered a slice of ham over a slice of turkey on my sandwich. "So why don't you move out?"

"We will." Abby wiped the tip of the mustard container with a paper towel. "But it's complicated out here. Most of the strays didn't get any help or guidance after they were infected. They figured out on their own that exposing themselves to humanity would be a bad idea, mostly from TV and movies full of government labs and scientists. And those the council knows about got warnings about following all the rules. But until Titus took over, there was no real regulation out here. They're used to living however they want."

"Like the Wild West," I mumbled.

"Yeah. Kind of. And these cowboys have never met a cowgirl of their own species. Most of them are just curious, but…" She shrugged, and her sandwich flopped in her hand.

"But until the law gets a better hold, you're circling the wagons."

Abby nodded. "I think we've pretty much exhausted that metaphor."

I laughed. "Agreed."

"Fine," Jace growled from across the kitchen. "But if it starts to go south, let me talk to Faythe. She'll listen to me."

"It's not going to go south." Titus turned to me, holding his cell, with Faythe Sanders's contact page on the screen. "You're up, Robyn."

FOUR

Titus

"We're in trouble here. Do you want my advice or not?" Jace snapped softly, while Abby and Robyn assembled sandwiches across the kitchen.

The Alpha in me wanted to growl "No." But my human half, which had spent the past five years expanding my father's multi-billion-dollar corporation, knew better. A CEO is only as strong and as smart as the advisers he listens to.

The same, presumably, went for Alphas.

"Yes," I said at last. "I want your advice, but this is my territory. The decision is mine."

Jace's jaw clenched briefly, and I saw him struggle to unlock it. I knew exactly how he felt. As valuable as he was as a friend and an ally, and as grateful as I was for his help and advice in forming my own Pride, we'd gotten along much better when we'd worked together from a distance—him in his territory and me in mine.

"If the decision were mine," Jace began. "I'd send her back."

"Now?"

"As close to now as possible. I'd call Faythe and tell her what happened, then have her send someone to meet us at the border. With Abby. For a friendly handover."

"Because with the council chair's daughter in the line of fire, they're less likely to let things escalate."

Jace nodded. "Exactly."

"And if Robyn won't go?"

"That's not up to her."

I sipped from my glass to hide my smile. "Better not let Abby hear you say a woman can't make her own decisions."

Jace rolled his eyes. "That's not what I'm saying. Robyn already made her decision. She made a deal with the council. She has to honor her word. That's no different than a plea deal would be in the human justice system. For a man or a woman."

"But the US Department of Justice wouldn't try to marry her off." I watched as she took the first bite of her sandwich, leaning with the curve of one well-formed hip against my countertop.

Jace's gaze narrowed on me, and I jerked my focus from Robyn with more effort than the act should have taken. "Titus, *don't do this*."

"Do what?" But I knew damn well what he meant.

"Do *not* look at her like that."

I didn't even bother trying to stifle the soft growl of warning clawing its way up my throat.

His scowl deepened. "Falling for her will cost you everything you have. Everything *we* have."

"Like falling for Abby cost you?" I snapped.

"Exactly. But she and I had somewhere to go. If you lose this territory, that won't be the case for any of us."

"It doesn't have to end like that."

"You know they'll fight for her return, and if we fight to keep her, no stray Pride will ever be recognized."

"They didn't fight over Abby," I pointed out.

"Yet." Something uneasy swept briefly over his expression. "But Abby can't help them figure out how human women can survive the infection. Or whether or not a female stray's kids would be shifters," he adds, and again, the thought of some other man ever touching her made me unreasonably, inexplicably angry. "Robyn represents the future of the US territories, and they're not going to let her go without a fight." Jace took a deep breath. "Either she goes to the Prides, or they'll come in and get her."

"I know." He was right. But Robyn was also right. She was a stray, and I'd sworn to fight for the rights and acceptance of strays under my protection. That was the only reason I'd been able to recruit twelve enforcers and command the loyalty of my other Pride members.

That was something I *believed* in.

Returning Robyn against her will would be a violation of everything I'd sworn to uphold as the first stray Alpha.

But if I kept her, my days as Alpha would be numbered.

I *had* to send her back.

"Why don't you let me make the call?" Jace offered. "I've known Faythe her whole life."

"No." If I let Jace make the call, it would look like he was in charge. My Pride. My decision. My responsibility. "I got it."

"Fine," Jace growled. "But if it starts to go south, let me talk to Faythe. She'll listen to me."

"It's not going to go south." I pulled up Faythe Sanders's contact information on my phone. "You're up, Robyn." I pressed "call," then tapped the speakerphone button and set the phone on the island. She looked up at me, panic shining in her big blue eyes, and hurriedly swallowed the bite of ham sandwich she'd been chewing. "I'll start," I said, as the ringing echoed around my kitchen. "But then it's all you."

Static cut into the ringing, then there was a brief silence. "Hello? Titus?" Faythe said.

Robyn sucked in a breath and held it. She looked terrified, but determined.

"Yeah," I answered as I sank into one of the bar stools. "Are you alone?"

"Um...I can be. One minute." Hinges squealed over the line, then a door clicked closed. "What's going on, Titus? We have our hands full here."

"So do we. I have a problem."

"What kind of problem?"

"The five-foot-eight, blue-eyed brunette kind of problem." I glanced at Robyn and found her carefully peeling the crust from the top slice of bread on her sandwich. Watching me nervously. "The kind that sneaks into your car and hitches a ride out of her territory completely without your knowledge."

"Shit." Springs groaned softly over the line as Faythe sat. "Robyn?"

"Yes. And let me reiterate that I crossed the border with no idea she was in my car." My phrasing was careful, but accurate.

Faythe sighed over the static. "Who else knows

about this?"

"Just the four of us," Jace said. "Me, Abby, Titus, and Robyn, of course. And a few of Titus's enforcers."

"Robyn's there now?" Faythe asked, and I could practically hear the frown in her voice. "Is she listening?"

"Yeah," my uninvited guest spoke up, at last. "I'm sorry. I didn't mean to rile everyone up. I only—"

"Stop talking, Robyn," Faythe ordered, and in that instant, despite all the other roles she played in her life, she was all Alpha. So Alpha, in fact, that the hairs on my neck stood up, as I became instinctively affronted by the assertion of her authority in my kitchen. "I'm going to ask some questions, and I want you to answer as succinctly as possible. With no extraneous information."

Because she'd be obligated to report everything Robyn said to the rest of the council.

"Okay…" Robyn glanced at Abby, who gave her an encouraging nod. Then she looked at me.

I wanted to tell her to relax. That everything would be fine. But I couldn't figure out how to do that without lying.

"How did you get into Titus's car?" Faythe asked.

"He left it unlocked."

"And you knew it was his car?"

"Yes," Robyn said. "I knew he'd be leaving—"

"That's enough," I cut in. "Only answer what she asks."

"Did Titus know you were in his car?" Faythe continued, as we all stared at my phone on the white granite countertop.

"Not until I showed myself. After we'd already

crossed the border," Robyn added.

"Okay. Titus, I have to ask..." Faythe said, and I closed my eyes. I knew what was coming. "Why didn't you smell her?"

"Because she hid in the back, beneath the clothes from my gym bag."

"She hid herself in your scent."

"Yes." And the fact that she still smelled like me made it difficult to concentrate, with her standing so close.

"All right. Titus—"

"This is my fault," Robyn interrupted, a bit of bread crust crushed in her fist. "I snuck out. Titus had nothing to do with it. Don't penalize him and his Pride for what I did."

"Unfortunately, it's not that simple," Faythe said. "But you can fix this—"

A door squealed open over the line, and Faythe's chair springs creaked again, as she swiveled. "Faythe? We..." Chairman Rick Wade's sentence faded into nothing. "Who's on the phone?"

"It's Titus," Faythe said, and everyone in my kitchen went completely still. "The good news is that Robyn's safe."

"Damn it," Wade swore. "I assume the bad news is that he has her?"

"Yes, but he didn't *take* her. She stowed away in his car. He and Robyn are on speaker phone."

"Give it here," Wade said, and I realized Faythe hadn't mentioned Abby or Jace. "Titus, take me off speaker."

I picked up my phone and tapped the speaker button to turn it off. "I'm here. Listen, I—"

"Send her back," Rick Wade interrupted. "I'll have

someone meet you at the border. That's the only way to keep this thing from—"

I stood so fast my barstool nearly fell over. "With all due respect, Mr. Chairman, I don't take orders from you."

The chairman's silence was swallowed by twin groans, one from Faythe over the line, and one from Jace, in my kitchen.

"Titus, I want you to think carefully about how you answer my next question. Are you saying you won't return Robyn? And please keep in mind that you have no standing on the council and no business interfering in the council's affairs."

"Robyn made this my business. I didn't take her. She snuck out. And she doesn't seem inclined to return."

Robyn's eyes widened, but Jace scowled. "Don't," he mouthed silently.

I marched out of the kitchen, down the main hallway, and into my office, intentionally cutting everyone else out of the discussion. This was my problem. I would deal with it my way.

"Mr. Alexander, you have a petition sitting before the council right now," Chairman Wade continued, as I closed the door. "Do you really want to shoot yourself in the foot?"

"Are you saying you won't approve the petition if I don't send Robyn back to you? Against her will?"

"Of course not!" Faythe spoke up, her voice thin over the distance. "The council cannot be bribed, and we don't operate through coercion!"

"I'm saying that what you've done won't garner any good will with the other council members." Leather squeaked, and I recognized the sound from

Bert Di Carlo's office couch as Wade took a seat. "But doing the right thing here could buy you some good will."

"The right thing? Dragging a woman across territorial boundaries so you can lock her up again?"

"Giving her a safe escort into the Southeast Territory, so she can honor the deal she made. That's in everyone's best interest, Titus. Including Robyn's. And if you make this easy for everyone, I'd be happy to let the other council members know how instrumental you were in returning Robyn to us safely. Beyond that, Faythe and I will call in every favor we owe. We'll do everything we can to get your petition approved. You'll be Alpha of the first new territory this council has acknowledged in two centuries. You'll be the first stray to ever sit on the council."

"Marc sits on the council," I pointed out, and the fact that he couldn't seem to remember that gave me little faith that he would remember the promises he was making to me. Or that I'd be taken seriously on the council, even if I were granted a seat.

"Marc is a co-Alpha," Wade insisted. "He and Faythe share a vote. You'll have your own. We're ready to move into the future with you and your Pride, Titus. But we need you to show a little respect for the institution you want to join. Robyn made a deal with the council. If you want to sit on that council, you have to uphold its interests."

Well. That couldn't be any clearer. I sank into my office chair and closed my eyes. "So, I scratch your back and you scratch mine."

"It sounds bad when you put it that way," Faythe said. "Look, I sympathize with Robyn's situation more than anyone. If I could give her freedom, I would. But she agreed to the terms of her training and rehabilitation, and the council can't afford to set a precedent by letting her walk out on an agreement. Beyond that, Titus, she killed four people. Four *humans*."

"Four humans who knew about shifters and were actively hunting them," I reminded them, mentally searching for a way out of this. A way to make everyone happy. "Four humans you'd have taken out yourself, if you'd known what was going on."

"Four humans we would have dealt with much more carefully, with as little media coverage as possible. Look, we all want what's best for Robyn, but we can't let her out into the world until we're sure she can control herself. Until we're sure life won't trigger instincts she can't yet control. That's in everyone's best interest. Help us help her. Please."

"Fine." I didn't really have any choice in the matter. "But let me do it my way."

Rick Wade growled. "This isn't a negotia—"

"What's your way?" Faythe interrupted.

"Robyn came here to see Abby. She feels isolated and disenfranchised. So let her spend time here with her friend. With a fellow tabby."

"Absolutely not," Wade snapped.

"If you don't, she'll fight us all, every step of the way," I told them. "And she'll run away from you again, the next chance she gets. If you want her to stay, you're going to have to show her why she should."

"What makes you think she won't run from you, like she ran from us?" the chairman demanded.

"We have Abby." That was a low blow to a father missing his daughter. But it was the truth. "She's the only person Robyn trusts. And if that doesn't convince you, you have my word that I won't let her out of my sight."

"How much time would you need?" Faythe asked, over Wade's disgruntled mumbling.

"Give us two weeks with her, and we'll convince her to return on her own. She'll finish out her training in the Southeast, fulfilling her obligation to the council. You'll be the Alphas who got her back without spilling a drop of blood, and I'll have 'earned goodwill' by returning her willingly and in good spirits. Everyone wins."

Everyone except Robyn, who would not want to return. Even after a two-week reprieve.

"That won't work," Wade insisted.

"It'll be a hard sell," Faythe admitted.

"So do what I'm going to do. Make it work." I ended the call and sank into my chair, my eyes closed.

How the hell did this happen?

Going into the council meeting, Faythe, Jace, and I had agreed that our petition had about a fifty percent chance of succeeding. Not great odds, but not bad for a first attempt. We were prepared to be turned down and ready to appeal the decision.

Worst case scenario, we were prepared to wait for Blackwell to die. His son-in-law was rumored to be much less old-fashioned. His grandson even less so.

But if the council didn't get Robyn back—soon, unscathed, and willing to cooperate—they would blame me. At the very least, my abilities as an Alpha would be called into question, and if I was found lacking, I would not get a second chance.

Thanks to Robyn.

Yet even knowing all of that…I wanted her to

stay. She was as smart and fierce as any of my enforcers, and she was a damn sight prettier than any of them. She was also a stray who personally understood what most of my men had been and were still going through.

Robyn *felt* like a Mississippi Valley Pride member.

I exhaled deeply, then slid my phone into my jacket pocket as I stood. All eyes turned my way when I stepped into the kitchen.

"Well?" Abby stood from her barstool, holding a half-eaten sandwich.

I turned from her to Robyn, who'd hardly touched her food, other than to shred the crust. "I bought you two weeks."

Robyn swiveled on her stool until she faced me, brows drawn low over wide blue eyes. "Two weeks of what?"

"Hiatus. Vacation. Interlude."

"Vacation." She looked like she'd bitten into a clod of dirt. "And then what?"

"Then you go to Atlanta and finish your training." I picked up my glass and took a sip. "After that, when the council is sure you're no longer at the mercy of your instincts, you'll get your life back."

"In what form?"

"What do you mean?"

Robyn pushed her plate away and stood. "I'll get my life back in what form? Can I finish school? Can I go see my parents, instead of checking in over the phone on approved calls, so they know I'm still alive?"

I shrugged. "Of course."

"Maybe," Abby said.

Jace exhaled slowly. "The school thing is

complicated, Robyn. You only have one semester left, right?" he asked.

She nodded. "For my bachelor's, anyway."

"So you'd need permission from your Alpha—whoever that turns out to be depends upon what Pride you join—for a leave of absence, of sorts. And permission for temporary residency from the Alpha of the territory where the school's located. That's Abby's brother Isaac."

"My understanding is that that's routine," I added, when Robyn's scowl began to deepen. "My toms will have the same privileges, once our Pride is recognized."

"It is routine. That's how I was able to go to school in Jace's territory. And Isaac will totally give you permission," Abby assured Robyn.

"Unless the council doesn't want him to." Jace drained his glass and reopened the bottle. "Isaac's the junior-ranking council member, and I can tell you from experience that that position comes with pressure from all sides. You vote with a senior ranking Alpha on something he wants, and he'll vote with you on something else. Or vice versa."

"So, to finish school, I'd need permission from two different Alphas?" Robyn glanced from Abby to Jace, then back. "But I won't get that without approval from the council? How is that freedom?"

"Well..." Abby picked up her glass and stared into it.

"Our society works differently from the human world." I pulled Robyn's stool out for her and sat in the one next to it.

"So I've noticed." But she didn't sit.

"Most of the rules are out of necessity," Jace said.

"The rest are to accommodate instincts that make cats territorial. You can't walk into someone else's territory without permission. That would trigger aggression, on both a personal and a societal level."

"It's like that for all of us," I explained. "Even cats with no authority or seniority feel possessive of their own space, be it a neighborhood, a house, or even just a bedroom."

"I don't have a space of my own," Robyn said. "My bedroom used to be Sara's, and it's like living in a shrine."

Oh. Suddenly her impromptu defection made even more sense. "I suspect that's part of why you're unhappy with the Di Carlos. You're living in someone else's space." And they'd taken away everything familiar to her. School. Her best friend. True contact with her human family. "When you return, I'm sure they'd be happy to let you make the space your own."

"Yeah. They're totally going to want to box up their dead daughter's stuff so I can hang my own posters and sleep under my own comforter."

"It's been five years," Abby said. "They need to move on."

"*I* need to move on." Robyn finally sank onto the stool next to me. "What if I don't want any part of this territorial system? Can I opt out entirely? Like Abby did?"

"When you've completed your sentence, you can try to defect," I told her. "But that will only get you stuck in one of the free zones, without access to friends, family, and schools in any of the other territories."

"And that's why you're doing this?" Robyn turned to me. "That's why you're giving up autonomy in the free zone and subjecting yourself to the rulings of some arbitrarily manned committee?"

"It's not arbitrary," I told her. "And I won't just be subject to it. I'll be a member of it. Part of the decision making process. I'll be in the position to make things better for my men. And women," I added, when her brows rose.

"As long as those men and women are willing to live by your rules."

"They're not my rules. They're *the* rules. And they're there for a reason."

"Fine." Robyn stood again and took a deep breath. "Let's get this 'vacation' started. Where can I shower?"

Abby stood. "I'll show her."

As the ladies headed out of the kitchen, I watched Robyn with a heavy feeling in my heart and Jace poured another inch of bourbon into my glass. "You know she has no intention of leaving in two weeks."

"I know. I have two weeks to change her mind." And to get myself on board with what I had no choice but to do.

"How are you going to do that?"

I drained the glass. "I have no fucking clue."

FIVE

Robyn

"Abby and Jace are across the hall, and I'm a few doors down," Titus said from the bedroom doorway, his arms crossed over a suit jacket that looked preposterously over-the-top for one in the morning. "In case you need anything. But this space is yours, for as long as you're here. Please feel free to make it your own."

I sat on the bed and pulled the bathrobe closed to cover my knees, while my wet hair dripped on his guestroom comforter. "Make it my own." The words sounded as meaningless as they felt. "The problem with seizing the moment is that the moment is typically too brief to accommodate advanced planning."

Titus laughed, and for a second he looked like a normal-yet-abnormally-gorgeous guy who didn't have eight bathrooms, and hundreds of human employees, and a dozen shifter enforcers, and millions of dollars. And a smile that lit up his gray eyes like a lightbulb shining through a smoky room. "You didn't bring any of your stuff?"

"There wasn't time to pack a bag." I hadn't even thought to grab my shampoo or my makeup. "But I'll do my best to take ownership of the designer colors and meaningless art your interior decorator chose." I lifted one corner of the comforter beneath me. "Is this silk damask? Would you call the color 'antique red' or 'blood of thine enemies'? Because I know which way I'm leaning."

Titus's left brow rose, and his amused gaze sent heat blazing toward the most private parts of my body. "You're making fun of me?"

"I'm trying. What do I have left, if not my sense of humor?"

"Your life." Abby shimmied through the doorway from behind him, her poof of red hair brushing the shoulder of his jacket. "Your friends. A two-week reprieve from Donna Di Carlo and her collection of ceramic angels." She sank onto the bed next to me with a folded stack of spare clothes. "How many does she have now? Last time I was there, I counted more than a hundred."

"There's easily double that now. And they all look like Sara. Which is super-creepy."

Abby's smile wilted like a dead rose.

"I'm sorry." *I am* such *an asshole.* "You knew her, didn't you?"

"Yeah. I...um." Abby cleared her throat and set the clothes on the bed between us. "I saw her die."

"Oh. Shit. I'm sorry, Ab."

"It's okay. That was a long time ago." She shook her head, and her smile returned. "I brought you something to sleep in, and some clothes for tomorrow. These are all I have that might fit you.

67

We'll go shopping in the morning and get everything else you need."

"We can get a new comforter," Titus added with a grin. "If you'd rather have 'dark as the stain upon my soul' with black velvet trim."

"Ha. I think I can make do with the red, thanks."

"Okay. I'll see you ladies in the morning." He backed into the hall and closed the door.

Abby turned to me with wide brown eyes. "I can't believe you did that!"

"Criticized his decor?" I grabbed a pair of pajama shorts from the pile and stepped into them beneath the borrowed robe. "He's an Alpha, not a god."

"I can't believe you snuck into his car! You put him in a really tough position."

"You mean like the position you put Jace in?" I let the robe fall and pulled a soft pink T-shirt over my head.

Abby rolled her eyes. "That was different."

"I was making a point, not an accusation. We do what we have to, right? *You* told me that."

"I know, but…"

"Look, Ab, I had no idea they'd hold him responsible for what I did. I'm not trying to make enemies."

"Good, because if you want to stay here, Titus is the friend you need to make."

I crossed the room to hang the robe on a hook on the bathroom door. "Who says I want to stay here?"

Abby frowned. "I thought you didn't want to go to the Southeast Pride."

"I don't. But it's no better here. It sounds like this isn't the free zone anymore, and it doesn't do me any good to step out of one cage and into another. And that's exactly what Titus is turning this place into."

"Okay, but it'll be different here," she insisted.

"No, it won't. Titus couldn't get his Pride accepted if it weren't just like all the others. Well, *almost* like the others."

Shit. I sank into the desk chair as the truth hit me like a blow to the gut. What kind of revolutionary activist gives the disenfranchised and underrepresented a *vacation*? I asked for sanctuary. Autonomy. Instead, I got two weeks in a beautiful mansion with a gorgeous young Alpha.

But what's in it for Titus?

"He's in acquisition mode for the element he's missing," I mumbled. "*Damn* it, Robyn!"

"What are you talking about? What element?"

"He needs a wife, Abby. You can't have a Pride without an Alpha *and* a dam. But he can't have you, because you're with Jace. Which is why he's being so nice to me. And that means he's no different than any of the others."

"You think he wants to keep you here?"

"Considering he looks at me like he's starving and I'm the last scrap of food in the fridge? Yeah. I think this is an audition. At the end of this two-week 'vacation', he thinks he'll have a decision to make. Whether to send me back, or keep me for himself."

"He may think you're pretty—I mean, the man has eyes. But he wouldn't use you to complete his Pride, Robyn."

"Of course he would. He's an Alpha. Running other people's lives is what they do."

My eyes flew open in the dark as footsteps pounded down the hall toward my door. I sat straight up in bed, panting as if I'd been running for my life, and if I'd woken up a second later—

I shook my head, dislodging the nightmare and my narrow escape from human hunters determined to hang my severed head on their wall. Was I screaming? Is that why someone was running toward my room?

I glanced to my left, expecting to see Sara Di Carlo's green alarm clock numbers, but found a window instead, where moonlight gleamed through sheer curtains.

Oh yeah. I was in the not-so-free zone.

I looked to the other side and found red numbers floating in the darkness above the marble-topped nightstand. Three-oh-four. I'd only slept for an hour and a half.

"Titus!" a voice whisper-shouted from the hallway, and on the tail of his name, I heard three sharp thumps that could only be a fist hitting a door. But not *my* door. "We got another one!"

Heart racing, I threw off the covers and jogged across the large bedroom. When I opened the door, I found Abby and Jace standing in the doorway of their room across from mine, staring down the hall.

"Titus!" Drew Borden knocked on a double set of doors at the end of the hall, a cell phone clutched in his right fist, baggy jeans hanging low on his hips beneath a white tee. "Spencer's on the line. He's bringing in another one."

The left-hand door opened, and Titus appeared, wearing nothing but a pair of sleep shorts, which showed off his *nicely* sculpted chest.

Stop it! You're not attracted to him, Robyn. Your body thinks

70

you should be, because you're a tabby and he's an Alpha. But it was my eyes, not my hormones, noticing how soft his lips looked, and how his biceps bulged, and how pretty his steely irises were. Titus Alexander was an attractive man by any standard. With or without shifter impulses pushing me toward him.

I had no intention of being used by him, but that didn't mean I couldn't look. Right?

"Sorry. My cell was on silent." Titus took the phone from Drew. "Spence? How far away are you?" He listened for a moment, and though I could hear a deep voice over the line, I couldn't make out the words. "Okay, take him downstairs as soon as you get here. We'll get a space ready."

Titus pressed a button on the phone, then handed it to Drew. He disappeared into his room for a minute, then came out wearing jeans and holding the button-up shirt he'd worn beneath his suit jacket the day before. "Jace?" Titus asked as he passed me, pushing his left arm through the sleeve of his shirt. "Up for this?"

"Always." Jace kissed the top of Abby's head, then gave me a polite nod and followed Titus and Drew toward the staircase at the other end of the hall.

"Where are they going?" I asked, as three sets of heavy footsteps clomped down the wood treads.

"Spencer's bringing in a new stray," Abby said, on the tail of a yawn.

"Spencer's one of the enforcers?"

"No, just a Pride member. He works in the ER. Every now and then, they get a case of scratch fever mistaken for the flu. Spencer gives them IV fluids, and when they're released, he brings them here. Titus and his men can help better than any ER doctor, and the fewer blood tests run on new strays, the better."

"Because someone will eventually find something weird in the sample?"

"That's the fear, yes." She nods. "But it's not likely as long as they're only testing for specific illnesses, like strep and flu."

"So, where are they taking this new guy?" A door squealed open downstairs, then everything went quiet as it closed again on three sets of footsteps.

"They use the basement beneath the guest house as an infirmary."

I thought about that for a second. Then I headed for the stairs. "Let's go!"

Abby caught up with me in the kitchen, carrying a pair of slip-on shoes, but I headed into the backyard barefoot. The tiles were cold against my feet as I raced across the porch and down the steps. I passed the pool, which was covered for the winter, then crossed a small patch of grass in front of the guest house.

The door was ajar, so I went in without asking and followed the echo of voices to a stairwell off the small, high-end kitchen.

"Robyn!" Abby called as she followed me down the stairs. "Wait!"

At the bottom of the steps, I could only stop and stare. The basement was small but brightly lit, and divided into two distinct halves. On my left, steel bars were set into the floor and ceiling forming two old-fashioned jail cells. Both stood open and empty. Each cell held a stainless steel toilet and sink, as well as a twin-sized bed bolted to the floor. As I watched, Drew made the mattress in the farthest cell up with a clean fitted sheet.

"You keep new strays in prison cells?" I demanded.

All three of the toms looked up, obviously surprised to see Abby and me, in spite of my stomping down the stairs.

"It's a precaution," Titus said. "We don't close the cells unless we have to, and there's a private bathroom over there." He pointed to an open door in the other half of the basement, past shelves of medical supplies, a kitchenette, and a small round breakfast table. "We modeled it after the one in Faythe's basement."

"With improvements," Jace said.

"Hers doesn't have a kitchenette," Abby added. "And hers is for detention, whereas we mostly use this one for acclimating new strays."

"Think of this more as a hospital than a prison," Titus said. "We only lock the cells if the patient gets violent, and that's as much for his good as for ours. But most of them are just sick."

"Like you were," Abby reminded me.

The guesthouse front door squealed open upstairs. "Hey! A little help?" a new voice called, and in answer, I heard the clomp of more footsteps, coming from the second floor of the guest house.

"Move over." Titus tugged me away from the stairs as a tall, fair, shirtless man came down backward, carrying the lower half of an unconscious guy by the ankles. As he twisted to spot the next step, a loose strand of dark blond hair brushed his left shoulder blade from a rapidly unraveling man bun. His chin and upper lip were covered by a neatly trimmed full beard and mustache a shade darker than his hair.

Higher on the stairs, the unconscious stray's shoulders were carried by a man in greenish scrubs, with warm brown skin and eyes glowing a rosy hue of amber in the clean white light falling from the ceiling of the stairwell.

"We're ready for him in here," Drew called, as he set a freshly cased pillow on the twin bed in the far cell.

"Spence, can you tell how long ago he was infected?" Jace asked as he pulled a forehead touch thermometer from a drawer in the kitchenette.

"He'd been there for hours when my shift started. His temp was 102 in the ER, so I'd say it's been at least a day since he was infected," the man in scrubs—clearly Spencer—said. "Which would mean…Thursday night, maybe? But I don't think he's shifted yet."

"Where's the wound?" Titus followed them into the cell as the other men laid the stray on the bed. The patient's face was pale, and his clothes were soaked with sweat.

"Did I look like that?" I whispered.

Abby nodded, her eyes wide.

Spencer carefully lifted the man's T-shirt to reveal a bloodstained bandage wrapping around his lower ribs toward his back. "He told the ER doc a cougar attacked him in the woods. Animal control issued an alert and they're sending people out to look for it at first light."

"What was the diagnosis?" Titus asked.

"The doc thinks the fever is from an infection," Spencer said. "She gave him IV antibiotics and ibuprofen, but those weren't working, so I had to talk him into checking out before they ordered blood tests."

"How did you do it?" I asked, and when Spencer turned, seeming to notice me for the first time, I realized I'd wandered to within feet of the cage where the new stray now lay on the twin mattress. "How did you get him to check out?"

"Who...?" Spencer aimed a questioning frown at his Alpha.

"Spence, Loch, this is Robyn Sheffield. She'll be with us for the next two weeks. Treat her like you treat Abby."

"Only better," Abby said with a grin.

Spencer gave her a friendly wink, then turned to me. He inhaled deeply, and I tried not to be offended or weirded out, but I still couldn't get used to the way cats sniff each other all the time. Even if the human-form version was much more polite than a house cat's butt sniffing.

I braced myself for his reaction. For the subtle staring and less-than-subtle excuses to touch me. But Spencer only shrugged and held out his hand to be shaken. "Hey. I'm Spencer Cole."

"Lochlan Hayes." The tall, blond tom stuck out his hand, peering at me through light hazel eyes, and I could only stare at them both. Though I caught their Alpha looking every time I turned around, they seemed totally unaffected by the presence of the only female stray known to exist in the US.

Spencer laughed and lowered his hand, when I failed to reply to his introduction. "Nice to meet you anyway. And to answer your question, I told him I knew a specialist who was familiar with this particular infection. Then I offered to treat him for free. No need to file anything with his insurance. That last part usually seals the deal."

"Do we have a name?" Titus asked.

Lochlan pulled a worn leather wallet from the pocket of his gray jogging pants and handed it to his Alpha. "Corey Morris. Looks like he's a freshman at Ole Miss."

"Any idea why he'd go to the hospital in Jackson?" Jace asked. "That's a two-hour drive south of Oxford."

"Maybe the way *you* drive," Abby said. "It'd take me two and a half."

Drew shrugged. "Poor kid's just eighteen years old."

"His life isn't over." Titus stared at the unconscious new stray, while Spencer pulled an IV bag full of clear liquid from one of the upper cabinets on the other side of the basement. "It's just a lot harder now."

My chest began to ache as his words dug into me like the claws that had simultaneously shredded my skin and ruined my life. I couldn't think of a truer statement in the world. My life wasn't over either, but since I'd been scratched by a dying stray in a cage more than four months ago, everything had gotten infinitely, immeasurably harder.

Every decision seemed complicated by a whole list of consequences and considerations I'd never had as a human. Each breath brought with it a banquet of scents my sluggish brain struggled to identify and classify. Every beat of my heart pumped blood-borne instincts and cravings I fought to resist. Every square foot of earth belonged to some Alpha who would only let me stand on it if I promised something in return. Loyalty. Obedience. Marriage.

Corey Morris would wake up in a world he no longer recognized or truly belonged to.

I knew exactly how that felt.

Spencer crossed the cell and hung the IV bag from a hook on the wall above the twin bed. While he opened a packet of sterile IV tubing and supplies, Titus knelt next to the bed until his nose was inches from the bloody bandage. Then he inhaled deeply. "He definitely hasn't shifted yet. I can't smell his infector's scent in his blood."

"What does that mean?" I whispered to Abby.

"The way my dad puts it, sampling someone's scent is like tasting wine," she whispered, while we watched from the other side of the cell. "You know how when you smell a person, you get the primary scent, but also subtle layers of other things? Fear. Health. Pregnancy, if that applies."

I nodded. It had taken my human-born nose a while to learn how to find and interpret those things, and the truth was that I was still learning what each scent meant.

"With a stray, you also get a trace of the cat who infected him. But that doesn't kick in until after the first shift, when the infection has thoroughly permeated the bloodstream."

"So, in a few hours, we'll be able to tell who infected him, just from smelling him?"

"If the scent belongs to someone we know." Abby shrugged. "But that's not likely. Titus's goal is to identify and reach out to all the strays in his territory, but the reality is that that's quite an undertaking. Most of them aren't volunteering to be counted in the census."

"So, what's with the IV?" I asked, as Spencer

carefully slid a needle into Corey Morris's arm. "They're medicating him?"

"No." Titus leaned against the bars to my left, to get out of Loch's way. "Hydrating him. The fever leads to dehydration, and IV fluids help fend off the worst of the sickness."

Abby gave me a sad look. "I didn't know that when you were infected. Sorry."

I linked my arm with hers. "You did what you could. Without you, I'd probably be dead by now."

And without Titus and his friends, Corey Morris might die too. Or he might live, then infect someone else.

The sick stray's free arm twitched on the bed.

"He's waking up," I said.

"Damn," Spencer swore, still holding the needle in the stray's other arm. "Someone hold him still."

Titus and Jace stepped forward and carefully held the patient steady by his shoulders and calves, while Drew stabilized Corey's arms.

Spencer finished the IV with speed and skill that hinted at years of experience. He was throwing away the medical waste when his patient's eyes fluttered open.

Everyone stepped away from the new stray as one, as if their movements had been choreographed.

Everyone except Titus.

"What's going on?" I whispered, as Abby tugged me out of the cell.

"Titus needs to take the lead, to establish his authority from the beginning," she whispered.

"Where am I?" Corey blinked several times, struggling to bring his vision into focus, and suddenly I felt like I was right there with him. Blinking at Abby from that filthy couch, in that cabin deep in the woods. I hadn't been able to bring her into focus, but I'd known she was there, even when she wasn't talking.

Somehow, I could *smell* her. And I'd known I wasn't alone.

"Is this a hospital?" Corey lifted his arm, frowning at the needle secured to the inside of his elbow with medical tape. Then his gaze wandered farther into the room, and his eyes widened. "Am I in jail?"

"No. You're in my basement. We use it as a makeshift infirmary," Titus said. "You're very sick, Corey, and that's going to get worse over the next few hours. But then you'll start to get better. You're going to be fine. But you're going to be different."

"Who're you?" The patient's words were slurred, his face bright red with fever.

"My name is Titus Alexander. I'm your Alpha."

SIX

Titus

"You should get some sleep." Jace sank into the chair across the small table from me, and he looked as tired as I felt. "I'll take a shift."

I shook my head. "It needs to be me."

"Morris won't forget you're his Alpha if someone else is there the next time he wakes up."

"You don't understand," I said, and Jace rolled his eyes. A growl rumbled up from my throat, and I let it echo between us for a moment. "You may be tired of hearing it, but it's the truth. We weren't born into this. We didn't see the appropriate behavior modeled for us in a Pride full of toms," I told him. "Corey Morris won't be conforming to an intrinsic set of instincts when he wakes up. He'll be fighting to reconcile everything he ever knew and felt in his human life with a series of bizarre and terrifying new impulses. He will be at war with himself, almost literally."

"I know," Jace stood and pulled a mug from the cabinet. "You say this every time."

"But you can't truly understand it, because you've never felt it."

"If you use the childbirth analogy again, I'm going to break this pot over your head." He lifted a half-full glass carafe from beneath the coffee maker. "I don't have to give birth myself to know that it hurts."

"Spoken like someone without a uterus," Abby said as she jogged down the steps, red curls bouncing around her face.

Jace took a third mug from the cabinet for her, wordlessly inviting her to sit with us.

"How's Robyn?" I asked as I pushed a chair out for Abby with my foot.

"In bed, but not asleep." Abby sat, then aimed her worried gaze at me. "Titus, she thinks you want to keep her here."

I leaned back in my chair until I could reach the counter, where I snagged a box of sugar packets and avoided meeting her gaze. "Why would she think that when I agreed to personally hand her over to your father in two weeks?"

"She thinks this 'vacation' is some kind of audition. That if you like her, you'll try to make her stay. For the same reason the Di Carlos want her."

I frowned. "To study her? Why would I—"

"For a smart guy, you're pretty stupid." Jace set a full mug in front of Abby, then dropped into the only remaining empty chair. "She thinks you want to marry her, Titus. To use her as your dam, to start a true Pride."

My frown became a scowl. "This *is* a true Pride. I don't need her for that."

"Not officially," Abby said. "But traditionally, it'd be pretty hard for an Alpha to hold onto his territory if he can't deliver a daughter, to...propagate. To insure the continuation of the species."

"That's ridiculous." I stood and grabbed the carafe, then filled my own mug. "Our species isn't dying out. There are more toms in Mississippi than I can keep up with."

"Those are strays," Jace pointed out. "They don't count."

A growl rumbled from low in my throat, and he held up both hands, palms out. "That's not coming from me. It's the council's perspective. They'll think the same thing Robyn does, if she's not in Atlanta within two weeks. That you're making a play for their new tabby, to cement your authority."

"That's such bullshit. She's a person, not a chess piece."

Jace laughed. "I wish you'd known Faythe in college. You might have given Marc a run for his money."

Abby snorted. "She'd have fed you your balls in a sandwich. Robyn may still."

"I can't tell if you're joking or—"

The mattress squealed behind me, and I turned in my chair to find Corey Morris trying to sit up in bed.

"How do you feel?" I set my mug on the counter and crossed into the occupied cell. "Any nausea? Do you need the bucket again?"

"No." Morris's voice cracked on that single syllable. "I don't... I don't understand."

I picked up a half-empty bottle of water from the floor and handed it to him.

Morris pulled the top off the bottle and gulped until the water was gone, slaking a thirst that persisted in spite of his IV. "What's going on?" He held the empty bottle out, and I set it on the floor again. "Where am I?"

"You're at my house, about an hour north of Jackson. You went to the emergency room at Baptist Medical Center around midnight, and my friend brought you here because we're better equipped to treat the infection you have."

Morris blinked heavily, then ran both hands over his short, sweat-damp hair. "What do I have?"

He wasn't ready for the answer. I knew from experience that he wouldn't believe the truth until he could feel his first shift coming on. Until the newly feline half of him ripped its way through his human form. So instead of answering his question, I asked one of my own. "Mr. Morris, I understand you're a student at Ole Miss. Can you tell me why you went to the hospital in Jackson, instead of in Oxford?"

Morris blinked again, trying to follow my subject change in spite of his high fever. "Um. My best friend's girlfriend goes to Millsaps and he said I could come to a party with them in Jackson if I gave him a ride."

"When was this party?"

"Thursday night. I was going to drive back to Oxford Friday morning. But..." He glanced around the basement again, as if seeing it for the first time. "What's going on? What's in there?" He moved his left arm, which tugged on the IV bag.

"You're dehydrated from the fever, so we're giving you intravenous fluids. There's nothing in the bag but sterile solution." I cleared my throat and pulled a folding chair closer to the bed, so I could sit. "Mr. Morris, you told the nurse at the ER that you'd been attacked by a large cat in the woods. Can you tell us where that happened?"

"After the party—"

"The party was on the Millsaps campus?" Jace asked, from the breakfast table where he and Abby still sat.

"Yeah." Morris frowned at him, then his tenuous focus slid to me. "Afterward, I went with my friend Leland and his girlfriend into the woods east of the highway."

"I55?" I asked.

Morris nodded, then closed his eyes for a second, as if he were fighting nausea from the movement. "South of the city. There's a bunch of dirt roads and creeks out there, and Leland's girlfriend's family has an old hunting lodge. It was more of a shack, really. Leland and Ivy started getting hot and heavy, but I was like a third wheel, so I took a walk, you know?"

"And that's where you saw the cat?"

"I didn't see it. I heard something following me. Twigs snapping. Heavy breathing. The sounds started freaking me out a little, so I ran toward the shack, and the damn thing…pounced. It landed on my back and clawed up my side. I started screaming, and it ran off. Like *I* scared the damn *cougar*."

"You're sure it was a cougar?" Jace asked, and I resisted the urge to turn and glare at him, keeping my focus on the new stray.

Morris shrugged. "It was behind me until it ran off, and I couldn't see it very well in the dark. But it was definitely a cat, so it had to be a cougar, right? Unless something bigger escaped from the zoo." He pushed himself up, and I could see him fighting vertigo as he clutched the mattress. "*Did* something escape from the fucking zoo? Should I get a lawyer?"

I gave him a small smile. "I don't think this would be much of a lawsuit. It was a wildcat."

"He showed no stealth and was easily scared off," Jace said, and I looked up to see him cradling his coffee mug. "I think we're looking for someone recently infected."

"What does that mean?" Morris's wide-eyed glance flicked from Jace to me. "What's wrong with me? Did I catch rabies?"

"No." I picked up the thermometer from an inverted bucket being used as a nightstand and swiped the sensor across his forehead. "One-oh-three. You're still sick, Mr. Morris. Why don't you try to get some sleep? Spencer will replace your IV bag in a couple of hours, and when you're feeling better, I promise I'll explain everything."

He looked like he wanted to argue, but then he fell against his pillow, as if arguing would be too much work.

"You two go get some sleep," I said as I sank into my chair at the small round table in the kitchenette.

"You sure?" Abby asked.

"He's sure." Jace stood and tugged her up. "I'm sure we can find something to do on our own."

"What happened to getting some sleep?" She grinned as she snuggled up to him.

"I think that phrase is open to interpretation," Jace said, one arm around her waist.

I tried not to listen to their private, largely explicit chatter as they headed up the steps, but a cat's hearing is both a blessing and a curse. And not for the first time, I wondered if I was wasting my time petitioning for a Pride with myself as its Alpha. Jace had more experience and first-hand knowledge of the inner workings of the Territorial Council. I couldn't help thinking that he stood a better shot of getting the Pride recognized.

Yet he and Abby swore the opposite was true. That Jace was *persona non grata* to most of the council, having been permanently exiled from all ten territories. For crimes he didn't even commit.

He'd accepted responsibility for what Abby had done to hide and protect Robyn from the council. Because Robyn had killed the men who'd infected her and murdered her friends, and in the process, had uncovered a ring of human hunters.

Robyn Sheffield, with her big, innocent eyes, had a higher kill count than most of my enforcers, and her targets had been actual, dangerous criminals, rather than strays who'd gone bad because no one was there to teach and assist them when they were newly infected, terrified, and confused.

Robyn was the most infuriating woman I'd ever met. Yet somehow she was also the most beautiful, fascinating stray I'd ever come across.

And she held the fate of my Pride—the trajectory of the rest of my life—in her graceful, deadly little hands...

A soft huffing sound wormed its way into my dream, and I woke up with my forehead resting on my arms, which were folded on the edge of the table. I blinked, and my bare feet came into focus on the concrete floor, between the legs of my chair. A soft beam of sunlight shone over them from the narrow window high on one wall.

Morning had come.

That sound came again—a deep huffing exhalation—and I sat straight up, my pulse rushing in anticipation.

Somehow, I'd slept through Corey Morris's first shift. He sat on his haunches a few feet in front of the table, with his tail curled around his legs and his back to me. Glossy black fur covered a sleek but powerful feline musculature. He was slender in human form, but in cat form, he wasn't much bigger than Abby.

Despite the groan of my chair when I sat up, he ignored me, his silent focus trained inside his cell at…Corey Morris?

Morris stood on two human legs in sweat-drenched clothes, staring through the open door of his cell at—

I sniffed the air, and her scent flooded my nostrils. I stood so fast my chair clattered to the floor.

The cat wasn't Morris. It was Robyn.

She glanced over one shoulder at me, and the graceful arch of her neck gleamed in the florescent utility light hanging from the ceiling. Robyn blinked once, then dismissed me with a soft snort as she turned to Morris.

His eyes were wide, his forehead shiny with sweat. His cheeks practically glowed with fever. His gaze seemed to swim in and out of focus.

He probably thought he was dreaming. Or hallucinating.

"Robyn," I whispered. "Come here."

Instead, she stood and padded silently into his cell. Morris took a shaky step back. His chest hitched with deep, quick inhalations until his jaw snapped shut and he drew in a breath through his nose. Then he froze.

Recognition flickered across his expression, followed almost immediately by confusion. He wasn't afraid of her, but he didn't understand why. He recognized something about her scent, but he didn't understand that either.

I remembered being where he was, but the first time I saw a fellow shifter was a week after my infection. I'd been stuck in cat form for days, and I was starting to wonder if I'd only imagined ever being human.

Robyn made a soft cooing sound deep in her throat, and Morris's tense frame relaxed a little. He knew that sound—that gentle chorus of comfort and acceptance—though he'd likely never heard it before that moment. He reached out to her with one trembling hand.

She stepped forward and pressed the top of her fur-covered head against his palm, like a giant house cat demanding to be petted. He ran his hand over her head and as far down her spine as he could reach without moving. Wonder played across his flushed features.

"Who are you?" he whispered.

Robyn brushed the side of her face across the outside of his left thigh, marking him with a trace of her scent. Labeling him as a friend.

Irritation shot up my spine. "Robyn," I snapped. She didn't have permission to bond with my new tom. *I* was supposed to help him through the transition. *I* was the one he needed to trust and depend on.

I had to establish my authority over and responsibility for him from the very beginning.

Yet that wasn't why I'd snapped at her.

She hadn't marked *me* as a friend. She'd hardly even touched me, and I'd given her sanctuary. All Corey Morris had done was stare at her in a fevered haze.

I recognized the irrationality—the blatant envy— of my own thought even as Robyn turned to blink lazily at me. She seemed unmoved by my irritation, but I heard the spike in her heartbeat. Try as she might to hide it, her instincts responded to displeasure from an Alpha.

You could be her *Alpha*, a traitorous voice whispered from deep inside me. *Or you could just be hers…*

I dislodged that thought with a single shake of my head. "Come out of there. What are you doing here?"

"Who is she?" Morris whispered as Robyn padded toward me. He knew she was female, and he knew she was a who, not a what. But he didn't seem to know *how* he knew any of that.

"Corey Morris, this is Robyn Sheffield. She's a stray. Like you." Well, not *entirely* like him.

"Like me?" Morris frowned. "Is this a dream? This doesn't feel real."

In my experience, there were two types of newly infected strays. The first responded to their own transitional state with fear and aggression, snapping and hissing at anyone who came close. Even in human form. Even before they understood the nature of the infection.

The second kind reacted with disbelief, confusion, and—often—the fear that they were losing their minds. Morris, thankfully, seemed to be the second kind. He might be harder to convince, but he'd be easier to handle. At least physically.

"This is real. She has the same infection you have.

So do I. This is what it does to you." I nodded at Robyn. "What it turns you into. You can choose to accept that, along with both the advantages and disadvantages your new life brings. Or you can fight it, and live the rest of your life in misery."

His focus slid from me to her. "I don't understand. Why do you have a panther?"

"She's not a panther. 'Panther' isn't a species." *And I certainly don't have her. Alas.* "Robyn?" I said, and she turned to look up at me. "Would you like to demonstrate?"

At first, she only blinked at me silently. Then her head bobbed, and she made a soft purring sound, evidently pleased to have been asked.

"Holy shit." Morris's eyes widened until I worried that they might pop from his skull. "Did the cat answer you?"

"Yes, and that's the most succinct answer I've ever gotten out of her," I said.

Robyn snorted. Then she padded into the space in front of the stairs and stared at the floor.

"Wha…?" Morris's question faded into nothing when he heard the first gristly pop.

A low groan rumbled from Robyn's throat, and a ripple of popping sounds washed over her body as her joints began to dislocate. As her bones began to shorten and elongate, accommodating their individual transformation.

"What the hell?" Morris backed up until his legs hit the side of the bed, but his gaze stayed glued to Robyn as all over her body, fur began to recede into her skin, like grass growing in reverse. "Seriously, man, what the *fuck*? What did you put in my IV bag?"

"You're not hallucinating, Corey," I said as

Robyn's groaning reached a higher pitch. "This is real. What's happening to her will happen to you soon. Maybe as early as a couple of hours from now, but definitely by tonight. It's a natural transition, but that doesn't mean it's easy. Or comfortable."

"What's happening to her?"

Robyn lay on the floor on her side, writhing in pain as her skeleton broke itself apart and knitted itself back together. As her joints realigned and her muscles stretched and bunched to fit the new structure.

"This is the most vulnerable moment in a shifter's life," I said, keeping Morris in my focus and Robyn's demonstration on the edge of my vision. "We're defenseless while we shift, and the fact that she's willing to do this in front of you should mean a great deal to you."

And to me. Instinctually speaking, she had no reason to trust either of us not to kill her while she lay helpless on the floor. Did that make her rash, or simply eager to help a stray she obviously identified with?

Or was she trusting me to protect her? Putting her life in my hands...

A proud, pleasant warmth settled into my chest with that thought.

"I don't... I can't..." Morris stammered, his wide-eyed gaze glued to Robyn as her facial features slowly attained a recognizably human structure. Cheekbones. Brow bones. A delicately pointed chin.

And all at once, after several minutes of a grotesque and obviously painful transformation, Robyn lay on the cold concrete floor, naked and breathing heavily as her body fought to recover from the self-induced trauma.

"Holy shit." Morris swiped his left hand over his sweaty hair and sank onto the side of his bed. "How the...? Holy *fuck*."

"Articulate, isn't he?" Robyn smiled as she sat up slowly, and long dark hair fell over the graceful curve of her shoulder. But it covered very little else.

I began unbuttoning my shirt, intending to offer it to her.

Robyn frowned. "What are you doing?"

My fingers paused three holes down. "Being a gentleman."

She stood, both hands propped on her hips. Her curvy, bare hips... "You mean being a prude? If I'd wanted clothes, I would have brought some with me."

My hands fell to my sides, and for the first time since I was thirteen years old, I had no idea what to do with them.

Look at her eyes.

Only her eyes...

Robyn laughed, as if she could hear what I was thinking. Or read it on my face. "It's my understanding that nudity is par for the course for shifters, and that it doesn't mean anything sexual unless it's accompanied or preceded by some sort of overture. At least, that's what the natural-born cats tell me. Is that different for strays? Are your men shy?"

"No. But they're...men." I hesitated, unsure how to proceed without sticking my foot in my mouth. "I assumed a woman who didn't grow up in this lifestyle would be...hesitant."

"Maybe you should stop expecting different things

from me just because I use a stall rather than a urinal."

"That's not—" I bit off the explanation because I didn't owe her one. But the truth was that I was making an educated guess, not a sexist assumption. Abby put her clothes on as soon as she was done shifting, which had led me to believe that Robyn would as well. That tabbies were more modest than toms.

"She turned from a *cat* into a *woman*, and the part you can't understand is nudity?" Morris said, and we both turned to him in surprise. I'd almost forgotten he was even there. "I'm less worried about her clothes than about her fur. What the hell just happened?"

Robyn's soft smile was part amusement, part...nostalgia? "I know, it looks weird. And it feels even weirder. Actually, it hurts like hell. And I wish I could say you get used to it, but you don't. I haven't, anyway." She crossed her arms beneath her breasts—*look at her eyes, Titus!*—and padded into Morris's cell on two bare human feet. "But maybe it'll be different for you."

"You're saying that's going to happen to me?" Morris said, and I realized that now *they'd* forgotten about *me*.

"Yeah." Robyn shrugged, and more hair fell over her shoulder. "You got scratched, right? I saw the wound last night. The cat that scratched you was a shapeshifter, and now so are you." Another shrug. "But you're way luckier than I was. Titus has a sweet setup here. I was totally incoherent by this phase, but you seem mostly okay."

"We've kept him hydrated," I said. "That makes all the difference."

Morris laughed, but rather than joy, the sound held an edge of mania. From the fever.

"What's funny?" Robyn asked.

"The IV." Morris dragged one hand through his hair. "This whole thing is absurd. I got attacked by a fucking panther. I went to the ER for the infection, then got in a car with a stranger and woke up in a jail cell in a basement, surrounded by even more strangers who smell…weird. Yet weirdly familiar. Then there's you." His eyes narrowed as he studied her, and my hands clenched into fists because he did *not* look just at her face. "You were a panther, then I *saw* you turn into a woman, and now you're naked. Yet somehow, the thing that feels most preposterous of all is this damn IV." He raised his hand, and the tube coming from his arm rocked the bag hanging from a hook on the wall. "It's so normal and logical that it shouldn't have any place in this nightmare."

"Again, this is not a dream," I said.

Robyn laughed, as if I hadn't even spoken. "For me, it was coffee." She stepped into the cell and dropped into the bedside chair, then crossed her legs at the knees. "I got infected in this horrible cabin. There were cat heads mounted on the wall—I didn't know they were dead shifters at the time—and there was blood everywhere. My friend Abby and I had to stay in the cabin, because I was too sick to hike out of the woods. I was in and out of consciousness with a raging fever, vomiting every hour or so, but through it all, I kept smelling coffee. The good kind. French Vanilla or chocolate biscotti, or something sweet like that. I thought I was hallucinating, but it turns out the asshole hunters who kidnapped me and dragged me to their shifter slaughterhouse had some fancy coffeemaker, and Abby drank cup after cup so she could stay awake and take care of me."

"What happened to the assholes?" Morris asked, and I stared at Robyn in astonishment. He should either have been backing into a corner of the room, sweating terror from every pore, or convinced that he was either dreaming or hallucinating the whole thing. Yet Robyn had him talking coherently. Asking questions, in spite of a fever that should have knocked him on his ass.

"Abby killed them while I was unconscious, then Jace swooped in and cleaned the whole thing up." She made a swooshing gesture with both hands, and my gaze snagged on the swell of her left breast, where her elbow grazed it.

Eyes, Titus.

"But at that point, neither of them knew I was infected."

"So you really were kidnapped?" Morris asked, leaning on his pillow.

"Yeah." Robyn's expression seemed distant for a moment, and I could tell from the set of her jaw that there was more to it. Some part she didn't want to talk about. Then she shook that off and reached over to give the new stray's shoulder a little shove. "Let's just say that your origin story isn't half as traumatic as mine, so if I can get through this, so can you."

I couldn't take my gaze off her.

It's not like I'd never seen a beautiful woman naked. But I'd never met a woman as comfortable in her own skin as Robyn clearly was. I'd never seen anyone bond so easily with a newly scratch-fevered stray, even though that was *my* job.

Robyn was as fascinating as she was irritating, and

suddenly, I wasn't sure at all that I could give her back.

SEVEN

Robyn

A knock echoed against my bedroom door, and my breath caught in my chest. "Robyn? I need to talk to you for a minute," Abby called out from the hallway as I wrapped my wet hair in a towel.

I swallowed an unexpected twinge of disappointment—I'd hoped it was Titus—then shoved my arms into the borrowed robe. "It's unlocked!"

Abby opened the door and stepped into the room. Holding a duffel bag.

Hair stood up all over my body.

For a human, that means goose bumps, but for a shifter, body hair rising away from the skin is an actual physical reaction to a perceived threat. Physical or emotional. Like a kitten whose fur puffs up every time she's startled, I hadn't *quite* learned to control it yet.

"Why are you packed?" Suspicion echoed in my voice.

"Isaac called." Abby set her bag on the floor and

tugged me down on the bed next to her. "The council has temporarily lifted Jace's travel ban. So he can go to the ceremony."

The wedding. Jace's sister, Melody, was marrying Abby's brother Isaac, the new Alpha of her territory and father of her unborn child. That scandal was the only thing anyone in the Southeast Pride was talking about, other than the unprecedented discovery of a female stray.

You'd think notoriety would've given Melody and me something to bond over. But you'd be wrong.

I swallowed my nerves. Surely it only *looked* like Abby was about to abandon me in a house full of strange toms. "So, when is this shotgun wedding?"

"There's no shotgun," she insisted. "They *want* to get married."

"You're avoiding the question."

"No." Abby pushed a poof of red curls from her face. "I'm avoiding the answer. The ceremony's on Thursday. If they wait any longer, she won't fit into her dress."

I fiddled with the sash around my robe, to have something to do with my hands. "That's five days from now, and it's, like, an eight-hour drive. Why are you already packed?"

Abby shrugged, but the gesture tried too hard to be nonchalant. "Isaac wants Jace to be one of his groomsmen, so he has to get fitted for a tux, and Melody seems to think she can get a dress altered for me in a couple of days, so I'm going to be in the ceremony too. And there's the bachelor party and the bridesmaid's brunch. And the rehearsal dinner. And I think they're going to squeeze in a baby shower too. This isn't a one-day event."

"So you're just going to leave me here?" Panic echoed in my voice, loud and clear.

"No!" She grabbed my hand and held it so tightly my fingers began to tingle. "I want you to come with us! We'll only be gone for six days, then we'll come back here. You'll still have a week of…vacation."

"You know damn well this is no vacation!" I snapped. But anger was a poor disguise for my fear and frustration. I'd come here to be with Abby—my best friend and the person most able to convince her father, the council chairman, to let me off for time served.

Letting me off for good behavior seemed like a long shot at best.

"I know. I'm just not sure what else to call it." She turned to face me on the end of the bed and squeezed my hand again. "Come with us, Robyn. It'll be fun!"

"I can't go to a shifter wedding with you!" The whole place would be crawling with eligible toms itching to make a play for the only of-age, unspoken for tabby in the country. "Hell, Melody will probably throw the damn bouquet right at me!"

"So duck." Another shrug. "There'll be dancing and an open bar. Think of it as a party. A chance to let loose."

"While everyone's staring at me like a fish in a bowl? Sounds like torture."

"It'll be whatever you make it, Robyn. But either way, Jace and I are going. This could be his last chance to see his mother and his sister for *years*."

"That's ridiculous." I stood, suddenly itching to be moving. To…run. Instead, I grabbed the clothes I'd worn when I fled the Southeast Pride—someone had done my laundry while I'd slept—and shrugged out of the robe to pull on my underwear. "Jace's family could come see him here even if the council never lifts his exile."

"But they won't," she insisted. "Melody and Patricia don't feel safe in the free zone, and they won't even after it's officially a Pride. They're kind of…precious."

"So I recall." I'd only met Melody and her mother once, but that was plenty. "Abby, if I go back, they'll never let me out of their sight again."

She shook her head. "Faythe and my dad gave you their word. They won't break it."

"They said I could stay with Titus for two weeks." I pulled my jeans on over my underwear. "They didn't say they'd let me leave again if I came back early. And anyway, the whole council's already broken their word, letting Jace visit after they said—" I gasped as the truth hit me like a slap to the face. "That's what this is about."

Abby gave me a confused look as I buttoned my jeans and reached for my bra. "What are you talking about?"

"They're trying to lure me back early. They don't think Titus will keep his word." And I was starting to hope they were right. Titus might be trying to turn the free zone into another Pride territory, but that was like trying to build a brick house out of rough-cut stone. His "house" was never going to look like all the others, because he was using different building materials. Strays, instead of Pride cats. And if I could make him understand that his territory *shouldn't* be like all the others—that he didn't need to give his Pride a dam—then there was no reason a female stray couldn't live in peace there like all the others.

"You think my brother's wedding is a ploy by the council to get you back?" Abby frowned. "Robyn, they've been engaged for two months. You're starting to sound paranoid."

I shook my head as I shrugged out of the robe. "Not the wedding. Lifting Jace's exile." I hooked my bra into place, then pulled my shirt over my head. "They're letting you and Jace come to the ceremony because they think I'll come with you. And once I'm there, I'll never get out again."

"I doubt they've put that much thought into it."

"She's right," Jace said, and I looked up to find him in the doorway, leaning against the frame. "They're making a play for Robyn, and she can't come with us unless she's willing to go to Atlanta after the wedding."

Abby crossed her arms over her chest. "You really think my dad and Faythe would do that?"

He shrugged. "I think they only make up one-fifth of the council, and even if the other four-fifths agree on nothing else in the world, they agree on getting Robyn back. For the research potential, at the least."

"I hate to think they'd be so duplicitous about it," Abby murmured.

Jace stepped forward and pulled her up by both hands. "Your faith in people is adorable." He kissed her on the forehead, and they looked so sweet together that I almost gagged.

When I looked past them, I saw Jace's packed bag lying on the floor in the hall, next to their closed bedroom door. "When are you leaving?"

"After breakfast." Abby turned around in Jace's embrace until she was pressed against his chest. "Robyn, you *will* be okay here. Titus won't let anything happen to you."

"Nothing you don't want, anyway," Jace added, and my pulse spiked at the thought. Abby elbowed him in the gut, but he hardly even flinched. "I'm kidding," he amended. "The man's a perfect gentleman. And he's not looking for a wife."

I could feel my face flame. Abby told him about my suspicion. Jace must have thought I was a total egomaniac. "Good." I cleared my throat and pushed past my own embarrassment. "I'm only here because the alternative is Atlanta."

Abby stepped out of Jace's embrace and looked up into my eyes. "Robyn, *promise* me you'll be here when we get back."

I shrugged. "Where else would I go?"

"I just… Don't run, okay? It's not safe out there by yourself. If you really don't want to go to Atlanta, we'll figure something out after the wedding. You have my word."

Jace laid a hand on her arm. "Abby, don't make promises you can't keep."

"I…" She didn't seem to know how to finish that. Instead, she nodded. "We'll be home in a week. Stay put, okay?"

"I will." *Probably.*

After the paper plate revelation of the night before, I'd expected breakfast to consist of two or three enforcers in jeans and dark tees eating cold cereal and slopping milk on the countertop. What I got instead were Jace, Abby, and six toms in various stages of undress, pouring coffee from a French press, squeezing orange halves in a steel-handled juicer, and devouring homemade waffles.

On paper plates.

Though I'd already met several of them, I lingered in the arched entryway for a minute, watching. Trying to decide how—and whether—I fit in. Trying not to be intimidated by the crowd, and by how close they all obviously were.

I'd spent more than two months with the Di Carlos and never felt like I knew a soul, other than Dr. Carver, who only visited to draw my blood.

"Hungry?" a voice asked from my left, and I jumped, startled to find that Drew Borden had snuck up on me. Only he hadn't really snuck. He'd probably just walked with a cat's inherent silent grace.

Even in human form, my hearing was excellent when I paid attention to it. But I hadn't yet mastered the art of listening to my surroundings without conscious effort, something a natural-born shifter never had to learn, as far as I could tell.

But these weren't natural-born shifters. I was finally among people who truly understood what I'd been through and what still lay ahead. I should have been thrilled for the company—for the commiseration—yet the thought of stepping into Titus's kitchen made my chest feel tight.

My presence had put them all at risk from the US Prides. They would either hate me for bringing war to their doorstep or be all over me, because I was only the second tabby they'd ever met.

I gave Drew a hesitant smile. "Yeah, I could eat, but…" I let the statement trail off when I realized how pathetic my fear of a hot-or-cold welcome would sound. I'd made my own bed.

Drew smiled. "They don't bite. Not in human form, anyway." He'd exchanged last night's jogging pants for a snug pair of dark jeans, but instead of an enforcer's typical black tee, he wore a navy polo, which distinguished him from the other enforcers laughing and talking as they put away massive quantities of food. And somehow, Drew wore the minor wardrobe upgrade as if it were a hand-tailored suit.

Still, though I could see in an almost academic way that he was hot as hell, I felt no real attraction to him. So how come every time I got even a whiff of Titus, I wanted to rub myself all over him until we both smelled like each other?

Maybe it was his scent. I'd spent four hours in Titus's, yet I hadn't really gotten close enough to the others to notice anything from their scents other than the obvious trace of werecat.

Indulging a sudden impulse, I stood on my toes and pressed my nose against Drew's neck, inhaling deeply. He smelled good. Clean and masculine. Yet...nothing.

He chuckled. "What was that for?"

I shrugged. "Just testing a theory." Then I turned to the kitchen and changed the subject while my face flamed. "How long have you known them?" I asked him.

"About a year and a half, for most of them." His gaze scanned the kitchen, and I could practically smell pride emanating from his pores as he studied his fellow enforcers. "Nearly a decade, for Titus. We met in college. He got me a job at his dad's company a couple of years before his parents died and he took over the reins."

"You were friends *before* you were both infected? That's a hell of a coincidence." *Or maybe not.* Being Abby's friend is what got me infected.

Drew nodded, arms crossed over his polo. "We were actually scratched on the same night, at a work event, and were dragged into this whole shifter thing together. We came up with the idea for a stray territory over fish tacos and imported beer about a year later, and look at it now." He spread his arms, full of pride for what he and Titus had created, and I couldn't resist a smile.

"Yeah, you guys are doing good work." But then I glanced again into the bustling kitchen, and my insides began to twist with nerves.

Drew stepped over the threshold and tugged me along gently by one arm. "Hey!"

All laughter and conversation came to an abrupt halt as everyone turned to look. Abby's green eyes brightened when she saw me, a bite of whipped cream-covered waffle inches from her mouth.

"For anyone who hasn't heard, this is Robyn Sheffield. She'll be staying with us for a couple of weeks, so I want you all to dust off your manners and put them to use. When she goes back to her territory, we'd like her to have only good things to report about the world's first stray Pride."

"Does that mean I have to put on a shirt?" the youngest tom in the room asked with a light-hearted grin. He was about my age, with dark brown hair artfully tussled all over his head and the suggestion of a six-pack peeking through the bare, tanned skin above the waist of his jeans.

"It means you have to eat with a fork and pretend there's a target in the bottom of the toilet bowl,

Brandt." The tom manning a matching set of rotating waffle irons dropped a fork on the younger man's half-filled plate. Except for his face and the palms of his hands, every visible inch of the cook's skin was covered in swirling geometric-patterned tattoos, from his neck to a low-hanging pair of jeans. "Hey, Robyn, come grab a plate."

I dragged my gaze up from the fascinating canvas of his sculpted chest to his face, frowning as I searched my memory. He spoke to me as though we'd met, but I would have remembered those tattoos.

Then I saw his eyes. Brown with a ring of gold around the outside. Just like the cat who'd growled from Titus's front porch the night before. "Knox?" A single sniff in his direction confirmed my guess. "I didn't recognize you." Without fur.

He laughed. "I don't hear that often. Here." He held out an empty heavy-duty paper plate, and I took it, grateful to have recognized one more not-unfriendly face. Knox motioned to the rotating waffle iron on the left. "This one will be done in a few sec—"

The waffle iron beeped, and Knox flipped it by the handle, then opened it to reveal a perfectly toasted Belgian waffle. He pried it loose with a plastic spatula, then slid it onto my plate.

"We have butter—whipped or melted—fresh berries, chocolate chips, and chopped bacon," he said, waving one hand down the long kitchen peninsula at a series of disposable paper bowls and platters. "Also caramelized banana slices, toasted pecans, chocolate and caramel drizzle, and my favorite: homemade whipped cream, in the mixer at the end."

"Homemade...?" I looked up at him, wide-eyed. "Did you make all this?"

"What, like waffles are so hard?" Drew grinned as he reached around me to sprinkle a heaping spoonful of chopped bacon on his waffle. "The directions are on the back of the box."

"Blasphemy!" Knox accused. "Bisquick is for soccer moms."

"I'm kidding." Drew slapped one hand onto Knox's shoulder. "Alistair here was a chef in Baton Rouge before he came face-to-face with a stray in the bayou a couple of years ago."

Knox mumbled some colorful expletives under his breath over the use of his first name as he poured more batter into one of the waffle irons.

"And the others?" I whispered to Drew as I drizzled melted butter over my waffle.

"You met Spence and Lochlan in the basement last night. Er, this morning."

"Yes. Good morning," I said, as I passed them, eating on stools on the other side of the bar.

"Morning." Spencer gave me a tired smile as he stirred a spoonful of sugar into a steaming paper coffee cup.

"You're a doctor?" I asked as I dumped a spoonful of sliced berries onto my plate.

"A triage nurse." His scrubs were gone, but he still wore exhaustion from his shift at the hospital, followed by a night spent helping Titus with the new stray. "*He's* a doctor, though." Spence elbowed the man on the stool to his left.

Lochlan rolled his eyes, and a tumble of dark blond waves fell over his shoulder. No man bun today. "Does that never get old, man?"

"I don't understand," I said as I dug a spoonful of toasted pecans from the next bowl. "Are you not a doctor?"

"I used to be an Associate Professor of Philosophy at Duke."

"Ah." My brows rose. "A PhD. That's my plan too. History."

Loch nodded. "Unfortunately, Duke isn't in the free zone, so..." He shrugged, then cut a bite out of a waffle half-buried beneath caramelized banana slices.

Duke University was in Abby's father's territory. No strays allowed.

"Loch and Knox both lost their jobs and their homes when they got infected," Drew said. "But all that should stop once we're officially recognized by your council."

It's not my *council...*

"But not you?" I said with another glance at Spencer.

He shrugged. "I'm local."

"What about him?" I nodded at the youngest tom as I followed Drew farther down the peninsula.

"That's Brandt Fischer. He was infected a few months ago, but we didn't find him until after his first shift. We brought him here for acclimation, and he just doesn't seem to want to leave."

"You know I can hear you, right?" Brandt spoke up from the breakfast table, where he sat at Abby's left.

Drew rolled his eyes. "That's a somewhat selective ability, in your case." Then he leaned closer to whisper into my ear. "He wants to be an enforcer, and no one has the heart to tell him he's too young and inexperienced. He mostly tags along after Knox and Naveen, doing whatever grunt work they throw his way."

"Naveen?" I asked, glancing around the kitchen.

"Over here." A man with thick, glossy black hair and piercing brown eyes stood from his stool at the end of the peninsula, holding an empty paper plate smeared with whipped cream and syrup. "Naveen Madan." He extended his hand to me across the granite. "You're Abby's friend?"

"Yeah." I transferred my plate into my left hand, so I could shake his. "We were college roommates until…"

"Until you were infected?"

"Well, until the council found out I'd been infected. But that was my own fault." Turns out that killing four people—even bad guys—will quickly bring you to the attention of the authorities, both shifter and human.

And suddenly I was uncomfortably aware that if any of the men around me had done what I'd done, even if they were as traumatized as I'd been, they would have been executed for their crimes. Quickly, and quite possibly brutally.

But I saw no sign that they knew what I'd done. If Abby hadn't told them, I probably shouldn't either.

"Ready?" Drew asked with a glance at my plate.

"Almost." I took a scoop of luxuriously thick homemade whipped cream from the mixer at the end of the peninsula, then drizzled chocolate syrup over my mountain of food and followed him to the round table, where there were two seats left. "Is breakfast always like this?" I asked as I slid into the chair across from Abby.

She shrugged. "Sometimes there are omelets with

arugula and pesto, or basil, chili, and parmesan."

"Oooh, or smoked trout and fennel," Brandt added.

I turned, wide-eyed, for another look at Knox, the tattooed chef.

Most of Di Carlo's enforcers had sworn oaths of service and loyalty shortly after graduating high school. Serving as an enforcer and protecting a Pride had been their lifelong ambition—an inevitability from the time they were small.

But Titus's men were a little older than the average enforcer and they'd obviously developed lives, careers, and talents of their own before they were infected. Before they came to work for their Alpha.

Lives and careers many had been forced to give up when they were exiled to the free zone.

Jace set his fork on his empty paper plate. "Robyn, I hate to eat and run, especially since you just got here."

"But…" I could practically hear the word hanging from his tongue.

"But we need to get on the road."

Abby swallowed the last bite of her waffle and stood, plate in hand. "I'm sorry. But we'll be home in a week."

"I know."

She dropped her plate into a trash compactor, then pulled me up for a hug. "You'll be fine here. There isn't a man on Titus's team who wouldn't die to protect you," she whispered into my ear. "They take their enforcer duties very seriously, because they all feel like they have something to prove."

"To the council?"

"And to Titus. And now to you. They're good

guys."

"I'm sure they are." But they were also *big* guys, with the strength of several very large human men apiece. Big guys who had two solid reasons to dislike me, whether they knew it or not.

But I'd put myself in this mess.

"Give them a chance," Abby whispered as she let me go. I tried not to panic as the men around me shouted out jovial goodbyes.

Chewing my first bite of a truly spectacular waffle, I listened to Abby's and Jace's footsteps fade as they headed down the long main hallway toward the front of the house. Only once the sound of Jace's engine had faded from my ears did I notice that the Alpha was missing.

"Where's Titus?"

"In the infirmary," Lochlan said from his seat at the bar while he pulled his long blond hair back and secured it with a rubber band.

"Still? Doesn't he ever...delegate?"

"I'll go down to give him a break soon, but he tries to stay with new strays as long as possible," Spencer said. "It lets the stray form an immediate connection and establishes Titus as an authority figure from the beginning."

"Does that help?" I asked.

Drew shrugged from the chair to my left. "Natural-born cats rarely question the societal structure and authority figures they're raised with. Titus is trying to replicate that by being present in the infancy of a stray's transition. I guess time will tell if it works. He's only been doing this for about a year."

Drew stood to get a second helping, but I could only stare at my plate as his words played through my head again. I'd totally lost my appetite.

"What's wrong?" Naveen slid into the vacated chair on my left. "You look like you were personally betrayed by that waffle."

"I…" I shook my head and stabbed a chunk of pecan with my fork. "It's nothing." My complaints would sound like spoiled whining to men who wanted nothing more in the world than to gain official standing in the council's eyes. To truly belong in a world that's held them at arm's length for generations.

A smile lingered at the corner of his beautiful, full mouth. "You're a *really* bad liar, Ms. Sheffield."

"I don't get much practice," I admitted. "My thoughts typically pour forth like Niagara Falls."

Naveen laughed. "What's holding you back today?"

We'd just established how bad a liar I was, so… "I'm afraid you'll all hate me if you knew what I was thinking."

"Unless you're about to say you're a UNC fan, I don't think you have much to worry about." When his eyes went wide, I realized he'd misinterpreted my silent confusion. "Oh shit, you *are* a North Carolina fan!" He lowered his voice to a conspiratorial whisper. "Loch bleeds Duke blue and white, so let's keep this between the two of us."

Finally, I understood. He was talking about a college sports rivalry.

Naveen laughed again at my expression. "Not much of a basketball fan, huh? So then what's the big secret?"

"There's no secret. I just…" I stabbed at another pecan and broke it into three chunks. Then I dropped my fork and looked him straight in the eye. "I don't understand why you guys are trying so hard to turn yourselves into something you're not, when what you are right now is awesome!"

Naveen gave me a baffled frown. "What we are right now?"

"Free," I said. "Independent, and of no real interest to the council. They don't care what you do, as long as you're not killing or infecting people, so you could do whatever you want out here. Why form a Pride and pay dues, and conform to their rules and archaic social conventions if you don't have to?"

For a moment, my soft outburst met with surprised silence. Then Naveen smiled. "First of all, we don't pay dues. Titus is a billionaire. He doesn't need to tax Pride members to pay his enforcers, like the other Alphas do."

"Oh. Well, that's…"

Billions? My cheeks felt like they were on fire.

Naveen studied my face. "You didn't know?"

"I knew he ran some big corporation, but no. I didn't know *that*." And I wished he hadn't told me.

His frown deepened as he studied me. "Knowing about the money makes you uncomfortable?"

I shrugged. "In my experience, money gets in the way. People who have it think everyone and everything is for sale."

Naveen chuckled softly as he cut another bite from his waffle.

"What's funny?"

His fork paused on the way to his mouth. "You'll understand once you get to know Titus."

"I know what I need to know. Wealthy or not, Alphas are all cut from the same cloth. They have a pathological need to issue orders and to…procreate."

Naveen leaned back in his chair, studying me with a new intensity, as if he suddenly understood...something. "You think Titus wants to, what? Father your kids?" He laughed again, as if the concept were truly ridiculous. "You have a very robust self-esteem."

"That's not—" My face was on *fire*. "It's not that I think Titus can't resist *me*. It's that Alphas are *driven* to reproduce—I learned that, if nothing else at the Di Carlos'—and I'm the only eligible tabby around."

"Sorry." Now Naveen looked embarrassed. "I didn't mean that the way it sounded. You're totally hot, and if Titus—if *any* of us—were looking to start a family, you'd be at the top of the spousal wish list. But that's not something many of us think about, out here in the free zone."

"But this won't be the free zone for long. And that's what all Alphas want," I insisted, as my cheeks continued to burn. "They're biologically driven."

His smile returned, and somehow, despite the mortifying turn our conversation had taken, there was no patronization or teasing in his expression. "Robyn, I don't think you fully understand the goal. We may be modeling our Pride after the others, but we have no desire to replicate their system exactly. With a few exceptions, Pride cats have always held themselves above us. The *last* thing any of us wants is a gaggle of natural-born princes and princess running around, looking at us as if we're subjects sent to serve them in the family castle."

"But if Titus doesn't have a daughter...?" Shifter society was patriarchal, but matrilineal. The men were in charge, but control of a territory was passed from the Alpha to his daughter's husband. At least, until

Faythe. And Abby.

Which was why the loss of Sara Di Carlo—and now Abby—was devastating for the US Prides. Their territories now had no dam to give birth to the next generation.

Naveen seemed to understand what I hadn't managed to voice. "We don't need shifter babies, because our population is not in decline. Citizenship in our Pride isn't limited to natural-born shifters. We're bursting at the seams."

I thought about that for a second, and the tension building inside me began to ease. This is what Jace and Abby were trying to tell me. "So, Titus doesn't need to claim me for his Pride?"

Naveen shook his head. "Nope. Out here, you are worth no more than any of the rest of us. Except perhaps as an initial curiosity."

I should have been relieved. So why did that thought suddenly feel like a slap in the face?

EIGHT

Titus

"Okay, now breathe deeply and try to relax all your muscles," I said as Corey Morris collapsed to the concrete floor on his knees. His flesh looked pale and oddly lumpy from the transformation of muscles going on beneath his skin. "I know that sounds impossible, but the tenser you are, the more this will hurt and the longer it will take."

Morris rolled his eyes at me, and if he'd been capable of speech with a mouth caught somewhere between a cat's muzzle and the human arrangement of teeth, I'm sure he would have been sharing quite a repertoire of expletives. Which would have been considered an insult to any other Alpha.

In theory, I had no interest in censoring my enforcers' language, but I'd already come to understand the logic behind the "no cursing at your Alpha" rule, which was standard in the officially recognized Prides. An Alpha who lost the respect of his enforcers would soon lose the respect of the rest of his Pride members.

Then he'd lose the Pride itself.

Morris groaned through clenched teeth as his jaw began to ripple, taking on an even more feline shape. His ears seemed to twist as they were re-formed, migrating slowly from the sides of his head toward the top. But the visible part of that transformation barely scratched the surface of the pain he would feel below the skin, where the true change was ripping its way through his muscular and skeletal structures.

"When I was new at this, I found it easier to lie down." But the frustration in Morris's eyes said he couldn't figure out how to make his muscles obey that command. He wasn't in control of his own body, possibly for the first time in his life, and I knew as well as anyone how terrifying that feeling was.

Especially the first time.

Soon, he'd learn to control his shift. To bring it on at will. But for now…

"Try to let the changes roll over you. Give yourself up to the process. As cheesy as that sounds, it's the best advice I can give."

Finally, as fur began to sprout from follicles all over his body, Corey Morris either figured out how to relax his muscles or lost control of them entirely. He fell over on his side with a solid thud. A choking sound rattled in his throat, as his larynx and esophagus began to shift.

"Just breathe…" I felt like I should put a hand on his shoulder, or make some other comforting gesture, but I knew better than to touch a stray during his first shift. Or right afterward, before he's gained his bearings. Before he realizes he can still access his human thoughts—and boundaries—while in cat form.

That's what had gone wrong with Robyn, according to Jace. Abby had done her best to help her roommate through the transition, but she was brand new to the process—they both were—and she didn't expect Robyn to live. Though there'd been vague rumors of female strays surviving in Central and South America, none ever had in the US, so in the beginning, Abby'd believed that all she could do was comfort her friend as the fever slowly drained the life from her body.

By the time she'd realized her roommate would survive, Robyn had already shifted, in the very cabin her kidnappers had dragged her to. Where she'd witnessed several deaths. Where she was surrounded by the scent not just of the cat who'd infected her, but by the scents of the men who'd assaulted her and tried to kill Abby.

Robyn was born into the shifter world in a violent event as rife with blood and pain as any real birth would have been. It was a miracle she'd come out of it with her mind intact.

Mostly.

The shock and trauma Robyn had undergone—the inability to process or control instincts making demands she couldn't understand or master—was what strays in the free zone had been enduring for generations. What I was trying to prevent with Corey Morris, and with all the other toms in my territory.

"It's almost over now," I said softly, as the river of fur flowed to cover his belly and the lower halves of all four of his legs.

When the transformation was complete, Morris lay panting on the floor on his side, staring at the basement as if he couldn't see it. I knew from experience that he wasn't processing anything yet, other than the end to a massive and unanticipated amount of pain. Pain in places he hadn't even realized he could hurt, like the insides of his elbows and the tops of his feet. The ends of his fingers and toes, and that fleshy place between his thumbs and forefingers.

I stood, and the movement caught his eye. "I'm going to get you some food and water. You might not feel like eating yet, but you'll be famished soon." Because shifting burned an enormous number of calories. And because he'd been too sick to eat or hold down any food for the past twelve hours, at least.

Morris grunted from deep in his throat, a sound that could have meant anything from "Thanks" to "Fuck you very much."

On the other side of the basement, I opened the refrigerator and pulled out a pitcher of cold water and a hunk of raw rabbit, left over from Knox's hunt the night before. I poured water into a bowl, put the meat on a paper plate, and set them both on the floor a few feet from Morris, so that any initial misfiring of his new arrangement of muscles and nerves couldn't knock them both over.

I'd just poured myself a fresh cup of coffee when my phone rang, and Faythe Sanders's name and number appeared on the screen.

"Faythe?" I fought not to yawn into the phone. "It's been a long night here. What's up?"

"I spoke to Jace and Abby," she said, over a background of road noise. "They said Robyn isn't coming with them."

"To the wedding?" Another yawn. "Did you really think she would?"

"I think it would have been better for everyone involved if she had." Something brushed the phone on her end, then her voice was muffled. "Greg, no! Put the straw back in the cup!"

"Are you driving?" I asked.

"No, Marc is. We're on the way to Kentucky for the wedding." A child's laughter rang out over the line, and Faythe heaved an exasperated exhalation. "Greg! Please put the *straw* in the *cup*!"

"You sound like you've got your hands full. Are you supposed to travel this far into a pregnancy?"

"Don't even try that 'go home and rest' crap with me, Titus. Girls run the world. I believe Beyoncé said it best."

I laughed. "Then I guess I should let you get back to business."

"Not yet. Hang on." Something brushed the phone again. "Greg, put your headphones on. I'm going to play the movie. Just put them... Yes, over both ears." Then she returned. "Titus, please tell me you're not having second thoughts about sending Robyn to Atlanta."

The truth was that second thoughts were the only thoughts I'd had. Robyn didn't want to go back. "I would have thought that you, of all people, would understand where she's coming from, Faythe. She doesn't want the council to run her life. Doesn't that sound familiar?"

"Yes, and if she hadn't made a deal with them—if she hadn't given her *word*—I'd be on the other side of this argument with her. And after she's fulfilled her half of the deal, I *will* be on her side, if she still wants to leave. But until then, I can't support any attempt to weaken the authority of the council I'm a member of, when it's acting in good faith and in the best interest of the community it serves."

"And if it weren't acting in the best interest of that community?"

"Then I would go to bat for the community. But that's not what we're talking about here, Titus. You have to bring her back so she can finish her training. What she decides to do after that is up to her."

"Is it really? Because she overheard your council arguing over whose son gets first dibs on her. And she said you were in on it."

"Damn it. That's not..." Faythe's words trailed off with a huff of frustration. "Yes, they were discussing the possibilities. They each want to be a grandfather, and most of them are old-school. But I wasn't advocating marrying her off. I was pointing out that if she doesn't *like* any of their sons, the whole discussion is pointless. No one will make Robyn do anything she doesn't want to do. You have my personal guarantee on that."

"Mine too," Marc said, his voice fainter, because he was farther from the phone. "Robyn can see—or not see—anyone she wants. But..."

His hesitation set off alarms in my head. "But what?"

"But she needs to wait to make any ...romantic decision," Faythe finished for him. "Until after she's finished her training and is officially on her own."

"And is the council willing to commit to a timeframe for that?" Not that I had the authority to negotiate on Robyn's behalf...

"It's kind of a self-paced program, Titus. The deeper her commitment, the faster it will go. And the council thinks she should concentrate on her own mental and emotional health until she's learned to control herself in both forms."

Those alarms coalesced into a full-fledged siren. "What are you saying? She's not allowed to date? That's not your decision to make." Why did I suddenly sound so defensive? "Don't you think that making positive connections might help her gain control over the wilder side of her instincts?"

For a moment, I heard nothing but road noise over the phone, and I had no doubt they were mouthing things silently to each other as Marc drove.

"She killed people, Titus," Faythe finally said. "She *couldn't help* but kill people. This is in her best interest, but it's also in yours."

"Mine? You think Robyn and I—"

"I meant 'you' in the plural sense," she clarified. "This is in the public's best interest, so to speak."

But that wasn't entirely true. That much was clear in the newly tense tone of her voice. "Why don't you say whatever you're dancing around, Faythe?"

She exhaled slowly. "The council has asked me to make sure you understand how vulnerable Robyn is at this point in her acclimation. She's still having flashbacks and nightmares, and they're afraid she might misunderstand any overture of friendship on your part. That she might…form an attachment. And that you might let her."

"You think I'm taking advantage of her?" I demanded.

"No. I don't," Faythe insisted. "I know you better than that. But I also know that things happen without planning, especially when the people involved are vulnerable or in pain." The sincerity in her voice sounded visceral and very personal. As if she were reading a page from her own history. "Mistakes are made, and they can't be taken back."

And suddenly I understood. *She's talking about Jace.* About their affair, years ago, before she'd married Marc.

Yet she was also talking about Robyn and me. Did that make me the potential mistake Robyn would one day regret?

"Okay, look," Marc said. "This isn't personal. We have to make sure you understand your position here, since Jace and Abby left her alone in your territory. Her safety is *entirely* in your hands. You're an authority figure. You can't sleep with her. No matter what."

"You're questioning my ethics and taking charge of a decision that belongs to Robyn." My voice had become a growl. My temper was a storm surge battering the walls of a weakened dam.

"Titus…" Faythe groaned. And that's when I realized how my protest sounded.

"I'm not arguing. I'm saying that this entire phone call is an insult. The council has no right to question my behavior and no right to tell Robyn who she can't…be with."

"You're right. That's not our place. And I promise I wouldn't be asking, regardless of what the council wants, if I didn't think this was in her best interest," Faythe said. "You're her Alpha, at least for the time being. Do the right thing. Guard her while she's with you, both physically and psychologically."

"Robyn's well-being is foremost in my mind," I assured them through clenched teeth. "And you have my word that I have no plans to seduce her. But I won't tolerate having my judgment questioned again. Is that understood?"

"Perfectly," Faythe said, while Marc grunted over the line. "Thank you, Titus."

I echoed Marc's grunt. Then I hung up the phone.

"How is he?" Robyn said from halfway up the stairs, and for a second, I thought she'd heard Faythe ask me not to abuse my authority as an Alpha by sleeping with her. As if I would ever abuse my authority. During that second, I found myself in a rare moment of speechlessness, unsure how to cover my own humiliation.

Acknowledge the awkwardness and joke it off?

Ignore the whole thing?

But then Robyn jogged down the rest of the stairs with her gaze glued to Corey Morris, who still lay panting on the floor, and I saw no sign that she'd overheard. "Lunch. From Knox." She dropped a brown paper bag on the table in front of me, and I could already smell the sandwich inside. "When did he shift?" she asked as she crossed the concrete toward the open cell at the end of the basement.

"Just now."

"So can you tell who infected him?"

"Not yet. But soon, hopefully. His scent will begin to develop, now that he's shifted."

"Like an old Polaroid?" she asked, and I laughed.

"Kind of. It'll happen once he's recovered from the shift, and that'll be faster if we can get him to eat something and drink more water."

She glanced at the rabbit meat on a paper plate in his cell, then marched forward with clear purpose.

"Wait!" I reached for her arm as she passed, but she dodged my grasp. "He might not—"

"Corey?" Robyn dropped onto her heels in front of the new stray, and I followed her into the cell, prepared to get between them if Morris had a bad reaction to being approached for the first time in cat form. "You need to eat something. Trust me, you'll feel one hundred percent better once you do." She reached for him as if she'd stroke his head, but I darted forward and pulled her away.

"Don't touch him yet. Let him get used to—"

Robyn pulled her arm from my grasp and scowled at me. "He won't hurt me."

"You don't know that. He's not himself yet. Don't you remember how confused and terrified you were right after your first shift? His instinct will be to snap or swipe at anyone who comes close, and if he hurts you before he knows what he's doing—" *I will never forgive myself.* "—the guilt could color his perception of his feline half forever."

She frowned. "What do you mean?"

"Morris needs a positive outlook on his new form. He needs to understand from the very beginning that this new part of himself is powerful and sometimes dangerous, but not inherently bad in any way. If he hurts you before he's had a chance to come to terms with what's happening to him, his initial impression of this new form could be that it's monstrous or somehow wrong. Or worse—uncontrollable."

Her frown faded. "You're not trying to protect me from him. You're trying to protect him from himself."

"I'm doing both," I said as I watched Morris breathe heavily on the floor. "That's my job."

"You really care about him. About all of them." She sounded surprised by the realization, and I tried not to be offended by that.

"Why would I be here, if I didn't?"

"I don't…" Her frown became a slow smile. "You're not what I expected from an Alpha."

I couldn't resist the opportunity to throw her own words at her. "Maybe you should stop expecting me to be like all the other Alphas. We're breaking new ground here, in case you haven't noticed."

"I *have* noticed," she said. "And I want to help." Robyn turned and squatted to put herself closer to Morris's height. But she preserved the distance I'd put between them. "Corey? I want you to nod if you understand me. Titus needs to know that even though you look like a cat, you're thinking like a human. That's something I didn't even know was possible at your stage in the game. So can you give us a nod?"

Morris lifted his head and pushed himself onto his haunches. He blinked slowly. Sluggishly. Then he nodded.

Robyn's smile looked young and excited, as if she'd just seen her first rainbow. "Good. Now we need you to eat something. The faster you recover, the faster we can get a good whiff of your scent and find out who did this to you. That way we can—" She stood in a single graceful motion, frowning at me. "What will happen to whoever infected him? That's a crime, right?"

"Yes. But the consequence depends on the circumstances. If he was infected by a new stray who didn't know any better—who didn't intend to hurt him or infect him—we'll focus our efforts on rehabilitation. On teaching him how to be a productive and safe member of the Pride."

"And if he can't be rehabilitated?" There was something fragile in her voice, as if she had some personal stake in my answer. And of course, she did.

Robyn was in the midst of that very rehabilitation process. The council considered her sentence to be training and rehabilitation rather than punishment, but I could see in her eyes, and in the sudden, defeated slump of her posture, that she wasn't sure it would work. That she wasn't sure she could truly learn to control her feline self, which had been acting on an unchecked instinct telling her that bad men deserved to pay.

"Robyn, you're going to be fine," I whispered, to keep the conversation as close to confidential as I could.

"Yeah. I know." She blinked, and that glimpse of vulnerability was gone, buried beneath the very bravado that had steeled her spine when I'd caught her in my car. "I'm talking about whoever infected Corey."

"With any luck, he'll be okay too."

A gristly sound caught our attention, and we turned to see that Morris was finally gnawing on the hunk of rabbit meat, not yet sure how to separate flesh from bone in his first cat-form meal.

Robyn smiled. "It helps if you use your paw..."
This time I didn't try to stop her when she knelt and crawled closer to Morris, but I did follow her. I had to be close enough to pull her out of harm's way if the new stray decided his meal was being threatened. Because as Faythe and Marc were determined to remind me, her safety was entirely in my hands.

NINE

Robyn

I closed the guesthouse front door, and finally, I could exhale.

Robyn's well-being is foremost in my mind. And you have my word that I have no plans to seduce her.

Titus's words echoed in my head, and a bitter taste filled the back of my mouth.

He didn't seem to know I'd overheard his phone call. And I hadn't, really. All I'd been able to make out was the last few seconds of the conversation.

Why would he give Faythe his word that he had no plans to seduce me, unless she'd made him promise not to?

Where the hell did she get off, deciding who I could and couldn't sleep with? After Abby's stories, I'd expected that from the rest of the council, but coming from Faythe? After she nearly tore the council apart over her right to marry—or not—as she chose?

I had no plans to seduce Titus either. But a girl has the right to change her mind, and that hungry way he looked at me when he thought I wasn't watching made me want to find out whether he tasted as good as he smelled...

If he truly wasn't using me to provide a dam for his Pride, then I would damn well decide for myself whether or not to reciprocate any hypothetical interest from the world's first stray Alpha.

I would *not* let my private life be scheduled or restricted by committee.

"Whoa, those aren't paper plates!" I stopped in the entryway to the dining room, stunned by the display laid out before me.

Titus's dining room table—a massive slab of wood shaped like a vaguely oval leaf, with copper veins running through it—was set for eight. Each place setting included a bowl nested inside a broader, shallower bowl, set on top of a large matching plate with fancy scalloped edges. There were four forks, two spoons, two knives—one laid across a small plate set to the left—and stemmed, gold-rimmed glasses for three kinds of wine, as well as a water goblet.

"It's Titus's mother's china," Brandt said as he rounded the table, setting the smallest wine glasses in place. "He said he'd skin me alive if I dropped anything."

I ventured closer, studying the beautiful, complex scrolling pattern on the edge of the shallower bowls. "What's the occasion?"

"I believe you're the occasion," Lochlan said from

behind me, and I jumped, startled by his sudden appearance. Evidently, I would *never* get used to how quietly shifters moved around.

"Me?" My heart thudded harder, and when he smiled, I realized he could hear it.

"Don't take it personally. He's been looking for an excuse to use them. His mom broke them out for every holiday before she died."

"Oh." Yet my pulse remained elevated. The pendulum swing from paper plates to heirloom china was extreme, no matter what Loch said.

"It's a lot of dishes, huh?" Brandt ran one finger over the gold-rimmed plate on the bottom of the nearest place setting. "This one's called the service plate. You don't put food on it. It stays there because there isn't supposed to be an empty place on the table until dessert is served. So all your other plates and bowls sit on top of the service plate."

Wow. I was way out of my league. "What's that glass for?" I nodded at the last one, as Brandt set it carefully on the table.

"It's the dessert wine glass."

"Don't look too impressed," Loch said. "He had to look up 'how to set a formal table' online."

"I had to look it up because no one else knew either," Brandt said with a scowl.

"True," Lochlan conceded. "We've never used the full set before." He turned to Brandt. "Knox says we'll be ready to eat in ten, and we'll be forgoing formal dress, since our guest of honor has no luggage." He glanced at me with a grin, and I laughed. "We got sidetracked today by the new arrival, but tomorrow, someone will take you shopping."

"Wait, there was going to be formal dress?" Brandt

appeared suddenly worried. "The most formal thing I own is my good T-shirt."

Lochlan smoothed a loose strand of blond hair toward his bun. "Well, save it for another day. You're off the hook." Loch somehow looked well-put-together yet casual in a navy wool cardigan with leather elbow patches, over his black enforcer's tee. "I have to get to the kitchen before Knox starts yelling."

I followed Loch—and the sounds and scents of a serious culinary undertaking—to find the rest of the enforcers at work in various stations around the huge gourmet kitchen, chopping, stirring, and blending under the supervision of our illustrious chef. Knox's tattoos were temporarily covered by an honest-to-goodness white chef's coat with a double row of dark buttons, accented by a knee-length black apron. He definitely looked the part, and the speed and skill with which he was toasting the tops of a series of small custard-filled dishes with a tiny blowtorch said that his former restaurant's loss was our gain.

"Wow! You've got your own little sweatshop in here!" I said as my gaze wandered over the meal courses, in varying stages of near-completion.

"Out!" Knox ordered, pointing toward the hallway with one finger. He never even looked up from his torch. "The guest of honor isn't supposed to see the preparation."

"You're thinking of the groom seeing the bride before the wedding," I said as I backed away from the kitchen, a smile taking up most of my face. The food smelled *amazing…*

"Ten minutes!" Knox called after me.

I wandered from room to room on the first floor of Titus's home, through the theater, a formal living room centered around an enormous marble fireplace, a sunroom with huge sliding glass doors, a room with no clear purpose, other than playing video games on the massive television and mixing drinks at a full-scale bar, then into the glass-walled wine cellar nestled beneath the curving marble staircase in the foyer.

But my favorite space was an informal den, one wall of which held a collection of framed photographs of what could only be Titus's family. Two boys, several years apart, grew in age over the course of the display. With them in most of the shots were a mother with long dark curls and a father with piercing gray eyes and a thick head of prematurely white hair.

Their clothes were nice and obviously expensive. The locations were often tropical or historical. But the family itself could have been anyone, at any time. They looked so…normal.

As I studied the pictures, the whisper of a shoe against the hardwood floor at my back warned me that I was no longer alone.

I turned to face Titus with a triumphant smile. "I heard you coming that time," I said, and his soft laugh made me frown, even as the sound sent delicious little shivers up my spine. "You made noise on purpose, didn't you?"

He shrugged. "It doesn't feel fair to sneak up on you, when you've had so little practice listening for us."

"I was infected four months ago. This should be coming easier for me by now, shouldn't it?"

Titus ran one hand over his short scruff of beard, and my gaze caught there as I wondered, not for the first time, what his stubble would feel like against my palm. This time, instead of squelching the dirty fantasy that thought inspired, I let it play out a little.

Cold night. Warm bed. Bare bodies. Titus's hands sliding over my—

"I'm sure the learning curve is different for everyone," he said, evidently unaware of the salacious turn my thoughts had taken. "And I'm just as sure that there are things you're better at than I am."

"Any idea what those things are? Because off the top of my head, all I can come up with is menstruation and makeup application. And I couldn't swear to that second one."

Titus laughed, and the sound filled me with joy in a deeply felt but incomprehensible way. As if his mood were connected to mine through some psychological puppet string.

Would it be like that with any Alpha? I hadn't spent much time around any of the others—an intentional choice on my part.

Did that connection work both ways? If I smiled, would he feel happier?

My gaze wandered over the photographs again. "These are your parents?" I asked, cringing over how obvious the answer must be. But he only nodded. "May I ask what happened to them?"

"Car crash." Titus slid both hands into the pockets of his casual slacks. "I was twenty-five, and my brother was fourteen."

"How awful!"

"Really. It's okay. It was five years ago." He turned to a freestanding bar along the wall and pulled a crystal decanter full of amber liquid from the shelf. "What about your family?"

"My parents are still alive, in the clinical sense, at

least. Though neither of them has had anything I'd describe as a real life in at least a decade."

"And how would you describe a 'real life?'" He poured an inch of whiskey—as my nose labeled it—into a short glass, then wordlessly offered it to me.

I shook my head to decline politely. "I'd be happy if either of them ever left the house for something other than work and grocery shopping. Though I'm not sure they actually leave to shop anymore, since my sister showed them how to order groceries online."

"And your sister? What's she like?"

"Married with a two-year-old daughter. Dana's a guidance counselor at an elementary school in Kentucky, in a town full of women just like her. Seriously, she wouldn't stand out in a random sampling. But at least she and her husband have a date night every Friday. She's the one who encouraged me to apply to graduate school."

"How much do they all know about what happened to you?"

"Nothing." Despite the size of the room, instead of echoing, that word hung there in front of me, like a cloud of smoke in the air, tainting every breath I took. "The council said I couldn't tell them anything, for their own good. And I'm only allowed to talk to them on supervised phone calls." My voice dropped into a bitter growl. "The Di Carlos confiscated my cell phone until I'm 'rehabilitated'."

"We keep several disposable cells on hand. I'll have Naveen set one up for you after dinner. And of course, you're welcome to call your family while you're here." He took a long sip from his glass. "Do they know you're no longer in school?"

"No. But I told them I'd need another semester to graduate. That I was short two classes. With any luck, I'll be finished serving my sentence in time to graduate next December."

"I'm sure you will be."

I kept my doubts to myself and changed the subject. "What about—"

"Knox says it's time to eat," Brandt said from the doorway. "He made me actually come find you instead of shouting. It's not a very efficient system."

Titus chuckled. "Sounds like the manners are chafing."

"Like burlap underwear," Brandt confirmed.

The guys were already in the dining room when we arrived, each standing behind one of the eight chairs in a very formal posture, in spite of the fact that they all wore jeans. At each place setting, nested inside the other dishes, sat a steaming bowl of orangish soup. A beautifully browned dinner roll lay on the small plate at each setting.

Brandt took up his position behind one of the empty chairs, leaving only Titus's seat at the head the table, and mine to his right. Titus pulled out my chair for me, and only once I was seated did the others join me.

I'd never felt more conspicuous in my life. Or more...esteemed.

If this is what chivalry looks like in the twenty-first century, sign me up.

"Since we have no service staff, this will only be a semi-formal dinner," Titus announced as he took his seat. "Please forgive any breaches of etiquette caused by the lack."

"I wouldn't know the difference," I mumbled as I

stared down the length of the polished, leaf-shaped table. The most formal meal I'd ever attended was my high school's annual honor's banquet. Which was a buffet.

"Knox, what are we starting with?" the Alpha asked.

"Our first course is curried pumpkin soup."

"The soup spoon is the one on the far right," Brandt stage whispered from across the table as he lifted his. I couldn't resist a laugh as I dipped my own spoon into the gold-rimmed bowl atop my nested place setting.

I moaned around the first bite, then glanced around the table in embarrassment. Which turned out to be unnecessary. Most of the guys had their eyes closed, their expressions frozen in near orgasmic pleasure.

"Holy shit, man, that's really good!" Brandt said.

Naveen laughed from his left, and Titus shot the kid a censuring glance. "While the phrasing is coarse, even for a semi-formal meal, I do agree with the sentiment!" our host declared.

Knox shrugged off the compliment, but I could see that he was pleased.

"So, if you *can* eat like this, why bother with the paper plates?" I asked as I lifted another steaming bite toward my mouth.

Drew huffed. "You'll understand when you see the pile of dishes waiting in the kitchen."

"My mother's china is hand wash only," Titus added. The table groaned unanimously.

Spencer pointed his spoon at his Alpha. "I know I'm only a guest here, but it seems to me that he who requested the formal dinner—and didn't help cook—

should do the dishes."

A chorus of cheers went up around the table.

"Insurrection already? The Pride hasn't even been formally recognized!" Titus laughed. "Fine. I'll do the dishes. You can all relax and eat."

When we'd finished our soup, Brandt and Drew cleared our bowls while Naveen and Lachlan brought the next course in shallowly curved plates from the kitchen. "This is a kale salad with candied pecans and pomegranates, served in a cucumber 'bowl'." Knox informed us.

The dish was so beautiful I wasn't sure how to eat it without tearing it apart, until I watched Titus cut his "bowl" open with his fork.

"Do you think Corey will be able to eat with us tomorrow night?" I asked as I carefully speared a chunk of candied pecan. "Or will he already be gone by then? How long do new strays have to stay here?"

"I think you mean, how long do they *get* to stay here," Brandt said around a mouthful of kale. "And the answer, in my case, is 'indefinitely.'"

Naveen rolled his eyes at the kid. "Most of them are ready to go home by the time they're able, so we keep pretty close tabs on them for a while afterward, to make sure they know they're not alone. Morris might be ready to join us tomorrow. He's already shifted, right?"

Titus nodded. "A few hours ago."

"So soon we'll be able to smell his infector's scent. How does that work?" I asked.

Drew set his fork on the edge of his plate so he could gesture with his hands. "Picture a scent as a woman's hair braid. Or Lochlan's."

Loch flipped Drew off while everyone else

chuckled.

"Anyway, a braid is made up of multiple strands, right?"

"Yes." My sister and I had grown up braiding each other's hair, and the memory made me miss her. "Three of them, in a standard braid."

"Okay, but each of those strands is made up of hundreds of individual hairs, right? In this analogy, each of those individual hairs is an element of the scent. The infector's scent is like a ribbon woven into the braid. Something thin. Like, a strand of yarn. It's thicker than the individual hairs, but a very small part of the overall bouquet. It's difficult to detect at all, if you aren't already familiar with the infector's scent."

"So, what happens if you are?" I asked as Drew rose to clear my empty salad plate. "You go round him up?"

"Yes." Lochlan came in from the kitchen carrying two plates. He slid one onto the service plate in front of me and the other in front of Spencer, on my right. "For questioning, at the very least."

"Knox, this looks amazing!" Titus said, and I had to fight not to pick up my fork and knife until everyone had been served.

"Thank you. Tomorrow night we're ordering pizza." Knox cleared his throat as Lochlan and Naveen sat in front of their own entrees. "Tonight's main course is an Indian-style leg of lamb with Dijon-glazed carrots and roasted baby leeks with bacon. *Bon appetite.*"

I cut into my lamb to find it perfectly cooked and tender. "So, when you go after infectors, are they usually just waiting for you? I mean, don't they know infection is a crime?"

Drew groaned with pleasure as he cut into his meat. "The ones whose scents we recognize know that infection is a crime, because we taught them that. If we hadn't already had contact with them, we wouldn't recognize their scents."

"Sometimes they're already on the run before we get there," Lochlan added with a speared hunk of carrot halfway to his mouth. "Sometimes they have no idea we're coming."

"From what I understand, if the infection was an accident, you try to rehabilitate the infector, for lack of a better word. Right?" I asked.

Drew nodded while he chewed.

"It's more like behavioral counseling," Naveen elaborated, and Knox snorted.

I cut another tender hunk from my lamb. "What if the infection wasn't an accident?"

Utensils went still all around the table. Men stopped chewing. Everyone looked my way. Then their gazes slid toward Titus.

"Unfortunately, sometimes by the time we get there, circumstances have created an unwell state of mind beyond anything we're equipped to deal with. Delusions. Uncontrollable rage. An inability to cope with the sudden onslaught of feline instincts and territorial impulses. And every now and then, a stray turns out to be a bad apple for no reason involving his infection. When that happens, we have to execute."

"You put him to death?"

"In as humane a manner possible," Drew said. "For the greater good. To protect us all."

"Who—" I cleared my throat. Lamb that had been delicious seconds before had suddenly lost all taste.

Would I have been executed for my crimes if I'd committed them in the free zone? And if I'd been a man? "Who does it?"

"It's always either Drew or me," Titus said. "Or sometimes Jace. We can't ask the other men to do a job we're not willing to take on ourselves, as leaders, and the emotional burden of carrying out an execution… Well, it's not something to be taken lightly."

"And on that note…" Knox stood with his plate. "It's time for dessert."

Again, Drew and Brandt cleared the dishes—including the service plate—while Loch and Naveen helped Knox bring out our final course. Titus poured sherry as the dessert wine, but Spencer and I—both guests—were not allowed to help with anything.

Dessert turned out to be crème brûlée, in the very dishes I'd seen Knox toasting earlier.

"There's a plate for Morris on the kitchen island," he said as he set the final dish in front of Titus. "When we're done, Spencer, you're welcome to take it out to him."

"Not on my mother's china," Titus insisted.

Knox rolled his eyes. "It's on a paper plate."

I'd never had crème brûlée before, and I had to watch the others break the sugary crust on top to be sure that's what I was supposed to do. When the first bite nearly melted on my tongue, I realized that my own culinary skills weren't up to the challenge and I wondered if I could achieve the same effect by taking a lit match to the top of a vanilla pudding cup.

After dinner, I brushed off a chorus of objections as I helped carry the dishes to the kitchen, where I found Titus at the sink with his sleeves rolled up, elbows deep in steaming sudsy water.

I laughed as I set a stack of small, shallow dishes on the counter to the left of the sink.

"What's so funny?" he demanded, as he ran a soapy cloth around the inside of a soup bowl.

"I didn't expect to find dishwashing in your skill set."

He blew a damp lock of dark hair off his forehead. "I'll admit, it's a relatively recent acquisition."

"So I see. You should rinse in hot water, not cold. It dries faster and leaves fewer streaks." I flipped the faucet lever to the left and reached into the soapy water for the bowl he'd just washed, and my fingers bumped his. I went still, reluctant to end the accidental touch.

His gray-eyed gaze found mine. He took my hand beneath the bubbles, and for one brief moment that neither of us knew how to acknowledge, we were not Alpha and tabby, embroiled in a political shitstorm. We were not lawbreakers, or revolutionaries, or rebels. We were only a man and a woman, holding hands. Wishing for a little more.

"Hey, Robyn, I set this phone up for you," Naveen said as he stepped into the kitchen. "I've programmed all of our numbers into it, and you should have plenty of data to get you through the next two weeks."

Titus let go of my hand as Naveen set the new cell phone on the counter next to the large wire dish drainer.

"Thanks." I dragged my gaze from Titus to find the enforcer watching us with a quiet, knowing smile.

"No problem. Enjoy," he added on his way out of the room, and I wasn't entirely sure he was talking about the new phone.

Titus held the bowl under the hot rinse water and cleared his throat. "You know how to dry them even faster?" he asked as he reached past me to set the bowl in the drainer.

"How?"

"With this." He pulled out a drawer next to the sink and plucked a dishtowel from inside, then tossed it over my face.

I laughed as I removed the towel with my wet hand and ran my dry one through my messy hair. "Does the guest of honor traditionally help with the dishes after a formal dinner?"

"No. But neither does the host. As with everything else in the former free zone, we're forging new territory here." His gaze caught on mine again, and we suddenly seemed to be talking about something else.

I stared up into his gray eyes, lingering in another small moment. "How could I possibly argue with that?"

Titus washed, and I dried, then stacked the clean dishes carefully on the white granite countertop. "You're pretty good at that," he observed after a moment of quiet so profound I realized the other guys must have retired to the guest house to avoid being recruited.

I rolled my eyes at him. "This is not a recently acquired skill for me. Nor is it complicated." Yet I was never called upon to help at the Di Carlos'. Donna seemed to think that would have been taking advantage of my non-voluntary resident status.

"So your childhood was full of dirty dishes?" Titus asked.

I lifted one eyebrow at him as I slid my new phone into my pocket. "Was yours full of silver spoons?"

"I—"

The kitchen door suddenly flew open and smacked into the wall. Spencer appeared in the doorway, carrying the sturdy paper platter still full of Corey Morris's dinner.

"What's wrong?" I asked, clutching a wet plate to be sure I wouldn't drop it.

Spencer set the platter on the nearest counter top. "The basement is empty. The stray is gone."

TEN

Titus

"Okay, Lochlan, you and Naveen start at the property boundary and head west into the woods, one on two legs, one on four. Drew, you and Knox go east. Same instructions. If you haven't found any trace within a mile of the property, call in for new directions. He's hardly over scratch fever and he doesn't yet know how to control his urge to shift. That means he should be easy to find, but his behavior will be unpredictable and possibly irrational." And dangerous, of course.

"What about me?" Brandt shifted his weight from one foot to the other on the wood floor of the office, visibly eager to help. Or rather, to be included.

"I appreciate all your help around here," I told him. "But you know I can't send you into the field. You're too young and too new. You're not an enforcer."

"So I'm good enough to set the table, but not good enough to help where it really matters?"

"Of course you're good enough. You're just not

experienced enough." But my explanation only seemed to frustrate him further.

"I'm not trained as an enforcer either," Spencer said from his seat on the edge of the leather couch. "But I'd like to help. Why don't Brandt and I team up and take a look around the grounds. It's possible that Morris hasn't made it off the property yet."

I hesitated, trying to phrase a careful explanation. "He's obviously confused and possibly scared," I said. "And he might still have a low fever. He could lash out without even realizing what he's doing."

"We'll stay in human form," Brandt said, hope riding high in his voice. "And we won't approach him if we find him. We'll call it in. Come on, Titus. Let us help."

"Fine," I said at last. "But you stay together, and keep your phones handy. Call me if you find any sign of him."

"We will!" Brandt took off toward the foyer, his jacket in hand. Spencer signaled his thanks to me as he followed the kid toward the front door.

As soon as they were gone, I sank onto my desk chair with a sigh. Then I moved the mouse around to wake up my computer monitor and began pulling up aerial shots of the property, so I could start marking up a search grid.

When Robyn sank onto the couch in front of my desk, I glanced up, startled. "Now who's stealthy?" I asked, trying to force a smile when I saw how worried she looked.

"I want to help."

"I appreciate that, but there isn't much you can do. You don't know the property."

"But I know Corey Morris. As much as any of you

do, at least. And I may know his thought process even better, being a recently infected stray myself."

I nodded. "Valid point. But I can't send you out there on your own."

"Then come with me." She stood, and the determination drawn in the line of her jaw told me she would not be refused.

"I need to stay here, to coordinate communication and draw up a search grid."

"That's an *old* Alpha's answer." She waved off my objection. "The grids can wait, and thanks to the miracle of cell phones, you can coordinate on your feet. Don't you think we'd both be more useful out there looking for him?"

Without a doubt. But new strays act unpredictably, and if Robyn got hurt on my watch, the council would never forgive me.

If she got hurt, I'd never forgive myself.

"You're staying here to babysit me, aren't you?" She sounded almost as insulted as she looked. "I can handle myself. In fact, according to the council, I can handle myself a little *too* well."

"Against humans," I agreed. "But you've never fought a fellow shifter, outside of sparring, have you?"

She blinked and suddenly looked more irritated than insulted. "No, and I don't plan to fight Corey Morris. I'm going to look for him. If you want to 'protect' me, you'll have to come with me." With that, she marched out of the office and down the hall, toward the kitchen.

"Wait!" My chair rolled toward the shelves behind me as I stood and jogged after her. "I don't suppose it'd do me any good to order you to stay here."

She turned to walk backward, one eyebrow arched at me. "Are you still planning to send me to Atlanta?"

An ache spread through my chest. "You know I have to."

"Then you're not my Alpha." She shrugged and headed down the hall. "Order away. But tie your boot while you talk."

I looked down to find that my right boot was indeed untied. By the time I caught up to her, shoelaces trailing behind me, she had one hand on the kitchen door. "Wait a minute, Robyn!" I dropped into a squat to tie my boot, and she let go of the doorknob. "Did you follow orders this well in Atlanta?"

"Nowhere near this well," she said with a grin.

"Then I'm almost surprised they want you back."

She shrugged as I stood. "Me too. Let's go."

I followed her out the door onto the patio, where she stopped to look over the pool and hot tub—both covered for the winter—and the tree-lined path leading to the tennis court. "So, what's the plan?" I asked.

"Well, cats don't track by scent, like a dog would. Man, was I disappointed to realize that."

"You're not the only one."

"But a while back, I had some pretty good luck tracking people using my other senses—eyes, ears, and common."

I couldn't resist a smile, despite the circumstances. "Okay, then, work your magic. Where do we start?"

"At the last known location." Robyn headed around the pool at a jog, and I followed her through the front door of the guesthouse and down the stairs. In the basement, she stopped and looked around again, and I was starting to wonder if she was part bloodhound.

Or a police detective.

She marched into the empty cell and picked up a sweat-stained shirt from the pile of clothing discarded on the concrete floor. "Okay, his clothes are here, so he's probably in cat form."

"Or naked," I offered.

"That's possible, I guess, but not likely."

"How do you know?"

"I know because in the very darkest part of my post-infection period, I wanted to kill the people responsible—the need was so strong I could hardly think about anything else—but I never went outside naked, unless I was on four paws. I might have been on the edge of sanity, but I wasn't crazy. And neither is Corey Morris. In fact, he seemed pretty coherent a couple of hours ago."

"Okay." I tried not to sound too impressed by her empathy and understanding. "So he's probably covered in fur. Where would he go?"

"That depends on why he left. He could have been hungry, especially so soon after shifting. Maybe he went out to hunt."

"But there's more meat in the fridge. I told him to help himself."

"Yes." She stood and glanced across the basement at the kitchenette. "But if he can't control his shifts yet and got stuck in cat form, he may not have been able to open the refrigerator."

"Well, if he went into the woods, we'll find him eventually."

"Or he'll wander out of the forest on the other side and be spotted by motorists. Or hunters." She frowned as she rounded the table, her gaze narrowed on something behind one of the chairs. "Was Corey wearing a coat when he got here?" She squatted, then stood with a dark green quilted jacket.

The shredded remains of one, anyway.

"No, that's mine." Damn it. And it was my favorite.

Robyn held the scraps of material to her face. "It's covered in both your scent and his. Why would Corey tear up your jacket?"

"I have no idea." But that did not bode well for my attempts to bond with the new stray.

"When was he last seen?" Robyn asked.

"I saw him a couple of hours ago. I don't think anyone else was down here after me, until Spencer brought his dinner."

"And the doors were unlocked?"

"Of course. We don't lock up new strays unless they're dangerous, in more than a reactionary sense."

"Meaning...?"

"Meaning new strays will often snap at or strike out at people who get too close, but if they're not aggressive when given their own space, locking them up only makes things worse," I explained. She seemed both relieved and frustrated by the answer. "We've never lost one before," I added. "Most new strays seem comforted by the scents of their peers and wary of striking off on their own, at least at first."

"Well, Corey doesn't seem to have been comforted by your scent." She held my ruined jacket up for emphasis. "But even if he wasn't locked in, the doors were still closed, right?"

"Yes, but you may have noticed that all of the doorknobs are actually levers." I gestured at the one at the top of the stairs for emphasis. "After I was infected, I had the knobs all replaced so I could get in and out without thumbs."

"So he had a bad reaction to your jacket, and he let himself out sometime in the past two hours." Robyn looked up at me. "I assume he's never been on or near your property before?"

I nodded. "Not that I know of. We've certainly never caught his scent around here."

She exhaled heavily, a rare glimpse of defeat shadowing her blue eyes. "I think it might be time to get your property grids. How much land do you have here, anyway?"

"Twenty acres, all unfenced. Half of it wooded." I followed Robyn up the stairs and through the guesthouse, my gaze focused on the jacket she still held, while I tried not to notice the sway of her hips. Or think about her hand, warm in mine in the dish water.

Why would Morris shred my jacket?

In the main house, I headed for my office, then turned to ask Robyn a question, but she was gone. She was getting *really* good at stealth. "Robyn?"

"In here!"

I followed the sound of her voice to the utility room, where I found her standing over an overturned basket of unwashed clothes. "Did you stop for an emergency rinse cycle?"

Robyn knelt and lifted a gray workout shirt by its collar. I could see the far wall through the huge rips in the material. "I assume this is yours? And this?" In her spare hand, she pulled the matching pair of equally shredded running shorts from the basket.

"Yeah. You think he came in the house just to tear

150

up more of my clothes?"

"That's what it looks like." She stood, my shredded clothing still dangling from her grip. "Why would he do that, Titus?"

"I don't know." I took the clothes from her and dropped them onto the pile, then tugged her up by one hand, glad for a legitimate excuse to touch her. "But he's angry, and he may still be in the house. I want you to stay here while I search—"

Her eyes widened. "I think I know where he is!" She stepped past me and took off down the hall, and I had to jog to catch up with her.

"Wait! Where are you going?"

"He's destroying things that smell like you. He's probably in your room."

"Shit." I overtook her on the stairs and raced past half a dozen doors to my suite at the end of the hall, on the right. But then I stood in front of the double doors for a minute, listening.

I heard nothing. No scratching. No growling. If Morris was in there, he wasn't actively damaging anything.

As Robyn stopped at my side, I inhaled deeply through my nose, but with the doors closed, all I could smell was her, and I found her scent very distracting, in the best—and worst—way.

"Step away," I whispered. But Robyn didn't move, and I was starting to understand that she wouldn't move unless I moved her.

Instead, I opened the door.

Corey Morris sat on the floor at the end of my bed, naked and wet, and dripping on the hardwood. He smelled like my shampoo and fresh water, and he held one of my shirts in his lap. His eyes were shiny with tears, but his jaw was clenched in anger.

The door to my bathroom stood open, and a series of wet footprints showed his path across the room to where he sat.

What the hell...?

"Corey?" Robyn spoke softly, like one might speak to a spooked horse, but she didn't try to enter the room. "Are you okay? What's going on?"

Morris's focus locked on me, as if he hadn't even heard her. "Why would you bring me here? Why pretend to help me?"

"I'm not pretending." As I watched, a drop of water fell from his hair onto his arm, then rolled onto the floor. "I truly want to help you. We all do."

"You're *lying!*" Morris shouted, and Robyn flinched. I stepped in front of her, instinctively shielding her.

Traumatized or not, Corey Morris needed a reality check. "I don't know why you would say that, and I don't know why you're in my room right now." Or why he'd obviously showered in my bathroom. I took one firm step over the threshold. "We need to get you back to bed, so Spencer can examine you. It sounds like your fever's back." I could think of no other explanation for his certainty that though we'd treated his illness and I'd talked him through his first shift, I was only pretending to care about him.

"You're everywhere." Morris didn't seem to notice that I'd entered the room. He lifted my shirt to his face and inhaled, then threw it across the floor. "No matter where I go, I smell you. You're *all over* me, and I can't wash you off!"

On the edge of my vision, Robyn turned to me, and though I couldn't see her expression, I was sure it

152

reflected my own horror. I'd never touched Corey Morris, yet he seemed to believe he was somehow covered in my scent. As if he'd been wearing my clothes or rolling around in my bed.

His strange delusion made my skin crawl.

"It could be transference," Robyn whispered as she stepped up to my side. "Like, a misapplication of emotion or aggression. There was some discussion after my trial theorizing that I had 'transferred' my hostility toward the cat who accidentally infected me onto the human men I killed. That was total bullshit. My hostility toward those murdering bastards was aimed right where it belonged. But it could be a legitimate problem here."

"Why?" I studied Morris, trying to understand. "How?"

"Maybe you did your job too well? I know you were trying to bond with him, but if he smelled too much of your scent too early and began to associate it with the pain of shifting—or with his fever—he could be subconsciously blaming you for what happened to him."

I shook my head slowly. "Nothing like that has ever happened before. And this doesn't look very subconscious." In fact, it looked bizarrely, inappropriately conscious.

"Corey?" Robyn turned to the stray. "What happened to you wasn't Titus's fault. He's trying to help you. He's your Alpha now, and that's what they do."

I glanced at her in surprise. Her previous statements about Alphas hadn't been anywhere near as flattering.

Robyn sank onto her knees and sat on her heels,

putting herself at the same height as Morris. "We all want to help you. We've all been where you are. Do you remember me telling you about how I was infected?"

Morris nodded, and more water fell from his hair. "You killed the men responsible."

"Yes, and Titus and his men are going to find the shifter who did this to you. He will be dealt with."

"What the hell are you talking about?" Morris's frown looked almost coherent. As if Robyn were the one not making sense. "Is this some kind of sick game? Why would you people bring me here? To *him*?" His tortured focus found me again, and it felt accusatory.

Robyn turned to me, her brows drawn low. "He seems to be blaming you for all of this. We need to get him back to bed, and maybe give him a sedative."

I nodded. I wasn't sure a sedative would cure Morris's delusion, but at least it would give us time to figure out what had gone wrong with his adjustment.

"Let's get you something to wear." Robyn started to stand, then turned to me instead. "He probably shouldn't wear something that smells like you. Ideas?"

"There's a clean robe hanging on my bathroom door," I told her. "I haven't worn it yet."

Morris's gaze followed Robyn nervously as she walked past him into the bathroom. A second later, she brought out the robe, and even from my position in the doorway, I could smell the fabric softener used on it. "Okay, Corey." She sank onto her knees and draped the robe over his shoulders. "We're going to take you to the basement and Titus is going to call Spencer to come take a look at you. Okay?"

"As long as *he* stays back." Morris's anger was like

a knife to my gut. I'd helped at least a dozen strays acclimate to their new lives in the past year, and none of the others had blamed me for what happened to them. I'd had varying levels of success in the bonding department, but my efforts had never backfired before.

How could I be an effective Alpha to a man who hated the very sight—and scent—of me?

"Fine." I stepped away from my own bedroom door. "You can deal with Robyn and Spencer for now."

Robyn gave me a relieved smile as she helped Morris slide his arms into the robe sleeves, and I realized how lucky the new stray and I both were to have her around at that moment. She genuinely wanted to help him, and he seemed willing to let her. She was just as good at this as I was. Maybe better.

"Let me help you up." Robyn looped one of her arms around his and started to stand. Then she froze, her face inches from the stray's bare neck. "He smells different." Her wide-eyed gaze caught mine. "I've never met a stray before his scent changed before. This is fascinating! He smells like—" The light in her eyes died beneath a confused frown. She backed slowly away from the stray and rose to her feet with a cat's effortless grace. "Titus, he smells like *you*."

"I know. He's been all over my clothes and he showered with my shampoo." I gestured one-handed toward the wet footprints leading from the bathroom. "Can you get him to stand up?"

"No." Gravity echoed in her voice as Robyn's gaze narrowed on me. "He doesn't smell like your clothes or your shampoo. He smells like you. That ribbon of his infector's scent braided through his is *you*, Titus."

ELEVEN

Robyn

"What?" Titus crossed the floor toward us as if shock had obliterated any trace of the Alpha's typical caution.

Corey Morris scooted away from him frantically, but Titus dropped into a squat at his side. He inhaled deeply, and his bearing changed in an instant. Tension tightened his entire body until I worried that his muscles would snap, like cords under too much pressure. "That's not possible."

"So you didn't infect him? Then why does he smell like you?" I inhaled again, to verify what my nose was already sure of. "Why is he tearing up your clothes and showering to try to scrub your scent off himself?"

Titus moved slowly away from Corey, and I could see no sign that he'd even heard me. His eyes were wide and uncomprehending, his forehead furrowed, as if his features couldn't decide whether to look shocked or confused.

"Titus?" I reached for him, but he stepped back. "What's going on? Did you do this to him?"

His phone buzzed from his pocket and he blinked

as he pulled it out, as if he'd just woken up from a long nap. "Drew and Knox are heading home. I need you to take Morris to the basement while I clean this up." His gaze followed the trail of footprints.

"Titus, what's happening?" I whispered, while Corey watched us warily from several feet away.

"Get him to the basement," he repeated, and his expression was suddenly as featureless as a concrete wall. He'd thrown a shield over his thoughts and shut me out. "Now." Then he disappeared into the bathroom and closed the door.

"Okay." My heart pounded, not from exertion, but in sympathy and synchronicity with the stress Titus was emitting like radiation from a cracked reactor.

As if he were my Alpha.

Despite the evidence, Titus seemed to have no idea why Corey Morris carried an unmistakable, if faint trace of his scent.

"Come on, Corey, let's get you to bed." I gave him my hand and was relieved when he let me help him up.

"What's going on, Robyn?" he asked as I looped my arm through his and guided him toward the hall.

"I'm not sure. But I *am* sure that this isn't what it looks like." It couldn't be. Titus was *completely* shocked by Corey's post-shift scent.

I escorted Corey down the stairs, through the kitchen and into the guesthouse, inhaling deeply through my nose, hoping with each breath to discover that I'd been mistaken. That he wasn't really carrying Titus's scent.

But he was. He couldn't escape it, and neither could I.

I got Corey to rest on the bed in his cell, and while

I was pouring him a glass of water from the pitcher in the fridge, the front door squealed open upstairs. Boots clomped on the steps, and I was surprised to realize I could already recognize the cadence of Titus's footsteps.

"I need you to go get Drew from the main house," Titus whispered. "Just Drew. Do you understand?"

I nodded, though I understood little of what was happening.

I found Drew in the kitchen with Knox, Spencer, and Brandt, brewing a pot of coffee. I tossed my head toward the door I'd just come through without breaking eye contact, and Drew followed me out onto the patio.

"Titus needs to see you. But only you," I whispered, when Brandt's focus followed us through the kitchen window.

Drew took off down the tiled walkway leading around the pool, leaving me to follow.

In the basement of the guest house, Drew followed his Alpha's focus to Corey Morris, who sat on his bed, his wary gaze trained on Titus. "What—"

"It's his scent." Titus no longer looked confused. His voice was low and steady. He sounded…resigned to some inevitability I couldn't yet understand.

Drew stepped into the cage and approached the new stray carefully. He inhaled deeply through his nose, then he coughed, practically choking on the scent in shock. "Titus…" he turned to face his Alpha, eyes wide. "What the hell happened? Why didn't you tell me?"

"It's not what it looks like. Er…what it smells like," I said, and Drew turned to me with one brow raised. "Titus didn't do this."

"It's exactly what it looks like." The Alpha sank into a chair at the table and poured whiskey into his coffee mug from a half-full bottle he'd evidently found while I'd fetched Drew. "I have a decision to make, and I need your advice."

"Wait, what are you talking about?" I asked as Drew sat next to Titus at the table, but neither of them seemed to hear me.

"The council will find out, and they'll never recognize our Pride with me as Alpha. Not now." Titus tried to screw the lid on the whiskey, but Drew took it from him and gulped straight from the bottle. "We need to do some serious damage control."

"This doesn't even make sense." I slid into a chair across the table from him. "Cory was infected on Thursday night. Where were you on Thursday?" Maybe his alibi would at least contradict the evidence.

"I took a patrol. Alone. I needed time to think before the meeting in Atlanta."

Okay, no luck there. "But I saw your face when you caught Corey's scent. You were *shocked*. What's going on, Titus?"

Finally, Drew looked at me. Then he turned to his Alpha. "What's she talking about?"

"Nothing." Titus leveled a serious gaze at me. "I'm not going to ask you to leave, because the others would try to interrogate you about this meeting. But this is none of your business, Robyn." His tone was polite, but firm.

I had clench my jaw against an argument. Because he was right. *Still...*

"Maybe if we explain the circumstances," Drew said, already back on topic. "It was self-defense, right? Or an accident? We all know you'd never infect someone on purpose. The Pride will stand behind you."

I stared at Drew, puzzled by their DEFCON 1 reaction. I knew better than most how strong the council's responses could be, but they wouldn't act without a trial. Titus *would* get a chance to tell his side of the story.

"The circumstances won't matter," Titus insisted. "An Alpha has to be above reproach. Especially the first stray Alpha."

"Okay. Well, we still have options." Drew shrugged. "The council doesn't have to know. Even if they decide to do an inspection or official tour of the territory, they don't ever have to meet Corey Morris. We can send him home with Spencer, to recuperate in private."

Titus took a long drink from his mug. "Even if I wanted to start my official relationship with the council off with a lie, that won't work. This is a long-term problem. Anyone who *ever* smells Morris's scent will link him to me, and eventually, that information *will* make it to the council. And that would be worse than owning up to it in the first place."

"You're right." Drew's frown deepened. "We need something more permanent."

"Whoa, wait a minute." I stared from one to the other as chills blossomed the full length of my arm. "You can't just kill him!" I whispered, well aware that if Corey knew enough to use his feline hearing, he'd hear me anyway.

Finally, they both turned to look at me, wearing identical scowls. "We don't kill people, Robyn," Titus said. "He's talking about a more permanent solution to the Alpha problem. Not the Corey Morris problem."

Oh. Wait. "What does that even mean?"

Titus exhaled heavily. "I have to step down." He met my gaze with an iron determination. "That's what's best for the Pride."

"What's best for the Pride is you as its leader." A few hours ago, I couldn't understand why Titus would want to turn the free zone into another Pride-controlled territory, but now the thought of him losing something he'd worked so hard for—something intended to help strays abandoned by the existing system—was breaking my heart. And pissing me off. "This is *your* Pride!"

Titus shook his head. "It'll never be recognized as a Pride at all with me as the Alpha."

"He's right," Drew said. "We need to face the reality of the situation, which is that the odds are already stacked against us. We have to work harder and hold ourselves to a higher standard than natural-born cats just to get a seat at the table. We can't ask for recognition with this hanging over our heads. They already think most of us are savages."

"You're wrong!" I insisted. "Faythe and Marc know better. Abby's dad knows better."

"They're a minority of the council," Titus pointed out. "They can't outvote the others."

"Look, I know this is none of my business. And I know we only met a couple of days ago. But I also know that whatever happened, you couldn't have *intended* to infect Corey Morris." I was more certain of that than of anything else I'd learned since sneaking out of the Di Carlos' territory. "So tell them what happened and let the facts stand on their own. Tell *us* what happened."

"We're beyond that. What matters now is getting in front of this before it can hurt the Pride." Titus stood and dumped the rest of his mug into the sink. "Drew, call a meeting."

I stared at them both, frustration pounding in my head like a migraine. Why are Alphas so *stubborn*?

Drew stood. "Should I call in the patrols?"

"No, just the toms currently in residence. I'll draft a letter to everyone else. We'll meet in the study in twenty minutes."

Drew gave him a sharp nod, then disappeared up the steps. Titus sank into a chair at the table again and crossed his arms over his chest while he stared at Morris, who lay on his bed, facing the wall. The Alpha was clearly lost in his own thoughts until I pushed my chair closer to the table and it scraped against the concrete floor.

"Robyn." He seemed surprised to see me still there. "I could use time alone."

"Tough. What's going on, Titus?"

"The world is crumbling beneath my feet. Is that not obvious?" His scowl felt like clouds rolling in front of the sun, an effect that even Bert Di Carlo's disapproval hadn't had on me. With a brief beat of panic, I realized what that meant—my shifter half had come to recognize Titus's strength and authority. To feel it in my bones, like some incontrovertible truth.

This is how it happens. How shifters come to follow men like Titus and women like Faythe—people willing to put the good of those they lead over their own well-being. And the natural-born probably never even felt it. Or rather, they were born feeling it, thus likely never noticed.

Bert Di Carlo was not my Alpha—that much was

suddenly perfectly clear. But Titus Alexander *could* be.

Assuming he would ever be anyone's Alpha.

"I saw your face." I leaned across the table and took his hand, refusing to let go when he tried to pull away. "You didn't infect Corey Morris. Not on purpose, anyway. You had *no idea* you were going to find your own scent when you tested his."

His eyes narrowed. "You don't know me well enough to know that."

"Bullshit." I tried to pretend that didn't hurt. "Surprise looks much the same on any face. And if you had infected him, you wouldn't have kept him here, waiting for your own guilt to emerge. So what's going on?"

Titus exhaled, then firmly removed his hand from my grip. "Robyn, go upstairs and wait with the others in the study. Now."

He hadn't made a request. He'd given me an order.

I stood to follow that order, even though my human half wanted to protest, but then the guesthouse door opened overhead. Footsteps thumped down the stairs, and Brandt appeared on the landing, then jogged the rest of the way down. "What's going on, Titus? Drew's calling a meeting, but he won't say…" Brandt's words faded into nothing as his gaze fell on Corey Morris. "Is this about the infector? Are we going to bring him in?"

Titus's jaw clenched, but Brandt hardly noticed as he crossed the concrete floor toward the open cell at the end. He took a dramatic whiff at the threshold, and his entire body tensed.

"What the *fuck*, man?" Brandt spun faster than any human could have without losing his balance. "All I've heard from you since I got here is how we're never, ever supposed to do to someone else what was done to us. The guys lost their jobs. They got kicked out of their homes when they got infected. They can't get married or ever have kids because we're not allowed to tell anyone else what we are. How could you preach one thing, then do the opposite?"

"This is a little more complicated than it looks," Titus growled, staring at the hands he held clasped tightly on the table, and my pulse leaped with hope at the first acknowledgment I'd heard from him that all was not as it seemed.

"Bullshit!" Brandt growled.

I stood so fast my chair scraped the floor behind me. "Do *not* curse at your Alpha!"

Titus's head swiveled toward me, his brows almost comically high.

Brandt looked at me through eyes haunted by betrayal and shiny with unshed tears. I understood how he felt, having obviously lost an idol. But that didn't excuse his behavior.

The young tom tore his pained gaze away from me and aimed it at Titus. "Sack up, man. Take responsibility, like you're always saying. Did you infect that poor guy?"

Titus stood slowly, as if the motion actually hurt. "Yes. I infected him," he said, and the words seem to drain the steel from his spine. The strength from his soul. They seemed to break him, like nothing ever thrown at him, including his own infection, ever had. "I'm sorry I let you down."

Brandt blinked tears from his eyes and stood straighter. He'd obviously expected Titus to deny it. To somehow explain away the evidence we could both smell clearly. When that didn't happen, he turned and ran back up the stairs. A second later, he slammed the guest house door.

Hands clenched into fists at his sides, Titus unleashed a roar so visceral and deep that his vocal cords must have shifted, though no visible part of him had.

In his cell, Corey Morris whined, and I wondered for the first time how much he'd understood of what he'd heard.

According to his own narrative, Corey hadn't attacked the cat who'd infected him, and I had no reason based on his scent or body language to believe he'd been lying about that. And since he hadn't gotten a good look at his attacker, there probably wasn't much he could reveal about Titus's involvement, one way or another.

"I'm sorry," Titus said through clenched teeth, and it took me a second to realize he was apologizing for losing his temper.

"If you're going to be sorry about something, be sorry about lying to Brandt."

His gaze narrowed on me. "I didn't lie."

"Yes, you did. And now you're doing it again. I know what a man looks like when he lies to my face."

Titus exhaled and sank into his chair again. "The facts and details aren't as important as the greater truth; which is that the only thing I can do for Brandt and the others now is step down. Shifters live and die by their senses, Robyn, and what our senses are telling us is that I infected Corey Morris. Whether you like it or not, I'm a liability to the Pride."

I sat in the chair next to him and ducked to catch his gaze. "But there has to be some—"

"Robyn." He took my hand and looked right into

my eyes. "I appreciate your trust, and on some level, I even appreciate your indomitable spirit, as infuriating as I find it in this moment. But for the next half hour, I'm still the Alpha here, and you are not allowed to argue with the Alpha."

That was the first thing he'd said in the past few minutes that made sense.

"Fine. So, who will replace you? How does that work, anyway? You appoint someone?"

"Yes. I think. Though technically anyone can challenge the Alpha to a fight, at any time, and if the challenger wins, he's the new Alpha."

"Or she."

That drew a smile from him. "Yes. Or she."

"So it doesn't really matter who you appoint?"

"If the men still have any respect for my opinion and experience after they hear about Morris, then they'll believe that whoever I appoint is the man most worthy of the job. If not…" he shrugged.

"They know you better than I do. If I can tell that this is more complicated than a simple attack, they'll believe that too." Yet Brandt hadn't, because… "If you *let* them believe that."

Titus gave me a quiet smile, but he looked unconvinced.

"So, who will you appoint? Jace?"

"Jace is the most qualified, but…"

"But he's not here?" I guessed, when Titus's voice trailed off.

"That, and he's natural-born. They like him, and they're fine with him here in an advisory position. But they won't want to be led by someone they think holds himself above them."

Did they really think of Jace like that? What about

Abby?

"My other concern with Jace is that he's already insisted that putting him in charge won't help our case with the council. If they wanted to recognize Jace as an Alpha, they wouldn't have exiled him in the first place."

"So then, Drew?" I guessed.

Titus nodded slowly.

"You look doubtful."

"I'm not sure he's ready, but he's my only real option. Fortunately, he has the best interest of the Pride at heart, and he's been with me from the beginning. I'm sure he'll accept advice from both Jace and me behind the scenes." Titus blinked, then shook his head, as if he were trying to wake up from a long nap. Or emerge from shock. "I'm sorry. That's nothing you should have to worry about."

Which was clearly just a nice way to say it was none of my business, and if he'd been thinking straight, he would never have revealed an Alpha's private doubts to an outsider.

Titus stood and squared his shoulders, and I could practically see him donning determination as if it were an article of clothing. "You don't need to come to the meeting. None of this has anything to do with you."

"Seriously?" I stood and stepped into his path, so he'd have to stop and reconsider. "So once you step down, your deal with the council will be void? I can take off whenever I want?"

"That's not what I meant." Titus ran one hand through his hair. "Drew will uphold our agreement. That's in the Pride's best interest. You'll get the rest of your two weeks."

"And after that? What if I don't want to leave

here? Does Drew have the experience and backbone to stand up to the council?" Would he do that for someone he'd just met? Someone who wasn't ready to pledge loyalty to him as an Alpha?

"I don't know. I'm sure he'll do the best he can." He tried to step around me, heading for the stairs, but I grabbed his arm to stop him.

"Titus. What's going to happen to them without you? Where will your enforcers live? Can Drew afford to pay them? I may not know much about the inner workings of a Pride, but I know they can't operate without enforcers. Or funds."

"He'll figure something out. Alphas have been running territories for generations without a fortune to fall back on." Titus shrugged. "I'll fund them for a while and then maybe he can get a day job and charge dues, like the other Alphas. But that'll be up to him. I can't really think about that right now. I have to…" He gestured for the staircase, then stepped around me and took the steps two at a time.

I followed him out of the guesthouse, around the pool, and into the kitchen, where he stopped. Listening.

"You can't be serious." I recognized Knox's voice from down the hall, and even most of the wordless grunts of agreement following it sounded familiar. "This is a joke."

"Go see for yourself," Brandt said. "I wouldn't have believed it either, if I hadn't smelled him."

Titus took a deep breath, then marched forward with his shoulders square.

"You don't have to do this," I whispered as I followed on his heels. "Tell them the truth. Whatever that is, it can't be worse than losing your position.

Than losing their respect."

"I've made my decision," he growled softly.

I shrugged and stepped past him. "Fine. Then I'll tell them you're hiding something."

"Robyn." Titus grabbed my arm, his eyes flashing with the first beats of anger I'd seen from him. "This is my last order to you as an Alpha. *Keep your mouth shut.* Do you understand?"

His order resonated through me with the authority behind his words. The shifter half of me demanded that I obey. But if I could choose to fight my attraction to him—just another instinct to be conquered—I could fight the order too.

Or…

"I tell you what." I stood on my toes so I could reach his ear, and his scent triggered a rush of my pulse. "I'll keep my mouth shut during the meeting if you give me your word that you'll tell me the truth afterward."

Titus's eyes narrowed. His brows dipped low. His grip on my arm tightened. "Just you?" he demanded softly, and I couldn't quite smother the chill his whisper sent through me. "And you'll keep it to yourself? You swear?"

"I swear on the very concepts of feminism and independence."

His left brow arched. "Those are odd things to swear by."

I shrugged. "Those are the parts of me most threatened by my new life as a shifter. They're what I cling to, so that I know I'm still me, even when the fur takes over. Even when I follow orders. Take it or leave it."

Titus's puzzled expression melted into…surprise.

"Alphas aren't typically given ultimatums. I'll take it. But don't make this a habit." He let go of my arm, then leaned down to whisper again into my ear. "And do *not* break your word, Robyn."

The fierce edge in his voice called out to something primal deep inside me. I nodded, then I followed him down the hall and into a two-story study that I might have called a library instead. Three of the four walls were lined with shelves packed with hardbacks—mostly old leather-bound editions. In one corner, a tall ladder rested on a rail that would carry some lucky reader all the way around the room and up to the shelves at the top of the high ceiling.

In the center of the room, Brandt and the resident enforcers were seated on a cluster of leather furniture arranged around an old Persian rug in shades of red, brown, and dark blue.

A few feet away, Drew Borden sat on the edge of a massive, ornate wooden desk, one foot planted on the floor. He cleared his throat when we stepped into the room, and everyone got quiet as they turned to stare.

Titus stopped inside the doorway. "I'm not going to drag this out," he said. "I'm stepping down as Alpha, effective immediately. Recent developments have made it clear that my leadership will do more harm than good for the Pride. I ask that you accept Drew Borden as your new Alpha."

Drew looked humbled by the nomination, but not truly surprised. "Titus, I'm not sure—"

"You'll be fine," Titus insisted. "And both Jace and I are on call to advise, as often as you need us. I will call Faythe Sanders and report the change. Expect to hear from her later today." He closed his eyes and inhaled slowly. Then he focused on Drew again.

"You'll need to make other housing and finance arrangements, but for now, you're all welcome here. I will be taking a short trip so that my presence won't interfere with your transition into a leadership role."

With that, he turned and headed for the staircase at the front of the house.

I lingered in the study doorway, watching as shock rippled across the small crowd. For a couple of seconds, no one spoke. Then Brandt let out a disgusted huff.

"I told you. He did it. He got caught, so now he's quitting. He's a fucking hypocrite!"

"Brandt." Lochlan twisted his long blond hair into a bun as he spoke. "Shut up and let the grownups think."

"He's understandably frustrated," Drew said. Then he turned to Brandt with a stern expression. "But that's no excuse for the name-calling. Whatever's happened doesn't change the fact that Titus has been a great leader and he's put nothing ahead of the good of the Pride. The very fact that he's stepping down illustrates that."

Brandt nodded, staring at the hands clasped in his lap.

"Let's keep this under wraps until Titus and I have a chance to notify the rest of the Pride. I'll be putting together a new patrol schedule and will be selecting a second in command within the next day or so…"

Reeling, I backed away from the study, trying to wrap my head around events still unfolding. How could Drew already have a game-plan minutes after losing his Alpha, when I was still stunned by the change of leadership?

When Titus was still obviously in shock.

Titus.

I jogged up the stairs and down the hall, then planted one foot in Titus's bedroom doorjamb just in time to stop it from closing. Too late, I remembered I wasn't wearing shoes. "Ow! Wait." I pulled my foot free and rubbed it while I hopped on the healthy one, grateful for the cat's balance that kept me upright. "You gave me your word."

Titus pulled the door open and looked at me. I stopped hopping and set my throbbing right foot on the floor, suddenly aware of how stupid I must look. "Come in. But we'll have to talk while I pack."

"Where are you going?"

"I'm taking a leave of absence. Like I said."

"Yes, but *where* are you going?" I stepped into his room and was surprised to find it nearly spotless in the wake of Corey Morris's invasion. No more torn clothing on the floor. No more wet footprints. The exception was his bed, which still looked very much slept in, with the dark gray comforter askew and the crimson sheet hanging from one side. "Where does a billionaire go to get away from his problems? Europe? The Caribbean?"

"Jackson." Titus opened a door on the far wall and disappeared into a closet the size of my former dorm room, lined with racks of hanging slacks and suit jackets.

"Jackson, Mississippi? As in, an *hour* from here?"

The grunt from the depths of his closet sounded vaguely like an affirmation. A second later, he emerged with a carry-on sized designer suitcase.

"Why the hell would you go to…" My question faded into nothing. The answer was suddenly obvious. "Jackson is where Corey Morris was infected. You're not trying to get away from this. You're digging deeper into it."

Titus wouldn't investigate something he already understood. But if he didn't understand how Corey Morris was infected, why would he accept the blame for it? Why would he give up his territory and leadership position?

He set his suitcase on the bed and flipped it open without even a glance in my direction. While he returned to his closet, I closed the hard shell case and sat on it. He returned with an armload of clothes and stopped short when he saw me.

"Spill it, Titus. I'm not going to move until you do."

TWELVE

Titus

Robyn sat on my suitcase in those snug jeans, her legs crossed at the knee and dangling down the side of my unmade bed. The sight of her there, so close to where I wanted her, sent a spike through my pulse.

But she'd never been mine, and I no longer had the luxury of pretending otherwise.

I laid my clothes across the footboard, trying not to notice that she twisted to watch me, then I headed into my closet. "Do you honestly think I only own one suitcase?"

When I came out with a spare, she was sitting on my clothing, her legs now dangling against my footboard.

"I know you have more clothes," Robyn said, looking up at me with her arms crossed beneath her breasts. "And more suitcases. And probably duplicates of everything you own. I can't stop you from running out of here without keeping your promise. But I don't think you'll do that. A good Alpha keeps his word."

"I'm not an Alpha anymore," I pointed out as I eyed the wrinkles her shapely thigh was pressing into my favorite shirt. Wishing I was wearing it at that moment.

"You're not *their* Alpha. But you're still an Alpha. According to Abby, the position of 'Alpha-as-leader' isn't the same as being *an* Alpha. Her brother Isaac is in charge of his Pride, but he's not truly an Alpha yet. And Jace is an Alpha with no Pride to lead. That's why you two keep butting heads. You're like him now. A displaced Alpha. But a good one. You'll keep your word." Her mischievous smile stirred a heat deep inside me. "And in case I'm wrong about that, I'm fully prepared to obstruct you every step of the way until you start talking."

I could see that she wasn't bluffing. And I *had* given my word.

"Okay, but this is for your ears only, Robyn. You can't tell Drew. You can't even tell Abby. I need you to swear, and I need to know you mean it."

"I swear." Her smile faded into a look of concern. "What's going on, Titus?"

I pulled her to her feet and hung my clothes over my desk chair, then sat in the chair. Robyn sank on the edge of the bed again, facing me, worry dipping her brows lower over her big blue eyes. I exhaled slowly. Then I met her gaze.

"You were right. I lied. The scent woven through Morris's isn't mine." I could see the questions already forming on her tongue, but I pressed on before she could ask them, because once Robyn started talking, it was hard for anyone else to get a word in. "It's my brother's. The scents of same-sex full-blood siblings are very similar. Have you ever smelled Abby's

175

brothers?"

Robyn shook her head. "I've met Jace's brothers, but at the time I was too preoccupied with the charges against me to notice what they smelled like." She shrugged and dropped her gaze to the floor. "And that was before my mandatory training, so I wasn't really tuned in to how much you can learn about a person from his scent. Other than the obvious advantage for identifying the bastards who did this to me."

"Well, if any of them had had brothers, you might have made some big mistakes," I told her.

She snorted. "The current consensus is that I *did* make some big mistakes." She blinked, and I could practically see her dragging her focus back to the present. "Tell me about your brother."

"Justus is eleven years my junior. He was a freshman in high school when our parents died." He'd been devastated, and being there for him had let me defer my own mourning until he'd left for college, which had turned out to be both a blessing and a curse. "Now he's a sophomore at Millsaps. In Jackson."

Her frown deepened as the location sank in. "Where Corey Morris was infected. Do the guys know?"

"That Justus exists? Of course. There are pictures of him all over the house. His bedroom is the one across from mine and next to yours, but he never comes home anymore, and Drew's the only one who's met him." A very deliberate decision on my part.

"So they'll assume Morris is carrying a trace of your scent for the same reason I did," Robyn said, clearly thinking it through. "Because they've never smelled your brother. But if Drew's met him, why doesn't he recognize Justus's scent?"

"He'll figure it out eventually. But so far, it hasn't occurred to him that my brother could have infected Corey Morris because Justus is human. At least, he was when I saw him over the holidays. I've been very careful to keep him out of all Alpha-related business. He didn't even know shifters exist. Though he clearly knows now."

The thought of what my brother had been through—the inevitable trauma of his infection—made me want to put my fist through the wall. I'd jumped through every hoop imaginable to keep him safe and in ignorance of the violence that had become my life since my own infection. In ignorance of the struggle to protect the strays in my territory, often from each other and from themselves.

But obviously my efforts had been spent in vain.

"I should have told him." I leaned forward with my head in my hands, devastated to realize that my attempts to keep Justus safe had actually put him in more danger. "If he'd known we existed, he would have come to me when he realized he was infected. He would have known how to handle his own transition." I sat up and met her gaze with an anguished one of my own. "Robyn, if I had let him meet the guys and see what we're doing, he wouldn't be out there infecting other innocent people."

Corey Morris's infection was my fault, even though I'd never laid a single claw on him. In that sense, what I'd told my men was true.

"Second guessing yourself now won't help," Robyn insisted. "Hindsight is worthless unless you can learn from it, and what could you possibly learn from this? You can't just announce our existence to the world so that the next person who gets infected understands what's happening. That's against the council's rules."

Which was one of the reasons I hadn't disclosed our existence to Justus—telling him would have been violating one of the Shifter world's most important prohibitions and likely would have kept me from being acknowledged as Alpha.

Had I sacrificed my brother's safety for my own ambition?

"Titus, I don't even understand this." Robyn's frown became a wide-eyed look of confusion. "How could you possibly keep this from your brother, logistically speaking? Doesn't he come home on school breaks? How do you explain the parade of totally ripped men walking around half-naked in your home? Some halfway house for reformed male strippers?"

A laugh snuck up on me, and when I saw her small smile, I realized she'd startled me out of self-pity.

"Justus used to come home during his breaks, but when I decided to turn my home into Pride headquarters, I started sending him on trips during the holidays, instead. I can't go with him, unless we vacation in one of the free zones, so we've rented this cabin up in the Montana free zone for the past two Christmases. And there are no shifters native to island nations, so in the summer we spend a couple of weeks in the Bahamas or the Caribbean, before I send him to Europe for the rest of his break." I shrugged. "I don't know how long that routine would have held up, but it's worked so far."

"But did you think that for the rest of his life he'd never make a surprise visit? Did you *truly* think you could keep this from him forever?"

"Of course not. I knew I'd have to tell him something once the Pride was recognized." But in addition to it being against the rules, jumping the gun felt like jinxing myself—a superstitious end to the possibility that the Pride ever *would* be recognized.

"Okay. So if Drew will eventually figure out the truth about your brother, why bother hiding it? Or stepping down? As Alpha, wouldn't you be in a better position to help Justus?"

"I don't think so." I'd thought about little else in the past hour. "And trying to help him might endanger my position anyway. Creating a stray is a capital offense. A mandatory death sentence."

"So is killing a human, yet I survived. And Abby said that Faythe infected someone years ago, and she's in charge of a whole Pride now. They found her guilty, but gave her a light sentence because the infection was an accident. It could go the same way for your brother."

I shook my head. She still didn't understand. "You're both women. The council values your lives over male lives. Especially over *stray* male lives. Most of the members will take any excuse to execute a stray, and I can't let that happen to my brother. I have to find out what really happened before anyone else figures out that he's involved. Thus the suitcase." I stood and flipped open one of the hard shell cases, then began folding the clothes draped over the back of my chair.

"Okay." Robyn stood and headed for the door. "Let me get my stuff. Which is pretty much the extra toothbrush you gave me yesterday."

"Whoa, wait," I said, but she kept walking, so I had to jog past her to block the bedroom door. "You have to stay here."

"Why? Do you think the council will keep its word, now that you're not the Alpha? Because *I* think they'll use this as an excuse to make me go to Atlanta immediately. Especially now that Abby and Jace aren't here. They're not going to leave one of their precious tabbies in the hands of a bunch of strays they've never even met and have no reason to trust."

"Robyn, I gave them my word." Breaking that now would only make things worse for both of us. And for Justus.

"But you never told them I'd stay in this house for two weeks. What you told them was that you'd protect me, and you can't do that if I'm here and you're in Jackson. What if something happens to me while you're gone? They'll hold you responsible. You *have* to take me with you, Titus."

Son of a bitch. Robyn had me. And it was *possible* I didn't try very hard to convince her otherwise.

"Fine. Go get your…toothbrush. I have to make some calls."

Robyn looked satisfied, if not happy, as she raced into the hall and closed my bedroom door behind her.

I called Jace first, while I packed. He answered on the third ring. "Hey, Titus, what's up?" Highway noise and the use of a hands-free speaker made him difficult to understand, but cat's hearing gave me an advantage. "Robyn driving you nuts already?"

The grunt immediately following his question told me Abby had elbowed him. Or punched him in the arm.

"No. Well, yes, but that's not why I'm calling." I rolled a wrinkle-resistant button-up shirt and wedged it into the suitcase between a pair of spare shoes. "Shouldn't you guys be there by now?"

"We stopped for a long lunch," Abby called out. "We're about half an hour away."

"Has Drew been in touch?" I asked.

"No." A steady ticking sound came over the line as he used his blinker. "Why would he?"

"Because I just stepped down as Alpha and put him in charge."

"Whoa, what?" Abby demanded, as brakes squealed over the line. "Jace, pull over."

"Working on it," Jace said. "Titus, what's going on?"

"I don't have much time, so I'll let Drew go into the details later. But the quick version is this: I've been implicated in the infection of the stray Spencer brought in last night. I stepped down to keep that from affecting the Pride's chances of acceptance."

"You can't really stop that," Jace said.

"I know, but they're better off without me at the moment."

"What happened?" Abby demanded. "What do you mean by 'implicated'?"

"I'm not going to go into that right now. What I can tell you is that it's not what it looks like, but it's every bit as bad as it sounds. I'm leaving for a few days to figure this whole thing out, but I'll have my phone with me. I told Drew that you and I would both be available in an advisory capacity."

"Of course," Jace said.

Abby sighed. "Jace, maybe we should go back. You're more qualified than Drew…"

"Yet less likely to be acknowledged by the council. I'm no good to the Pride except in an advisory role," he insisted, echoing what he'd already told me a dozen times.

"But we can't leave Robyn there now. Everything will be chaotic, and Drew will be distracted from looking out for her."

I added another rolled up pair of jeans to my suitcase, then threw in several pairs of boxer briefs. "Robyn's coming with me."

"What? Where are you going?" Abby demanded. "You can't parade Robyn around the free zone. It isn't safe."

"There won't be any parading. And since I gave my word that I'd protect her, I kind of have to bring her."

Jace chuckled. "That was her idea, wasn't it?"

"It doesn't matter whose idea it was. I'm hanging up now so I can call Faythe." I said as I flipped my suitcase closed. "But don't worry about Robyn. She'll be fine. I swear on my life."

"What about you?" Abby asked. "Will *you* be fine?"

"You'll know as soon as I do." With that, I hung up the phone and sank onto the edge of the bed. The most difficult call was yet to come.

I dialed Faythe's cell phone while I closed the clasps on my suitcase, and I was almost relieved when her voicemail kicked in. I left the basics—I was stepping down for the good of the Pride, and Drew Borden would be taking over—in my message, as I threw toiletries into a small leather case in my bathroom. When I emerged from my room, fully packed, I almost ran smack into Robyn, who stood in the middle of the hall. Holding a toothbrush.

"Abby took all her toiletries with her, and since she's the size of a fourth-grader, all her clothes look like dirty Halloween costumes on me." She shrugged and gestured with the toothbrush. "So it looks like I'm packing as light as I thought I'd be."

"I have soap and toothpaste and we can stop for clothes and things once we get there," I told her. Robyn nodded, but didn't look entirely happy with that thought. "Let's go."

"Don't you want to say goodbye to the guys?" she whispered when I marched down the stairs and headed straight for the front door, carrying my suitcase in one hand.

"No." The truth was that I had no idea what to say to them, and I wasn't prepared for the inevitable questions. Any answers I gave could expose my lie, and until I knew exactly what had happened to my brother, I wasn't going to risk revealing his part in the infection of Corey Morris.

"Well, *I* do." Robyn's shoes squeaked on the marble floor as she spun and headed toward the kitchen, where I could hear most of my men speaking in soft voices. "Hey, I just wanted to say goodbye before we go," she said, and I closed my eyes and prayed for patience.

"Where are you going?" Knox said. "Aren't you supposed to stay here?"

"Yes." Concern rode Drew's deep baritone. "She is."

I exhaled slowly, then set my bag down and headed for the kitchen. "I told the council I'd protect her, and I can't do that if she's not with me," I said from the doorway.

"Are you sure about that, Titus?" Drew asked, and

his concern raised the hairs on the nape of my neck. It was only natural that he would challenge me, considering his battlefield promotion to Alpha.

And it was only natural that his challenge would irritate me.

"I'm sure." Even though Robyn had to talk me into it.

"I hate to question your judgment, man. Especially in your own house. But you gave your word as Alpha of this Pride," Drew said, and the collective focus of the enforcers volleyed back to him, as the level of tension in the room rose. "Shouldn't that promise be transferred along with the position?"

"No." I didn't bother to elaborate, because outlining my reasons would make it look like I felt the need to justify my position. Or that the matter was up for debate. Neither of which was true. "Robyn, say goodbye. We're leaving."

Drew opened his mouth, obviously ready to argue, but Robyn pulled him into a hug before he could. "It was great to meet you, and hopefully I'll see you again before they drag me back to Atlanta." She let Drew go and looked up at him with gratitude so earnest it could only be an act. A manipulation. "It's so awesome of you to step up to help Titus. Hopefully, he won't have to impose upon your generosity for very long."

Drew stared at her, stunned by her blatant characterization of his tenure as temporary. In front of all of the enforcers.

I fought not to laugh out loud. Robyn might be smaller than the toms, but that woman's mind was *badass* in a way that no enforcer's claws or incisors would ever be.

She went around the room, hugging my men, saying something nice and personal to each of them, but when she got to Brandt, her hug lasted longer than it should have. Because she was whispering something in his ear.

When she finally let him go, his gaze fell on me, and he appeared—if not friendly—a little less hateful than he'd looked half an hour ago, in my study.

"What did you say to Brandt?" I whispered as I grabbed my suitcase on our way toward the front door.

"I told him that sometimes you have to trust the people you know and love, despite what logic seems to be telling you. After all, logic tells us that humans can't turn into cats, but we all know that's not true."

"Wow." I tried not to look too impressed. "Thanks, Robyn."

She smiled as she pulled open the passenger door of my car, and a single raindrop hit the tip of her nose. "Does that mean I can ride up front? Or do I have to hide under your clothes all the way to Jackson?"

THIRTEEN

Robyn

Titus drove us south toward Jackson, in the dark and the rain, and we arrived at the Millsaps campus around ten o'clock. But the car didn't stop.

"Where are we going?" I asked as we rolled past the campus's concrete-and-brick welcome sign.

"My brother has an apartment off-campus. I figured we'd start there."

Justus Alexander's apartment turned out to be a thirteen-hundred-square-foot space with two large bedrooms, two baths, hardwood floors, and walk-in closets. I'd seen smaller houses.

"I'm guessing your brother got an inheritance as well?" I said as I ran my fingers across the granite countertops in the generous galley-style kitchen.

"Yes, but he won't get the first lump sum until he turns twenty-five. I pay for the apartment. Which is why I have my own room, for when I visit." Titus pushed open the door to the back bedroom and flipped a switch to turn on the light. "But I'll take the couch tonight. You can have the bed."

"Thanks," I said. But I personally thought the overstuffed couch piled with designer pillows looked pretty damn comfortable—until I stepped into Titus's room-away-from-home.

The bed was smaller—full-sized instead of king— but the mattress was tall enough that it had to be padded and the bedding looked plush and soft. And it smelled like him.

The sudden, visceral need to roll around on Titus's comforter took me by surprise so strongly that I'd taken two steps toward the bed before I realized what I was doing. Mortified, I stopped, pivoted, then marched past him and out of the room, my cheeks flaming at the puzzled look he gave me.

And I certainly did *not* inhale his scent as I passed him on my way out the door.

The living room was freshly swept and smelled clean. The kitchen was spotless, and I didn't see even a hint of dust buildup on the full-sized washer and dryer peeking from behind a set of bi-fold doors off the living room. "Your brother's even more of a neat freak than you are."

Titus snorted. "No, he has a bi-weekly cleaning service."

"Of course he does." I tried not to roll my eyes or sound too jealous of a nineteen-year-old attending a private college with no student debt, living alone in an expensive apartment with someone else to clean up all his messes.

Justus's life was not without problems. Thus the reason for our visit.

I set my toothbrush on the glass coffee table. "Okay, I'm unpacked. So, where do we start?" Titus had been calling Justus every few minutes since we'd left the mansion, but he'd gotten no answer. "Is he on your cell plan? Can you track his phone?"

"Yes. But I'm going to give him one more chance to answer." He tapped a name in his contacts list, then held his phone up to his ear. It rang once from Titus's end—then again from the front bedroom.

"He's here?" I whispered, suddenly unnerved to realize we weren't alone in the apartment.

"I doubt it." Titus marched across the room and pushed his brother's bedroom door open. "He would have heard us." He flipped a switch on the wall, and light flooded the room.

I followed him through the doorway, then stopped short, staring at the colossal mess. "Definitely not a neat freak." But maybe an actual freak. "Does it usually look so…?"

"Destroyed?" Titus supplied, as he ended the call, and I nodded. "His room is only ever clean on cleaning days, but this is…excessive."

"When was cleaning day?"

He slid his phone into his pocket and stared through narrowed eyes at the mess. "Thursday. Two days ago."

"And he's been here since then."

Titus dropped into a squat at the edge of the bed and inhaled deeply, to verify through scent that Justus had trashed his own room. "Yes. And he's definitely a shifter." He sank onto his heels. "I don't think I truly believed it until now."

I took a deep breath through my nose. "Wow! He smells so much like you!" Even though the lingering scent in his room could be from before Justus was infected.

"I know." Titus stood and moved around the bed,

stepping over clothing, video game controllers, and an open jar of guy hair gel on his way to the built-in shelves lining one wall beneath a row of windows.

"Can you tell who infected him?" I couldn't detect anyone else's scent woven through Justus's, but that could be because I didn't know his infector.

"No. It's probably too faint to catch in trace scents. We won't know until we can actually smell my brother in person, and chances are we won't know even then. He could have been infected by someone we've never met. The vast majority are infected by strays totally off the radar."

"Well, we can't track him if he doesn't have his phone. So, what, we just wait here for him? How long does he usually stay out?"

"He's nineteen years old. He could be out all night." Titus plucked his brother's laptop from a pile of laundry on the floor. "While we wait, we snoop."

I spotted Justus's phone on top of his chest of drawers, peeking from beneath a battered chemistry textbook and a wrinkled jumble of note cards. The device was locked, but when I woke it up, missed call alerts lit up the lock screen. I scrolled to the beginning, past nearly a dozen calls from Titus.

"Well, we could have plenty of time to snoop." I held the phone out so he could see the list. "He hasn't answered a call in forty-five hours."

"What?" Titus took the phone from me and scanned the alerts. "So, what? Justus got here right after the apartment was cleaned, tore up his room, then left, never to return? That doesn't make any sense."

"Or maybe it does." I knelt to pull a scrap of lace and wire from another pile of clothes and held the shredded bra up for him to see. "Unless your brother has a pretty big secret, this might be about a girl. Was he dating someone?"

"More like everyone. Justus is very...social. I probably didn't set a good example in that department."

A bolt of jealousy shot through me. How many girls had Titus brought home?

Titus scrubbed one hand over his face, and sleep deprivation seemed to catch up with him all at once. "And that's only one on a long list of regrets over how I took care of my brother after our parents died."

"This isn't your fault. You didn't infect him." A photograph caught my eye from beneath the rim of an overturned aluminum mesh trash can, and I nearly tripped over a dumbbell on my way to it. "Are you sure he didn't have an actual girlfriend?" I asked as I studied the photo. Which was actually half a photo, showing a smiling young brunette woman with a man's arm wrapped around her waist. The rest of the man was on the missing half of the picture. "Because this looks like fallout from a bad breakup to me."

"That would be a new development, but certainly possible." Titus took the photo and stared at the girl. "So, two days ago, he trashes his room—possibly over a girl—and disappears. That night, he infects Corey Morris in the woods east of I55. How are those connected?"

"Let's find out." I took the laptop from him and picked my way across the cluttered floor. "In the living room."

I settled onto the couch with Justus's computer on my lap, and Titus headed into the kitchen. "I need a snack," he said. "Are you hungry?"

"Always." I opened Justus's computer, and the screen blinked to life instantly. And asked for a password. *Damn it.*

"I'm no chef, but I can handle a couple of sandwiches." Titus pulled open the fridge and rummaged inside, then set half a loaf of bread on the counter. "Ham or turkey."

"Surprise me." I typed "password" into the prompt screen, and was denied access to the computer. "Hey Titus, I don't suppose you know your brother's password?"

"No. Try his middle name."

"Okay." I frowned at the computer balanced on my knees. "With a first name like Justus, his middle name must be Truth, or Patience, or something like that."

Titus laughed. "Anthony."

"Justus *Anthony* Alexander," I said as I typed his middle name into the field on the screen. "Nope. What else you got? Favorite book?"

"I'm not sure he's read anything other than a textbook since he was about ten years old. Back then, he liked Harry Potter."

"Okay." I tried every character name I could remember from the series. No luck. "What's your middle name?"

"Nathaniel. But he wouldn't use that." Titus looked up from spreading mustard on a slice of bread. "Try our mother's name. Penelope."

I typed that in, and the lock screen disappeared. "Yes!" Then I frowned. "I'm calling this a win for now, but when we find your brother, you need to tell him to use random words or phrases for his passwords."

Titus chuckled. "When I was in college, my passwords were the first six digits of Fibonacci's sequence or the first ten digits of pi, depending on the device."

"And, the Nerd of the Year Award goes to Titus Nathaniel Alexander..." I said without turning away from the screen. "It looks like his computer is set to remember his other passwords, which is a security nightmare, but convenient for our well-intentioned but illicit purposes."

"Turkey, pepper jack, and pickles. Justus doesn't stock tomatoes or lettuce, or anything fresh. At all." Titus sank onto the couch next to me holding two sandwiches. Each on its own paper plate. His leg touched mine from hip to thigh, and I could feel the warmth of his skin through both layers of denim. "So what do we know so far?"

I accepted my plate and set it on the couch cushion on my other side, trying not to think about how warm his leg felt. About how his shoulder brushed mine as he leaned in to see the screen. About how, if I turned, my lips would be less than two inches from his, and he'd be damn near *obligated* to kiss me. Or to hold still and let me do it.

"Well, it looks like he hasn't posted on any social media in nearly a week," I said, trying to purge thoughts that made me feel warm and raw all over. "But six days ago, he put up a shot of himself and the girl from the picture having lunch from a food truck. The caption reads, 'Me and Ivy at Molly's Tamales'."

"Ivy. Shit," Titus said around his first bite. "Wasn't that the name of Corey Morris's roommate's girlfriend? The one who owned the cabin where he was attacked?"

I closed my eyes, trying to remember everything Corey had said about how he'd been infected. "I think so. Maybe it's a different Ivy."

Titus huffed. "That'd be a hell of a coincidence. The more logical conclusion is that Justus was involved with Morris's friend's girlfriend. Or she was cheating on Justus with Morris's friend." He leaned closer to glance at the laptop screen. "Do we have a last name?

"No, but he's tagged her. Just a sec." I clicked the link and took a bite of my sandwich while the page loaded. "Ivy Lowe. She's a sophomore at Millsaps. There are several pictures of her in a dorm room, so it looks like she lives on campus. I bet her number's in his phone. Why don't you call her?"

Titus set his plate on the coffee table and pulled his brother's phone from his pocket. He typed a four-digit number into the lock screen, and it disappeared.

"You knew the password?"

"No, but I can see the pattern. It was the date our parents died."

Morbid, but understandable.

Looking over Titus's shoulder—and breathing in his scent, inches from his neck—I could see that there was no Ivy in Justus's short favorites menu. I took another bite, watching while Titus scrolled through the longer contacts list, then stopped. "Ivy Lowe. Cross your fingers." He pressed CALL, then held the phone up to his ear, and I could hear perfectly well when her voicemail picked up. "Well, that's not good."

"Maybe she's in class." I licked a smear of mustard from my upper lip, pleased to find him watching my mouth.

"At ten-thirty pm?"

I shrugged. "Maybe she's studying. Or working. Or driving with her phone on do not disturb." I took another bite and spoke around it. "She'll probably text you back any minute in all caps, yelling at Justus for whatever he did to break them up."

Titus glanced at me with one brow arched. "You're assuming *he* broke them up?"

"Your brother trashed his room, shredded his girlfriend's underwear, and infected a stranger. Even if he didn't mean to be, chances are that he was the problem."

"If that's true, she may have blocked his number." Titus frowned. "We probably shouldn't show up at her dorm room in the middle of the night."

"No," I agreed. "But I might be able to 'run into' her tomorrow on campus."

"And how would we know where she'd be?"

"Through the miracle of cyber-stalking. How do you think I tracked down certain dead psychopaths who shall remain nameless?"

Titus laughed, then waved one hand magnanimously at the computer on my lap. "Go for it."

While he finished his sandwich, I scrolled through Ivy Lowe's posts on every social media account I could find for her. In spite of their apparent breakup, she and Justus were still friends online, so I was able to see pictures that would otherwise have been hidden on her private accounts.

"Well, Ivy plays tennis for Millsaps, but she doesn't win much. On the weekends, she works at a vintage clothing store. And she eats enough ice cream to keep a dairy farm in business all on her own. Not that you can tell it from her pictures." I frowned as I took another bite of my sandwich. "Maybe it's low-fat yogurt."

"Can you tell where she gets it? We could people-watch at an ice cream place tomorrow."

"I can't see the name of the shop, but it has a pink logo, with—"

A phone rang, and I thought it was Justus's until Titus pulled his cell from his pocket. "It's Faythe." His heartbeat took up a rapid, stressed cadence, and mine raced to match its pace. And again, that connection surprised me. Do all Pride cats have sympathetic physical reactions to their Alphas' stress? Or excitement? Was that part of some weird Pride bonding?

Did my reaction mean that my feline half recognized Titus as its Alpha? Or was the connection more personal in nature?

My pulse raced even faster with that thought.

"What are you going to tell her?" I asked, dragging my thoughts back on track.

"I don't know. But I owe her an explanation."

I grabbed his phone and pressed the button to reject Faythe's call.

"Robyn!" Titus took his phone.

"You can't tell her much without incriminating your brother, so let her get the scoop from Jace and Abby for now. We'll call her when we have more information."

He scowled, disapproval radiating from his gray gaze, and I had to push past my inner cat's instinct to cower. But then he took the laptop from me and set it on the coffee table, next to my toothbrush. "If that's the plan, let's go get that information."

When he stood, I stood with him, my pulse racing again. After two months of metaphorically sitting on my hands at the Di Carlo compound, a chance to play detective with Titus—and help his brother, a fellow stray—felt like waking up from a psychological coma. "Where? How?"

"We're going to start in the woods east of I55. If Justus infected Corey Morris there, it might be his regular hunting grounds. For however long he's been a shifter." His eyes narrowed in thought. "I have no idea how long that is. How can I not even know how long ago my own brother was infected?"

"This isn't your fault, Titus." I sat again and opened the laptop. "If we're going to the woods in the middle of the night, we need a plan. Or at least a starting point."

"Okay…" He sat next to me again, his warm leg pressed against mine, and watched while I pulled up a map of Jackson, Mississippi, online and clicked on the satellite filter. "Okay, east of I55. North or south of the city?"

"South. Isn't that what Morris said?"

"I think so." I zoomed in and panned around in the wooded areas until I found a cabin. The satellite view wouldn't let me see the small building up close, but it gave me the longitude and latitude.

"How do you know that's the right cabin?" Titus asked, so close that I could feel his breath on my neck. I had to concentrate to keep my focus on the task at hand.

"I don't." I jotted down the coordinates, then panned around on the map a bit, but only found one other cabin nearby. "Okay, these are the only two they could have gotten to without having to cross a river. It's a good starting point."

"Great. Let's go."

I set Justus's laptop on the glass coffee table and Titus reached down to pull me up from the couch, his gaze locked on mine. His grip on my hand loosened and lingered until he was just...holding it. Renewing the connection.

That sweet, innocent contact—his hand warm against mine—should have been nothing, but it felt like...*something*.

Something that I wanted, for the first time since the night I'd been scratched.

I slid my free hand up his arm and around his neck, then I stood on my toes and kissed him. Before I could talk myself out of the impulse.

Titus made a satisfied sound deep in his throat. His hands found my sides, then roamed up my back. I sucked on his lower lip, tasting it, then slid my tongue into his mouth. He groaned.

Then, suddenly Titus was gone. I opened my eyes to find him four feet away, staring at me in a pained mixture of desire and guilt. "I *really* wasn't supposed to do that."

"Why not? Because the council told you not to?"

Titus frowned. "You overheard my phone call?"

I shrugged. "Just the part where you promised Faythe you had no intention of 'seducing' me."

He exhaled slowly. "I didn't say that because the council doesn't want us together. I said it because they're right. You're young, and new, and vulnerable. And I'm an authority figure. It's wrong."

"You're not *my* authority figure anymore." Not officially, anyway.

"Robyn…"

"No, seriously. You're not the boss of me, and I have no intention of following any order you try to give. Ergo, you are not my authority figure. You're not taking advantage. You're not even instigating this." I stepped forward and kissed him again, and this time when he tried to pull away, I gently bit his lip.

"Robyn, you can't—"

"Fuck that." I stepped back, anger firing in my veins. "I was starting to think you were different from the other Alphas, but here you go, telling me who I can and can't kiss. If you don't want to kiss me, then make that decision for yourself. As a man turning down a woman, not as an Alpha using a position he doesn't even hold anymore as an excuse. But don't you *dare* say you're doing this for me.

"I can damn well make my own decisions."

FOURTEEN

Titus

The highway was dark, the asphalt still slick, though the rain had ended an hour before. My phone buzzed in Robyn's hand, and the call interrupted the map app, obscuring the latitude and longitude we'd been navigating by.

"It's Faythe again." She held the phone up for me to see as I drove slowly along the shoulder of I55. "I assume you don't want me to answer?"

"You assume correctly."

"Maybe I should, though. She might quit calling if she knows I'm okay."

"Then text her from your phone. It was your idea to put off talking to her, and I don't feel like being bitched at again."

"I didn't bitch at you." Robyn rejected the call on my phone, and the map reappeared, lighting up the interior of my SUV.

"I didn't mean you."

But she made no reply as she set my phone in the dashboard mount, so I could see the map, then dug her new phone from the pocket of the black wool coat I'd lent her. She was still mad, and I couldn't blame her.

It had taken every bit of willpower I'd had to stop kissing her, and though my head had told me I'd done the right thing, my heart was far from convinced. As was my body.

You're not the Alpha anymore. I had no authority, and I probably never would again. Kissing Robyn would constitute no conflict of interest or abuse of position. And she *clearly* wanted to be kissed, almost as badly as I wanted to kiss her.

So apologize. I could stop the car, right there on the side of the road, and kiss her. I could tell her how much it meant to me that she wanted to help my brother and the other disenfranchised strays. And me. I could fix things between us, because knowing I hurt her feelings, when all I'd wanted to do was kiss her, made me feel like an ass.

I glanced at Robyn and found her typing a text to Faythe.

Hey, this is Robyn. I'm fine. Titus is fine. We're safe, and he'll call you as soon as he can.

"Okay, we need to turn left as soon as you find a way into the woods," she said with a glance at the map, but there was a distance in her voice. A distinct lack of warmth. "We're coming up on the coordinates." Her phone buzzed in her lap, and she glanced at the text. "It's Faythe. She wants us to call her. I'm going to put it on do not disturb," she said as her fingers tapped the screen, then she turned to the road without even a glance my way. "I think I see a dirt path up there. Do you see it?"

I squinted into the darkness. "Yeah." I glanced at the rearview mirror, then turned across both lanes of the highway onto the small road cut into the woods. The headlights shined on several sets of tire tracks in the dirt.

"I don't suppose you recognize any of those tracks?" Robyn asked, squinting at them through the windshield

"No. I'm better at recognizing paw prints than tire tracks, and I doubt I'm as good at that as most natural-born toms." Who were practically born tracking prey in the woods.

After a bumpy mile and a half of watching our progress on the GPS map, Robyn told me to stop. "We're half a mile away. If we go much farther in the truck, the light and engine noise might spook him."

She was right. And I was impressed, especially considering that her somewhat illicit tracking skills were self-taught. However… "If he's out here in cat form, he'll already have heard us," I said. "Looks like we're walking from here."

Robyn nodded. "You want to shift, or should I?"

I glanced at her again in surprise, and she rolled her eyes. "I've spent the past two months surrounded by enforcers. I know that two-man patrols work with one person on foot and one on four paws, so the team has access to advantages in both forms—a cat's eyes, ears, and nose, and a human's thumbs and cell phone. But…" She sighed. "I haven't exactly *totally* mastered my instincts in cat form. And by instincts, I mean bloodlust." The face she made suggested that the admission actually tasted bad on her tongue.

I shrugged. "Okay, I'll shift. But if you're going on

two legs, you have to carry this." I leaned across her to open the glove box, and she shook her head before I even got it open.

"I don't know how to shoot a—"

"It's a stun-gun." I pulled out the blocky plastic pistol with a clunky square barrel and dropped it into her lap. "Just in case. You point and shoot."

"Okaaay." Robyn slid the gun into the right pocket of her borrowed coat.

"Did you really think I'd let you shoot my brother?" I asked as I got out of the car.

"No." She laughed. "Though that would hint at an interesting family dynamic." Her teeth began to chatter the moment she opened her car door—even in Mississippi, February was a cold month—so I rounded the front of the vehicle and folded the collar of my coat up over her neck and chin.

I didn't realize what I was doing, or how intimate a gesture that was, until she looked up at me from inches away. Evidently surprised that I'd voluntarily touched her.

When I inhaled, her scent mixed with mine from the borrowed coat, and the combination made my heart beat harder. That moment felt...right. As if it could have been removed from our current mission—plopped down in any time or place—and I could be bundling her up in my coat on a snowy day on vacation in Europe. Or for a brisk afternoon walk on our own property.

And suddenly I wanted both of those things. Moments with Robyn that weren't overshadowed by danger and stress. By the possibility that I had permanently lost my Pride and that my brother might soon lose his life.

Startled by that realization, I cleared my throat and stepped back.

"So, what's the plan?" Robyn asked while I rounded the car again and took off my coat. "We're going to walk around and hope we run into your brother?"

I folded my coat and set it on the driver's seat. "We're going to walk in the direction of the cabin and, yes, hope we find my brother. Or at least some trace of his scent, to confirm that he's been out here recently." I pulled my shirt over my head, and I was unsurprised, but definitely pleased, when she studied my chest with no hint of shame or timidity.

I'd been pursued by women before—most were more attracted to the me they read about in Forbes "30 Under 30" list than to the actual me—but Robyn was uninhibited and confident in a way few of the other women had been. She wasn't arrogant, or presumptuous, or coy. She was just...open. Honest about what she wanted, not just with everyone else, but with herself.

"What if we don't find Justus?" she asked, casually watching me over the hood of my car while I unzipped my pants. "Or any trace of him?"

"Then we go back to the apartment and get some sleep, and tomorrow we stake out all of his classes and try to get ahold of Ivy Lowe." I stood fully naked and goose-pimpled in the moonlight and was suddenly glad that the front of the car shielded me from sight from the hips down—no first impression of an intimate nature should *ever* be made in sub-freezing temperatures.

I opened the rear driver's side door and took a backpack from the floorboard. "I need you to carry this," I said as I stuffed my keys and clothes into the bag, then tossed it to her over the hood of the car.

While I shifted, Robyn turned off the car lights and locked the doors, then she leaned against the hood and studied the GPS map until I finally stood on four paws.

"Wow, that was fast." She settled the straps of my backpack higher on her shoulders. "Will I get faster with experience?"

I bobbed my muzzle at her. Then I tossed my head toward the east, in the general direction of the cabin. Corey Morris had told us he was attacked within fifty yards of the cabin. I was far from convinced that we'd find Justus out in the forest, but he wasn't at home, and he had to be somewhere.

"Yup. Let's go." She headed into the woods, to the east, and I padded alongside her.

Her human footsteps were clumsy and obvious, at least to my cat's ear, but she was clearly trying to be stealthy.

"Sorry," she whispered the third time her boot snapped through a twig.

I gave her an amused snort. It didn't matter how loud her steps were. If Justus was out there in cat form, he would hear her coming even if she could manage not to stomp on every crisp fallen leaf. Unless, like Robyn, he hadn't yet mastered the art of listening without conscious effort.

A light blinked deeper in the woods and I froze, my frame tense. I inhaled deeply, but caught no out-of-place scents.

"What? Do you smell him?" Robyn took an exaggerated whiff of the air, but I could tell from her frown that she smelled only the same woodland inhabitants I had: skunks, beavers, raccoons, and somewhere nearby, a very nervous deer.

I shook my head and stared straight ahead, trying to direct her gaze in the right direction, absent the ability to speak. When she only squinted into the woods, I realize we weren't close enough yet for her human eyes to register the light. So I kept walking, and she followed as quietly as she could.

Twenty yards later, she gasped softly. "A light. Is it the cabin?" The light had a yellowish hue, but lacked the jumpiness or warm look of a flame. "It's dim, at least to my human eyes, but according to the GPS—" She held the screen out for me to see. "—it's coming from the direction of the cabin."

So we pressed on. "Still no scent of him?" she whispered as we continued.

I shook my head.

The closer we got to the cabin, the more detail I could see. It was old and small—probably only one room—with a rusted metal roof. The windows were grimy, but both of those facing us were lit by what appeared to be a single dim bulb.

At the top of a set of warped wooden steps, the front door stood ajar.

"Shit," Robyn whispered. "No one over the age of eight leaves the front door open."

She obviously hadn't spent much time with Brandt. But her point was valid.

My muzzle bobbed as I scented the air in several short sniffs.

Death. Decay. Rot. Feces.

My pulse exploded into a frantic rhythm, and I took off for the cabin as fast as I could.

"Wait!" Robyn called as she raced after me, all

caution abandoned. She obviously couldn't yet smell what I'd scented, but she could tell something was wrong.

She burst into the cabin a moment after I did, then pulled up short, one hand covering her nose when the smell hit her. Then she gagged and staggered onto the porch.

Unpleasant scents are weaker in human form, but much more difficult to tolerate. Especially if you're unaccustomed to them.

While Robyn gulped breath after fresh breath through her mouth, I stared up through the wooden railing at the second-floor loft directly over the cabin's small kitchen, breathing deeply to analyze the details of the tragedy I smelled upstairs.

"Sorry," Robyn murmured as she stepped into the cabin, clutching the straps of my backpack, her teeth clenched against an obvious gag reflex. She sucked in another long, slow breath and I could see her fighting to control the impulse to flee the stench. "There's a corpse?" she asked, and I nodded, still staring at the loft.

She glanced over the worn living room furniture, the small, grimy kitchenette, and a fireplace full of ash, but found no obvious source for the stench of death. And finally, her gaze traveled up toward the loft, where my feline nose had already pinpointed the source. "It's up there?"

I padded toward the threadbare couch, where a woman's purse sat on the edge of the left-hand cushion. Reaching up, I nudged the bag with one paw, and it fell, spilling makeup, tissues, and assorted other belongings across a wood plank floor worn smooth by years of traffic. I sniffed the contents, familiarizing myself with the trace scents of the owner.

"Is it Justus?" Robyn whispered, dragging her gaze away from the loft.

I shook my head. Then I lay down on the floor and began to shift, because there wasn't much more I could tell her—or that I could do—in cat form.

While my body tore itself apart and slowly, painfully reassembled itself in a human configuration of muscle and bone, Robyn set my backpack on the floor next to me, then crossed the small room toward the narrow staircase.

I wanted her to wait for me—she shouldn't have to find a decaying corpse by herself—but until my shift was complete, I could only listen to the wood creak as she climbed the stairs.

As my shift wound down with a few soft, gristly pops and deep bone creaks, Robyn gasped. I sat up to find her standing hunched over in the loft, because of the valued ceiling, which only reached its eight foot height directly above a full-sized bed, the end of which I could see through the railing.

I dumped my backpack on the floor and scrambled to pull on my pants, then raced up the steps two at a time. The smell of decay was distinctly weaker in human form, but immeasurably worse, because my human brain processed not just the facts—rot equals death—but the more complex and devastating emotional reality.

Someone has died.

Someone female, whose purse still sat abandoned on the floor of the cabin.

The dead girl lay on the bed—the only piece of furniture in the cabin loft—atop the rumpled, old-fashioned bedspread. She was fully dressed, her sightless eyes staring up at the ceiling. Though the stench was terrible, there was no visible sign of decay. Her identity was clear. We'd found Ivy Lowe.

But someone else had found her first.

Chunks of flesh were missing from Ivy's left calf. Something had been *eating* her. There was relatively little blood on the blanket beneath her, which meant her heart had stopped beating before the meal began.

Still... "Son of a *bitch*," I whispered.

"I don't... I can't..." Robyn's words seemed to get lost on their way out. I wrapped my arms around her and turned her to face the stairs. Slowly, her hands found my back, until she was squeezing me in a desperate hug. "Someone was *eating* her, Titus."

"We don't know that it was a shifter." *Please, God, don't let it be Justus...* "The door was open. Anything could have gotten into the cabin."

"How did she die?" Robyn's focus was glued to my face as if she couldn't stand to look at the body anymore.

"My guess would be scratch fever." I stood and lifted Ivy's arm, where an inflamed but visibly shallow set of scratches marred her flesh. I repositioned her arm at her side, and when I backed up, my heel hit something. "She had a rifle." I knelt to pick it up, then slid back the lever on top. "The round is jammed." I thought for a moment. "Okay. So maybe Justus came to the cabin after he infected Corey Morris. Which could still have been an accident," I insisted. Robyn didn't argue. "Ivy got scared, obviously, but her rifle didn't fire." *Miracle of miracles.* "Maybe she swung it like a bat and fought him off, or maybe she dropped it. Either way, he infected her."

"You don't know that," Robyn pointed out. "She never shifted, and her wounds are too shallow to get much of a scent out of, so we can't be sure who infected her."

"We can make a reasonable assumption. Justus was the only shifter out here that night, and we know he infected Corey Morris. Who was here with Ivy and…" I frowned. "What happened to the other guy? Morris's roommate at Ole Miss. What was his name?"

"Leland something. He was Ivy's boyfriend." Robyn frowned. "Except we don't know whether she was cheating on Justus or on Leland. Either way, that would definitely be enough to set off a newly infected stray. Especially if your brother smelled the other guy on her."

"So, what, we're thinking that Justus followed them out here, maybe to confront them, maybe to confirm his suspicions? Then he got upset and lost control?"

Robyn shrugged. "That's happened to me."

"That's happened to all of us. But most of us don't kill."

"I don't think he meant to." Robyn gestured to Ivy's arm again. "Her gun didn't work, yet he barely scratched her. If he was newly infected himself and didn't have the benefit of the counseling and information you give your new strays, he probably had no idea that scratching her would kill her. He may even have been defending himself from a rifle used as a baseball bat."

"Okay." The temptation to cling to her interpretation of events was strong. I didn't want to think that my little brother had become a murderer. But I couldn't just dismiss the other possibilities because I loved Justus. "We'd know for sure if we could find him."

"He's not the only one missing. According to Corey Morris, Leland was with Ivy in the cabin when he was infected."

"You think Justus infected him too?"

Robyn shrugged. "Chances of him leaving unscathed are slim, right?"

I nodded. *Especially if he was sleeping with Justus's girlfriend.* Even in humans, that kind of betrayal often led to violence. To a newly infected shifter unable to control his instincts and urges…?

"This is why the Pride has to be recognized. New strays need structure and assistance. Education. Support. If Justus and whoever infected him knew what they were becoming, they wouldn't have spread the infection." I *had* to believe that.

"Agreed. So, what do we do with her?" Robyn braved another glance at the body. "I assume we can't call the police."

"You assume correctly. If she made it to the morgue, at the very least, they'd put out a warning about large cats, and hunters would flock to the area hoping to bag one."

"So what are we supposed to do with her? We can't leave her here."

"We'll bury her. We can do that, at least."

"But this is her family's property," Robyn pointed out. "When they realize she's missing, won't this be the first place people look? They'd notice a fresh grave."

"Yes, but we're burying her out of respect and to delay the inevitability of discovery, not to hide anything," I explained. "An autopsy would turn up no evidence of foul play, other than the burial itself, and if they test her blood, the lab will likely assume the sample was contaminated by the cat that scratched her." I shrugged. "The cops will have a mystery, but no true crime to investigate."

I glanced around, hoping for a throw blanket or something to cover her with, but there was nothing except the bedding she was already lying on. "Hopefully there's a shovel in here somewhere."

The cabin itself turned up nothing more useful than a few large spoons in a drawer beneath the microwave. But a small shed stood in the clearing out back, and inside we found an ax for chopping firewood and two shovels.

One of them was broken.

While I started digging the grave, among the trees well behind the shed, Robyn wrapped poor Ivy in the blanket she'd died on and brought her outside.

"She can't have been dead for more than a day," Robyn said as she carefully laid the body on the ground, near the still-shallow hole. If she weren't a shifter, she never could have carried a woman nearly her own size down the stairs by herself, in a cradle hold. "How can she possibly smell so bad?"

"From the amount of ash in the fireplace, I suspect the fire burned for a while after she died. That would have kept the cabin warm, even with the door ajar, which accelerates the decomposition process." I threw another shovelful of dirt onto the growing pile next to the grave. "Even so, we're much more aware of the smell than any human would be."

Robyn brushed her hands down the front of the black wool coat she'd borrowed from me. "I think you're going to have to burn this. And not just to get rid of evidence."

"Fortunately, Justus has a fireplace."

For a while, I dug in silence, except for the thunk of the shovel into the soil and the chorus of crickets. Robyn stared at the blanket-wrapped bundle, and she was quiet for so long that I started to worry.

"You okay?" I finally asked, wiping a thin sheen of sweat from my forehead, in spite of the cold.

"Is this what would have happened to me, if I hadn't survived scratch fever?" Her voice sounded strained. "Would Jace and Abby have buried me in an unmarked grave in the woods where I died?"

"You didn't die."

"But if I had?"

She was going to make me say it. "If you'd died, then yes. They would have done the best they could by you, which probably would have meant digging two feet deeper than the six-foot hole I'm digging for Ivy." I'd never had to dig an entire grave on my own. In the past, I'd had enforcers with shovels of their own to help. The work wasn't difficult, with a shifter's strength. But it was tedious.

"What about her family?" Robyn asked. But what she really wanted to know about was her own family, in the event of that hypothetical death. "They'll never know what happened to her, will they? She'll just be…gone."

"With any luck, yes." I pushed the shovel into another clump of packed earth and wrenched more dirt loose. "At least this way, they can hope she's still alive somewhere. Isn't that better than knowing how she died?"

"No." Robyn didn't hesitate. "False hope is never better." She stood and brushed dirt from her pants and the back of my coat. "Here, let me dig for a while."

"No need. I'm nearly done."

"I'm bored." She took the shovel from me, and after five minutes of watching, I was ready to pull clods of dirt from the earth by hand, just to have something to do.

"Why don't you see if there's anything to drink in the cabin?" she said when she noticed me fidgeting.

"Thirst-quenching or recreational?"

"Thirst-quenching." She pushed hair from her face and left a smear of dirt across her forehead. "You know. Because of all the shoveling."

"I'm on it." I circled to the front of the cabin and was pleased, when I stepped inside, to find that the smell of decay had faded significantly with the removal of Ivy's body.

The refrigerator held nothing but an out-of-date box of baking soda, and the cabinets were empty, so I grabbed the empty water bottle from my backpack and refilled it from the sink. I was halfway to the door again when I heard a scream and a thud from outside.

Alarm raised every hair on my body. Pulse pounding, I raced down the front steps and around the small cabin, then past the shed, where a growl clawed its way up my throat from my gut.

Robyn lay pinned to the ground by a large shifter with his front paws on her shoulders, his muzzle inches from her neck.

His head snapped up when he heard me, and his gaze met mine. A low growl rumbled from his throat.

I skidded to a stop in the dirt, my hands up to show him I meant no harm, still holding the water bottle. I knew with one look at him that this cat wasn't Justus. There was no recognition in his gaze.

Shoving down the fury raging inside me at the sight of Robyn in danger, I spoke in a low, even voice to keep him calm. "Hey. It's okay. We're not here to hurt you, and we don't want anything."

He continued to growl, but softer than before.

"My name is Titus Alexander. The lady you have pinned down is Robyn Sheffield. We're shifters. Like you."

The cat's head cocked in an oddly human look of confusion, and I took that as confirmation that he was listening and that he could understand me. Though something in my statement had clearly puzzled him.

"Smell her," I said, but the cat only blinked at me. "Seriously, smell her."

Robyn gasped when he lowered his muzzle to her neck, and for a moment I wondered if I'd made a huge mistake. If he bit her throat instead of smelling it, she was as good as dead.

If that happened, nothing would keep me from ripping him apart with my bare hands.

But the cat only sniffed her skin, then turned to me.

"Smells familiar, right? That's because she's a shifter, just like you. Just like me. You seem a little confused about what's happened to you, so I'm going to take a guess, and you nod if I'm right. Okay?" I said, but he only stared at me, still standing on Robyn's shoulders while she took even, measured breaths, obviously trying to lie very still. "I'm guessing you were attacked by a cat who looked like you do now, a couple of days ago."

I wasn't close enough to get a good whiff of his

scent with my human-form nose, but unless we'd stumbled upon a scratch fever epidemic, there was only one logical conclusion for me to draw, having concluded that this shifter was not my brother. "Is your name Leland?"

The cat cocked his head to the side again, silently asking me a question.

"It was an educated guess. We met a friend of yours yesterday," I explained. "Corey Morris. He told us that you and he had come out to the cabin the other night with Ivy, and that a cat had attacked him. He didn't know that cat was a shifter until we explained it to him, and I'm guessing you didn't either." I gave him a second to respond, but he didn't seem to know how. "If I'm right, you can nod your head."

Leland's muzzle bobbed up and down, hesitantly at first, and I could practically see the lightbulb flare in the air over his head. With that one gesture, he'd bridged the gap between his feline and human halves. Understanding that he was capable of human thought and communication even in cat form was the first step toward the harmonious co-existence of both parts of himself.

"Good. Now, if you'll let Robyn up, she and I can finish giving Ivy a proper burial, and if you want, we can talk you through shifting back into human form. Have you done that yet?"

Leland slowly shook his muzzle back and forth.

"Well, we'd be happy to help."

"If you'll get off me," Robyn reiterated, her words strained by the weight on her chest.

And finally, Leland backed carefully off her.

"Thanks." Robyn sat up slowly, careful not to

spook him with any sudden movements. When he seemed calm, she stood, just as slowly, and began brushing dirt and leaves from the back of her—my—wool coat.

It took all my restraint to keep from pulling her into my arms, away from him, and kissing her. From telling her how stupid I'd been to push her away. She could have died. I could have *lost* her.

But I couldn't tell her any of that with him listening. A new stray should not know how much power he'd wielded. Or how close I'd been to killing him.

"Is it okay with you if we finish burying Ivy?" Robyn asked, impressively composed, after what she'd been through.

After a long moment of hesitation, Leland nodded.

"Why don't I do that while you talk him through a shift?" I picked up the shovel where it had obviously landed when he'd pounced on her, prepared to use it as a weapon, if I had to. The sooner we got Leland in human form, the sooner we could question him about Justus. And disarm him of his claws.

Robyn shrugged with a glance at Leland. "I'm game if you are."

FIFTEEN

Robyn

Still spooked from my near-death experience, I walked Leland away from the grave, hyper-conscious that if I startled him, I could wind up right back in the dirt, with him on my chest. Leland's infection and transition had obviously been even more traumatic than mine, and until then, he'd never even met another shifter. He would be taking his very first behavioral cues from us, and I understood that if he didn't trust us, rather than helping a stray, we'd be creating a rogue. A *true* wildcat.

While Titus finished digging the hole, I gave Leland softly-voiced, patient instructions for how to take his shift into his own hands. "You aren't at the mercy of it," I told him. "I know you didn't have any choice that first time, but you do now. And the same goes for all your new feline instincts and urges. No matter which form you're in, *you* are in charge of your body, not the other way around. But sometimes the easiest way to exercise that control is to relinquish a little bit of it. Your body knows what to do. All you have to do is get out of your own way."

By the time the hole was deep enough, Leland was nearly finished with his shift. As Titus lifted Ivy's lifeless body and lowered her into the grave, Leland carefully rose from the leaf-strewn dirt—finally human and naked—to watch.

"She deserved better." His voice cracked on the last word. "I didn't mean to… I was just so hungry." Chill bumps stood out on his arms, but he didn't seem to notice the cold.

Titus hesitated with the first shovelful of dirt. "Do you want to say anything to her?"

Leland nodded, and light from the waning moon shined on his dark hair. He stepped forward until he could see into the hole, wincing when his heel snapped through a twig. "I'm so sorry, Ivy," he whispered. "If I could take it back, I would." Then he stepped away with a somber nod, and Titus began shoveling dirt into the grave. After a few minutes, I grabbed the bottom half of the broken shovel from the shed and began to help. Then Leland pitched in with his bare hands.

By the time Ivy was properly buried, we were all three covered in dirt and sweat.

Titus took the broken shovel from me and set both of them inside the shed. "Come on, Leland…what's your last name?"

"Blum. Leland Blum," the naked stray said.

"Come on, Leland Blum." Titus gestured for him to come with us into the cabin. "Let's get cleaned up and find you something to wear. I think I have some spare clothes in my backpack."

"Do you always travel with extra clothes?" I asked as we rounded the side of the cabin, headed for the front door.

"I started carrying a spare set after I was infected, because I tended to lose track of where I'd left my clothes after I shifted." He glanced at Leland, clearly eager to begin...mentoring. "That's what we call the transformation from human to cat, and vice versa."

Leland rolled his eyes. "Wow. That's not cheesy at all."

"Right?" I said, surprised by his sarcasm. Frankly. I was impressed that he wasn't curled up in a corner, whimpering, considering what he'd been through.

Inside, I found rags in one of the kitchenette drawers, then wet them at the sink and passed them out. "This would be a lot easier if there were a bathroom," I said as I scrubbed dirt from my forehead. "Or a mirror."

Titus grunted as he brushed loose earth from the front of his jeans.

"This place pre-dates indoor plumbing." Leland rinsed his dirty rag, then began scrubbing his left arm. "Ivy said her grandparents put the kitchenette in, but her grandfather refused to add a bathroom, when he could just pee out the back door."

"I wonder what her grandmother thought of that?" I mused as I ran my rag over my throat and the grimy skin exposed above the collar of my shirt. For a couple of minutes, we worked in silence. Then Titus rinsed his rag again and turned to Leland.

"How long were you and Ivy together?" he asked, and though Leland probably didn't pick up on it, I could tell how much the answer meant to him by the too-casual tone of his voice. By the tension in his shoulders.

"Nearly two years. Since our senior year in high

school."

Titus stiffened almost imperceptibly. Ivy was cheating on her boyfriend with Justus. Titus's brother was the other man.

I rinsed my rag under the faucet, then draped it over the divide in the sink to dry. I was as clean as I was going to get without a shower. "Leland, can you tell us what happened the other day? The night of the attack?"

The new stray frowned first at me, then at Titus. "I thought you already knew."

"Corey Morris gave us the broad strokes, but he only knew what happened to him." I sank to my knees next to the couch and began putting Ivy's things into her purse. "He had no idea you and Ivy were infected. You'd be helping us out if you could give us the details."

"What details do you want?"

"Did you know the shifter who...infected you?" Titus asked.

Blum's bewildered expression said as much as his answer did. "I don't know *any* shifters. I didn't even know there were shifters, and I didn't know that cat was one until you told me." He dropped his rag into the sink without bothering to rinse it, then plucked the last clean one from the drawer. "All I know is that Ivy and I were on the couch, getting...intimate." His gaze strayed to the couch while he ran hot water over the clean rag. "Then we heard Corey shouting from outside. I opened the door but before I could even step onto the porch, this cat was there. He was *huge*. Bigger than a bobcat—more like a mountain lion, but solid black."

"Yes, we're all black in cat form." I set Ivy's

repacked purse on the scuffed up coffee table, and I wondered if we should have buried it with her.

"Well, he just pounced on me. He drove me to the floor, and his claws dug into my shoulders. See?" Blum wiped the dirt from his left shoulder, exposing four small puncture wounds, crusted with dried blood. "They're deeper than they look. I thought he was going to eat my face off or something, but then Ivy screamed and ran up into the loft. The cat went after her, and I froze. She was terrified. Screaming. And all I could do was stand there."

"She had a gun?" Titus prompted, when Leland seemed lost in the memory.

"Yeah. Her dad kept an old hunting rifle under the bed. But it wouldn't fire, so she swung it at the cat. Hit him several times. Finally, he took off, right out the front door. I locked it behind him and went to check on Ivy."

"She was scratched?" Titus said, when the new stray's gaze lost focus in the direction of the loft.

Leland nodded. "On one arm. It bled a little, but it was nothing fatal. For a while, we stared out the window, trying to see if the cat was still out there. We thought Corey was dead, but we were scared to go check, and he wasn't answering his phone." He bent to wipe the dirt from his bare legs, without pausing in his story. "When we were finally sure the cat had left, we took a couple of knives from the kitchen and went to look for him. We found his phone, but Corey was gone. So was the car. He just...left us out here."

"I'm so sorry," I said, gutted by the look on Leland's face. "Corey got scratched pretty good, and he drove himself to the emergency room. But you should know that he had no idea you and Ivy were hurt."

"Not that it matters now." Leland wiped the last of the visible dirt from the top of his right foot, then tossed the second dirty rag into the sink. "Walking through the woods in the dark seemed stupid, with a wild cat on the loose, so we decided to stay in the cabin for the night. But by then, we were both running a fever. I tried to take care of Ivy. I brought her water from the sink and gave her some ibuprofen from her purse. But then I passed out." Leland closed his eyes. "When I woke up, she was dead."

"That wasn't your fault." Titus unzipped his backpack and pulled out a spare shirt and pair of jeans. They'd be big on Leland, but better than nothing. "Women never survive the infection. Well, almost never," he said with a glance at me. "There's nothing you could have done for her."

Leland accepted the pants Titus held out. "I could have not eaten her."

"You were terrified and in shock," I said as he stepped into the jeans. "And probably ravenous after your first shift." I remembered that blind hunger. But when I'd gone through it, I'd known who and where I was. I'd known what was happening, because Abby was there to explain everything. I couldn't imagine suffering through what Leland had.

"Yeah." He buttoned the jeans, then took the shirt Titus gave him. "That, and I was locked in here. The front door was closed, and once I turned into a cat—I thought I was losing *my mind*—I couldn't get it open. And after a while, nothing felt real. I couldn't really be a cat, and if I wasn't really a cat, I thought maybe Ivy wasn't really dead. I mean, maybe her body was a hallucination. And I was *starving*."

"How did you get the door open?" I asked.

"I kept trying. Like, fifty thousand times. Pushing down on one side of the knob with one paw. Eventually, it turned enough for the latch to disengage. That was last night, I think."

"So, you've been in the woods since then?" Titus asked, digging through his bag for more clothing.

"Yeah. I ate some squirrels. A rabbit. I slept under a tree. Then I heard a car engine. I watched you guys go into the cabin. Then you came out with Ivy, and..." He shrugged and pulled Titus's shirt over his head. Then he frowned and pulled the hem of the material up to his nose. He inhaled deeply. Then he fixed an accusing gaze on the Alpha. "Is this your shirt?"

"Yes." Titus put the bag down and gave Leland his full attention. "But it's not what you think."

"I don't know what I think." Leland frowned. "I know this scent. Why do I know your scent?"

I watched Titus, waiting for some hint about how to proceed.

He exhaled and gestured toward the couch. "Leland, why don't you sit down, and I'll explain."

"I think I'll stand." The new stray's fist clenched around a handful of Titus's shirt, and I realized he was seconds from coming to the same erroneous conclusion Corey Morris had come to. That Titus had infected him.

"That's fine." Titus kept his voice low and even. "My scent is similar to my brother's. And you probably recognize his scent, at least subconsciously, because my brother, Justus, is the cat who infected you."

"Your *brother?*" Leland demanded. "Your brother

turned me into this? And killed Ivy?"

"We think that was an accident." I stood, careful to give him some space. "If Justus had wanted either of you dead, he could have killed you. And he probably had no idea that scratching you would infect you."

"Probably?" Leland turned to Titus, but kept me visible in his periphery.

"Justus is newly infected, himself. We're still trying to find out what he knows," Titus said. "The last time I saw my brother, he was human. I have no idea who infected him, or how much he understands of what he is, and I won't know any of that until we find him. That's why we're here. Looking for my brother. I don't suppose you know a student at Millsaps named Justus Alexander…?"

"No."

"Are you sure?" I asked.

"I think I'd remember if I met someone named Justus. It sounds like it came from a superhero name generator. You know, 'He defends truth, Justus, and the American way!'"

I pretended to scratch my nose, disguising a smile. And the fact that I'd had a very similar thought, earlier in the evening.

"I mean seriously," Leland said. "Whose name is Justus?"

"My brother is the only one I've ever met," Titus admitted.

"Okay, so now what?" I said. But what I truly wanted to ask was, "What do we do with this new stray?"

And the answer was no simpler than the question. We couldn't just let Leland Blum go. He needed to know what to expect in his new life. He needed to know there was a support system in place for him. He needed to know the rules. But we couldn't take him Titus's house.

No one could know that Justus Alexander had created two strays and accidentally killed a woman. At least not until Titus and I could find him, find out exactly what had happened, and come up with a reasonable defense.

Titus shrugged, glancing from me to Leland Blum. "Now...we'll have to take him with us."

"So, what?" I whispered, when the sound of running water from the bathroom told me that Leland was in the shower. "We're going to put him up in your brother's apartment? What happens if Justus comes home?"

"We count ourselves lucky to have found him," Titus said as he pressed buttons on a fancy built-in coffee maker I couldn't make heads or tails of.

"True, but Justus won't be happy to see his girlfriend's other boyfriend." I rubbed my forehead, fending off a headache from hunger, lack of sleep, and contemplating the consequences of a shifter love triangle gone wrong. "Do you think he knew Ivy was cheating with him, or you think she kept both men unaware of the other?"

"I have no idea," Titus said. "We don't even know for sure that she and Justus were more than friends."

"He must have thought they were," I said. "Otherwise, why would he follow her to the cabin in the first place?"

Titus exhaled slowly. I could see his reluctance to think ill of his brother, but the evidence was not in Justus's favor. "Either way, we can't leave Leland alone so soon after being infected, and we can't turn him over to Drew without incriminating my brother. So he has to stay with us, and we have to stay here, at least for the rest of the night, in case Justus comes home." He glanced around the kitchen with a confused, frustrated expression.

"I get that." I handed Titus the mug he seemed to have forgotten he'd taken down from an upper cabinet. "But this seems like a bad idea, considering how territorial some shifters are."

"Well, if you come across a better idea, let me know. In the meantime, there's another shower." He pointed over my shoulder to Justus's bedroom, which had a small bathroom of its own. "Why don't you get cleaned up while I make us all something to eat?"

That was the best idea I'd heard in days.

I turned on the shower in Justus's spotless bathroom—his tantrum hadn't extended that far—and while I waited for the water to warm, I ventured into his trashed bedroom out of curiosity, and the overwhelming urge to straighten up.

I turned his laundry hamper right-side up and began collecting the clothes strewn all over the floor. The hamper was nearly full, but the room looked much better, when I picked up a shirt discarded in the corner near the closet, and my fingers brushed something stiff. Dried blood, surrounding several three-inch long claw-shaped rips in the fabric.

A quick sniff confirmed that the blood was Justus's, and that he'd still been human when he'd shed it. He'd been wearing the shirt when he was infected. But I could detect no ribbon-scent of an infector. Surely he'd been wearing more than just the shirt when he was attacked…

Steam rolled into the bedroom through the bathroom doorway, but I ignored it as I sat on my knees in the middle of the newly tidied floor and dumped the hamper out.

"Robyn?" Titus opened the bedroom door in time to catch me sniffing a pair of his brother's pants.

"Hi." I dropped the jeans onto the pile. "This isn't what it looks like. Though I'm not really sure what this looks like."

He glanced into the living room, then stepped into his brother's room and closed the door, his brows arched in amusement. "I'm going to need a little more information than that."

"Okay. I thought I'd do some detective-slash-cleaning work while the shower warmed up, and I found this shirt with your brother's dried blood on it." I tossed him the shirt, and Titus caught it in one hand. "I think that's what he was wearing when he was infected, but you can't tell anything from his blood, because he hadn't shifted yet. Then I thought that his attacker might have left a scent on whatever else Justus was wearing…"

"Which is why you're sniffing the crotch of my brother's jeans?"

"Yes. No." My cheeks flamed, but Titus only laughed. "I wasn't sniffing his crotch specifically. Would you like to join me?"

He laughed again. "That is the single most bizarre invitation I've ever received from a woman, but yes. I'll join you in sniffing my brother's jeans."

We went through Justus's dirty pants

227

systematically, and after the eighth pair, I decided he had much too large a wardrobe. But finally, Titus held up a faded pair of jeans in triumph. "More blood." He held the stain beneath his nose and inhaled, then frowned. "It's Justus's. If there was ever a trace of his attacker, it's faded too much for me to detect. Which probably means he wasn't infected in the past week."

"I'm sorry. I was hopeful." I grabbed an armload of his brother's dirty clothes and stuffed them into the hamper.

"It was worth a shot." Titus stood and headed for the door. "Go ahead and shower, then you can join me and Leland for a three AM snack and a quick rundown on shifter dos and don'ts."

"Give me five minutes."

Only once I stood wrapped in a towel, dripping shower water on the bath mat, did I realize I had nothing to wear that wasn't covered in dirt and leaves.

I tightened the towel around my chest, then ventured into the living room. Though I had no modesty issues with nudity associated with a shift, I wasn't going to walk around naked all night in a stranger's apartment. Especially considering that our new stray hadn't yet been truly introduced to the ways of life as a shifter.

"So Alpha is a job?" Leland said from the leather arm chair as I stepped out of the bedroom. "Or more like a rank?"

"It's both." Titus's hair was damp, and I could smell his shampoo from across the room. Somehow, he'd beaten me out of the shower. "And those usually go hand in hand. Shifters with the most strength and leadership potential typically rise organically to the position of Alpha. Though there are exceptions. For instance, until this evening, I was an Alpha."

"You're still an Alpha," I said, and they both turned to look at me. "You're just not currently in charge of anyone."

Titus's brows rose again with a glance at my towel. "Oh." I shrugged. "Yeah, we forgot to go shopping."

"I'm sure I have something you can wear." He stood and disappeared into the spare bedroom, then returned with a clean T-shirt and a pair of jogging pants. "They'll be big, but they'll work until we can wash your clothes again. And in the morning, we'll go shopping."

"Thanks." I took the clothes back into Justus's room to change. The jogging pants had a functioning drawstring, thank goodness, but the shirt would swallow me whole. It was clean, but not unworn. Or maybe it had simply mingled with other clothes that held his scent in his suitcase. Either way, I pulled the shirt over my head, and the next breath I took was like inhaling Titus. Like how you can walk by a lotion and soap store in the mall, and for a second, the whole world smells like vanilla and lavender. Except my world now smelled like him.

Fascinated, I pulled the collar of his shirt up over my nose and inhaled again. A bolt of warmth trailed down my stomach to settle into lower, more sensitive places. Every inhalation I took reminded me that he was there. That he was close. That I wanted to touch him.

I towel-dried my hair, then rejoined Titus and Leland in the living room, just in time to hear the Alpha explain exactly why the new stray couldn't tell anyone about what had happened to him. "I swear to you there's a network in place to help you. People you can talk to, who can teach you everything you need to know. As soon as I get this situation with my brother figured out, I'll take you to them. Until then, it's just me. But you can ask me anything."

"Me too." I squeezed between Titus's knees and the coffee table, then plopped down on the couch next to him. From the chair across from us, Leland offered me a tray of pita chips and hummus, and I gladly accepted. "I'll tell you anything you want to know."

"Is there a cure?" Leland asked without hesitation. "Or will I be stuck like this?"

"There's no cure," Titus said. "Your body has been changed on a genetic level. But you're not stuck. With practice, you'll gain total control of the shifting process, and I promise you that after that, being a shifter has more advantages than disadvantages."

"Unless you want marriage and kids," I said around a mouthful of pita and hummus. When Leland gave me a horrified look, I realized my mistake. "I'm sorry." I swallowed my bite. "I don't want marriage and kids, and most of the men I've dated have claimed to feel the same, so I assumed…" Which made an ass out of me, as the saying goes.

"Ivy and I were going to get married," Leland said. "I hadn't asked her, or anything, but we'd talked about it. I always assumed that after college…" His voice trailed off as his gaze lost focus.

"I'm sorry. And I wasn't clear," I admitted. "It's not that you can't get married or have kids. It's just that because of the gender imbalance, that's very difficult to do without exposing yourself as a shifter. Which is completely off limits."

Leland frowned. "What if someone who's already

married gets infected?"

We both looked to Titus for the answer to that.

"So far, that hasn't happened, that we know of. But the potential for situations like that is one of the reasons we're working so hard to get our Pride recognized by the larger shifter social and political structure. For guidance. And support. And resources."

Leland's eyes had glazed over again.

"Why don't you get some sleep?" I turned to Titus. "We should give him the guest room." Because if Justus came home and found his dead lover's boyfriend on his couch...

"Of course." Titus stood with Leland's empty glass. "The bed is freshly made. Help yourself to whatever you need from the closet and the dresser. Though, fair warning, everything in there carries my scent."

"Thank you." Leland stood, and I watched him shuffle into the bedroom and close the door. He looked tired and unsteady enough to fall over.

"I'll make up the other bed for you," Titus said, as I bit into another pita chip.

"You can have it." I patted the soft leather couch. "This thing seems pretty comfy."

Titus backed into his brother's room without breaking eye contact. "Justus shouldn't find you on the couch for the same reason he shouldn't find Leland there."

I glanced at him in amusement. "Because I slept with his girlfriend too?"

He rolled his eyes. "Because you're a stranger. I'll stay in the living room."

"Fine." I set the tray on the coffee table and

followed him into his brother's room. "But let me help with the bed."

While he pulled the used bedding from his brother's mattress, I set the laundry hamper against one wall. As I lifted the bloody pair of pants to set them inside, a folded sheet of paper fell from one of the pockets.

I dropped the pants into the hamper, then picked up the paper and unfolded it. "Um...Titus?"

"Yeah?" He pulled a pillow from its case, then dropped them both on the floor.

"Did you know your brother went to the ER two weeks ago? The paperwork says he had lacerations consistent with an animal attack, and an infection." I scanned the paper. "I guess now we know when he was infected."

He let go of the second pillow he'd picked up and took the receipt I held out to him. "He went to Baptist. Spencer must not have been working that night."

"Would he have recognized Justus?"

"Probably, from the pictures in my house. And he definitely would have recognized the symptoms of scratch fever." He frowned, reading silently from the discharge page. "Two weeks. He's been dealing with this for two weeks, and I had no idea."

"This *really* isn't your fault."

Titus folded the paperwork and slid it into his back pocket. "We have to find him."

"We will." I circled the bed and pulled the fitted sheet free from the top left corner of the mattress. The sheets smelled like Titus, and I—

No, the sheets smelled like *Justus*. Not Titus. *This is not Titus's bed.*

"I can do that." He tried to take the sheet from me, but I stepped past him and unhooked another corner, then pulled the sheet completely off the bed. "Just throw it in the hamper," he said, pulling the top sheet free from a tangle with the comforter.

I dumped the material on top of Justus's bloody pants, then grabbed the clean fitted sheet he'd set on top of the top of the dresser.

"You don't need to make the bed." He tried to take the sheet from me, but I pulled it out of reach.

"I want to."

"I'd rather you didn't," he said.

"Why?" I studied his face, confused by his insistence. "If you're trying to prove you don't think only women are suited to domestic work, you can relax. I've already seen you wash dishes, prepare food, and help strip the bed. You're scoring points for feminism left and right."

Titus smiled. "It's because you're my guest. I'm supposed to protect you and show you hospitality, yet I've dragged you out of my home, rather than making you comfortable in it, and I let some strange stray pounce on you in the woods. I've failed in every duty a host has, and if I let you make your own bed, that'll be one more failure."

I stared at him for a moment. Then I burst into laughter.

"Why is that funny?"

"Because you didn't drag me out of your house. You didn't even invite me into it. I broke into your car. I slammed into your life like a fucking missile, throwing up shrapnel. But you fed me and gave me somewhere to sleep. Hell, you gave me your clothes. If that's not proper hospitality, I don't know what is."

Titus's gaze strayed to my shirt—to *his* shirt—and stuck there. Heat flared behind his gaze. "You smell like me," he growled, but his tone wasn't angry. It was the floodgate holding back some primal need churning behind his eyes.

"Yeah." I ran one hand over the front of the shirt, holding his gaze. "It's distracting, honestly. I can smell you *all over me*."

Titus dropped the sheet and pulled me closer by a handful of the borrowed shirt. I laughed and wrapped my arms around his neck, as his hands found my hips, over the bunched waist of the drawstring pants. He kissed me. And his scent swallowed me whole.

"Wait, I thought we weren't supposed to do this," I said when his mouth trailed down my neck.

His deep chuckle sent a thrill through me. "I thought this was what you wanted."

"It is," I groaned, fighting the urge to abandon words entirely as his mouth traveled over my shoulder, pushing the broad neck of the borrowed shirt out of the way. "But I need to know it's what *you* want. In spite of the consequences." I'd made my point—it was none of anyone else's business if I wanted to kiss Titus, Alpha or not. But I couldn't cause him any more trouble, especially considering everything else he was already dealing with.

Titus stood straight, and the heat in his eyes nearly roasted me alive. He pressed the length of his body against mine, and I could feel how badly he wanted me. "Any more questions?" The gravely quality of his voice resonated deep inside me, and I wanted to roll around in that sound. I wanted to hear it in the dark, in the middle of the night.

I wanted to hear it in my dreams.

But…

I put one hand on his chest and took a step back. "Wanting this right now isn't enough, Titus. I don't want to be what keeps you from leading your Pride. From getting it officially recognized. From helping all the people who need you."

"You aren't the problem," he said. "The council is the problem. Their rules don't allow for the fact that strays face a different reality than natural-born shifters. For the reality of mistakes made before we even know they're mistakes. But at some point, they're going to realize that their world is changing. That a political power structure that doesn't support the majority of its citizens—whether or not they're acknowledged as citizens—can't stay in power for long. I believe that time is coming, with or without me. With or without you. And I'm no longer willing to pretend I don't want to touch you just so they *might* consider acknowledging a populace they have no right to reject in the first place."

I smiled up at him, my pulse racing in response to his. "You're hot when you get political."

His arms slid around me, and the stubble on his chin caught in my hair. "I can recite the US presidents in chronological order," he whispered.

"That's a shame," I whispered back. "You might get laid if you could do it alphabetically…"

"John Adams. John Quincy Adams." He pulled his shirt off and dropped it on the floor, his heated gaze challenging me to make good on my word. "Chester A. Arthur. James—"

SIXTEEN

Robyn

"—Buchanan."

I laughed as I pushed him onto the bed, suddenly glad we hadn't made it past the fitted sheet.

Titus looked up at me, and his grin kindled a fire in low and sensitive places. "Do you need to hear more, or are you convinced?"

I settled onto the bed over him, straddling his hips, and the position gave me a tantalizing sense of control. And another intimate brush with the very warm, very hard evidence of his arousal. "I'm convinced of your alphabetical proficiency, Mr. Alexander. But I might need you to demonstrate a few other critical skills…" I rocked forward, pressing myself into him.

Titus groaned beneath me, and that sense of control swelled into a provocative sense of power. What other noises could I get out of him?

Intrigued, I leaned forward slowly, holding his gaze as long as I could, until my cheek brushed the stubbly length of his jaw. I bit his ear with just enough pressure to draw a little gasp from his throat. Pleased with the sound, I rolled my hips again and sucked his earlobe into my mouth, grazing it with my teeth.

Titus moaned softly. His hands found my hips, and he guided them back, then rocked me forward again, pulling me firmer against him. Tearing a groan from me.

Eager now, I shimmied down the length of his body, dragging my tongue along his neck. His hands slid over my waist and beneath my shirt, skimming my ribs, then circling to my spine. Leaving chills in their wake.

"Mmmm..." I mumbled against his chest, between nibbling kisses. I inched my way lower, trailing my tongue over the peak of his left nipple, then down the hard planes of his chest. Every inch of his skin was stretched taut over well-defined muscle. He was pure power, draped in human flesh and held in check by an iron will I suddenly had the desperate urge to test.

I nibbled and licked my way down his chest, delighting in every groan and inhalation, and the lower I went, the higher Titus's hands pulled my shirt. By the time I dipped my tongue into the well of his navel, he was breathing in short pants, his hands fisted around the hem of the shirt caught beneath my breasts.

"Robyn..." he moaned, and the throaty sound of my name sent a lick of heat south of my own navel.

Titus sat up, pushing me back, but his hands steadied me as I stood. He pulled the borrowed shirt over my head with agonizing slowness, his fingers skimming my arms as they went. Finally, the shirt hit the floor

He let his hands glide down my sides, warm against my skin, but his gaze was the more intimate touch as it slid over my breasts, then found its way to my face. "God, you're beautiful." He pulled me into a deep, hungry kiss, as my hands explored his chest.

Titus groaned again and picked me up as he stood. I wrapped my legs around him, then he turned and placed me on the bed. "Pants," I gasped.

Titus unbuttoned his jeans and pushed them to the floor. He stepped out of his pants and socks and stood in front of me wearing nothing but a pair of black boxer briefs straining against the demands of his erection.

I started to untie my borrowed sweats, but he pushed my hands away with a growl, and I laughed as more chills slid down my spine. Titus lowered himself onto one elbow next to me. His mouth found my left breast, hot against my sensitive skin, and I buried one hand in his hair, arching into his touch.

His tongue flicked over my nipple, and my eyes fell closed. His hand glided over my stomach, and I caught my breath. His fingers slid between my thighs over my sweats, and when he began to stroke me through the cloth, my hand tightened around a handful of his hair.

"Oh…" I breathed, my voice hoarse with need. "Titus," I moaned, and his patience evaporated in a throaty growl.

The bed rocked as he stood, and I opened my eyes when he tugged impatiently at the waist of my pants.

"Drawstring," I murmured, too lost in desire to be more articulate.

Titus tugged the drawstring until the bow slid loose, and I lifted for him so he could drag the material over my hips. He pulled the sweats down slowly, in spite of the impatience clear in the hungry way he watched me. Chills followed his fingers as the material skimmed over my legs, then disappeared. The sweats landed across the room, then he appeared over me again, need burning in his eyes.

Titus put one knee on the mattress, but I sat up, my hand on the flat plane of his lower stomach. "Wait." He stood and I slid my hands beneath the last bit of material separating us. I pulled his boxer briefs down, freeing that last bit of him, proud and thick, straining toward me even as the rest of him clung to a thin thread of restraint.

I looked up at Titus as I wrapped one hand around him. His groan was almost too low to be human. Encouraged, I slid my hand down his firm length, then grasped him at the base. An inarticulate sound of pleasure rumbled up from his throat, and he gasped as my mouth closed over him.

"Robyn…" His hands slid into my hair, encouraging, but not demanding.

When I felt him at the back of my throat, I pulled away, sucking a little harder, until I could trace a circle around his head with my tongue. Then I took him in again, as deep as I could.

He groaned again and again as I stroked and sucked, his hands tightening in my hair until—

"Robyn." Titus pushed me back gently. I looked up to find desperate need firing like sparks behind his eyes. "I have to slow down. I was infected three years ago, and since then, I haven't…"

"You haven't had sex in three years?" I frowned up at him. "Why not?" I hadn't slept with anyone since I was infected either, but for me, that was a matter of *months*.

"Because of Faythe."

"*What?*" I leaned back on both hands, staring at him in shock and confusion. "You and *Faythe?*" The married, pregnant Alpha of another Pride?

"No!" Titus sat next to me. "Faythe's a legend, even to us out here in the former free zone. She's the reason we all know about the partial shift, and she discovered that during a very *intimate* moment."

My confusion must have shown.

"She infected her boyfriend during sex, when her teeth started to shift, and I couldn't take the chance that that might happen to some poor human girl. Because of me. Especially considering that women don't survive infection. Well, until you."

"So you were going to, what? Take cold showers for the rest of your life?" Because there were no tabbies in the free zone, other than Abby. And until me, there'd been no real prospects. "Am I just…convenient?"

"*No.*" Titus pulled me closer, and his lips skimmed my temple as he spoke. "You are *anything* but convenient."

"Ha, ha."

"I'm serious. You are beautiful, and brave, and bold, and…uninhibited. And I love all of those things. But you're the least convenient prospect I've ever had—and I mean that in the best way. You're not just a sudden opportunity to be grasped, and I don't want you to feel like one. If you don't want this, we can stop right now."

I looked into his gray eyes. Assessing.

He meant it. He hadn't had sex in three years, but he'd rather go without than let me believe I was scratching an itch any female shifter could have scratched.

"So then, if I'm not convenient…what am I?"

"You're unforgettable. Irresistible," he said, and suddenly I felt like I was in freefall on a swing set, waiting for my stomach to catch up with the rest of me. "I've hardly been able to think about anything else since the moment you popped up in my rearview mirror." He shrugged. "Since the moment I saw you in the Di Carlo's dining room, actually. And every time I think you can't get any more incredible, you come up with some possibility I haven't thought of, or you shut down some bullshit I don't even realize I'm spouting, and you do it all with this sexy little smile." Titus took my hand. "I don't want to give you up, Robyn. I want you here with me, even if I never get the Pride back. If you're willing to stay."

My heart pounded so hard I felt dizzy. "But you told the council…"

"When Blum had you pinned, I thought I was about to lose you, and I realized I *could not* let that happen. Not to him. Not to the council. Not to anyone. We'll figure something out. If you want to stay."

Looking up into his eyes, I believed him. Titus was a different kind of Alpha, and not just because he wasn't natural-born. "I want to stay with you," I said, and he looked so relieved I almost laughed. I wanted to help him guide and support new strays, whether or not he ever got his Pride back. I wanted to see him looking at me with that hunger in his gaze every day. Every night…

I smiled and ran my hand over his side, to the lateral bulge of muscle at his hip. "So, you stopped me so I'd know I'm…inconvenient?"

"No." His face flushed a little. "I stopped you because it's been a while for me, and…" He brushed hair from his forehead. "Your turn."

Titus knelt in front of me at the side of the bed, his gaze burning into me. He put a hand on each of my knees and pushed them open, and anticipation gathered low in my stomach. Then he pulled me forward as I lay back on the bed and closed my eyes.

His hands disappeared, leaving me cold and exposed for a moment. Then his fingers skimmed from my knees up my inner thighs. Parting them wider.

I moaned at the first touch of his tongue, wet and blisteringly hot against my most sensitive parts. He started off with long, slow caresses, the tip of his tongue teasing me at the end of each stroke. Then my hands found his hair, and he licked faster, harder. He stroked deeper, longer, until a blissful pressure began to build up, tightening with each touch of his tongue. Each breath came short and fast. My hands clenched around his hair, and I arched up, aching for more from each little bit of contact.

"Titus. Please…" I begged, each word a throaty whisper.

"Not yet." He rose, and I let go of his hair reluctantly. "Wait for me, Robyn." I propped myself on one elbow, watching as he fumbled in his brother's nightstand, then tore open a condom. A moment later, he settled over me, supporting his weight on his elbows. His tongue trailed up my neck, pushing my head to one side as he sucked my earlobe into his mouth. "Almost…" he whispered, as he positioned himself between my thighs. Then he slid inside me in one long, smooth stroke.

For a moment, neither of us moved. I tightened around him, enjoying the pressure and friction, and he groaned softly in my ear. Then I rocked beneath him, and he groaned louder.

Titus pulled back, then sank into me again. And again. We found our rhythm, and I rose to meet him over and over. Soon that pressure built again, an ache made of promise.

When I couldn't wait any longer, I wrapped one leg around Titus's thigh and pushed on his shoulder. He slid one arm around me and rolled us over.

Pleased, I sat up, both hands braced on his sweat-damp chest, and took control of the rhythm. Driving us faster and faster as I chased that swelling, spiraling release.

"That's it," he moaned as I rode him. "Show me what you like." Titus's hands slid down my waist to grip my hips, pinning me to him, increasing the friction as I set the pace.

"Robyn," he groaned, his fingers digging into my hips. He was close.

"Almost," I panted. I sat upright, my hands in my own hair, grinding into him at a new angle, and suddenly everything tightened.

Pleasure erupted through me, tearing a cry from my throat as I rode him frantically, and for a moment I was aware of nothing but the release washing over me with every rock of my hips. Every new jolt of friction.

"Robyn!" he cried as he came, thrusting into me, pinning me against him as he bucked up from the mattress.

I rode my release until it ebbed into an aching

satisfaction. Until finally, I collapsed against his shoulder, my hair spread over his arm. We breathed in sync, his heart pounding frantically beneath my ear.

Still buried inside me, he throbbed, and little aftershocks of pleasure fired through me as I tightened involuntarily around him.

"Three years, huh?" I teased, running one hand down his side. "That was some pretty impressive control."

"It was an effort," he admitted. "But it can only get better, right?"

I groaned. "I'm not sure I can handle anything better than that."

He laughed, one hand wrapped around my back, holding me to him. "I have confidence that you're up to the challenge." Then he rolled us over and withdrew as he stood. "Be right back."

I got up to find the pillows, and Titus returned as I was spreading the flat sheet over the bed. "Oh good. I was afraid you'd be dressed."

"Nope." I crawled onto the bed, beneath the top sheet, and he curled up next to me. Around me. One arm draped over my side. "I like naked."

"So I recall." He chuckled. "I like you naked too."

"Is it weird that we're in your brother's bed? Do you think he'd mind?"

"I know for a fact that he would not. He's always been generous with his things."

I huffed. "Probably because you always had the money to buy more things." Then a new thought occurred to me. "Do you think that's changed, now that he's been infected? Some shifters are highly territorial."

"Yeah, maybe." Titus brushed my hair up over the

pillow and away from his face. "But if anyone is likely to recognize me as an Alpha, it's my baby brother. I was the only authority figure in his life long before either of us were shifters."

"What's Justus like?" I asked, snuggling against him. "I mean, before he was infected?"

"He's a normal nineteen-year-old. Young and stupid, in a lot of ways. But he's a good guy. Generous, like I said. Funny. He likes video games and movies, but he also watches the news, if you can believe that."

"I actually *can* believe that. I hate the news, but Abby was a political science major. In school, she was always talking about the distribution of power and how some laws were written to hold people back, rather than protect their freedoms. What I study in the past, she studies in the present. Without the benefit of historical hindsight."

"I have to admit, that's come in handy out here. We're building all that from scratch, and we could use both current and historical expertise." Titus exhaled against my neck, and chills shot up my spine. "I always thought Justus would have been interested in what I'm doing, and now I guess I'll get to tell him about it. Assuming we ever find him. And the council doesn't have him executed."

I rolled over to face him. "Your brother's going to be fine, Titus. He didn't mean to infect anyone. Leland already told us that. The council is a pain in the ass, and they're way too stuffy for their own good, but Faythe and Abby's dad will never let them execute Justus for something he did by accident. Something he didn't even know he was doing. They're old and mean, but they're not psychotic."

Titus frowned. "Robyn, the council has been executing strays for doing exactly what Justus did, under those same, ignorant circumstances, for generations. If I want to save him, I'm going to have to come up with something a lot better than 'he didn't know what he was doing'."

"Maybe not." I shrugged, and the pillow moved with the motion. "Maybe it's as easy as giving them something they want more than Justus. Like whoever infected him."

SEVENTEEN

Titus

My brother's bedroom had no curtains, so when the sun rose, I did too. Careful not to wake Robyn, I rolled over and stood to dig my phone from my jeans pocket.

The clock on the lock screen read seven minutes after eight am. I'd gotten less than four hours of sleep, but my body refused to submit to any more with my brother still missing. Even with Robyn's naked warmth calling to me from the bed.

The only thing resembling breakfast in Justus's kitchen was half a box of frozen toaster waffles and a four-pack of energy drinks. The boy lived on carbs and caffeine.

Grumbling, I put on a clean shirt from my suitcase and walked down to the cafe on the corner for breakfast burritos and four large paper cups of coffee that I didn't have to brew myself. Blum and Robyn were still asleep when I returned, so I dumped a packet of sugar into one of the coffees and called Spencer Cole.

His phone went to voicemail on the third ring, and

I hung up without leaving a message. He was probably working. So I tried Drew next. His phone went to voicemail on the first ring.

"Hey, Drew, it's me. I have a hospital question for Spence, but I can't get through to him. Can you have him give me a call if he checks in with you?"

By the time I'd finished my first coffee, I could hear Robyn moving around, so I took a still-steaming paper cup into Justus's room for her.

The bed was empty, but the bathroom door was open. Robyn stood in front of the mirror, brushing her teeth. Wearing my too-big-for-her shirt and nothing else, that I could see.

Memories from the night before washed over me. Her soft flesh in my hands. The taste of her on my lips. The sight of her riding me, eyes closed, hands in her own hair…

Robyn turned, her toothbrush dripping in one hand. "Guess who didn't have any nightmares last—?" She laughed with a pointed glance at the bulge in my pants. "You are an early riser, huh?"

"And you are the most confident, least inhibited woman I've ever met."

She spat toothpaste into the sink, then frowned at me in the mirror. "I can't tell whether that's a compliment or a criticism."

I pulled her close and pressed myself against her bare leg. "Now can you tell?"

"Mmm…" she murmured, her minty breath warm against my ear. "Men's bodies are sometimes easier to interpret than their words."

"I'd say the reverse is true. Women are usually more comfortable showing you what they want than telling you. But you're the exception."

"You're saying I talk too much?"

I laughed. "Nope. It's nice to know where I stand with a woman for a change."

"I'm pretty sure no one has *ever* had to wonder what I'm thinking for very long." She rinsed her toothbrush and set it on the bathroom counter, next to Justus's hair...goop. And his toothbrush.

Huh. Justus didn't take his toothbrush. Nor did he pack anything, from what I could tell. Which meant he couldn't be planning to stay away too long. Or maybe he wasn't *planning* to stay away at all. What if he was stuck in feline form somewhere, like Blum had been, with no idea that he could shift, much less how to do it?

"Speaking of speaking my mind, I'm hungry," Robyn ran her fingers through her hair, then went up on her toes to kiss me. "Let's find something to eat."

"For once, I'm a step ahead of you." I held up the coffee. "And there's food in the kitchen."

While she rewarmed two of the burritos, I called Spencer again. And again, his line went straight to voicemail. "*Damn* it."

"What's wrong?" Robyn cradled her cup in both hands, as if for warmth.

"I keep calling Spencer, hoping he can get Justus's record from the ER, but his phone goes straight to voicemail."

The microwave beeped, and she pulled out our breakfast. "Why don't you try Drew?"

"I did." I removed the lid from the extra coffee and dumped in a packet of sugar. "I got his voicemail too."

"Here." She set the plate of burritos on the coffee table. "You take one of these, and I'll try Drew. He has to answer my call."

I peeled back the paper wrapping from one of the burritos. "In case you're in danger from the big bad rogue Alpha?" If anything, the opposite was true. At least, once the council found out that I had no intention of returning her.

"Exactly." She read aloud as she typed a text. "Hey Drew, it's Robyn. Call me as soon as you can, please." She turned to me with a mischievous grin. "What emoji best conveys fake fear for one's life, from the big bad Alpha? Screaming emoji, or frowny face with raised brows?"

"You need the poop emoji, because that is bullshit."

Robyn laughed. Then she unwrapped her burrito and took a big bite.

"You've got some...right...there." I leaned forward and kissed a dab of cheese from her nose.

Her brows rose, and I knew she was going to say something dirty before her mouth even opened. "Would you lick that off, no matter where I smear it?"

"Yes." I glanced at my bare wrist, as if I wore a watch. "In fact, we probably have time..."

"Don't you want some specifics?" she said. "What if I smear it on the bathroom floor?"

"I trust you."

"I—" Robyn's cell rang. She dropped the burrito onto her plate, then grabbed her phone. "It's Drew." She answered the call and held the phone to her ear. "Hello?"

"Hey, Robyn, what happened?" the new Alpha of my Pride asked, from over the line. "Are you okay?"

"I'm fine. Titus was trying to call you earlier, and

he said he couldn't get through."

"Is he there with you?" Drew asked.

Robyn glanced at me, brows raised, and I shook my head, then mimed zipping my lips. "He went out for breakfast," she said. "Why?"

"I don't want to make things worse, but I got tossed into this with no warning. Trial by fire. And I'll never be able to lead this Pride to the best of my ability if they still think of him as the Alpha. So I've asked the guys not to communicate with Titus until further notice."

Anger shot through me, like lightning shooting along every nerve in my body. My eyes narrowed, and my jaw clenched. I understood what Drew was doing, and I probably would have done the same thing in his position. Still...

"You cut him off?" Robyn stood, irritation sparking behind her eyes. "You're living in *his* house, spending *his* money." Her heartbeat quickened until it synced with mine, and some nearly imperceptible change in her pheromones seemed to be feeding my own anger.

She was angry because I was angry. Not because of what Drew was doing, but because of *how I felt about it.*

That had never happened to me with another shifter, not even those who recognized my authority. Not with my enforcers, and not even with Drew, who'd been with me from the beginning.

Was this about more than the relationship of an Alpha to his men? Er...people? Could this mean that I had become as important to Robyn as she had to me?

I gave Robyn a small head shake, calling off my fierce, beautiful would-be defender, even though every cell in my body wanted to watch her rage.

She frowned, but then nodded reluctantly.

"It's only temporary," Drew assured her. "Just until everyone's adjusted to the transition." He hesitated. "I don't know how else to do this, Robyn. In the wild, one Alpha fights—and often kills—another to take over a territory, and obviously that's not what we want here. But the Pride members need some signal that this change is real. Something symbolic, that they can understand on an instinctual level. A clean break is the best thing I could think of."

"If you're looking for a Titus palate cleanser, I think you're going to have to move out of his house," she snapped. "You can't subconsciously cut him out of their lives as long as they're surrounded by his scent, not to mention all those family pictures."

I shook my head at her again, silently asking her to dial down the anger, despite the fact that I was still bathing in it, but she only turned away from me. Her refusal of my order raised the hairs on the back of my neck, blurring the line between angry Alpha and proud lover. How could I be irritated at her and pleased with her at the same time?

"Where are you and Titus staying?" Drew's voice had a still quality, like the surface of a calm lake.

"We're...at a hotel."

"Then why would Titus go out for breakfast instead of ordering room service?"

Robyn turned to me, frowning. "Because I don't like room service." She rolled her eyes, obviously frustrated by her own improvisational skills.

I stifled a smile. But Drew was silent for several seconds.

"Robyn, are you sure you're okay? Titus isn't being

aggressive? He hasn't…tried anything?"

"You know he would never do that!" Her eyes flashed with anger, and gratification at her reaction flooded me.

"Until yesterday, I would have agreed with you. But if he's been out there infecting people, we don't know what he's capable of."

She rolled her eyes. "Drew, Titus didn't—"

I shook my head firmly. She couldn't tell him about Justus. Not until I'd figured out what had happened to him and come up with a strategy to defend against the charges that would inevitably be leveled against him.

"He didn't what?" Drew asked.

"He didn't try anything. He's not being aggressive. He's giving you the space you need and upholding his promise to keep me safe. He's not a bad guy."

"You seem to have gotten to know him pretty well."

Robyn rolled her eyes again. *Want me to ask about Spencer?* she mouthed, but I shook my head. "Yeah, I guess. Okay, I gotta go. Tell the other guys I said hi?"

"Of course," Drew said. "And Robyn, call me if anything changes. I can be there in less than an hour."

"Okay, thanks." She hung up the phone and frowned at me. "How does he know he can be here in less than an hour if he doesn't know where we are?"

"I'm sure he's figured out I'm visiting my brother. Which isn't great, but as long as he doesn't know Justus has been infected…" I shrugged. "Can I use your phone to call Spence? I understand where Drew's coming from." Though it pissed me off. "But I still need to find Justus."

She handed me her phone. "Where is Drew

coming from?"

"He's trying to be a good leader and to protect you. They all legitimately think I infected Corey Morris. Which means I could be capable of anything."

"If they know you, they should know that's bullshit." She picked up her burrito and took a big bite.

I gave her a grateful smile, then I dialed Spencer. He answered on the second ring. "I don't know this number. Who is this?"

"Hey Spence, it's Titus. I'm on Robyn's new phone. Don't hang up."

"Hey, man, we're not supposed—"

"I know Drew told you not to take my calls, and I'm sorry to put you in this position. But I need some information. It's important."

For one long moment, he was quiet, and I heard a voice speaking over an intercom system. "What do you need?"

"Are you at work?" I asked.

"Yeah."

"I'll be quick. I just found out that my brother went to your ER two weeks ago. Can you get to his record?"

"Your brother lives in Jackson?"

"Yeah. He goes to Millsaps. Can you help me?"

"Maybe…" Spencer exhaled heavily. "What's going on, Titus?"

"I'm not sure yet. But I wouldn't be asking if it weren't very important."

Another long pause. "Why can't you ask your brother?"

I hesitated, trying to decide how much to tell him. Spencer wasn't an enforcer and didn't live at my house, which meant Drew wouldn't know I'd called him unless Spence reported the call.

Holding the last two inches of her burrito, Robyn nodded at me, encouraging me to tell him something. To trust him.

"Spence, my brother's…unaccounted for. I came to his place when I left the house, but he was gone and I can't get ahold of him. I really need to find him."

"I'll see what I can do. What's his name?"

"Justus Alexander. J-u-s-t-u-s."

"Okay, I'll get back to you if I find anything." He hung up.

"You think he'll do it?" Robyn asked around a bite of burrito.

I shrugged. "There's an equal chance he'll tell Drew I called and wash his hands of the whole thing."

"This isn't right." She dropped the rest of her breakfast onto the paper plate, evidently too disgusted to finish it. "They shouldn't think you're dangerous."

"They should *always* think an Alpha is dangerous. And in this case, that's better than them thinking Justus is dangerous."

"Is it?" She tilted her head in an adorable gesture of acute skepticism. "He's newly infected. Don't you think they're more likely to forgive a newly infected stray—a kid—for acting on ignorant impulse than an experienced Alpha, who doesn't have any excuses?"

As usual, she had a point. "Yes, I do. But I can't risk the council—or Drew—finding out about Justus before I find him." Yet her skepticism remained. "If they know about him, they'll hunt him. They'll take him into custody—or execute him on the spot—and there'll be nothing I can do for him. I have to protect him, Robyn. I'm the only family he has."

Finally, she nodded. "Okay. Then we better find him."

The guest bedroom door squealed open, and Leland Blum stepped into the living room in his boxer shorts. "Find who? Justus?"

"Yeah." I waved at the bag on the kitchen counter. "We have breakfast burritos and coffee. And I'll grab your clothes from the dryer." I gave Robyn a reluctant smile. "Yours too." Though I was seriously considering giving her another of my shirts to wear, just so I could smell our combined scents all day.

Blum stopped on the way to the kitchen, inhaling in Robyn's direction. Then he sniffed in mine. "Why do you guys smell like each..." His brows rose when comprehension came. Then he looked sad, and I remembered that his girlfriend had just died. And I felt like a total ass. "No such thing as a secret among shifters, I guess?"

Robyn shrugged, and she looked as guilt-ridden as I felt. "Not for long, anyway."

Fortunately, Blum wasn't yet in contact with any other shifters, so we wouldn't have to make the moment even more awkward by asking him to keep the news to himself.

Half an hour later, we were all fed and dressed.

"Robyn and I have to run some errands," I told Blum, as I slid my brother's laptop into his satchel. "I'm not going to ask you to tag along, but I can't leave you here, either, in case he comes home. I could get you a hotel room...?"

"Or I could go to my dorm," Blum suggested.

"Do you have a roommate?" Robyn asked.

"No, I'm in a single."

"Okay, if you're comfortable staying there for a while, we'll meet up with you later." I opened the front door and held it for them both as they headed into the hallway. "I suggest you order in lunch. You've been through something truly traumatic, obviously, and that probably hasn't sunk in yet. And you haven't had a chance to learn to control your feline impulses, so you probably shouldn't try to go to class or anything just yet."

Blum nodded. He was surprisingly calm and agreeable for a newly infected stray.

"Would you like a ride?" Robyn asked him.

"Yeah, thanks."

We dropped Blum off at his dorm—room 204— then headed to the nearest department store, where Robyn chafed at the idea of letting me buy her clothes, until I pointed out that she was the closest thing I had to an enforcer at the moment, and a clothing allowance is typically provided for enforcers as part of the salary.

Afterward, as we headed for the closest coffee shop, her phone rang. "It's Spencer."

I pulled into the nearest lot and shifted my SUV into park. "Put him on speaker." Robyn answered her phone with a tap on the screen. "Spencer?" I said.

"Yeah. I got what you wanted, but I only have a couple of minutes."

"Do you have a break coming up?" I asked.

"Yeah. Meet me at the water fountain behind the hospital in ten minutes."

Nine minutes later, we found Spencer on a bench in front of the fountain. "We brought you a latte." Robyn handed him one of the cups she carried, then shoved her hand into the pocket of her new down jacket to shield it from the rare, truly cold Mississippi day.

"Thanks." Spencer scooted to make room for us on the bench, angling to face us both. "Your brother's bill says he was here on a Sunday morning, but that's just when he was released. He actually came in the night before, with wounds consistent with an animal attack and a fever." He opened the lid to let his coffee cool, and steam rose from the paper cup. "The attending thought the two were unrelated, because it was too soon after the attack for his wound to be infected, and it wasn't yet inflamed or warmer than the surrounding skin. They stitched him up, prescribed some ibuprofen and an antibiotic just in case, and sent him home with an order to stay hydrated."

"Did he say what had happened?" Robyn asked, her cheeks red from the cold.

"That's the thing." Spencer blew into his cup, and more steam rose from it. "Justus said he was at a party on the lake. He went into the woods to pee and something pounced on him. Knocked him flat on his face. He couldn't see the animal, but it ripped up his shirt and his back, then it took off into the woods."

"Like it got spooked?" I asked.

"Your guess is as good as mine." Spencer cleared his throat, and I knew what was coming. "Titus, is your brother infected?"

Robyn leaned back on the bench so she could see me. I raised one brow, silently asking for her opinion, and she nodded. She trusted Spencer.

"Yeah," I said at last. "We think he is."

"Shit, man." Spence was quiet for a moment. "You

didn't infect Morris, did you? It was Justus?"

"You can't tell anyone," Robyn said, before I could formulate a reply. I'd known there was a possibility that he'd figure it out, and I'd had no choice but to take that chance.

"You can't keep this secret forever," Spencer insisted. "People will know as soon as they smell him."

"Which is why we have to find him first."

"How weird that he was infected at a party." Robyn took a sip of her cappuccino, staring into the fountain. "Especially considering that Corey Morris and—"

I coughed, cutting her off before she could mention Ivy Lowe or Leland Blum.

"Considering that Morris was infected right after a party," she finished instead.

"It gets weirder than that," Spencer said. "We got another one late last night. Elliott Belcher. Twenty-year-old sophomore at Millsaps, attacked by an animal at a party."

"In the woods?"

"No, at a museum, after hours. He said he went out for some fresh air—"

"Or for some pot-scented air..." Robyn interjected.

"—and found a great big cat in the alley."

"He told you this?" I asked.

"Yeah. I was on duty when he came in. I don't know about the pot, but he was high on *something* when he got there, and everyone assumed he was hallucinating. Yet he clearly had wounds consistent with being clawed by a wild animal."

"Where is he now?" I asked.

"I took him to…well, to your house early this morning, then I had to get back to work a shift for the guy who took over for me when I left. I'm going on about two hours sleep, so the coffee is much appreciated."

"Has Elliott shifted yet?" Robyn didn't look at me when she asked the question, but I could tell from the tension in her frame that she was thinking the same thing I was.

"I doubt it." Spencer took a sip from his paper cup, then turned to me. "But if Justus is responsible, everyone will think it's you," he said, vocalizing what neither Robyn nor I wanted to say aloud. "How long are you going to let everyone think you did this?"

"At least until I find my brother and figure out what happened. Drew's trying to keep me out of everything. I understand why, but I need to know what happens with this new stray. Will you keep me updated?"

"Of course." Spencer glanced at his watch and stood. "Is there anything else I can do?"

"Don't tell them you saw us or spoke to us, obviously," Robyn said.

Spence's brows dipped even lower as he turned to me. "Does the council know you've resigned? Because when they find out, they're not going to want you running around with their prodigal daughter."

Robyn scowled. "You know, everyone thinks 'prodigal' means runaway, but it actually means 'wasteful' or 'lavish'." She gestured from herself to me, then back. "Between the billionaire and the poor college co-ed, who do you think better fits that description?"

"Oh. Sorry." Spencer grinned at her. "Did you

major in Bible story vocabulary?"

I laughed. "She just likes knowing more than anyone else."

"Screw you both," Robyn said. But she was smiling. "*The Real Story Behind The Bible Story*, on The History Channel. The Di Carlos don't get movie channels."

"Oh. You have my sympathy," Spencer said with a frown. "I have to get back, but if I hear anything else, I'll let you know." He raised his cup in Robyn's direction. "Thanks again for the coffee. And the vocabulary lesson."

EIGHTEEN

Robyn

Leland Blum didn't answer his phone. I was leaving another message when Titus got into the car with four foil-wrapped hot dogs.

"Voicemail again?" He set two of the dogs in my lap, and the combined scents of beef, relish, and mustard made my mouth water.

"Third time." I unwrapped the first dog and took a huge bite.

Titus laughed at my enthusiasm. "I promise I'll take you out for something nicer than burritos and hot dogs soon."

"Or maybe *I'll* take *you* out. And FYI, this is exactly the kind of high-class cuisine I can afford." I took another bite.

He laughed again, but then his smile faded as he stared through the windshield at the dorm building in front of us, his gaze moving from window to window, because we didn't know which one belonged to Leland Blum. "I think we should go check on him. I'm afraid he may be stuck in cat form again."

"Which would be hilarious, considering the college dorm setting, but probably less than reassuring for the local populace." I rewrapped what was left of my hot dog and set it on the center console. "Room 204. Let's go."

At thirty, Titus was older than the average college student, and older still than the average dorm resident, but I was in my natural habitat. No one gave us a second glance.

The door to room 204 was devoid of all personality. There was nothing stuck to it or written on the message board next to it. "It's definitely his." I knocked three times. "Leland? It's Robyn and Titus."

When we got no answer, Titus pressed his ear to the door. "I don't hear anything. This is a hollow door, and there's no seal at the bottom. If he's in there, I should be able to hear him moving around, at the very least."

I shrugged. "So—"

Titus gave the doorknob a quick, firm twist, and the door swung open.

"Oh shit," I whispered. Now we were breaking and entering.

He quickly pulled me into the room and closed the door behind us.

"We can't—" The rest of my objection was swallowed by horror. "Oh no…" Leland Blum lay on the floor of his dorm room, staring sightlessly at the ceiling. A pool of blood had soaked into the rug beneath his head, and more dripped from the corner of his nightstand. Where he'd clearly split open his scalp. Very recently, as far as I could tell. The blood hadn't yet begun to dry. "You think he fell?"

"I think that's what we're supposed to think."

Titus knelt next to the nightstand and sniffed the blood. "It's all his." He bent even farther to sniff Leland's hands, careful not to touch the body. "Fresh hand sanitizer. Either he just came out of the bathroom, or someone tried to destroy a scent."

"You think this was…" *Justus?* But I couldn't say his name. I couldn't theorize that Titus's brother was now a killer. "…a shifter?"

"A human murderer would have no reason to try to destroy his scent," Titus said. "They can't smell personal scents like we can. Try the doorknob." He waved one hand at the bedroom door, but I didn't understand what he wanted until I saw him bend to sniff the bathroom doorknob.

I squatted in front of the front door, but found only the metallic scent of the knob itself and… "More hand sanitizer." My gaze fell on Leland again as I stood. We'd dropped him off two hours before, alive and relatively well. A sick feeling twisted in my gut. "So we're pretty sure this is a murder?" If we'd kept him with us, he would still be alive.

This is our fault.

"Looks like it. Let's go." Titus took my hand as he reached for the door, but I pulled free.

"Wait, we can't leave him here."

"It's noon, Robyn." The sense of urgency in his voice, along with whatever Alpha pheromones were leaking from his veins, made me suddenly itch to get moving, even though I was morally opposed to that action. "We can't carry him out without being seen, and we can't call the police because eventually, they might be able to match my voice from the 911 call. And even if they can't, an anonymous 911 call will lead the authorities to investigate this as more than the accident it'll look like if the body is found organically."

"You don't think they'll know this was a murder?"

"Not unless they connect it with Ivy's disappearance. And we can't afford to be the ones who call this in, in case they do make that connection. Let's go."

Reluctantly, I followed him into the hall, then out of the building without making eye contact with the two people we passed on the way. Fortunately, they were both staring at their phones and couldn't possibly identify either of us, if asked to.

By the time we got to the car, the unasked question was like a hot coal sitting on the end of my tongue. "Was it Justus?"

"I don't know." Titus slid into the driver's seat, closed his door, and started the engine. "Accidentally infecting people, I can understand. He likely didn't even know that was possible. But murder? In human form?" He shook his head as he pulled out of the parking lot and onto the road. "He wouldn't do that. It's not Justus."

"So maybe it *was* an accident." I think I wanted to believe that as badly as Titus did. "Maybe he came to confront Leland about Ivy, and they fought. Maybe Leland hit his head, and Justus panicked."

Titus's gaze stayed glued to the road, but he didn't seem to see the traffic. "That's a lot of maybes."

"And I stand by each one of them. But there are other possibilities. There have to be. If it wasn't Justus, who else could it be? What are we missing?"

"I don't know."

"Who else would want Leland dead? Not that Justus would want him dead," I hurried to add. Which was when I realized I was making guesses about the motives and thoughts of a person I'd never even met. "My point is that we could be overlooking someone else's motivation. If this wasn't an accident, it was murder, and murder always has a motive, right?"

"I'm pretty sure that true psychotics murder people just for fun," he said through clenched teeth.

"Okay, but if Leland Blum got infected by a shifter, lost his girlfriend, and was murdered by a true psychopath, all in the span of two days, he's the unluckiest man on the face of the planet. Odds are that his murder and his infection are related. We just need to figure out how."

Titus stared at the road in silence.

I put one hand on his shoulder, half afraid he would shrug it off. "That doesn't mean Justus did it. That isn't what I'm saying."

"I know. But it's what I'm thinking. Who else would have anything against Blum?"

"We may not know that until we know who killed him."

"Or we may never know." Titus pulled the SUV into the parking lot of his brother's apartment building, then into Justus's designated space. He shifted into park, then folded his arms on top of the steering wheel and laid his forehead against them. "I can handle a brother who lost control of himself after being infected. But I don't know what to do with a brother who's a murderer."

"We don't know this is Justus. We have plenty of trouble on our hands. Try not to borrow more okay?"

Titus sat up, and his gaze caught on my mouth. For a second, I thought he was going to kiss me. Then he frowned. "I'm taking you to Drew. Let's run in and get your toothbrush."

"What? No! You promised the council—"

"That I'd keep you safe. That's what I'm doing. Leland Blum was murdered, Robyn. It's not safe for you out here anymore, and I *can't* let anything happen to you."

"I'm not going—"

"Yes, you are. You should be surrounded by enforcers right now. Come on." He got out of the car, and I had to follow him to argue with him. Yet on my way up the stairs, I realized there was no good argument to be made. I probably *would* be safer at his house, surrounded by enforcers. But the only thing I wanted to be surrounded by was Titus's arms.

"Hey!" I snapped as I jogged up the stairs after him. "I'm not—"

"Shh!" He turned to me with a fierce look, then pointed at the door to Justus's apartment. Which stood open about two inches.

"You locked it when we left," I whispered. "I specifically remember that."

"Yes, and I also *closed* it. Stay here." Titus pushed the door open, flinching when the hinges squealed, then stepped inside. "*Damn* it," he swore, but I couldn't see what the problem was until he headed for his brother's room, clearing my line of sight.

Justus's living room had been destroyed.

The glass coffee table lay in shards and chunks all over the pristine white carpet. The couch had been overturned, leather cushions tossed aside. Every cabinet and drawer in the kitchen stood open, and the bi-fold doors concealing the washer and dryer had nearly been pulled from their hinges.

"The bedroom's empty. And it's trashed again,"

Titus whispered on his way through the living area toward the guest room. "I don't think this was Justus. Whoever was here didn't have a key and seems to have been searching the apartment."

I tiptoed behind him into the kitchen, my new boots crunching on glass, and grabbed a butcher knife from the block on the granite countertop.

"Robyn!" Titus snapped softly. Then he pointed to the front door, silently telling me to go outside.

I held the knife up and mimed gutting the vandalizing bastard, but Titus looked distinctly unimpressed. He opened the guest room door, his entire body tense and ready to spring into action. Then his arms fell limp at his sides and his shoulders relaxed.

I looked past him into the room. It was practically untouched. The only thing out of place was...

"Um, Titus?" I edged by him into the room and picked up a wallet lying on the unmade bed. "Is this yours?"

"If my wallet were here, you wouldn't be wearing new clothes right now."

I sank onto the bed and opened the leather trifold. The clear ID pocket was empty, but the credit cards inside belonged to— "Shit. Leland left it here."

Titus sat on the mattress next to me and I gave him the wallet. He thumbed through the credit cards, then opened the billfold to find a thin stack of cash. "They only took his ID."

"Which means they were looking for him, right?"

Titus shrugged. "All I can say for sure is that this wasn't a robbery. But yeah, they could have been looking for Blum. Or they could have been looking for Justus, and found Blum's ID instead."

"So, whoever broke in here found Leland's driver's license, tracked him down, and killed him?" And that probably wasn't Justus; he wouldn't have to break into his own apartment.

"Looks like it," Titus said. "But ID alone wouldn't have led them to his dorm room."

"Because addresses aren't listed on college IDs and his hometown address would have been listed on his license." I nodded, thinking of my own university identification. "So how did the killer find his address?"

Titus frowned. "I think the more pressing question is 'Why would someone kill Leland Blum?'"

"Oh, good. A mystery. But I have to warn you, I've seen *every* episode of *Scooby Doo*. Even the ones where Scoob was a puppy."

Titus smiled, in spite of the circumstances. "Wow me, Velma."

"Okay, but I call dibs on ripping the rubber mask from the murderer, when we find him."

"Didn't the Scooby gang specialize in finding missing property?"

"Yes, but in my humble opinion, they never lived up to their true potential," I said, and Titus actually laughed. "You're taking this a lot better than I expected."

He shrugged. "I have to admit; I'm a little relieved to have potentially eliminated my brother as a murder suspect."

"Yeah. Okay, so whoever broke in here was either looking for Leland Blum, or was looking for Justus and found Leland's ID instead." I stood, and Titus followed me into the living room, while I closed the front door. The latch still worked, even though the lock itself was busted. "So who, other than the two of us, would be looking for Justus? And might also want Leland Blum dead? What's the connection between Leland and your brother?"

"The most obvious connection is Ivy," Titus said. "So maybe someone who knows they're connected to her disappearance?"

"Okay…" I got out my phone and pulled up Ivy Lowe's social media accounts, one by one while he tilted the couch back onto its feet. "But no one even seems to know she's missing yet. And here's why." I turned the phone around, and he read from the screen. "Thursday afternoon's post. Three days ago."

"'Heading to the cabin for a long weekend! Unplugging…now!'" Titus frowned as he replaced the couch cushions. "So it would have to be someone who knows what happened at the cabin. Which is you and me, poor dead Leland, my missing brother, and…" His frown deepened. "That's it. Corey Morris doesn't know that either Ivy or Leland were infected, and he has no idea my brother even exists."

"So then maybe Ivy isn't the connection." I sank onto the couch and pulled him down next to me, linking my arm through his. Holding him close. "What else do Leland and Justus have in common?"

Titus shrugged. "They're around the same age. They both go to Millsaps."

"Yes, but if that's the connection, every male Millsaps student is in immediate danger."

"Okay." Titus propped his feet on the metal frame of the shattered glass coffee table. "They're both newly infected shifters. And it's likely that neither of them even knew shifters existed until they became one."

"Now we're getting somewhere. They were both recently infected. And they're both connected to you. You're Justus's brother, and you found Leland at the cabin."

"Technically, *you* found Blum," Titus pointed out.

"Yes, but I have no connection to Justus. Oh shit!" I twisted to sit on my knees on the center cushion, facing him, as another connection came into sudden, horrific clarity. "Titus, they both know you're not the one who infected Leland and Corey."

"Which is why we were keeping Blum hidden. To protect Justus." Titus pulled his feet from the table and frowned at me. "Wait, you think someone killed Blum to keep anyone from finding out I'm innocent? I'm pretty sure I'm the only one who wants me to look guilty. I think we're veering onto the wrong track."

"Maybe so." I stared at the wallet I still held, suddenly acutely aware that I was holding evidence in a murder case. "I certainly *hope* so." *But...* I took Titus's hand as another disturbing idea emerged from the tangle of possibilities. "Titus, do you have any enemies in the Pride? Anyone who might want to see you...gone?"

"I'm sure I do." Though he looked bothered by the thought. "No leader is universally loved. But I can't think of anyone who'd be willing to kill innocent people to make sure I can't clear my name."

"But if there *were* someone like that...?" I let him fill in the blank for himself.

Titus's face went ashen. His grip on my hand tightened. "Then Justus would be in danger too, because he's living proof that I'm innocent. If someone wants me to go down for infecting Corey

271

Morris, then my brother's is the next name on the hit list."

"Or maybe his was the first." I let go of him and stood, my new boots crunching on broken glass as I paced. "Maybe whoever broke in here was looking for Justus—to make sure he can't clear your name—and found out about Leland Bloom when he smelled the scent of another shifter all over the place." I waved one hand at the guest room, where the sheets still carried Leland's scent. "That would explain why that room isn't trashed. The killer left the moment he realized he had another target."

"But who?" Titus grabbed my hand as I paced by and pulled me onto the couch next to him, where I leaned back and laid my legs across his lap. "Drew didn't even want the job. He tried to get me to give it to Jace. The rest of my enforcers are just as loyal. But our Pride is big. Twice the population of any of the others. It could be anyone."

"No, it has to be someone who knows you're here *and* knows that you're innocent. And no one knows…"

Titus's eyes widened. "Shit."

I exhaled slowly when I caught on. "Spencer. Titus, it can't be him. He helped us."

"I don't want to believe it, but he knows I'm in Jackson, and he knows about Justus. And he works ten minutes from here."

"And he brought Corey Morris to your house, which is what implicated you in the first place." I closed my eyes as I thought aloud. "But he couldn't have known that would happen. Morris hadn't shifted yet."

"Unless Spencer already knew that Justus infected

Morris."

My eyes flew open. "How would he know that?"

"He couldn't unless... Fuck!" Titus lifted my legs from his lap and shot to his feet, pacing so hard and fast I was afraid he would burn a hole in the carpet. "If Spencer infected Justus, he would already have known how much his scent smelled like mine."

"But why would he do that?" I had to agree; the evidence made sense. But... "Why would Spencer infect your brother? Have the two of you ever had a falling out? Or even an argument?"

"No." Titus stopped pacing. "But I did turn him down when he applied to be an enforcer."

"Why?"

"Because I thought he'd be more valuable to the Pride in the hospital, where he might be able to intercept new strays. And where he has access to a whole network of medical records. If I could, I'd put one of my men in every hospital in the state."

"And he resented being told to stay where he was?"

"Not that I could tell. He seemed to see the advantage of his position."

"Well, then why would he do this?"

"There's only one way to find out." Titus headed for the front door. "Come on, Velma, it's time to unmask the bad guy."

NINETEEN

Titus

"Call him again," I said as I stepped on the gas, and my car shot through the intersection beneath a yellow light.

"I've called him four times. He's not going to answer, Titus. But that doesn't mean anything. He's at work."

I swerved to avoid a car turning into our lane, and Robyn gasped.

"Slow down!" She grabbed her armrest and glared at me. "If we have a wreck—"

"Then the ambulance will get us to the hospital even faster."

"Okay, let's compromise. You slow down, and I'll call the ER. He'll have to take the call if it comes to him at work."

"Fine." I dropped the speedometer by ten miles per hour while she searched for the ER's phone number, using the browser on her cell. A second later, she held the phone up to her ear.

"Hi, this is—" An irritated female voice cut her

off. "No, it's not a medical emergency," Robyn said. "But don't put me on—!" She turned to me and spoke through clenched teeth. "I'm on hold."

"Naturally." I pressed harder on the gas as I changed lanes again, and again Robyn grabbed her door handle.

"Would you—?" She blinked as a voice came over the line again. "Oh hi, yes I'm here. I need to speak to Spencer Cole. I believe he's a nurse."

"Honey, if Spencer were here, we wouldn't be so slammed, and I wouldn't have had to put you on hold in the first place. He walked out a couple of hours ago."

"Do you know where he went?" Robyn asked, bouncing in her seat as I rolled over a bump in the road.

"No, and I don't care," the voice on the phone snapped. "But if you see him, tell him if he's not here at eleven, he's fired."

Robyn hung up her cell and dropped it into her lap. "Well, it looks like the ER won't be giving Spencer an alibi for Leland's murder. A couple of hours ago…" she said, clearly lost in thought. "Was that before or after we met him at the fountain? Would he have had time to go ransack your brother's place, then track Leland down, all after we spoke to him?"

"You can ask him that yourself, in a minute." I flicked on my blinker and pulled into a parking lot on the right, so fast that Robyn slid into the passenger's side door. "We're going to his apartment." I pulled into the first open space and slammed the gear shift into park, then tapped my cell screen to wake it up. Along with all the other official members of the

275

Pride, Spencer's address was in my contact information, along with his birthday, blood type, and every other bit of information I might ever need.

Robyn peeked at the screen. "Wow, you're super-organized."

I clicked on Spencer's address, and the map app opened, showing me the fastest way to get there. "It's in the job description." Even if I no longer officially held the job.

"Yet I'm pretty sure most of the other Alphas are still working from hand-written address books." Robyn cocked her head to the side. "Though come to think of it, I don't think many of them would ever need information like this on the go, because most of them lead from the rear. They're not all as hands-on as Faythe and Marc."

But I was hardly listening. I couldn't think about anything but Justus, and what had been done to him, and how that was spilling over to ruin lives and threaten the well-being of the entire Pride. And Robyn. I inhaled slowly, bracing myself for an argument. "When we get there, I want you to stay in the car."

Robyn snorted. "Would I be repeating myself if I told you to go to hell?"

"Do you want me to handcuff you to the steering wheel?" I took a left turn too sharply, and she had to grab her door handle again.

She snorted. "If you have handcuffs, last night would have been a good time to show them off."

"This isn't a joke." I let a bit of a growl leak into my tone. This wasn't a lover moment; this was an Alpha moment, and the fact that we were having trouble differentiating between the two was an unexpected complication. "We're going to confront a potential murderer, and I swore to keep you safe."

"Titus, I killed four murderers. By myself."

"I know, but they were human, and you had the element of surprise."

"You're saying I can't defend myself against a shifter?"

"I'm saying I can't let it come to that. If I have to handcuff you to keep you in the car, I will."

Robyn's brows rose in challenge. "You're welcome to try."

I drove in silence for the next five minutes, trying to decide whether locking her in the car for her own protection would be worth whatever hell she would unleash upon me afterward. She would forgive me. I had to believe that. The most important thing was that she live through this.

When we pulled into the parking lot behind Spencer's apartment building, she reached for her door handle.

"Hang on a sec." I leaned over to pop open the glove box and pulled out a set of handcuffs, each end already open and ready.

"Why—? You bastard!" She shouted as I slapped one open cuff around her wrist. Before she could launch herself into the parking lot, I slapped the other cuff around my steering wheel. "You *actually* have handcuffs?"

"I'm sorry, Robyn." Though clearly not as sorry as I would be very, very soon. "I know this isn't the most gallant solution, but I swore I'd protect you, and you're making that difficult."

"You haven't *seen* difficult yet!" she shouted as I got out of the car and closed the door. "And you haven't even begun to be sorry!"

"Call me if…anything goes wrong." I shoved back guilt as I jogged down the sidewalk toward building C. I could *not* lead her into a confrontation with a murderer.

Spencer's apartment was one of two on the top floor of his building. I took the steps two at a time, then knocked on his door. When there was no reply, I knocked again. Then I broke the lock with one twist of the knob and pushed right through the deadbolt, splintering the frame.

"Spencer?" I glanced around a small, neat living room and a tiny, galley-style kitchen. Three doors opened into the main area, and at least one of those would be a closet. I was still debating which of the other two to try first when the one on the left opened.

"Titus? What the hell, man?" Spencer held a bat at the ready. As if he'd forgotten he could rip a man's arm from its socket with his bare hands, now that he was a shifter.

"Put the bat down, before I break it over your head." My voice was half-growl.

"What?" Spencer blinked, evidently struggling to hold me in focus, but he dropped the bat without hesitation. "What are you doing here?" His gaze flicked past me toward the front of the room. "Did you break my door?"

"Where's my brother?"

"I don't know. What…?" He blinked heavily, then rubbed both eyes with the heels of his palms. "I have to be at work soon, and I *have* to get some sleep."

"That's not going to happen." I kicked the door closed behind me, but it swung open again with a soft squeal. "You're going to tell me where my brother is and why you killed Leland Blum, and *maybe* I'll let you live."

"What the *fuck*, man?" Spencer leaned against his bedroom doorframe, and swept one hand over his short cropped black curls. "I have no idea what you're talking about. Are you on something? Do you want to lie down?"

"I'm not fucking high, Spencer!" Blood pumped through my veins too quickly, and pressure began to build in my head. My hands curled into fists, and I fought to keep them at my side. "I just want to know where my brother is!"

"I don't know! I've never met your damn brother!"

The sound of fury that ripped its way up my throat was like no other sound I'd ever made in human form. Spencer stumbled backward and lowered his head in a feline stance of submission and respect.

Which was strange, coming from someone who'd had so little respect for my authority that he was willing to infect my brother and kill a newly infected stray.

"I think he's telling the truth."

I spun to the left, careful to keep Spencer in my sight, and found Robyn standing in the doorway. My steering wheel hung from the cuffs still fastened around her left wrist, dangling below her knee.

"*Damn* it, Robyn! You pulled off the steering wheel?"

"It was that, or chew off my own hand, so…" She shrugged, and the wheel bobbed with the movement. "I think Spencer's telling the truth." She pointed at him with her unencumbered right hand. "That's the face of a man whose nap was rudely interrupted, not the face of a man who killed someone, then stupidly went back to his own apartment to hide."

"She's right." Spencer cleared his throat, and I turned to him as Robyn stepped inside and pushed the front door closed. Then pulled a chair in front of it to hold it closed. "Some asshole at work scheduled me for the eleven-to-seven tonight, and I knew I'd never make it without some sleep, so I blew off the last half of my afternoon shift."

"And you've been here the whole time?" I studied his expression, looking for even a hint of a lie.

"Yeah. And I'd still be asleep if it weren't for…" Spencer frowned, glancing from Robyn to me. "What is this, anyway? You think I killed your brother?"

"No, he thinks you infected Justus and killed another stray." Robyn propped the steering wheel on an end table. "Do you happen to have a hacksaw?"

"No, sorry. But you're welcome to sit." Spencer cautiously crossed the room in front of me and sat on the end of the couch opposite Robyn. Leaving me the arm chair. But I remained standing.

"Why didn't you answer your phone?" I demanded, while Spencer dug through the drawer in his end table.

"Because I was sleeping. I put my phone on silent." He dug something small from the drawer and looked up at me. "I'm allowed to do that, because I'm not an enforcer, ergo I'm never on call for the Pride." He handed what turned out to be a paperclip to Robyn, whose eyes lit up.

"Thanks! It's been a while since I had to do this the hard way." She slid the paperclip into the lock mechanism and began gently twisting it.

I made a mental note to ask, once this was all over,

how and why she knew how to break out of handcuffs.

"Okay, wait a minute." I finally sank into the armchair and suddenly felt so tired I wasn't sure I'd be able to get up again. "If you didn't infect my brother or kill Leland Blum, who did?"

"Who's Leland Blum?" Spencer asked.

Robyn twisted the clip again, and the cuff popped open with a metallic click. "Yes!" She raised both fists in triumph, and though steering wheel remained on her lap, the open cuff still swung against her arm. "Damn it. I should have opened the other one." She bent over her arm again, this time working on the half of the cuff attached to her wrist.

"Robyn," I said. "Spence is the only one who knew about Justus."

"Yes. But he knows because we told him," she said with exaggerated patience as she twisted the clip. "We were wrong, Titus. Someone out there knows Justus is a shifter because he—or she—is the one who infected him. Although statistically, it's *highly* unlikely to be a woman."

"No kidding," Spencer said. "Aren't female shifters, like, only one in ten?"

"It's something like that for natural-born werecats, but women are dramatically less common among strays." The pin clicked again, yet her cuff didn't pop open. "But I don't have any numbers on gender imbalance among bruins, and from what I've heard, there is no imbalance among thunderbirds."

"Hey. Focus." Every second that passed reminded me that we were no closer to finding or helping Justus. "I'm still waiting for Nancy Drew to use her legendary powers of deduction to tell me who infected my brother."

Robyn looked up at me again, and her scowl was like a bolt of thunder. "I'm smart, but I'm not psychic. On the bright side, we've eliminated one suspect." She gave Spencer an apologetic smile. "But we may not know who the bad guy is until we actually pull off his mask."

"Isn't that more a Scooby Doo thing than a Nancy Drew thing?" Spence asked.

"Yes. But Titus is too upset right now to keep his dated pop culture references straight." Robyn gave the paperclip another vicious twist, and the last cuff popped open. "Thank goodness." She turned to me with fire flashing behind her eyes. "If you ever handcuff me to anything other than a headboard again, I will shave your *entire body* while you sleep. Including your eyebrows. And if you don't think I can pull that off, I will put you in touch with a couple of Pi Kappa brothers who can show you photographic evidence to the contrary!"

Spencer turned to me with arched brows. "Headboard?"

"Spence, may I use your restroom?" she asked, before I could decide whether or not to admit that Robyn and I were together. Assuming I hadn't ruined the best thing to ever happen to me.

"Of course." He pointed into his bedroom. "Through there, on the right. There're only two choices. The other one's a closet." When the door closed behind her, Spencer chuckled. "She's really pissed, man."

Yes. Yes, she was. "And yet I have more pressing concerns. Yesterday we found Corey Morris's fellow partygoers in the cabin where he left them. Ivy was dead from scratch fever, and Leland Blum was a newly infected stray, stuck in feline form. We kept Blum with us overnight, then dropped him at his dorm before we came to see you this afternoon. Afterward, we went to pick him up and found him dead in his own dorm room."

"Holy shit, Titus." Spencer leaned back on his couch, clearly stunned. "You thought *I* had something to do with all that?"

"Obviously I was wrong, and I apologize. But we're pretty sure that Blum's killer is going after my brother next, and I can't stop that if I can't find either of them."

"I might be able to help you there." Spencer stood and headed into his small kitchen, where he pulled a bottle of water from the fridge. "The stray who came in last night was in pretty good shape. His wound was so fresh it was still bleeding, and he didn't have much of a fever yet. On our way to your house, he told me about the party where he'd been attacked."

"The party at the museum. You told us that." Robyn came out of the bathroom smelling like hand soap.

"But that's only part of it. It's Blind Tiger week at Millsaps."

I shook my head, uncomprehending. "Blind Tiger?"

"As in, an underground bar?" Robyn frowned. "From the prohibition era?"

Spencer frowned at her. "How the hell do you know things like that?"

"History major. House arrest. Documentaries. We've been over this." She gave us both a cryptic smile. "You do *not* want to play Trivial Pursuit with me."

"I don't want to play Trivial Pursuit with *anyone*," Spencer said. "Anyway, Blind Tiger week is a series of underground parties, presumably serving alcohol to underage students. Each night is hosted by a different club, fraternity, or sorority trying to outdo all the others." He turned to me and held my gaze. "Both Corey Morris and this new stray, Elliott Belcher, were infected during or after attending Blind Tiger parties."

I closed my eyes, letting that sink in. A festival of unauthorized parties. Presumably hundreds of drunk, underage college students. And four new strays—two survivors—in the span of a week.

"Justus was infected a week before this Blind Tiger thing, right?" Robyn said.

"Yeah." Spencer cracked open his bottle of water. "But—"

"But if Justus ran across all four of his victims at Blind Tiger parties, chances are good that he'll be at the next party too," I finished for him.

"It's just a theory, but tonight's the last night." Spencer drained a third of his water in one gulp.

Robyn sank onto the couch, rubbing her wrist, where the cuff had chafed it. I wanted to kiss her wrist in apology, but I was pretty sure she'd punch me if I tried. "Please tell me you know where that party is, Spence," she said.

"I don't. But I know of two newly infected strays who might."

"Corey Morris and Elliott Belcher." I pulled my phone from my pocket.

"Let me do it," Robyn said. "They're more likely to talk to me than to you right now. Especially if Elliott Belcher has shifted and smells like you."

"Fine."

To my surprise, she selected Brandt from her contacts list, rather than one of the actual enforcers. "I think we have a connection," she explained as she pressed SEND to make the call.

Brandt answered before I even heard the phone ring. "Hello? Is this Robyn?"

"Yes." She smiled at me with the phone held to her ear. "How did you know?"

"Drew gave us your number and told us to answer if you called." He hesitated. "In case you need anything."

Translation: *In case Titus turns out to be the monster we all now suspect he is.*

"Well, that was nice of him. And I *do* need something."

"Happy to help." Brandt sounded as eager as a puppy with a bone. "What can I do for you?"

"I need you to put me on the phone with one of the new strays," Robyn said. "Preferably Corey Morris." With whom she'd already bonded.

"Oh…" Brandt hedged. "I don't think that's what Drew had in mind."

"I didn't call Drew. I called *you*, because I knew I could count on you. I'm trying to help Corey and Elliott. You and I have both been where they are, so I know you can sympathize. I need to talk to Corey for one minute. Do you think you can get into the basement without bothering Drew?"

"Yeah. He's out running an errand. Just a second."

Robyn made a scrawling gesture with her right hand, and Spencer dug a pen and a notepad from a kitchen drawer, while we listened to the familiar echo of Brandt's footsteps clomping down the basement steps.

"Corey?" he said, and the minor reverberation of his voice confirmed that he was in the basement. "You have a phone call. It's Robyn." In the pause, I heard the familiar squeal of mattress springs, as Corey sat up on his basement bed. "You wanna talk to her?"

There was no reply, but a second later Corey Morris was on the line. "Robyn?"

"Yes, it's me." She gave Spencer and me a silent "shh" gesture. "I have a couple of questions for you, if you don't mind."

"Okay…" But he sounded hesitant.

"The party you went to the night you were infected? Was it one of the Blind Tiger parties?"

"Um…yeah." He sounded…guilty. "But I wasn't drinking." There was a beat of silence. "How did you know about that?"

She gave me a wide-eyed, panicked look for a second. Then she shrugged and improvised. "There are posters all over campus, but they're surprisingly vague."

"They do that on purpose. The locations are spread through word of mouth. Which is texting, basically."

"The last party's tonight, right? Do you know where?"

"Um…maybe. Let me check my messages."

"Thanks." Robyn's voice betrayed none of the tension and anticipation I saw in the death grip she had on Spencer's pen.

"Oh! It's at the zoo," Morris said a minute later. "In the reptile house."

"Seriously?" Robyn frowned. "That's crazy!"

"That's the whole point." Despite the

circumstances, Morris sounded disappointed by the prospect of missing the party. "The hosting organization has to figure out how to get the security guards out of the way by midnight—without hurting anyone—and how to get food, drinks, and people in. All without getting caught. And everything has to be cleared out by five in the morning. There's *no way* they'll pull all that off at the zoo. But if they do, that party will go down in *history.*"

I had a feeling Morris was right, about the last bit, anyway.

"Thanks, Corey," Robyn said. "How are you, by the way?"

"Better. But I can't wait until they let me out of here. I need to sleep in a place that doesn't smell like *him.*"

Like me.

Like Justus.

Morris would never be able to escape that scent— it was a permanent part of him. But before long, he'd be so used to it that he wouldn't even notice it anymore. I knew that from experience.

"Hey, Robyn, why are you asking about the party?" Morris asked, "Are you going?"

Robyn hesitated. "Maybe," she said after a second. "I haven't had any fun since I had to drop out of school, and I saw the posters, so I thought I might check it out."

"If you do, get a picture for me, okay?"

She nodded, though Morris couldn't see her over the phone. "I will."

A second later, Brandt was back. "You're going to a party?"

"Maybe..." Robyn hedged. "Thanks again, Brandt.

I appreciate the help!" Then she hung up before he could ask any more questions.

"Well done!" Spencer said. "So, if you guys find Justus tonight, this whole thing'll be over, right? You can tell everyone the truth?"

"That's the hope, yes." I stood. "I have to find him before the council finds out about any of this, to keep them from taking him into custody or executing him on sight. I'm sorry about your front door. And I'm even sorrier about the favor I'm going to ask for next," I added as I retrieved my steering wheel from his end table.

"Let me guess. You want my car."

"I hate to ask, but..."

"Fine. If it'll get you out of here, so I can sleep. I can get a ride to work." Spence dug a set of keys from a decorative bowl sitting on his kitchen counter. "Just bring it back in one piece. With a full tank!" he added as I accepted the keys.

"Thank you. Seriously. I owe you."

"Damn right you do."

I gave his door an experimental swing, as if the problem were in the hinges. "I'll have a repairman over to fix this within the hour."

"No." He scowled. "I'm going to bed. Send him tonight, around nine. I should be up by then."

"Done."

Spencer closed his front door behind us, and a heavy scraping sound came from inside as he pushed something in front of the broken door to hold it closed.

"Wow," Robyn said as I followed her down the stairs. "I thought I was a natural disaster, but you're hurricane Titus. You took out his door *and* his car, in one fell swoop. Not to mention stealing his sleep and accusing him of murder."

"If you knew he wasn't the killer, why did you let me accuse him?" I demanded as I stared into the parking lot, looking for a Toyota that Spencer Cole might own.

"I didn't know for sure," she admitted. "I was planning to start that conversation with questions, not accusations, but you handcuffed me to a steering wheel!"

"Yeah. Just how mad about that are you?"

"Less so now than I was before I shredded your driver's seat, kicked in your dashboard, and slashed your tires."

I thought she was joking until I glanced past her at the space where I'd parked. How the hell was I going to explain *that* to my insurance guy? "Are you going to be this destructive every time I piss you off?"

"Did you not listen when the council warned you about my impulse control issues?"

"Not closely enough, apparently. Speaking of shocking revelations, why do you know how to pick open handcuffs?"

Robyn took Spencer's keys and pressed the lock button. A Corolla halfway across the lot beeped and flashed its lights. "Instead of answering that, why don't I show you how I acquired the skill…?" She pulled the cuffs from her pocket and dangled them in front of me with a wicked smile.

"You think I'm going to wear those?"

"I think we won't be even until you do." She backed toward the parking lot, and the sun glinted off the metal cuffs as she swung them. "Why? Is the big bad Alpha afraid to relinquish control?"

"To you?" I snorted and snatched the cuffs from her. "Hell, yes."

Robyn turned and took off for the Corolla, then called over her shoulder. "You should be..."

TWENTY

Robyn

The plan was to go back to Justus's place and take a nap before we had to head to the zoo. Titus was exhausted—he couldn't have gotten much sleep the night before—and he'd hardly eaten a thing all day. And with each mile we drove, he retreated a little more into his own head, until his eyes glazed over and his responses to my questions devolved into distracted grunts.

But the moment we stepped into the apartment, his bearing changed. Every muscle in his body tensed and his jaw clenched.

I glanced around the front rooms, expecting to find an intruder or some other danger that had triggered his internal alarm. The kitchen and living room were still trashed, except for the couch we'd put back in order, but the apartment was unoccupied, as far as I could tell. Titus's gaze locked on the guest room, which stood open and as empty as we'd left it. And finally I understood.

He wasn't bracing himself against a new threat. He

was still battling the last one. "I failed him. Blum is dead, and I was supposed to protect him. Maybe I should have handcuffed *him* to something."

Well, hell. No wonder he'd been so determined to keep me in the car. He blamed himself for Leland's death, and he couldn't stand the thought of the same thing happening to me.

I pushed the front door shut and put the chain on the hook, because the deadbolt was still busted from the break-in. "It's not your fault."

"Bullshit. I swore to protect them. I accepted oaths of loyalty in exchange for that promise. I told them I would lead them, and teach them, and defend them, and Blum got killed on my watch. Because I left him behind."

"Titus, we had no idea he was in danger. We took him to his dorm specifically *to* protect him. You can't blame yourself for this."

He sank onto the couch and bent forward with his elbows on his knees, his head cradled in his hands. "There's no one else to blame."

"Blame the killer. Tonight we'll find Justus, and we'll figure out who infected him. And who's trying to make sure you go down for the strays he's infected." Those *had* to be the same person.

"Does any of it matter? I'm a liability to the Pride, but without the weight of my position, I might not have the clout to help Justus." His expression cracked, exposing the pain beneath his anger. "Robyn, I can't let my brother wind up like Leland Blum. I can't let some psycho kill him, and I sure as hell can't let the council execute him."

"That won't happen." I took my new coat off and draped it over the arm of the couch, flinching as my boots crunched over glass ground into the carpet from the shattered coffee table. Then I sank onto his lap, straddling him. "You may not have the clout to make sure of that, but *I* do."

His hands settled onto my hips and he met my gaze, and for the first time since we'd left Spencer's, he seemed to be truly with me in the moment. "What are you talking about?"

"The council wants me back. You said they'd be willing to start a war to make sure that happens. Which means they're desperate, and desperate people are always eager to negotiate. So I'll agree to return peacefully—sparing everyone this 'war'—in exchange for Justus's clemency and the recognition of your Pride. With you as Alpha. Drew's doing the best he can, but *you* are best equipped to lead them." That much was obvious in the lengths to which he was willing to go to protect his brother.

"Robyn…" The objection was clear in his tortured expression, even if he hadn't found the words.

"I am the most valuable bargaining chip we have. I know you're willing to do whatever you can to keep me here, but the truth is that that's beyond your ability right now. Drew's in charge of the Pride, and he's too new to risk pissing off the council. But *I'm* the one whose life is being run by committee. If I have to go back, I might as well get something good out of it."

"I don't want you involved in this," Titus said. "Not any more than you already are," he amended, with a glance around the destroyed living room.

"Whatever. I brought war to your doorstep." I leaned down to kiss him, pressing as much of myself against him as I could while his grip on my hips tightened. "I owe you," I whispered against his stubble-rough cheek when the kiss finally ended.

"No." Titus's gaze burned into me. "You don't owe me anything, Robyn."

"Including obedience. This is my decision. And I've made it."

I tried to stand, but he held tight to my hips, and I saw myself reflected in his eyes. "You are the most fearless woman I've ever met. If it had been up to me, I wouldn't have locked you up. I would have set you loose upon the world and watched you soar."

My chest suddenly felt tight. "Before I met you, I was just angry. At the council. At the enforcers. At myself." I ran one hand down the side of his face, toward his chin, enjoying the rough brush of stubble against my palm. "Meeting you changed the way I feel about shifters. The way I feel about myself. I thought my life—at least as I knew it—was over. I was so obsessed with everything I lost when I was infected that I didn't take the time to truly realize what I'd gained. *You're* a big part of what I've gained, Titus. Your vision. What you're trying to do is more important than anything I've ever done in my life. If I can help put you in the position to do that, I will. Even if that means getting out of your way." Going back to Atlanta. I shrugged. "I got out once. I can do it again. Worst case scenario, I'll be back when my sentence is up."

Titus pulled me closer and buried his face in my hair. "I'm not done arguing about this."

"Okay, but fair warning, I'm not sure I've ever lost an argument."

"There's a first time for everything." His breath brushed my ear, and pleasant chills slid along my spine.

"Right now, I'm more interested in our second time." I slid my hands beneath his shirt, then dragged them up over the hard planes and angles of his chest. "This may be the last chance we get for a while…"

Titus pulled his shirt over his head and dropped it on the glass-littered floor. Then he stood with me still straddling him, and I wrapped my legs around his waist as my arms slid around his neck.

I kissed him all the way into the bedroom.

"The herpetarium." Titus stood on top of a commercial trash bin, staring over the Jackson Zoo's eight-foot exterior fence, squinting against the glare of the security light. "Who on earth would want to get drunk with a bunch of snakes and lizards?"

"You're showing your age, Mr. Alexander. But you're right. This would be much more awesome in the cat house."

"There's no cat house. They're in outdoor cages." He turned away from the fence and looked at me. "And even if there were a cat house, the lions and tigers would all *lose their minds* the moment they smelled us."

"Why? They're caged next to each other, and they don't kill themselves trying to get through the fence."

"I don't know. Maybe it has something to do with us smelling like humans *and* cats. Or maybe it's that we're walking around free when they aren't." Titus jumped down from the bin and landed right in front of me. "All I know is that I went to the zoo once, not long after I was infected, just to watch them. To see how much I had in common with nature's true predators."

"And what did you find?"

"That the cougars and leopards backed away from me, but the tigers were ready to rumble." He shrugged. "Maybe that's because they're so much bigger than we are. They know they have nothing to fear."

I watched him, fascinated by the thought of Titus staring through a chain-link fence, trying to figure out where he fit into the natural order. "What kind of cat are we, when we have fur?"

"No kind." He frowned. "No, we're *our* kind. A species of our own. We are like no other cat in the world." He pulled me close for a kiss. "And you are like no other woman in the world. Which makes you doubly unique and fascinating."

Grinning, I went up on my toes to give him another kiss.

"This is where you say something nice about me," he said.

I slid my arms around his neck and whispered into his ear. "You have a very limber tongue."

Titus laughed. "And you have a one-track mind."

"No, there are two tracks up here." I tapped my temple. "But one is totally dedicated to thinking and speaking from the gutter."

"And what is that other, more productive track thinking right now?"

"That it's my turn to go in feline form."

"No." Titus's dark brows dipped low. "If security thinks you escaped from one of the cat pens, they'll shoot to kill."

"The same goes for you. But that won't happen,

because the sorority hosting tonight's Blind Tiger party already got rid of security. Remember?"

He scowled. "I remember thinking that was a *terrible* idea, at a zoo."

"Agreed. But the worst the partiers are going to do if they see me is run screaming and call 911. Besides, you need to be able to talk to your brother, when we find him. Which you can't do in cat form. He won't recognize me. We don't even know if he'll understand that I'm another shifter."

"Fair point." But Titus didn't look happy about it. "Fine. But one of these days I *will* win an argument with you."

I grinned. "Don't count on it."

"Go ahead and shift. I'll stand watch." Because a shifter was never more vulnerable than when she was caught between forms, unable to defend herself.

I stripped behind the trash bin, tossing him each article of clothing as I removed it, knowing he could see me perfectly well in the dark, even with his human eyes. Titus stuffed my clothes into his backpack as I knelt on the grimy concrete, shivering.

As I shifted, breathing deeply through an agonizing dance of stretching muscles and dislocating joints, I let my mind drift to distract myself from the pain. Usually, that meant reliving a happy childhood event or a particularly satisfying college tryst. But something about the cold concrete and the unpleasant mix of scents wafting from the nearby trash bin called up less pleasant memories.

Hiding behind a pile of bulging black trash bags, staring through the grimy glass of a cabin deep in the woods, watching camo-clad, rifle-carrying men come and go. Waiting for my chance...

My knees cracked as they shifted, and the

traumatized muscles connected to them stretched so tight they felt ready to pop like elastic. If I could have unclenched my jaw, I might have screamed.

Teeth sinking through flesh into bone as I broke that redneck bastard's neck with one bite...

My rib cage expanded, each thin bone creaking as it moved into place until my chest felt like it would tear itself apart. My lungs burned—each breath felt like swallowing glass.

Racing through the forest, trying to outrun the stench of my enemies. The taste of their blood in my mouth. Knowing that I've lost control once more. That I may never truly be in control again...

My skin began to itch as fur sprouted all over it, sprouting like grass grown in fast-forward to cover my entire body. Pain shot through my teeth as they grew longer and sharper. As they rearranged themselves in my mouth, like the handiwork of some psychotic dentist.

And finally, when the ordeal was over, I lay panting on the filthy concrete, waiting for the echo of pain to fade from every nerve ending in my body. Stunned, as usual, I needed a moment of stillness—a moment of quiet—in which to understand what had just happened.

Would the process never seem natural? Would my mind never come to terms with the reality my body could no longer deny?

"Robyn?" Titus knelt next to me on the balls of his feet, looking more limber and agile on two legs than I was on four. "Are you ready?"

In reply, I stood, and with my first truly deep breath, alarm resonated through me like the echoing vibration from a cymbal. Never in my life had I smelled such an amazing and startling array of scents.

298

My muzzle bobbed as I sniffed the air, taking them all in.

Titus chuckled. "It's crazy, isn't it?"

Feline, bovine, porcine, equine, avian. I smelled moss, and mold, and rot, and bleach, and the dry, grainy scent of some kind of food pellet. And water. Not chlorinated or salted, like pool water, but fresh yet stagnant, like a pond with insufficient circulation.

There were so many scents I could hardly distinguish them. Too many to concentrate on, yet I couldn't afford to simply block them all out, because I was looking for one scent in particular.

Justus.

Like Titus, but not.

Unlike a dog, I wouldn't be able to track him, but if I could detect some trace of his scent, I'd know we were in the right place. We had come an hour early, hoping to see and smell all the partygoers as they arrived, including what would hopefully be the only guest on four legs.

Other than me.

"Let's go," Titus whispered as he climbed onto the trash bin against the fence at the back of the zoo. "You're first."

Instead of following him onto the bin, I hunkered down in a four-legged squat, muzzle pointed at the goal. *Eight-foot vertical jump. No problem.* I launched myself into the air with my rear legs. My whiskers flattened against my cheeks. The ground fell away.

My back feet caught the top of the fence, my paw pads curling around it for balance. My front paws hardly brushed the chain-link, then I pushed off against the fence, as I had against the ground. An instant later, I landed on concrete. Inside the zoo.

Chain-link rattled at my back. Titus landed in a squat, backpack square on his shoulders, one hand on the ground. His tongue wasn't his only limber body part. "Okay, let's find some place to hide, where we can see the entrance to the herpetarium."

Fortunately, the zoo's pathways were lined with flora to look like a wilderness trail, and in the dark, the gaps between the individual plants and shrubs would be even harder to see. At least for humans.

We found a spot behind several large ferns, and Titus squatted next to me, his arm stretched over my back, one hand on my shoulder. "Can you see anything?" He nodded to the herpetarium for clarity.

I stared at the low brick building. There were no windows. If anything was happening inside, I couldn't see it. Nor could I hear it, even when I rotated my ears to face the building.

"Well then, we'll just have to wait," Titus said. But we'd only been hiding a few minutes when I heard a shuffling sound from down the paved pathway in front of the herpetarium. Seconds later, I heard a giggle.

I whined, low and deep, and pointed my muzzle in the direction of the sounds, which Titus couldn't hear yet, with his human ears.

He stared down the path, and we both tensed when a small group of people came into view, arms weighed down by heavy bags, whispering softly to each other as they "snuck" toward their destination. As if somewhere nearby there was a sleeping security guard who might wake up if they spoke aloud.

I could tell from the way Titus dismissed them that Justus was not among the group.

For the next half hour, we watched small clusters

of people my age or younger walk in carrying bulging bags, pushing rolling beer kegs, and lugging cardboard boxes full of portable speaker components. But Justus did not appear, and the novelty of our stakeout soon faded.

No house cat in the history of either houses or cats has ever sat still for more than fifteen minutes without falling asleep, and by eleven forty-five, I was nearing my limit.

I stood and stretched. I yawned, subtly getting Titus accustomed to the idea that I could make small movements in the foliage without alerting anyone to my presence. Then I padded silently through to brush to the left, moving parallel to the path the party-throwers had all come down, combining reconnaissance with movement, to keep myself alert.

"Robyn!" Titus whispered fiercely. "Where are you going?"

I had no way to answer, so I kept moving.

Naturally, he came after me. "You can't wander around the zoo looking like a cat!"

If I could have spoken, I would have pointed out that wandering around looking like a human would have been just as dangerous, after hours, and probably more illegal.

No one ever accused a cat of trespassing.

"Robyn!"

But it wasn't Titus's irritation that brought me to a total standstill in the brush. My nostrils flared slightly, and my head bobbed as I scented the air, trying to pinpoint a direction.

Titus saw my reaction and dropped onto his heels. "Is it Justus?" He scanned what we could see of the path, and tension flooded his scent as clearly as it came through in his posture.

I gave him a small shake of my head. *Not Justus.* A scent I knew even better.

Leaves rustled across the path, and my focus homed in on the movement with an ease and precision my human eyes could never have managed. Cats may experience the world through taste and smell, but they hunt with their eyes and their ears.

Titus followed my gaze, and when the leaves rustled again, he spotted the movement.

"Not Justus." He set his backpack on the ground and dug quietly through the front pocket. "Do I need a weapon?"

I rolled my eyes at him, but I had no way to tell him that we were in no danger, except….

I looked down the path to make sure no one else was coming, then I stepped boldly out of the bushes onto the narrow paved road, staring right at the place where the leaves had moved.

"Robyn!" Titus called in a whisper hardly loud enough for me to hear, but I ignored him.

For a moment, nothing happened. Then Drew stood from his hiding place across the path. I could tell from the brief wash of surprise over his face that he hadn't known I was there. Yet after that initial shock, he seemed…relieved. As if he'd been looking for me.

"Come over here and let's have a chat." He spoke too softly to be overheard by anyone nearby. Anyone human, anyway.

Titus stood, and Drew's eyes widened.

Why would he be relieved to see me, but surprised to see Titus? Then I understood.

Corey Morris had told him that I'd asked about the

party. Or maybe Brandt had told him.

Did Drew really think Titus would let me go out alone, in a strange city with a shifter murderer on the loose?

Wait, he didn't know about the murder. And he thought Titus was the only thing to be afraid of in Jackson. Suddenly I was very glad we'd both showered after our latest...connection.

"Shit," Titus breathed. "We led him right to the party. We have to get him out of here before Justus shows up. Assuming he ever does. I'll talk to him. You get back in the bushes before someone sees you and panics."

Reluctantly, I slunk into the foliage to listen. And watch for Justus.

"I assume you spoke to Corey Morris?" Though Titus was whispering, I could hear him perfectly well.

"Brandt, actually." Drew glanced over Titus's shoulder at the brush where I was hiding, but I couldn't tell whether he could see me.

"If you came here for Robyn, there's no need," Titus said. "I'm not going to let anything happen to her."

"I believe you, but... Titus, the council wants her. When they found out I'd taken over the territory, but she'd left with *you*, they lost their shit. Abby's dad called to renegotiate. They're prepared to accept the Pride on a trial basis *right now*—if I bring Robyn to them. Tonight."

Damn it.

Drew's timing could not be worse. And he'd negotiated with my freedom. I'd been willing to do that for Titus and Justus, but not for a Pride without Titus as Alpha.

303

"A trial basis?" Titus crossed his arms over his chest. "That means they can change their minds whenever they want. Which'll be as soon as they have Robyn. It's not a real acceptance, Drew. They're manipulating you with an empty promise."

Drew bristled visibly. "It's more than they've ever offered you."

"Actually, it's *exactly* what they offered me. And it's not good enough. We can't accept anything other than full recognition by the council. And Robyn isn't a pawn to be sacrificed."

My chest suddenly felt too tight. As if my heart had swollen within it. If I'd been human, I would have thrown myself at Titus, arms wide open. But pouncing on him in cat form wouldn't have quite the same effect.

"No offense, man, but that's not your call anymore. She doesn't belong to us."

"No, but she does belong *with* us," Titus growled. "It's her decision."

"That's not how this works," Drew insisted. "This is our chance, Titus. This is what we've been working toward for years. We give them their tabby, and we get everything we've ever wanted. And it's not like they're asking for anything crazy. They want her to keep her word. Which is exactly what we want from them."

"You can't trust them—"

"That's *my call*," Drew said through clenched teeth, and a sinking feeling weighed heavy inside me. I recognized this conflict. It was the same one brewing between Jace and Titus. The same one that had come between Marc and Jace once upon a time, according to Abby.

Drew was an Alpha now. A dominant shifter on equal standing with Titus. Yet he lacked Titus's experience. He didn't yet know how to temper the instinct telling him to win this battle at any cost.

Titus wasn't willing to back down, and Drew didn't know how to. If something didn't change, they would come to blows.

Someone would get hurt.

I had no intention of going to Atlanta until I'd negotiated the return myself. But if Drew got a whiff of Justus while he was trying to talk me into leaving with him, he'd figure out how Corey Morris was infected—a capital offense the council would insist that he punish, even if only to show loyalty to the assembly he wanted to join.

Titus wouldn't be able to protect his brother.

The only way to get rid of Drew before Justus showed up would be for me to go with him. Maybe there'd be time for me to call Faythe and negotiate on the way to the border. If not…I'd escaped the Southeast Territory once. I could do it again.

I stood, ready to intervene, but before I could step onto the path again, a thud caught my attention from the right. From the direction of the fence Titus and I had jumped.

A second thud followed, then a third: shoes hitting the pavement.

Titus and Drew were still arguing. Their human-form ears hadn't picked up the sound.

I snuck through the foliage toward the fence, listening. Trying to decide what to do.

"Six parties in six days!" The voice was soft, yet obviously excited. "But you can't bail on us tonight, man. This is the last one." Three men rounded a curve in the path, still talking. Each carried an open bottle of beer, and none of them had any idea they weren't alone.

"I'm not going to bail," the guy in the middle said. "I got sick, I told you. Bad shellfish."

It was the familiar quality of his voice that made me look closer at him. But it was his face that drove a bolt of shock through me. Looking at him was like looking at a younger version of Titus. A younger *replica*.

Practically a clone.

A sniff in the kid's direction confirmed it. Justus Alexander had arrived. He had come to party. And threaded through his scent, I caught a ribbon of his infector's—

Son of a bitch.

TWENTY-ONE

Titus

"Okay, we're not going to argue about this." Drew swept one hand through his hair, and I had to fight for calm, when my instinct was to inform him that he wasn't *really* the Alpha. He was a pretender to the throne. A temporary fix until I could be sure I wasn't a detriment to the Pride.

He had *no right* to make demands of me.

"You stepped down voluntarily and asked me to do what's best for the Pride," he continued. "And that's what I'm doing. That's what I've *been* doing, since this whole thing was just a crazy idea you and I came up with in the middle of the night, several bottles in. And *this* is what's best for the Pride. It's not a death sentence, Titus. The council doesn't want to hurt Robyn. They want to do what's best for her."

"That's up to her to—"

A dark blur shot across my peripheral vision. Something seized the left leg of my pants, over my calf, and dragged me backward. Hard.

I stumbled, righted myself, and whirled around.

"Robyn! What the hell?"

She whined, deep in her throat. Obviously, she was trying to tell me something, but without words, all I could pick up clearly was anxiety. And urgency.

"You can't be seen. What's—?" Then I heard the voices.

"—make you forget about that lying bitch. You won't even remember her name."

"Ivy who?" The second voice laughed, and I turned, stunned, as my brother rounded a curve in the manicured path, sandwiched by two other kids in Millsaps shirts and light jackets.

"Justus?" Disbelief echoed in my voice. We'd discovered two corpses in our forty-eight-hour search for my brother, and there he was, laughing with his friends, carrying an open bottle of beer, as if he had nothing in the world to worry about.

"Titus?" He stopped, and his friends squinted in my direction. The humans probably couldn't see well enough in the dark to know that I was too old to go to a college party, and I could tell from the lack of panic that they couldn't see Robyn at all. Black fur blends well into the shadows.

Justus's gaze slid toward her and he frowned. "What's…going on?" His focus narrowed on Robyn, then flicked up to me, and I could see him trying to mentally connect dots that—in his mind—had nothing in common. His brother. And a big black cat.

He had no idea I wasn't human. Whether Robyn was a shifter or an escaped zoo cat, he didn't understand why she seemed willing to stand next to me, instead of fleeing into the foliage. Or attacking.

"You guys go on in," I said to his friends. "Justus will be there in a minute."

"Jus?" The one on the right squinted, trying to focus on me in the near-dark. "Who the hell is that?"

"It's okay." Though he sounded unsure of that. "It's my brother. Go on. I'll be right there."

His friends hesitated for a second, then turned right and headed into the herpetarium. Music and beams of brightly colored light fell onto the sidewalk, then died the moment the door closed behind them, leaving nothing but the soft thump of bass to remind us that the party had started. That the path we stood on would soon be overrun with more attendees.

"Titus, what's going on? And who the hell is that?" Justus stared at Robyn. "Is that...? Is she...?" He had no way to finish the question he didn't even really understand. He'd probably never seen a female shifter. He'd probably never seen another shifter at all, except the one who'd infected him, and surely he hadn't known that's what was happening to him, at the time.

I jogged down the path toward him. "I've been looking for you for *two days*," I said as I wrapped one arm around his shoulders, already guiding him toward the exterior fence and away from Drew. "Where—"

Robyn pushed her way between us. She growled, and I glanced down, assuming she was demanding an ill-timed introduction. But she only sniffed Justus's thigh. Dramatically. Insistently. And finally, I understood.

I pulled him into a hug and inhaled his scent right at his neck. Where it was strongest.

He smelled like himself. Like he always had. And he smelled like me, more now than ever. And he smelled like...

Rage burned through me, unburdened by logic. I

didn't understand what my nose was telling me, but I didn't doubt it.

"Drew!" I spun toward him, but he was gone. My best friend of nearly a decade. My college roommate. My trusted employee, even before we'd been infected.

The traitorous bastard who'd attacked my brother.

"What? Drew's here?" Justus asked, and with a sudden stunned comprehension, I realized he didn't know who'd infected him because as a human—even a newly infected stray—his sense of smell hadn't been strong enough to identify the cat who'd scratched him. He hadn't even known that was possible. And unlike Corey Morris, he hadn't yet connected his own scent to that of his infector.

Which could only mean that he hadn't smelled Drew since he'd shifted.

Focus, Titus. One thing at a time.

"Justus, this is Robyn. My…girlfriend." I laid one hand on her head, fighting for patience when every muscle in my body demanded that I find Drew and make him pay. "She's going to take you into the bushes, and you're both going to stay there until I get back," I said, talking over him when he tried to object. Or maybe ask a question. I turned to Robyn. "Can you still hear Drew?"

She went still, except for her ears, rotating on top of her head. Finding and categorizing sounds. Then she nodded, and her eyes narrowed. She pointed her muzzle toward the west.

"Thanks," I whispered. Then I took off running.

TWENTY-TWO

Robyn

Justus stared after his older brother in astonishment and utter confusion as Titus's footsteps pounded off to the west. Around a curve in the trail, several girls screamed, then burst into laughter, and I realized Titus had startled them as he raced by. They wouldn't recover so quickly from finding me on the path.

I seized Justus's jeans cuff between my teeth and tried to tug him toward the bushes, but he jumped back, startled, and the material ripped. His beer bottle exploded on the pavement. He blinked at me in the dark, uncomprehending, and I realized how little he'd understood of what had happened in the past minute and a half. So instead of trying to pull him again, I whined softly and turned toward the foliage, asking as clearly and politely as I could for him to follow me.

He stared at me for a second, and I recognized comprehension the instant it registered in his eyes. He'd finally connected me—a cat—with his brother's designation of me as his girlfriend. A descriptor that felt monumental, yet somehow insufficient.

And finally, as a group of six girls my age rounded the westward curve in the path, Justus stepped into the bushes with me and dropped into a squat.

"Robyn?" he whispered.

I nodded, and his eyes widened as if confirmation that I was a shifter—that I could understand and respond to him—was almost more miraculous than his mere suspicion that that was the case.

"You're with Titus?" he asked, and I nodded again. "And you're...like me?"

I bobbed my muzzle again, and his relieved exhalation was so deep and thorough that it broke my heart. "I hoped I wasn't the only one. Is...is Titus...?"

I nodded, wishing for my human mouth, capable of giving him the answers he needed. How could he think he was the only one? How could he know Drew, yet not know Drew had infected him? At least he wasn't stuck in cat form, like Leland Blum had been.

"What's going on, Robyn? Who are you? How do you know my brother? Why are you guys here?" Tears welled in eyes the same shade of gray as Titus's. His voice was thick with confusion. But without my human mouth, I could only rub my head against his arm, hoping he understood the comfort I was trying to communicate. "I don't know what that means!" His voice was getting louder, and I could hear more partygoers coming up the path. "Change back so I can talk to you!" he demanded in a loud whisper. "Please!"

Finally, I nodded, though I wasn't sure that was the wisest course of action, with so many humans nearby. But Justus needed answers, and I knew exactly how that felt. So I lay down with my legs folded beneath me and began the process.

Spurred on by his pain and the knowledge that we could be discovered any second, I managed my fastest shift ever, though it was still nowhere near what Titus could do.

"Holy shit!" Justus breathed when I finally sat up, naked and breathing heavily, covered in chill bumps from the cold. Exhausted by the process. "Is that what I look like? I've never seen it. It's pretty disgusting, in the middle."

"I know," I whispered. "And yes, that's what you look like." I crossed my arms over my chest, suddenly self-conscious about my nudity, now that Titus's little brother was staring at me. "Can you hand me that bag?" I motioned to the backpack, where Titus had hidden it behind a fern.

Justus handed me the bag. "You're my brother's girlfriend?"

I pulled my shirt over my head without bothering with my bra. "Yeah, I guess. It's a new development."

"And you're both…?"

"Shifters. Yes. I was infected a few months ago, but your brother's been like this for three years." I shimmied into my underwear without fully standing, then reached for my jeans. "I'm sure he'll tell you all about it when he gets back."

"Infected?" Justus frowned. "You mean I caught this, like a disease?" His eyes narrowed, and I could see him connecting the dots. "When I was attacked by something in the woods. I thought it was a wolf, or something. It was a…shifter?"

"Yeah." *Please don't ask me who it was.* I shouldn't be the one to give him that news. I wasn't family.

Instead, he asked for a much more difficult answer. "Scratching someone does this?"

I nodded as I stood to pull the jeans over my hips. "Or biting."

His frown became a look of pure panic. "But I scratched people. I didn't *know*." He scrubbed both hands over his face. "Ivy." He said the word into his palms, but I understood perfectly well. "And those guys at the cabin." He dropped his hands. "Are they...like me now?"

Damn it.

I pulled my shirt over my head. Then I knelt next to him and reached for his hand, silently hoping I wouldn't screw this up. That I wouldn't screw *him* up. "Corey Morris—the guy you scratched in the woods—he's a shifter now. And so is the guy from the museum last night." Justus's eyes widened, but he didn't ask how I knew about Elliott. "They're fine. They're at Titus's house. Friends are taking care of them."

"What about Ivy? And that bastard she was cheating on with me?"

"His name was Leland Blum. He died this afternoon. But that wasn't your fault. Someone..." I shrugged, then spat out the truth. "Someone killed him."

"And Ivy?" he asked again, as if he hadn't even heard what I'd said about Leland. Obviously, parts of the whole thing would take a while to sink in.

"She died from the infection a couple of days ago. I'm so sorry. Most women can't survive it. I'm an exception."

"She died because I scratched her?" His expression crumpled beneath an enormous burden of pain.

"No." I squeezed his hand, drawing his focus to me. "She died because someone scratched you, then didn't stick around to teach you anything. She died because you were infected and abandoned. It's an epidemic out here in the free zone, which your brother is trying to fix." But I could tell from the out-of-focus look in his eyes that he hadn't understood most of what I was trying to tell him.

"Who infected me?" Justus demanded in a low, gravelly voice. "Ivy's dead because of what that bastard did to me. Who is he?"

I hesitated, trying to figure out how to soothe the rage echoing in his voice and oozing from every pore on his body. But he misinterpreted my silence.

"Was it Titus? Did he do this to me? You said he's been a shifter for years, right?"

"No!" I put one hand on his arm, but he pulled away from me. "I mean yes, Titus has been a shifter for three years, but he didn't do this to you. It was Drew Borden. We didn't even know it was him until we smelled you a few minutes ago and made the connection. There's a trace of him in your scent now. And there always will be."

"Drew…" Justus's jaw clenched. His facial muscles began to ripple beneath his skin. "Why?"

"I don't know." His anger was bringing on a shift, and he didn't know how to control it. "Justus, you can fight this. You don't have to shift. Just calm down and listen to the sound of my voice."

"*Why?*" he demanded again, and there was little humanity left in his voice.

"Really. I don't know." Though there was no way in hell Drew had *accidentally* infected his best friend's little brother. "But Titus will find out. He'll fix this."

I regretted it as soon as I said it. Titus couldn't fix this. No one could. Justus would be a shifter for the rest of his life. Ivy's and Leland's lives were over. And there was nothing anyone could do about any of that.

Justus fell to the ground on his side, writhing in the dirt.

"Listen to me." I knelt next to him, whispering directly into his ear, softly stroking hair from his forehead. "Calm down. You're in control of your body. You can tell it to stop. You can stay human. You can fight this."

His eyes rolled up to look at me, and though his jaw was clenched tightly shut from muscles tensing as they shifted, I could see what he wanted to say clearly in his expression.

He didn't *want* to stop this.

TWENTY-THREE

Titus

"Drew!" I shouted as I raced through the darkened zoo, and only when I heard my own voice echo at me did I stop to wonder whether the party-throwers had gotten rid of the entire night security staff, or only those responsible for the herpetarium-side of the zoo.

Drew had a hell of a head start. I would never catch him if he didn't want to be caught. But he wasn't running to get away. He'd killed Leland Blum because Blum knew what he'd done, which meant Drew had no intention of fleeing the territory. He wanted to be Alpha, permanently, and for that to happen, he'd have to get rid of everyone who knew or could figure out the truth.

Me. Robyn. Justus. And maybe Spencer.

Drew wasn't running from me. He was running toward a position of advantage. A place to take his stand. Barreling head-first into his trap would only get me killed.

I stopped on the paved path, forcing myself to focus despite the rage pumping through my body with every beat of my heart. I detected no trace of

Drew's scent, in part because my nose was overloaded by an array and concentration of animal scents unlike any I'd ever experienced in nature. So I closed my eyes, concentrating on what I could hear instead. If Drew wanted to be found, he'd have to show me where he was.

Hooves shuffling in straw.

Birds squawking.

Monkeys howling, swinging on creaking branches from somewhere to the east.

The watery snort of something huge. A hippo?

Then I heard the familiar pounding of boots on pavement, accompanied by a breathless huffing. Drew was running.

I opened my eyes and took off after him. I ran past the carousel and the bathrooms, then across a grassy wooded patch of lawn. Drew's footsteps led me past a small amphitheater and a closed county-fair style cafe, then the scent of leopard overwhelmed me with its eerily familiar, yet unmistakably different pheromones.

One of the leopards growled. I couldn't see her, but she could smell me as well as I could smell her. I slowed to a jog. Drew was drawing me into the big cat area. In a zoo as small as Jackson's, that included only two more enclosures: the tigers and the cougars.

"Is this some kind of irony?" I called as I jogged toward the tigers. But Drew didn't answer, and I couldn't hear him anymore.

As I approached the enclosure, I slowed to a walk, listening for footsteps. Breathing. Watching for any out-of-place movement. But my senses were muted by the proximity of caged tigers. Two of them paced in front of the glass wall that let viewers get within inches of the great beasts. They were agitated by my presence and each huffing breath they drew into their huge lungs would obscure the sounds of Drew's breathing. And his footsteps, unless he wanted me to hear them.

"You couldn't just go away, could you?"

I spun toward the sound of his voice as Drew stepped into the covered viewing area. Holding a pistol.

"Drew..." Pulse racing, I held my hands up, palms out, my plan to disable him with no real care for his well-being temporarily stymied by the gun. "Why don't you calm down and tell me what this is about?"

"It's about the Pride!" He sounded exasperated. As if I should have known all along why he would turn into a violent sociopath. "That's all this has ever been about!"

"You infected my brother because you want to be Alpha?"

"I *deserve* to be Alpha." He gestured with the gun, and my focus followed the barrel. "I *am* Alpha. This Pride was my idea."

"The Pride was *our* idea." I tried to keep my voice calm. Even. "We said we'd run it together, and we *have* been. We—"

"Bullshit!" Drew roared, and the tigers stopped pacing to watch him warily. "It was *my* idea. I asked you to help, and instead, you took over. There was no discussion. No vote. You just assumed everyone would be better off with you in charge."

"Drew, I didn't..." Well, not exactly. I hadn't intended to take over. I hadn't even consciously thought about taking a leadership role. It just...happened.

"Being wealthy doesn't make you a leader," Drew insisted. "Running your dad's company doesn't qualify you to be in charge of people's *lives*. I was *summa cum laude*, and you were a B student. I worked for a living, and you practically lived on your trust fund until your parents died. The Pride was *my idea*, and you *took* it!"

"You're right." Though I would have conceded any point he made, while he had a gun aimed at my chest. "I didn't mean to cut you out. I didn't even realize you wanted to be Alpha." And the plain truth was that someone who had to *say* he wanted to be the Alpha—or waited for others to ask him to take the position—didn't stand much of a chance of actually attaining that goal.

Alphas step up because they can't *not* step up. They rise to a position of leadership and authority because people follow them, no discussion needed. No permission asked.

Drew hadn't done that. I had. And that had nothing to do with money.

"Right," he spat. "You just assumed that because you were everyone else's boss, that you'd be mine too." He raised the gun. "Turn around and start walking."

I almost refused. Then I realized that Robyn and Justus were waiting for me, just yards from a party full of unsuspecting college kids. If I didn't cooperate, would Drew start shooting? Was he that unstable?

He'd killed Leland Blum in cold blood.

I started walking, on alert for a chance to take the gun.

"So, you framed me," I said as we passed the leopards, headed back the way I'd come. "You infected Justus, knowing that whatever havoc he wreaked would be blamed on me, as long as no one knew he was a shifter."

"And as long as you had no alibi," Drew said, his shadow stretching out on the path in front of me in the glow from a security light overhead. "It took a lot of planning to get him to lose his shit while you were all alone. But I had no idea he'd keep infecting people. Cleaning up after your brother has become a real pain in the ass."

"And now you're done with him," I said, trying to keep him talking. The more distracted he became, the better chance I'd have of going for the gun. "You didn't come here for Robyn, did you? You came to kill my brother."

"I came to kill you both." His shadow shrugged on the pavement in front of me, and rage swelled like a roaring blaze inside me. "Since the council found out you infected and murdered poor Leland Blum, you've been declared public enemy number one. I *was* going to return Robyn and throw your corpse in as a bonus. Looks like now I won't be able to take her back alive." His silhouette shook its head as we passed the Elephant Cafe. "It's *such* a shame I couldn't get to her before you killed her too."

I had to swallow fury in order to speak. "You really think they're going to believe that?"

"I think they're going to believe their noses. Your scent is all over her. And they're going to believe the enforcers who've already testified via video that you admitted to infecting Corey Morris. You made it easy for me, Titus. And your brother was a far more accommodating—and prolific—infector than I could ever have hoped for."

Son of a bitch. Drew set the trap, and I walked right into it. He'd known all along that I'd take the blame to protect my brother. That I would tie my own noose, in front of my entire household.

"So, what, you infected Justus, then sat back to see what would happen?"

The silhouette of his head fell back as he snorted. "Do you think I would leave all this to chance? I made sure Spencer wasn't working the night I infected Justus so that he wouldn't be intercepted in the ER. Then, when you went on patrol by yourself, I anonymously emailed him a picture of his 'girlfriend' fucking her actual boyfriend—*that* was not easy to get—and told him where to find them. He did the rest on his own." Drew shrugged. "I'm sure he didn't *mean* to hurt anyone, but the newly infected have very little impulse control."

Bastard! How could I not have seen what was happening? How could I have lived and worked alongside Drew for years, yet had no idea how deranged his ambition was?

His shadow shrugged again as we passed the dark, frozen carousel. "New, untrained stray plus psychological trauma equals psychotic train wreck with the strength of several normal men. You remember that math, don't you Titus? You're the one who taught me the equation."

"So we could prevent it!" Anger thrumming through me, I stopped walking and turned slowly. "That wasn't an instruction manual, Drew! We're supposed to be helping people!"

"And now that I'm Alpha, I'll finally be in a position to."

"You got there by infecting and murdering people!

How could you do that to Justus? You've known him since he was nine years old. He thinks of you like a *brother!*"

Drew rolled his eyes. "Justus doesn't think about anyone but himself. But don't worry." He glanced pointedly at the gun still aimed at me. "He won't suffer much longer."

"You're psychotic," I spat, disgust riding every word. Rage fueling every breath.

Drew's eyes narrowed. He raised the gun until I was staring straight down the barrel.

My heart slammed against my rib cage, but even fear couldn't mute my fury. I had to get that gun away from him. "How are you going to explain the gunshot, Drew?"

"There are a hundred drunk college kids partying in the herpetarium. If they even hear the shot over their music, they'll assume some idiot took his second amendment rights a little too seriously."

My brows rose. "And the blood?"

"I don't have to explain that, as long as I'm not here when people find it."

"That's not what I mean. If the cops find blood with no body, they'll test the DNA to identify it. And what do you think they'll find?"

Drew shrugged, but couldn't quite hide his uncertainty. "Jace said they always assume the sample was contaminated with cat DNA."

"And how do you think the council will react to you giving them one more chance to figure out that's not the case?" I lowered my hands boldly and looked straight into his eyes. "Their most important rule isn't 'don't kill people'. It isn't 'don't infect people'. It's *do not under any circumstances expose us to the public*. Do you really want to crown yourself Alpha with that hanging over your head? Do you think they'll *let* you?"

Drew frowned. His aim wavered. "If I bring them your body, they won't—"

A dark blur flew out of the shadows. Drew screamed as he was driven to the ground. The pistol flew from his hand and slid across the pavement into the bushes. He landed on his back, a large black cat on his chest. Growling inches from his face.

I blinked, stunned, trying to process the sudden tackle.

"Robyn, no!" I shouted. The last thing she needed was another murder on her record. Justified though it may be. "Don't—"

She lunged for his throat and sank her teeth into his flesh.

The fragrance of fresh blood blossomed in the night air, and like the scent of a lover, it made me want things. *Crave* things. But I pushed those primitive urges back. "Robyn—"

"It's not me." She pushed her way through the foliage at the edge of the path behind the carousel. "It's—"

"Justus *no!*" The order rumbled from my throat with a depth and resonance no human could have produced. I lurched toward him, and my brother froze, his teeth still piercing Drew's flesh, on either side of his trachea. "Let him go."

Justus growled for a second. Drew's breath hitched, his chest stilled in panic. Then my brother let him go and backed away.

Blood spurted from both sides of Drew's neck onto the concrete.

"Shit!" Robyn rushed forward and pressed her

hands against the wounds, trying to hold them closed. I pulled my shirt over my head and held it out to her, but when she reached up to take it, more blood poured onto the concrete.

Drew's mouth opened, as if he wanted to say something.

"Don't talk. You're making it worse," Robyn whispered, tears filling her eyes. But by then his gaze had lost focus.

Drew sucked in one more weak breath. Then he went still.

"Motherfucker!" I shouted, and Justus whined, cowering on the ground in the shadow of a carousel horse. Dimly, I realized that his posture was the instinctual reaction of a Pride member to his Alpha. Something he hadn't needed to be taught.

If that instinct had kicked in a second earlier, Drew might still be alive. He might still be able to admit what he'd done in front of the council.

"We needed him," I whispered as I sank onto the concrete, wishing I had something to wipe my bloody hands on.

"Justus will be enough," Robyn insisted. "They'll be able to smell Drew in his scent."

"That won't excuse what he did. We needed Drew to testify to manipulating him. To sending him pictures of Ivy and Leland, knowing what would happen. Without that, he's just another rogue stray."

"We'll figure it out," Robyn whispered. "But we need to clean this up and get out of here."

She was right. "The Elephant Cafe." I pointed with one bloody hand at the closed restaurant. "There might be bleach inside."

Robyn stood and dropped my backpack at my feet.

"I'm on it. Clean up your hands and put a shirt on."

While she was gone, I dug carefully in my bag for a packet of antiseptic wipes, a must-have for any infant's diaper bag and shifter's supply pack. Justus watched me; his head cocked to one side.

"Don't worry," I said as I wiped blood from my hands and arms. "I'm going to take care of this. I'll protect you. I'll teach you." If I'd done that in the first place, Drew could never have gotten to him.

It took most of the packet of wipes to get me clean enough that I could wear the spare shirt from my bag without getting blood on it. As I tugged the top into place, Robyn returned carrying a gallon of bleach and a roll of brown paper towels that could only have come from a public restroom.

By then, Drew had stopped bleeding, but there was a large pool of blood beneath him. I rolled him over, and while we listened for any sign of approaching company, we sopped up as much blood as we could with the paper towels, shoving them into my backpack with the used wet wipes for disposal—or incineration—later.

When we'd done as much as we could, we doused the blood stain with bleach. That wouldn't erase any trace of blood, but it would destroy Drew's DNA and prevent his death from exposing the existence of shifters.

"Okay, I'll take these back and wipe down everything I touched." Robyn held up what remained of the bleach and paper towels. "Then I'll catch up with you."

"We'll wait here for you," I said, but she shook her head firmly.

"You have a dead body and a giant cat. You need

to get the hell out of here right now. I'll meet you at the car."

Unable to argue with her logic, I nodded and lifted Drew's corpse. "Come on, Justus."

Robyn headed for the Elephant Café, and my brother and I pressed on toward the exterior fence where we'd come in, hidden by foliage as much of the time as we could manage.

We could hear the party well before we got to it, and once we came to the herpetarium, it became clear why: the event had spilled outdoors.

"Fuck," I whispered, eyeing several dozen students holding beer bottles and cocktails in plastic light-up cups. Most of the girls wore cheap plastic headbands with panda or tiger ears on their heads, and several of the guys carried an inflatable giraffe or gorilla under their arms. And as far as I could tell, every single one of them was wasted.

Unfortunately, they were also between us and the section of fence I'd parked Spencer's car behind.

"Wow," Robyn whispered from behind me, and I nearly dropped Drew's body in surprise. Her stealth was rapidly improving. "What's the plan?"

"I don't know. I guess we go the long way."

Justus growled and shook his head. Then he stepped out of the brush onto the wide, paved walkway.

"Justus!" I hissed. But he only padded silently toward the party spilling onto the concrete in front of the reptile house. "What the hell is he doing?"

"Creating a distraction," Robyn answered softly. "He's got your brains and my sense of adventure. Admittedly a dangerous combination."

"Okay, when this is all over, we're going to have a

talk about how you're smart, and I'm exciting, but for now—"

A woman screeched. All laughter and drunken conversation died, leaving the music playing for a crowd that had stopped dancing.

They'd spotted Justus.

My brother stared at them, growling. His tail swished. He paced to the right, and panic washed over the crowd. Girls screamed. Guys dropped their inflatable animals. People ran in every direction, digging phones from their pockets.

In seconds, there wasn't a party-goer in sight.

"Come on!" Robyn called as she stepped out of the bushes onto the path. "They're all calling 911." Just as she'd predicted they would.

Justus raced after her, and I took up the rear, weighed down a little by Drew's corpse. My brother jumped over the fence with no problem. Robyn stared at it for a moment, then leaped several feet in the air. She landed less than a foot from the top, and while she climbed over, I contemplated the dead weight of the murderer I still carried like a sleeping child.

"I'm going to have to throw him over," I said at last. "So either get ready to catch him, or stand out of the way." The shuffle of shoes away from the fence told me which she'd chosen.

I sucked in a deep breath, then heaved Drew over the fence with as much height as I could give him. His jacket snagged at the top and a patch of material tore loose. But he made it over and crashed to the ground with a sickening thud.

I snagged the torn material on my way over the fence, then picked up the corpse and followed Robyn and Justus toward Spencer's car. Robyn got behind the wheel while I stored the body in the trunk, in a roll of plastic kept just for that unfortunate possibility—a tip from Faythe and Marc. Justus lay across the backseat, no doubt exhausted and starving from his shift.

"Where to?" Robyn asked as she pulled out of the parking lot into a long line of fleeing college kids. None of whom should have been driving.

"Home. I'll call Jace on the way." As she pulled onto the highway, I twisted in my seat to look at my brother, who lay with his muzzle resting on his folded front paws.

"We have a lot to explain to you, and it's going to come fast and hard. And the only thing I'm sure of right now is that the council's going to want your head. But I'll be damned if I'll let them take it."

Robyn

"You think they believe him?" Knox set a pesto, provolone, and mozzarella grilled cheese sandwich on the bar in front of me, cut into two triangles. On a paper plate. It smelled better than any three a.m. snack I'd ever tasted, but I had no appetite, despite the fact that I'd shifted two hours earlier and had yet to replace the calories that had burned.

"I don't know." Titus had been on a call with the council for more than an hour. Because they were gathered for Isaac and Melody's wedding, he'd caught several of them in one place and the others were all conferenced in, and everyone wanted a chance to talk. To yell. To make demands. To ask questions.

"Even if they don't believe him now, they will once they meet Justus," Lochlan said, cutting into a fresh omelet. "Drew's scent is on him, plain as day. They can't possibly think Titus infected anyone after that."

"Yeah, but that's part of the problem." I picked up half of my sandwich and truly contemplated taking a bite. "I think he'd rather take the blame than let them hurt his brother."

"How could they possibly hold Justus responsible for what he did, after Drew manipulated him?" Naveen demanded as he dumped a splash of whiskey into his coffee in lieu of cream. Or sugar. Or more coffee. They'd started drinking the minute they saw Drew's corpse and smelled Justus's scent, yet not one of the enforcers had so much as slurred a single word. Difficulty achieving intoxication was one of the benefits—and drawbacks—of a shifter's insanely quick metabolism.

"The same way they held me responsible," I told Naveen. "But since Justus isn't a woman, they have no reason to offer him the 'mercy' they offered me." And for the first time since my sentence had been handed down, I realized what a mercy it truly was.

Titus was afraid they'd execute Justus. Swiftly. The council needed me, but they neither needed nor wanted another male stray they weren't sure they could control. A stray who'd infected four people, including a woman who'd died from scratch fever. They had no reason to let him live.

My gaze fell on Justus, sleeping off his pre-dawn breakfast in clean clothes on the window seat at the back of the kitchen. He was only three years my junior, but he looked so much younger and more vulnerable than I'd ever felt, even after everything that had happened to me over the past few months. Justus was less than two years out of high school. He'd lost his parents. And in a way, he'd lost his brother, when Titus was infected and began putting distance between them in an attempt to protect him.

And if Titus couldn't pull off a miracle, he'd very soon lose his life.

TWENTY-FOUR

Titus

I pulled the heavy drapes closed and turned off the overhead light, then sank into my leather arm chair with my eyes closed, treasuring the final minutes of darkness before the sunrise would drag this nightmare into another day. An hour and a half was longer than any conference call should last, and sharing it with ten other Alphas—eleven including Marc Ramos—had made time seem to stand still.

And still, I had no answer.

They'd believed everything I'd told them, probably because I'd offered to ship them Drew Borden's body as evidence. But as usual, most of the council members had less use for the truth than they had for what it would buy them.

Faythe and Marc had argued on my behalf, of course. And Rick Wade had been a voice of reason, to the best of his ability. Which was limited because in many ways, he agreed with most of his fellow council members.

Justus *had* broken the law. He *was* dangerous. And

asking the council for a favor on his behalf wasn't a good way to engender their good will, considering that they hadn't yet ruled on my last request—to have my Pride recognized. And that I hadn't returned their wayward tabby.

Minutes after I sat, my phone rang from the arm of my leather chair, illuminating my darkened office with a bolt of bright white light. Rick Wade's name appeared the screen.

I took a deep breath and accepted the call.

"Okay, Titus, we're ready to make you an offer." Wade's voice echoed over the line, in that telltale way speakerphone mode has of making a caller seem a little too far away.

"I'm listening."

"As you know, infecting a human is a capital offense. Which carries the death penalty. The same goes for exposing our species to the world. By our count, your brother infected four people—one of whom didn't survive scratch fever—and took actions that could easily have exposed us at the Jackson Zoo. We are well within our right to demand his life on all five charges. But we're willing to spare him, considering the circumstances of his crimes. On one condition."

I knew what they were going to say before Wade could even form the words.

"You turn both Robyn and Justus over to us, and we'll take the death penalty off the table for your brother."

"So, I give you Robyn, or you kill my brother?" My voice sounded cold and dead. I didn't even have the energy to summon anger.

"That's not what we're saying. We're asking you to

do the right thing, for its own sake. And in return, we'll agree to see your brother disciplined and rehabilitated, rather than executed."

"Disciplined, how?"

"We haven't discussed that yet, but he's committed very serious crimes. The most common measures are incarceration, declawing, and the loss of both incisors. Though that last one's a bit archaic and unlikely."

"You want to lock him up and cut off the ends of his fingers?" I stood and began pacing at a feverish pace. "He didn't even know what he was doing!"

"We have to make a statement, Titus. If we let him off easy, we'll be eroding our authority. Inviting insurrection."

Bullshit. "What about Robyn?" I demanded. "How much is left on her sentence?"

Wade's silence made the hair at the back of my neck rise. "She broke her word. We can't let that go unpunished either."

"*You won't touch her,*" I growled, my hand clenching around the phone. "No one touches her." Too late, I realized they would hear the truth in my voice. In my words.

Fuck them all.

Suddenly it seemed so simple.

Robyn belonged with me, and if a single one of them tried to lay a hand on her, *I'd* bring the war to *them*.

"Of course no one's going to touch her," Wade insisted. "We're just extending her house arrest. To one year, from the day she returns."

"*A year?*"

"It's a very generous offer!" Paul Blackwell's

334

shaky, angry voice was easy to identify. I hadn't even realized he was on the call.

"Yes, and it comes with a time limit," Wade added. "You have twenty-four hours. After that, the deal goes away, and we'll have no choice but to come for Robyn and Justus. Do you understand what I'm telling you?"

Hand over my brother and my girlfriend, or you'll invade my territory, kidnap Robyn, and kill Justus.

Let them try it. We'd be ready for them.

"You're coming in loud and clear, Rick. You'll hear from me soon." I hung up the phone. Then I threw it at the wall.

My cell shattered into a thousand shards of glass, aluminum, and electronic guts.

The office door opened. Robyn's curvy silhouette appeared in the doorway, backlit by light from the hall. She squinted into the room, then turned toward the kitchen. "Hey Naveen, Titus is going to need a new phone!"

"I'm on it!" he shouted.

She stepped into the room and closed the door. "I take it that didn't go well?"

"See?" I smiled in spite of the circumstances and pulled her close. "I *told* you you were smart."

"Asshole." But she wrapped her arms around my neck and laid her head on my shoulder.

I buried my nose in her hair and inhaled deeply. "They offered me a deal. They said they'd take the death penalty off the table for Justus if I agree."

Robyn stepped back, her eyes wide. "That's great! What do they want…?" Her question faded into pained silence as comprehension crashed over her. "They want me."

"Yeah."

"Okay. Well, that's no real surprise." She nodded, thinking aloud. "I was prepared to ask for his immunity in exchange for my return anyway. And it's only temporary." She stood on her toes and whispered the rest into my ear. "I'll be back as soon as I can convince them I'm all better. No more than a month, and we'll have thirty days' absence to make up for."

"You'll be gone longer than a month, Robyn."

"What?" She dropped onto her heels and frowned up at me. "Why?"

"To punish you? To punish me?" I exhaled and spat out the rest of it. "They're extending your house arrest for a year."

"A year? A fucking *year*? With no school? No family? No...you?"

I nodded, my jaw clenched so hard my teeth were starting to creak.

"And if I don't go, I'll be signing your brother's death warrant."

"And even if you do, they're going to declaw him and lock him up in someone's basement." They'd locked Faythe up once. And one of her brothers, though I'd heard he'd deserved it. "But it's not going to come to that." I tilted her chin up until her gaze met mine. "We're going to fight."

Her frown deepened into skepticism. "What are you talking about?"

"I'm not giving either of you to the council, Robyn. I can't live with that. They're going to come in and try to take you, and we're going to fight. There are more of us. They don't even *know* how many more of us there are. They have no idea what they'll be marching into."

"No!" Suddenly she looked horrified. "Titus, most of your strays are untrained. Many of them are new and still adjusting, and fully half of them don't even recognize your authority yet. You promised to bring them acknowledgment, support, and respect from the council, but you're giving them war. They're not going to fight for you. And I won't ask them to fight for me. To die for a woman they've never even met. They deserve better than that."

"I know." As usual, Robyn was right. "But those are our options. And I'm *not* using you as a bargaining chip."

"Fine." She backed away from me, determination etched into her expression, and I could practically feel a gulf opening between us. "But this is my decision, and I'm going to make it. I'm not going to let everything you're building here fall to pieces because of me. And I'm not going to let them hurt your brother." She pulled her phone from her pocket.

"Robyn…" My voice held a firm edge of warning. "What are you doing?"

She clicked on a name in her contacts list, and I heard the phone ring. Then someone answered.

"Ms. Sheffield?" Rick Wade sounded as stunned as I felt.

"Yeah." Robyn turned away from me and paced across the dark room, toward the far wall of bookshelves. "I'm calling to renegotiate."

"Robyn, hang up the phone," I said, but she waved me off with a scowl.

"I'll turn myself in, and in exchange, you let Justus go. He had no idea what he was doing, and he'll never do it again. But I broke your rules on purpose. And

I'm the one you want anyway."

Wade cleared his throat. "I'm afraid we can't do that. However, we might be willing to reduce his sentence. But not unless you're willing to make more of a long-term commitment to the council."

"I wouldn't be calling if I weren't."

"Robyn!" I whispered frantically, panic bubbling in my gut. But again she ignored me.

"I'll join the Southeast Pride—as a permanent member—if you agree to…six months rehabilitation for Justus. No other disciplinary measures."

"No!" I reached for her phone, but she pushed me back, fire flashing in her eyes.

"That's an interesting proposal," Wade said over the line. "I'll take it to the rest of the council, and—"

"Not good enough," she snapped. "You commit *right now*, or I'm withdrawing my offer. I'll serve out my year with the Di Carlos, then I'll leave, just like Abby, and you'll lose me forever. Your call."

"Robyn, *please*…" I whispered, and everything else faded into the darkness of the room as I watched her. I couldn't see the shelves, or the couches, or my desk. Nothing else existed, except what I was about to lose.

The woman I was no longer sure I could live without.

"I can't do that without consulting—"

"Bullshit," Robyn spat into the phone. "You'll be a hero, and we both know it. Ten seconds. Nine… Eight… Seven…"

"Fine." Wade exhaled heavily. "You have a deal. Your permanent citizenship in exchange for a six-month rehabilitation sentence for Justus Alexander. Effective immediately. We'll send someone to pick you both up."

Robyn nodded, though he couldn't see her, and a growl rumbled up from my throat. "Send Marc Ramos," she said. "He's the only one I trust, other than Faythe, and I know she's exhausted."

"Done," Wade said. "He'll be there in eight hours."

She hung up the phone and turned to me. Tears stood in her eyes, but her voice was steady. "Take care of your brother, when he gets back. Take care of your men. And don't be so eager to get them all killed for a girl you just met." Then she turned and ran out the door.

"Robyn!" I shouted after her. But she was already gone.

I'd already lost her. The only woman I'd ever truly cared about, other than my mother.

Fuck. That.

I marched into the kitchen. "Knox, I need your phone."

"Sure. Here." He dug his cell from his pocket with one heavily tattooed hand and slapped it into my palm. I dialed by memory.

Marc answered on the third ring.

"It's me," I said.

"Hey, Titus, I'm so sorry about how that went down."

"I know." I sank into a barstool at the island, well aware that Knox was listening. "Are you alone?"

"Just me and little Greg. We're letting Faythe get some sleep. Why?"

"Rick Wade's about to call you. And I need a favor. From one stray to another…"

TWENTY-FIVE

Robyn

I closed the drapes in my bedroom and tried to sleep, but wound up staring at the ceiling instead. For hours. Trying not to think about what I'd done. About the rest of my life spent in Atlanta, where I didn't have a single friend.

How long would it take them to wear me down? How long before I agreed to marry some tom, just to shut them all up?

Never. Happen.

I didn't realize I'd finally drifted off until a knock on the door woke me up. "I'm busy!" I sat up and ran my hands through my hair. If I'd wanted to see Titus, I would have come down for lunch.

"It's me," he called from the hallway. I scowled at the door, ready to tell him that I *knew* who he— "Justus."

Oh.

"It's open."

The younger Alexander brother came in and closed the door, and to his credit, he didn't say anything about me lying alone in a dark room, in the middle of the day.

"Marc called." He sat on the edge of the bed, and I scooted forward to join him, my legs dangling over the side. "He's a few minutes away."

"Okay. Thanks."

"I want you to know that you don't have to do this." Justus pinned me with his serious gaze, and it was like looking at a younger version of Titus. "I made mistakes, and I'm ready to pay for them."

"You had no idea what you were doing." I scrounged up a small smile. "You need training and support, not punishment."

Justus nodded. And for a moment, we sat in a surprisingly comfortable silence.

"Are you packed?" he asked at last.

I glanced at the suitcase standing next to the door. I had packed it, but... "I'm not taking anything." Wearing the clothes Titus had bought me would only make it that much harder to forget him.

And I *had* to forget him. I couldn't spend the rest of my life in the Southeast Pride, thinking about what I'd lost. What I'd given up.

"Abby can have the clothes. She'll have to have them taken in, though." I shrugged. "Or the guys can donate them to charity."

"Robyn, I..." Justus cleared his throat and started over. "I wanted to say thank you. My brother would never have found me without you. Drew would have killed me." He threw his arms around me in a hug that smelled like Titus, but felt much more...fragile.

Justus felt *so* young.

"Oh, hon, Titus would never have let that happen." I rubbed his back, blinking away tears. "He would take care of you no matter what. He let himself get kicked out of the Pride to protect you."

"And you're doing the same thing. I just... I want you to know how much you mean to him." He let me go and met my gaze with a teary one of his own. "Titus has never called anyone his girlfriend before. It sounds stupid, but that's *huge* for him."

I sniffled back more tears.

From outside came the swelling rumble of an engine as it drove closer. Marc had arrived.

"Thank you for telling me that." I pulled Justus into another brief hug, blinking away my tears. "You're going to be fine. You're going to hate every second of their 'rehabilitation' but you're going to be fine."

The vehicle stopped out front, and the engine died. I turned to the window as a car door closed. *Time's up.*

I stood, and Justus stood with me. "At least we'll be together. For the drive, anyway," I said.

We found Marc in the kitchen, contemplating a leftover omelet Knox was trying to get him to eat. He seemed to be hesitating over the arugula.

They both turned when they heard our footsteps. "Robyn." Marc held his arms open, and I reluctantly accepted a hug, in spite of the tiny handprint-shaped stain on his shirt that smelled like SpaghettiOs. "And you must be Justus." He let me go and stuck one hand out for Titus's brother to shake.

"Yes. Sir." Justus accepted the hand and shook it firmly. He looked terrified, yet dignified. Just like his brother. "I want to say thanks for this."

"Don't thank me yet." Marc grinned. "You won't truly know what you've gotten into until Faythe hauls you out of the bathroom because pregnant women always have dibs."

What? Justus got to spend his rehabilitation with Faythe and Marc, while I got stuck with the Di Carlos?

"You ready?" Marc asked him, as Titus appeared in the doorway.

Titus looked at me, and a world of emotion swirled in his gray-eyed gaze. I wanted to go to him. I wanted to wrap my arms around him and kiss him goodbye, at least. But that would make this so much harder.

Justus nodded. "What do I have to do?"

"Just follow my lead," Marc said.

I glanced around in confusion to see that Lochlan, Naveen, and Brandt had all filed into the kitchen and stood watching, their expressions carefully blank.

What the hell?

"Justus Anthony Alexander, do you hereby vow to follow orders from your Alphas, to remain loyal to your Pride in all things, and to put nothing before the good of the Pride?"

"I sure as hell do." Justus looked straight ahead, his formal bearing in contrast with an answer that drew a chuckle from both Marc and Titus.

"Then I hereby accept you as a member of the South-Central Pride, on behalf of myself and of my co-Alpha Faythe Sanders, who is unable to be here, because the doctor said she's already traveled too much for her seventh month of pregnancy and needs to rest."

Titus and the other guys laughed.

I stared around the kitchen in absolute astonishment. "What?" I looked at Marc, wide-eyed.

"Did you just induct him into your Pride?"

"Yes." Marc shook Justus's hand again. "And now that he's officially a member, he's guaranteed a trial. A chance to prove himself innocent. No matter what."

"*What?*" I turned to Titus, mystified. "What's going on? What am I not understanding?"

He held up one finger, a small smile haunting the corners of his mouth. "Wait a minute. This is the best part." Titus pulled his new phone from his pocket and dialed. "Hello, Rick? It's Titus. I have an answer for you."

"Um…I don't understand," Rick said over the line. "Robyn already gave us an answer."

"She didn't have the authority to negotiate on behalf of my brother or me. Justus has just been sworn in as a member of the South-Central Pride. Which guarantees him the right to a fair trial, no matter what happens with my territory, or with Robyn. And since you no longer have any leverage over me, I think Robyn should have a chance to make a more informed decision. Hang on, and I'll let you talk to her."

Titus held the phone out to me.

Are you serious? I mouthed.

He nodded with a huge smile.

I looked around the room and found all of the guys—Marc and Justus included—grinning at me. They'd clearly known about this the whole time.

I held the phone up to my ear, my heart pounding deep in my chest. "Rick? Thank you so much for entertaining my earlier proposal, but as I'm not currently a member of one of your Prides, I'm withdrawing my offer in order to join the Mississippi Valley Pride. If you want to keep me under the council's authority and influence, you're going to have to acknowledge my Pride and the authority of my Alpha. Titus Alexander. We look forward to hearing from you when you have a decision for us. Bye!" I hung up the phone while Rick Wade sputtered in shock.

I gave Titus back his phone. My head spun. "I can't believe I just did that." My hands fell to my sides. "What if they invade?"

"They won't," Marc said. "Right about now, Faythe is reminding them that you never officially joined the Southeast, or any other Pride, which means that they have no authority over you. And that if they decide to fight the Mississippi Valley for you, they'll also be fighting the South-Central Pride. And the Appalachian Pride. They might be willing to go to war with Titus, but they won't be willing to fight another civil war so soon after the last one."

"How did this happen?" I whisper, stunned.

Titus pulled me into a hug and smiled down at me. "I called in every favor I could. Faythe and Marc stepped up. And Abby's brother came through, with Jace's former Pride. It turns out he's tired of being a pawn and ready to sit at the grownups' table."

"I can't believe you did this for me." I stood on my toes and wrapped my arms around his neck.

"I couldn't lose you, Robyn. You are the smartest, sexiest most infuriating tabby I've ever met. The Mississippi Valley Pride is honored to call you our own."

"Here, here!" came the chorus from around me.

"That's good!" I glanced around the room, tears in my eyes, a grin glued to my face. "Because you misfit bastards are all stuck with me!"

"They can welcome you to the territory later." Titus took my hand and tugged me toward the stairs leading to his bedroom, the heat in his eyes burning into me. "For the next few hours, you're all mine…"

Photo credit: Kim Haynes Photography

ABOUT THE AUTHOR

Rachel Vincent is a former English teacher and an eager champion of the Oxford comma. She shares her home in Oklahoma with two cats, two teenagers, and her husband, who's been her # 1 fan from the start. Rachel is older than she looks and younger than she feels, and she remains convinced that writing about the things that scare her is the cheapest form of therapy—but social media is a close second.

Made in the USA
Middletown, DE
05 January 2018